NO ALTERNATIVE

William Dickerson

Kettle of Letters Press
Los Angeles, CA 90027

The characters and events in this novel are fictitious.

ISBN-10: 0985188618
ISBN-13: 978-0-9851886-1-0

Library of Congress Control Number: 2012903381

DEDICATION

This novel is dedicated to my sister.

CONTENTS

NO ALTERNATIVE

"I would only wear a tie-dyed T-shirt if it were dyed with the urine of Phil Collins and the blood of Jerry Garcia."

– Kurt Cobain

"I would only wear a cardigan sweater if it were weaved with the pubic hair of Kurt Cobain."

– Bridget Harrison

WILLIAM DICKERSON

INTRODUCTION

Suicide is a universally human phenomenon. It's what separates us from the animals, despite the fact that people shun it and cloak it in taboo. Animals do not commit suicide, at least that's the common wisdom. It is this received wisdom that reveals something about our attitudes on the subject, as suicide is most always painted in the light of shame and pity, something we reserve for lesser beings than ourselves. In actuality, suicide is a refined and selfless act, usually a result of many thoughtful hours, days, months, or years of meticulous and steadfast preparation. Suicide is not thoughtless; it's precisely the opposite.

In order to commit suicide, one must be aware of one's life coming to an end – this awareness is wholly human, since animals are thought to be incapable of sharing this recognition. But how can we really know this? This is a purely clinical assumption. There are occasions when dogs sink into depression, whether as a result of old age or from a reaction to emotional stimuli such as a master dying, and they willfully stop eating, eventually starving themselves to death. Do they understand that if they do not eat, they will die? Perhaps not in any literal sense, but it's difficult to believe that such actions are taken without any awareness of the consequences.

Take as an example the story of one such case. In Rome, Italy, the owner of a Spanish Cocker Spaniel passed away. When paramedics removed his prone body from his house, the dog hurled itself from the third floor. The pet lived, suffering a broken leg. After being treated by the vet, its leg immobilized in a cast, it returned home in the custody of one of its owner's distant relatives. In spite of a profound difficulty moving, and the supervision of the relative, the dog broke free of its leash and again threw itself from the third floor of the house in which it was raised. This time, it accomplished what was pre-sumably its goal: it died.

Suicide is unbiased, non-partisan. It transcends gender, perhaps even species. In a biological sense, it's pure. At no other time in recent memory was suicide so prominent in the zeitgeist of Americana than in the early 1990's. The perceptive pop listener might argue that the 80's foreshadowed such a day of reckoning. In Billy Joel's song, *"We Didn't Start The Fire,"* history ended when the 80's did, as if each day that passed after his song debuted was one match strike closer to oblivion. Lis-teners were left longing for his song to stretch into the 90's, if for no other reason than to reference Crystal Pepsi in his "Cola Wars."

In a way, history did come to an end. There was an over-whelming stench of death in the air, emanating from the rotten music that decadent decade dished out. What was considered music in the 80's was reduced to ashes in the wake of the con-flagration of three unknown musicians from Seattle, Washing-ton – actually, two were from a shithole logger town called Aberdeen, and their drummer, Dave, was from Olympia. They declared war against the music industry, whether intentionally or not, and their declaration was a singular record album, *Nevermind;* an album on which there's not a single fade-out. Every song simply crashes to an abrupt and decisive end. As the band's front-man appropriately said in his suicide letter, it's *"better to burn out, than to fade away..."* That line was taken from Neil Young, but what 15 year-old nose-picker plugging his ears with punk knew that at the time Cobain quoted him?

What Billy Joel couldn't "take" anymore in his Billboard Top One Hundred tune was different from what teenagers at the time couldn't take anymore. To be quite frank, we couldn't take anymore of his fucking song. Or of Guns and Roses and their sweet children; or of Warrant and their baked goods; or of Def Leppard's sugar, some of which Warrant must have borrowed to make their cherry pie. The 90's ushered in an independent, do-it-yourself, ethic; a way to proactively and publicly flush the 80's down the toilet. Some music critics have argued that this was simply a resurgence of the punk rock ideology that thrived in the late 70's, and there's some truth to that. History is cyclical and not only was punk rock reinvented in the early 90's, so, apparently, was the suicide cult – what Jim Jones did for the *Peoples Temple*, in which he and 914 of his followers died in a mass murder-suicide at Jonestown in 1978, the charismatic David Koresh did for the *Branch Davidians*, and their 55 dead adults and 21 dead children, in Waco, Texas, in 1993. From Sid Vicious to Kurt Cobain, Jim Jones to David Koresh, artists and psychopaths alike were immersed in the cumulative whirlpools of thought, aggression, freshly clipped nerve-endings, disaffection, and the do-it-yourself zeitgeist of the moment.

Absolutely nothing is more do-it-yourself than suicide.

***

Suicide is the thing; the goal; the beginning and the end; the next big thing; the be all, end all; the eye in the sky – it's the Tylenol bottle with the 20 bonus pills, because swallowing an entire bottle of Tylenol can kill you.

Suicide is an option; it's an alternative; it's aqua seafoam shame; it's dead of a shotgun blast to the head.

Suicide is the lyric of a song; packaged inside a gold record.
Spinning.
Spinning.
Spinning.
Spin the black circle.

***

If the lyric is death, then the song is life itself, trapping its lyrics within a recurring embrace of murder and conception, all controlled by your Aiwa Minisystem's three-disc CD player, its repeat button the key to everlasting life. Some traditionalists will prefer the analogy of a vinyl record, the *black circle*, a turntable needle skipping along its groove; however, to recent generations, the *black circle* is a relic, just another obstacle to sidestep in the attic when it comes time to store your sweaters. To some boys and girls, the *black circle* is an object unknown. If you can't see your image reflected in it, it won't play your music. There's something appropriate about that.

There were still tape cassettes around in the 90's, stacked up on shelves somewhere, neatly organized in shoeboxes, an arm's length away for the convenient use of breaking up weed. By this time, though, they were mostly used to record rock bands in garages on four-track machines or used to record mixtapes to win the affections of girls – magnetic pleas for admittance into their unsullied jeans in the back of your Mom's Ford Taurus.

NO ALTERNATIVE

If you were a teenager in the early 90's, music as you knew it died on April 8th, 1994. The day the music died and grunge was born, but only grunge as a catchphrase, as an advertising motif. It was the beginning of a movement. Back when MTV actually aired music videos, rather than the onslaught of reality television programming they broadcast now, and viewers made a point to sit at home in their beanbags and watch those videos, on this day, they stopped airing their music videos, however briefly, and their perpetually coiffed and stoic news anchor, Kurt Loder, commandeered the airwaves to impart a Special Report to a legion of slacker viewers:

The body of Nirvana leader, Kurt Cobain, was found in a house in Seattle Friday morning dead of an apparently self-inflicted shotgun blast to the head. Cobain's body was discovered by an electrician carrying out repairs at the musician's house. Sources claim he had been missing for several days. The singer, whose band achieved global fame with the release of its album, Nevermind, in 1991, recently survived a drug and alcohol-induced coma in Rome last month. A statement from Nirvana's management company said: 'We are deeply saddened by the loss of such a talented artist, close friend, loving husband and father.' Police found what is said to be a suicide note at the scene, but have not yet divulged its contents.

***

Spinning.
Spinning.
Spinning.
Spin the black circle.

CHAPTER ONE

A pair of battered black and white Converse sneakers, lying on the floor next to a bed. The periwinkle eyes of a teenage boy open, blinking away the morning light, searching for focus. The eyes focus on the sneakers. Contrasting black canvas and white rubber soles, Jack Purcell's signature tennis shoe. Not the All-Star, like all the other kids are wearing, the tennis shoe, the ones with the reinforced rubber toe – the ones with the black smile at the tip – the ones his idol wore.

Lanky legs swing to the floor and frayed jeans with strategically torn holes in the knees are pulled over smiley-face boxers. In the late fifties, a style like this was born and dubbed shabby-chic, on account of the Kennedy boys and their ripped khakis and sockless docksiders. That was the first time America had witnessed children of wealth and privilege dressing down their airs. In the early nineties, there was a different name for this uniform. The teenager's hands reach down and pick up one of the shoes, fingering a tear in the rubber tip. It's the moment right after he wakes up when he's still disconnected from his brain, his limbs move, performing rudimentary functions, as though they're testing their joints, their mechanics, their overall design. He's not fully in control, he's not fully aware. Thomas Harrison likes this moment the best.

Thomas is tall, angular, and wide-eyed. He's the oldest child, the favorite, the only son. And sick of all that.

He steps to a wall calendar, the date: October 8, 1994.

***

Thomas slaps his shoe onto the faux-porcelain sink of the guest bathroom. He pulls a band-aid from the medicine cabinet and places it neatly over the slice in the footwear. He considers the utility of this addition, considers it in the context of his preferred style. He finds it pleasing, but you wouldn't know it. He closes the door with the ball of his foot and runs the hot water in the shower. Cracking his neck in the morning is not so much a ritual as it is a necessity and this discomfort is only the beginning of what will surely be a herniated disc later in life. The steam from the shower rises, its moisture wrapping the tile walls with a cloudy film. He breathes in the vapor, softening the mucus in his sinus passages. The hot mist flows through the nooks and crannies of his head, flushing out the waste below the surface of his face like the subterranean sewers of ancient Rome, the first sewer system in the world. Thomas should know; he built a working model of the system, replete with running water and miniatures of solid waste, for his Fifth Grade Latin Class. The whole class got to wear togas, made out of bed sheets. And sandals. He looks at himself in the mirror, looks at the sprout of fuzz curled around the base of his chin. He absently runs his fingers through the stubble.

As Thomas steps into the flowing water of the shower, he is emerging from his morning haze. He taps a foot, grabs a bottle of shampoo, clicks open the top, all in perfect rhythm.

Pivoting his foot, he returns the shampoo to its shelf. For a lanky white boy, Thomas has natural rhythm, but not the kind of natural rhythm a dancer is blessed with; he'll never breakdance. Thomas has metronomic timing. Thomas has the rhythm of a drummer.

He steps from the shower, dripping wet and unconcerned about anything as mundane as shower mats or the impact of water on the structural integrity of an ageing home. He grabs a towel, making a half-hearted effort at drying his wiry body. As he turns to close the shower curtain, a black blur in the bathtub brings him up short. Crouching down, he examines an enormous cockroach, its pin-sized antennae twitching as it scuttles about at the base of the bathtub, right where the silver-plating is beginning to peel off the drain. He picks up his sneaker, squats over the bug, squinting at it. What does it mean to be a cockroach? Is it simply a tiny machine of nature, randomly following scent paths through a meaningless life? Certainly, it's hard to imagine anything resembling thought passing through its tiny chitinous head. It seems so oblivious that it's hard to avoid the sense that it simply doesn't care about its impending doom. Thomas harbors no resentment toward the intrusion of the bug. Maybe he's simply following his own scent paths. He lines it up in his sight, casually. Then he slams the sole of his sneaker down on top of its furrowed, humpback shell.

The cockroach doesn't so much flatten as explode.

Thomas slips his foot into his sneaker, chunks of cockroach carcass stuck to its sole. He wipes the bottom of it on the bath mat, or what he thinks is the bath mat; since he didn't bother to glance down to make sure it was there. He grabs a toothbrush and continues his morning ritual.

***

Through an incongruously placed door in the living room and down a handbuilt staircase of two-by-fours, Thomas steps into a cluttered garage. His sister, Bridget Harrison, skulks in the far corner, pale white and inescapably preppy. At first glance, Bridget is an authentic slice of apple pie, but upon further scrutiny, you can't help thinking that the baker left out the cinnamon. Perhaps on purpose. She straddles a cushioned drum stool behind a painter's easel and is sketching a still-life of a bowl of fruit. Mostly apples and such, nothing a million painters before her haven't painted already. The myriad of eraser marks on the canvas evince her neuroses. This girl: trouble, troubling and troubled.

Thomas sweeps by, approaching a sheet-covered mass in the back of the garage.

"Can you please paint somewhere else?" he asks.

"I'm sketching," Bridget responds, without even looking up.

"Sketch somewhere else."

Thomas yanks the sheet off the mass, revealing a sizeable set of drums: the red sparkle finish is so thoroughly caked with dust and viscous residue that the aura of candy it once possessed is visibly diminished. There's a crack or two in the bronze cymbals, but cracks don't matter; they enhance the sound of the crash. Or as it's referred to in the current state of commercial song and sound, *the trash.*

Bridget continues sketching her apples and such, as if to say "I was here first."

Thomas adjusts his cymbals, finds a pair of chipped sticks. Bridget can't help but pry as he prepares to warm up his instrument, "You haven't played in months."

She looks at him sideways, recognition dawning.

"You must be done mourning."

Thomas is plainly annoyed. Bridget continues to sketch. Frankly, Thomas was annoyed the moment he encountered his sister in the garage inhabiting his space in the first place. Or what was his space. He ambles up to her, moving alongside her easel, and just stands there like a statue, or one of those metallic mimes in Times Square that pretends he's a statue, waiting for a pigeon to shit on him. Shit!: exploding onto his head like a water balloon.

"Okay, Jesus!"

Bridget springs up; she can't take people looking over her shoulder, or looking anywhere near her shoulder, or being too close to her, or being scrutinized, a set of character flaws that Thomas is aware of in the way that siblings are always aware of such things, because they are intent on exploiting them.

"Give me a break, will you?" he asks, pleading with her, shifting tactics and attempting to relate to her as one human being to another. "This is the only place I can play, you can sketch anywhere. In the house, outside…it's nice outside."

Bridget silently packs her pencils and fruit, folds the easel and departs up the stairs slamming the door behind her. Thomas ponders the nature of the slam, as most who are slammed upon do, post-slam. Was it a statement, or just the ricochet of her general presence? Her discomfort in the presence of others leads her to these periodic outbursts. Their mother, Maureen, often refers to her daughter as Hurricane Bridget, as her entrances and exits rarely go unnoticed.

Thomas gently lifts the drum throne and lofts it across the room, restoring it to its rightful kingdom. He sits down behind his drums, noticing for the first time how old and weathered his instrument has become. He extends his left hand, and then pulls his fingers back with his right, stretching them out carefully. They do not crack. He is acutely aware of this stretching as a ritual and not as a physical necessity. A drummer has his regimen: the location of the throne relative to the cymbals, the height of the snare, the easy tension of the bass pedal; the kit is a place as much as it is an instrument. Thomas rolls his head around his shoulders, winces a bit, then picks up a drumstick.

There had once been a folding ping-pong table in the place of these drums. After endless hours of practicing the game of table tennis, Thomas had developed a proficient ambidexterity that enabled him to switch his paddle from right hand to left and vice versa, in the middle of rallies, primarily to throw his opponent off balance. His father, William, a frequent opponent, did not take kindly to such trickery. During one of their matches, one in which Thomas's relentless trickery was heavily and masterfully employed, an argument ensued during match point over whether or not the ball had grazed the edge of the table.

Heated words were exchanged, but the specifics are not important. The specifics are never important. Memory has a way of flattening out the details of these kinds of disputes, laying waste to the volleys that escalate between the parties. You can never hope for complete lucidity, or even something resembling it, when trying to recall such events. What's important, and what Thomas can recall with crystal clarity, is the manner by which he chose to convey his final volley in the argument. Namely, that skillful turn of phrase and adolescent favorite: "Fuck you, Dad."

These words were a trigger, like in the sense of *The Manchurian Candidate*, that kind of trigger. In no uncertain terms, these words set William off – they set the Queen of Diamonds off spinning around his head.

Spinning.

Thomas was at the far end of the garage, so in order to escape he would have to proceed toward his father with the abandon of the reckless, dodging his inevitable grasp, swiftly ascending the stairs to his freedom. Thomas had size on his side; he was smaller, quicker, and lighter than his father. William had strength on his, and the unrelenting flow of parent-scorned adrenaline pumping through a spigot that's handle had completely blown off. His adrenal flow was akin to the surge from a freshly opened fire hydrant. However, he was modestly handicapped, having recently undergone inguinal hernia surgery. Thomas could always assume a defensive posture and kick him, but he hoped it wouldn't come to that. Even in his heightened state of fight or flight, he recognized that kicking his injured father might have dire and longlasting consequences well beyond the inappropriate use of expletives.

William threw his paddle to the ground, went right, then left, then right; each time Thomas refusing to take the bait. After several minutes of this, Thomas shimmied to his left, toward the door, and William went for it. In these instances, when the Queen of Diamonds began her revolutions, William didn't care much for patience. He was chomping at the bit and this was an elemental aspect of his personality. As William lunged at his son, Thomas slid under the table, tearing the seam of his jeans but narrowly avoiding his father's grasp. He popped out the other side of the table, like a Jack breaking free from the confinement of its decorative box, and lunged for the stairs. It felt like the slow-motion in dreams: you're trying desperately to run as fast as you can, to reach as far as you can, but it's like your body is encased in jell-o and you're struggling to wade through it. Once the sole of his buckskin saddle shoe (this was before he wore Converses) hit the first step, he leaped up the rest, three at a time.

And he was out that door in a hot flash.

As Thomas burst through the front door of his Tudor house in quaint Colonial Heights, his father was not far behind. They both hit the street. The race on the pavement proved impossible for William to sustain. As Thomas made his break up the street they call Grandview, William took immediate and definitive action. It was the end of fall and tree branches lined the trenches at the sides of the street. He leaned down, grabbing the largest one he could find, and heaved the rotting limb at his only son.

Thomas, with one eye on the middle-aged maniac pursuing him, zeroed in on the descending object and dove out of its way at the last second. But it was disturbingly close. It was at this explicit moment in time that William was forced, however reluctantly, to accept his inevitable defeat. This acceptance was a long time coming and applied to much more than a simple table tennis game or the failure to deliver an appropriate punishment for Thomas's teenage verbal transgression; this acceptance is something that no father takes lightly, even a father who wishes for his son to be better than him in every way.

William Harrison served his country as a Sergeant in the U.S. Army Special Forces, a Green Beret, to be precise, during the Vietnam War. He didn't wait to be drafted; he volunteered at the beginning of '64. And when his commander refused to honor his request in '65 to be dispatched to fight in 'Nam, he wrote his senator a handwritten letter – his senator at the time was Robert F. Kennedy of New York, brother of the recently slain President of the United States, John F. Kennedy. William explained that it was the President, his brother, who had instilled in him the confidence, courage and pride to join the United States Military and fight the Commies. He stated that his talent and commitment to the manifest destiny of Democracy was being wasted sitting on his well-trained hands and he asked to be let loose on the motherless heathens of North Vietnam, to be allowed not only to blow them to bloody bits but also to teach the motherless heathens of South Vietnam demolitions, so they might also blow the motherless heathens of North Vietnam to bloody bits.

Much to his commander's chagrin, there was no doubt his letter had been read because within a week, William was on a plane to Vietnam. Fortunately for his physical well-being, he was in the war early, when the fighting wasn't nearly so fierce. He did his duty, taught the heathens demolitions, jumped out of a few planes, saw the sights, and returned to America in '67.

William loved war, the idea of war, the idea of controlling chaos. There was a discipline to it that attracted him, but it was the tangible strategy of war that captured his imagination. The war was a chess game to William, with the pawns swapped out for gooks. If he could have stayed over there, he probably would have. He did make an effort to bring a piece of the war back with him: an M-60 machine gun that he hid in the false bottom of a military-issued cargo crate. The M-60 is the giant cannon of a gun that spits bullets from a bullet belt the shooter feeds into its side, the gun that was made famous by Sylvester Stallone in *RAMBO: First Blood, Part II*, a gun that is difficult for a single man to hold by himself. It's not exactly a weapon that's easily concealed in baggage.

William was detained at the airport in Syracuse, New York, by Secret Service, as the theft and transport of a weapon like this is a felony. After a detention marked only by its brevity, he was let go. Without so much as a slap on the wrist. This was right about the time when the country began to witness a blitz of fucked-up vets returning to the homeland. So they took pity on him, a sanctioned pity that the government took upon many, many others right up until the final days of the conflict.

Before shipping off to war, William had wanted to be a photographer. Perhaps serving in the war allowed him to dr- eam a little, as though being killed at any given moment issued license to the imagination, lent validity to hope — hope as a concept, as a democratic ideal. Throughout the Harrison home, there were leather-bound photo albums that William organized with photographs taken with a single lens reflex camera he bought at a thrift store in Cambodia. These photo albums were ultimately consigned to the role of an improvised step stool in the family room closet. Top among William's art shots was a close-up of an exhausted elephant resting its massive head on a crumbling brick wall bristling with spikes. The spikes were deliberately placed to deter ambitious animals from traversing the barrier into the unit's encampment. Clearly, ambition was not a factor for this particular elephant, as it sagged against the wall, the skin around its tusks pulled brutally down by gravity; the wall's designers had neglected to take exhaustion into account when building this thing. For the elephant, the hellish environment of the jungle with its stray bullets, exploding land mines and eruptions of napalm, led it to the inescapable conclusion that the spiked wall was one of its better options for some R&R. What William was able to capture, aside from the plight of this animal resting in the wrong place at the wrong time, was the orange sunset illuminating the sky around the animal, blazing through the trees, as though the branches and their leaves were incinerated by the film's overexposure. The sun didn't look like the sun, it looked like Mars, Mars on fire, and for William, this was Mars, the planet named after the god of war. He never felt more at home than when he was on Mars. Upon returning to the reality of the states, William came to realize that his goal of shooting plates for National Geographic or the glossy pages of Vogue might fall victim to the more realistic fate of becoming a wedding photographer. This was a fate that is the quintessential nightmare shared by every aspiring photographer with an itch to go professional, and it was a fate that William refused to accept. Thomas would often flip through the photo albums in the closet admiring the artistry, the framing, the meticulous attention to shutter speed and aperture, and he would wonder if it was an accident or if it was intentional. As a teenage son, he was biased in the reverse sense; in the same way that a father is almost always proud of his children, no matter how insignificant their accomplishments. In the photo albums, there were also scattered photos of Vietnamese captives, North Vietnamese since they were blindfolded with pistols pointed at the backs of their heads. William always claimed that he never saw much action. But Thomas couldn't help thinking that these pictures proved otherwise; that somewhere in the back of another closet or secreted away in a safety deposit box was a necklace festooned with the ears of a hundred dead gooks, a treasured souvenir that he *was* able to sneak past the Secret Service.

This man who just finished hurling a massive tree branch at his only son was no longer a Green Beret; he had become a State Supreme Court Judge, elected by the people to serve the people and determine who should go to jail and who should remain free. If William didn't follow his dream of becoming a photographer, he did find a way to make a lasting and meaningful impact on the community he loved. He found a way of controlling the chaos at home. Thomas ultimately escaped his sentence and loitered the streets of his neighborhood, in late fall, dressed only in a T-shirt, pajama pants and his buckskin shoes. It was a strange choice of attire, but his garage floor was too coarse for just socks, and he hadn't anticipated being seen in public. He sat down on a curb three streets away, folded his arms into his chest, and waited for his father to calm down and his mother to talk some sense into him.

As night fell, Thomas returned, just in time for dinner and an apology. Thomas apologized, too. The next day, his father decided to buy him the musical instrument of his choice, a gesture of amends, albeit an unabashedly material one. William had recently detected a passion for music blossoming in his son and he viewed this as an opportunity to encourage something productive in the life of Thomas.

What would annoy his father the most?

It was, of course, the drums.

Thomas sits behind his drums in the corner of the garage. He had been unable, or maybe just unwilling, to sit there since the death of his idol, as if the loss made his efforts seem misguided or insignificant, as if his aspirations were a poor reflection on the man he admired. He hefts the beat-up wooden drumstick between his restless fingers, ready to explore his musical pursuits again, feeling rusty but also right at home. In a flash, he recoils his arm, retracts his elbow, takes his aim, and strikes the stick against the scratched skin of his very highest tom. The blunt tip of the stick slices right through the head, perforating its deteriorated plastic.

He stares at the stick, protruding out from the head.

***

Leaves are turning on the stunted trees planted along the sidewalk on Mamaroneck Avenue in White Plains. Thomas stands at the display window of the Sam Ash Music Store scoping the plethora of musical equipment stacked up to the ceiling, gleaming like gigantic candies. Having removed himself from the study of his craft, he has the trepidation of an amateur as he steps through the front door.

Thomas wanders along symmetrical rows of amplifiers and racks of electric guitars, numerous noodlers sit on scattered stools testing guitars, flangelating the output of their nascent sound waves, ratcheting up the gain on their RAT distortion pedals. Thomas stops at a locked glass cabinet on the floor near the cash registers, inside of which displays a pristine sunburst Fender Jaguar electric guitar. He looks the instrument over, his eyes running along the hand-sanded curves and shimmering stainless-steel hardware, the knobs, buttons and dials like an echo from decades of rock royalty, the strings taut over the pick-ups. Like a lot of modern musicphiles, Thomas feels like the guitar is a *Playboy* model and he's the camera. Maybe *Hustler*. Okay, *Barely Legal* – a *Barely Legal* model. Whatever, same company owns the both of them.

Another teen, the precocious Connor Russell, slowly approaches Thomas from behind. Connor rocks matted blonde hair, not quite dreadlocks, more like *I don't give a fuck what my hair looks like*, and has a chain wallet stuffed in his back pocket. The chain is fashioned from the chain of a bicycle, and it hangs just below his ass. You know this guy; he's the guy who's kind of mad at the world for not recognizing his genius. Thomas spins around, recognizing his old friend immediately.

"No shit."

Connor, flipping the excess hair away from his eyes, takes a moment. He knows exactly who Thomas is, but he's added a three-second delay to his actions these days; it's an aesthetic choice, evidence of his personal flare as reflected in his interactions with others, a bit of *I'm too cool for me to recognize you, so you should recognize me first*. Or his hair has simply become a legitimate obstacle to his vision.

Connor nods, his chin bouncing, as a smile creeps onto his mug. The two kids slap a street shake. Street shakes have evolved over the years, since the greasers of the fifties casualized the greeting. There was the straight-five of the sixties, the high-five of the seventies, and the fist-bump that emerged in the eighties, all of which invited elaborate additions and augmentations. Even Michael Jordan helped evolve the gesture, bumping the knuckles of his opponents before a game; he preferred this to a handshake as a means of keeping talcum powder pressed between the palms of his hands. With the rise of hip-hop in the eighties, such modifications took on a level of attitude previously absent from the typical exchange. This attitude had shape-shifted across musical genres and come out in the grunge scene as well. The street shake that Thomas and Connor exchange involves a number of steps, including a grip, a snap, a lean-in and a push-away. The push-away is optional, reserved for older friends; it's not typically performed with an average slacker acquaintance. Connor looks Thomas over; he's not gay, but he tends to routinely assess the style of others.

"What're you doing here?" Connor asks.

"Buying some new skins for my drums."

Connor crinkles his brow at his friend.

"Didn't know you played."

"Took a bunch of lessons a while back," Thomas responds. "Nothing much, though. Dusted off my clunker of a kit this weekend."

Connor pumps his head enthusiastically, brushing the tufts of unwashed hair behind his ears, strapping them down. Connor and Thomas were briefly business partners around the end of sixth grade, beginning of seventh. They trafficked in audio-tapes of prank phone calls. They were part of a vast network of prepubescent pranksters who would crank-call people, mainly businesses, and record the hijinks. The recordings were then passed along to other pranksters across the county by way of the United States Postal Service. The process was deceptively complex. You'd get a tape in the mail along with a lean list of addresses. Some of the addresses were crossed out; the last one crossed out was yours. You'd usually accumulate a few tapes over the course of a few weeks, then, according to the rules of this underground railroad of infantile behavior, you'd listen to them, decide what calls you liked the best, which pranks elicited the deepest belly laughs, chortles and snickers, and you'd compile the winners onto another tape while sneaking your own personal exploits onto it as well. Then you'd pop it in the mail to the next address on the list. If, by the time you received the next tape, your phone calls had passed muster and appeared as one of the selections of your peers, you knew you'd done something right.

Connor had an obsession with Pasquale's Pizza in Bronxville, a couple blocks from St. Joseph's Elementary School. It was ideal for pranking because it had a payphone located directly across the street. So, at night, you'd be able to make calls from this phone, shielding yourself within the booth, and observe the resulting disturbance through the restaurant window in real time. A primitive multimedia, and boldly interactive, entertainment experience, which you'd record for the entertainment of strangers, at the expense of old man Pasquale, his banshee of a wife, and his customers. A typical conversation ended up etching itself into the minds of kids throughout Westchester County:

PASQUALE: *Pasquale's Pizza, how may'I'a'help you?*

CONNOR (voice forced three octaves lower): *Yeah, uh, I ordered a pizza 'bout an hour or, uh, two hours ago.*

PASQUALE: *Good'a for you. You wanna 'nother one?*

CONNOR: *No. I most certainly do not. I was calling to get my money back.*

PASQUALE: *Huh?*

CONNOR: *I ordered the pizza with pepperoni and I got cockroaches.*

PASQUALE: *Huh?!* [inaudible] *Whattayou say?*

CONNOR: *Cockroaches, instead of pepperoni. You heard me you son-of-a-bitch.*

PASQUALE: [inaudible, likely Italian expletives]

CONNOR: *I'm on my way back, with the pizza and a baseball bat, which I'm going to use to shove each one of these cockroaches I found on my pizza up your shriveled Italian ass.*

PASQUALE: *Who the hell is this?!*

CONNOR: *It's Mike.*

PASQUALE: *Mike? Mike'a who?*

CONNOR: *Hunt.*

PASQUALE: *I don't know who'a you are, but I'm'a gonna find out, and you'll be a'sorry.*

CONNOR: *The name's Hunt, tough guy. First name Mike.*

PASQUALE: *Mike...Hunt?!* (He puts the phone down, yells anxiously around his parlor) *Anybody know a Mike Hunt? Did he order a pizza? Mike Hunt?*

At this point, a couple of inebriated college smart-asses consuming slices at the corner booth couldn't help responding:

COLLEGE SMART-ASS: *I don't know your cunt, but me and my dick go way back…*

Pasquale, realizing his error —

PASQUALE: *Get out!*

The smart-asses amble out of the town haunt of tomato sauce and stale cheese, tossing what's left of their slices into the trash.

COLLEGE SMART-ASS: *…and it tastes just about as good as this pizza.*

PASQUALE (brings the phone back to his ear): *Oh, you motherfucker'a! You do come down here and you bring that bat, so I can show you how'a I fuck ya'momma as you daddy watch, ay? The cockroaches you found'a on your'a pizza, I found'a first in her ass!!*

That's about the time the boys would drop the act and start cracking up, as if on cue, like only two Catholic school sixth graders could while fleeing the scene of their delinquency. Not exactly original, but all such delinquencies seem completely original to the twelve year-old perpetrators who spread them around like a bad cold.

"Cool," says Connor, as he looks over his old friend, scrutinizing him. "So why you looking at guitars?"

Thomas knows exactly why, but pretends like he doesn't.

"Inside every drummer is a frustrated guitarist, I guess."

Connor leans down, like he's genuflecting in front of an altar, and points at the Fender Jaguar locked inside the glass cabinet. The instrument beckons Connor like the sword beckoned King Arthur from its stone. And, mistranslating the advice his insurance salesman father had once given him about sex, he believes it's up to him to pull it out.

"I'm saving up for that motherfucker."

Thomas is anxious to exhibit his expertise, perhaps to prove something to Connor, or at least to earn his slacker stripes in the eyes of this aficionado.

"Same one Kurt had," Thomas says.

Connor glances at Thomas, nearly impressed. "Almost. Kurt had a '65. This one's a reissue from Japan."

He then proceeds to describe the instrument in fetishistic detail and recite the history of Kurt Cobain's relationship to it:

"Same sunburst color and bowling-ball pickguard, but Kurt gutted the shit out of his. Got rid of that bridge 'cuz the strings popped out – it was supposed to be for surf music, like the Beach Boys, Jan & Dean, and Dick Dale and The Deltones, designed to sound like waves crashing. It couldn't handle the thrashing he was giving it, so he replaced it with a Tune-O-Matic. The strings stay put better, much better. He disconnected the on/off and phase switches. Biggest change was ripping out the single-coil pick-ups and replacing them with humbuckers: a DiMarzio PAF in the neck and a Super Distortion in the bridge, until the *In Utero* tour when he replaced it with a black Duncan JB."

Thomas looks at Connor like he's fucking crazy, but he's also extremely eager to respond: "He was a frustrated drummer, you know…wanted the adoration of John Lennon, but the anonymity of Ringo Starr."

Thomas's response comes across as though he had been rehearsing its words for months.

Connor is familiar with this story, more familiar than Thomas thinks; he doesn't like it one bit.

He flips his hair back in front of his face.
"Go fuck yourself."

CHAPTER TWO

William sips a cup of instant coffee at the kitchen table, reading the Sunday Edition of *The New York Times*. It's not that he dislikes coffee beans; he simply acquired a taste for stirring grounds into a steaming cup of water, because this was how they did it in the army. He's a creature of habit, a man who is happy with routine. He's also a sitting Supreme Court Judge, in the Empire State of New York, and he sits at his head of the table as though he's on the bench. He looks the part, he always looks the part, minus the robe. He has just settled into enjoying this weekend ritual when crunching guitar and thunderous drumming reverberate through the walls, circumventing the insulation, shaking the foundations of the house. He removes his reading glasses, looking up with subtle disdain.

In the lush backyard, Thomas's mother, Maureen, waters a flower garden. If Martha Stewart was a hippy with a biting sense of sarcasm, she'd be Maureen. Noticing the impending noise, she halts the hose. A small poodle and a Cavalier King Charles Spaniel skitter around her. The dogs of the privileged. The King Charles was bred to warm the bed of the King of

England, and warm the bed it did. Now they warm the beds of American politicians. The perfect lap dog, foot and leg warmer, cursed with a mouth filled with absolutely terrible teeth, either on account of generations of inbreeding, or on account of their British birthright.

Meanwhile, Bridget listens to rap music in her bedroom, her foot pumping anxiously at the base of her easel, as she continues to labor over the sketch of fruit. Bridget likes rap because her brother hates it, because her family hates it, her friends hate it. Thomas tried to sell her on the idea that if music is defined by the counterbalance of melody and rhythm, then rap is not really music, since it contains no discernable melody. It's nothing more than performance poetry set to rhythm. As if some grunge-addled white boy is in a position to define the merits of rap. Bridget, on the flipside, sees it as the most daring of contemporary music, full of energy and anger and perfectly expressive of her own teen angst. But is she really in any position to define it either? She stares blankly at her sketch. She hasn't made much progress. She feels like she's having trouble focusing. Understandable, given her nature. Bridget's appearance is neat, she's at least showered this morning, but her room is an abject mess: grimy plates tilted haphazardly on something that must be a desk; empty packets of cereal; half-full mugs of coffee; shattered pieces of saltines; pencils stuck in the ceiling, suspended above her like stalactites; globules of glue adhered to the fibers of her wall-to-wall carpet; a suspension bridge of empty Gobstoppers boxes connecting her dresser to her windowsill, just waiting for the wind of her presence to surge past and upend it.

Hurricane Bridget.

Posters of assorted hip-hop artists line the walls – *Wu-Tang Clan, and their 36 Chambers, ain't nothin' to fuck with* – and a spirited hamster, Bumpy, runs in a caged wheel on a shelf. Bridget erases an edge of a peach, which she's added to the apples, then stops, distracted by the repetitive assault of garage rock blasting from below.

"Fucking hell."

She cranks her rap music all the way up, adding insult to aural injury. Ol' Dirty Bastard's "*Shimmy Shimmy Ya*" promotes rawness, but in no way is that rawness associated with the low-end his clan produced in the studio. Unfortunately, the bass from Bridget's modest tweakers isn't nearly substantial enough to provide adequate consolation, but she bumps her boombox to the max anyway. It's the intention that matters to her.

In the garage, the scene of this domestic disturbance, Thomas pounds the skins of his new drumheads as Connor strums a hand-me-down Fender Stratocaster, its distorted sound driven through a decent combo amplifier, solid state, but doing its best to replicate the sound of vintage tubes. They play the same three chords over and over again, religiously, immersing themselves in a blanket of unadulterated noise. It feels like only this vibration exists, as though nothing else flows within the winds of this world. If all of humanity is connected by one underlying force, the unity proposed by followers of Yogis worldwide, surely it's connected via the vibration of the electric guitar. B, to C, to E minor. Power chords, the index and ring finger, clamping down on tinny and tiny strings, sliding from fret to fret, as if charting the path toward sonic salvation. Or oblivion, the apocalypse, depending on your point-of-view and taste in music.

The overhead light in the garage flickers on and off, three times in regimented intervals, as though William is trying to communicate a message in some kind of covert Morse Code, as he had once done as a soldier in the jungle years ago. Thomas and Connor cut the song short and look up at Thomas's 'rents, perched at the top of the small staircase. Maureen squints down at the teens.

"What are you guys doing?"

"We're playing," Thomas says.

"Can you play softer?"

"Not really...loud is the whole point. You said it was okay, Mom."

"I didn't know that Tinnitus was part of the deal."

The youngsters just stare at their elders, who in turn, stare back at them, a Berlin Wall of understanding between these people.

"If we're going to be forced to listen to you, how about playing something we like? Or at least know?" Maureen asks. "Do you know any Grateful Dead?"

"Don't you have to be on acid to enjoy that stuff?"

William, who's trying real hard to let Maureen do all the talking in this situation, can't bear it any longer. He chimes in, ominous and monotone: "Thomas…"

"You guys have one hour," Maureen says.

The parental units leave the teens to their order of business. Thomas and Connor erupt into a fit of laughter. Thomas turns to Connor, egging him on, "Turn that shit back up, man, and make it louder."

Connor grins like a spoiled little kid, "Fuck the Grateful Dead."

Thomas smacks his drumsticks together, firing off a four-count, launching them into the throes of the next song. If you can call it that.

It had been a long time since Connor had visited Thomas's house; he hadn't been there since the days of play dates and dodgeball in the backyard. He had once been a victim of Thomas's ambidexterity on the ping-pong table, a mistake he only made once. The rest of the time they spent playing *Contra* on

Nintendo, the only video game Connor could ever beat, which is why he'd play it constantly – especially in the presence of onlookers. In the game, you're one of two headbanded heroes with unabashedly heroic names: Clint or Lance. One of them looked uncannily similar to a chiseled Oliver North, not sure if it was Clint or Lance, and your objective was to destroy an international terrorist cell called the *Red Falcon,* an organization that was not so discreetly attempting to take over the world. Since this was the Reagan Eighties and the threat of Commies with bothersome nuclear weapons still very much permeated the air, red was an appropriate color for this symbolic bird of prey. As they finish up practice, Thomas hits the bathroom to wash the sweat off his face – he has an extremely fast metabolism and sweats and pees more often than most of his friends, something that sets him up for a fair amount of abuse. While he tends to his perspiration, Connor takes a stroll down the hall, wandering into his comrade's bedroom, closing the door behind him.

Thomas flushes the toilet and practically skips out of the bathroom, on a high after practicing, his ears ringing like an air raid siren is going off in his skull.

"Connor?"

As Thomas peruses the halls, he sees light at the bottom of his door. Thomas lives on the first floor. Not willingly, although as a teenager, he finds that this location is most certainly not a disadvantage. There are only two bedrooms upstairs, to the right is his parents', to the left is Bridget's, and straight ahead is the other bathroom. He cracks open his door, walks inside.

"Close the door, will you..." Connor spurts.

Connor crouches on the floor at the base of Thomas's entertainment center: a bookcase filled with CD's and VHS tapes, with a square cut out for a 27 inch tube television and two closed cabinets at the bottom. One of the cabinets is open and a number of editions of *Tennis Magazine* have spilled out onto the floor. Connor is swimming in them. He opens one of them up, revealing a centerfold of a buck-naked Gennifer Flowers.

"I see you're still using the covers of Tennis Magazine to hide your porn."

Thomas quickly closes his bedroom door, shaking his head.

"Gennifer Flowers, huh?"

"It's historic…it might be worth something someday," Thomas mumbles.

Gennifer Flowers is older than most of the models featured in *Penthouse Magazine*, sagging in places she'd rather not sag, but she did bang the president and there's something about a vagina that has been enjoyed by the leader of the free world that makes the organ more appealing than others.

Connor tosses the magazine back into the cabinet and leans backwards, lacing his hands behind his head.

"First time I masturbated was to Chelsea Clinton," Connor notes.

Thomas, tilting his head, "You mean, Hillary."

"No, I mean Chelsea. I just imagined she was older, is all."

Thomas begins to whistle an anonymous tune as he reaches out for the doorknob, cracking his door back open.

"I think that's enough jamming for today."

***

At approximately 8:05 a.m., Monday morning, the Metro North blue line commuter train opens its doors at Botanical Gardens Station and discharges the bane of the train's regular commuters: Fordham Prepsters.

NO ALTERNATIVE

Fordham Preparatory School is an all boys Jesuit high school in Bronx, NY, squirreled away in the back of Fordham University's Rose Hill Campus, adjacent to the college's industrial-sized garbage dumpsters. Its patronage consists mainly of two subsections: minorities and working class Italian Americans from the Bronx, and entitled white kids from Westchester. Even though they share a common racial heritage and socioeconomic background, it's the white kids who are the bane of the working man's existence on the commuter trains. These commuters have more sympathy for the hard-working Bronx minorities who may well be in the process of lifting themselves up by their proverbial bootstraps, laying claim to the American dream in the way that executives respect, through hard work and native charm. The white kids, on the other hand, have the arrogance of youth and the prerogative of the pampered. They're probably a lot like the children of the commuters and that makes the commuters less tolerant of them. The working men and women of Wall Street, Midtown law firms, and west side Fortune Five Hundred companies are forced to spend a considerable portion of their mornings listening to these brats causing a commotion through the stops of Crestwood, Tuckahoe, Bronxville, Fleetwood and Mount Vernon; then it's a long fifteen minutes before the doors open again at Botanical Gardens. These fifteen minutes usually involve streams of vulgarity, scratching tags into the high-density windows, slamming each other into the vestibule billboards, spitting chewing tobacco into empty Snapple bottles and rolling them under other commuters' seats like hand grenades, but when these troublemakers are finally released, it's in tandem with the release of harmonious sighs of relief among the remaining rail users who are finally halfway to Grand Central Station.

Thomas trundles through the back gate of the Prep, decked out in pleated corduroy slacks, paisley tie and a gingham blazer, bobbing to his headphones that are wired to the Walkman clipped to his canvas belt. Leather-bottomed Jansport backpack loosely slung over his shoulder, he walks in line with about a hundred other teenage boys, who are all dressed, more or less, exactly like he is. He flashes Henry Dukes, the skinny security guard standing inside a rickety booth, his laminated school ID as Henry gives him a pound, the pound he gives every other student, once authenticated as such, along with his signature morning greeting, "Wuz'up, guy?"

In the commons, the heart of the school's testosterone-heavy social scene and reliable provider of Grade D Jamaican beef patties, Thomas sits at a U-shaped corner table occupied mostly by preppy suburbanites. He sits next to his buddy, Jeremy Brewer, a rawboned dude with floppy hair pulled back in a headband and safety pins holding his jacket together. All this style seems to be hiding something sad. Alex Pappas, an extroverted version of Johnny Depp from *21 Jump Street*, but cursed to forever be seventeen, pontificates at the head of the table.

"I kid you not – this bitch knew how to give a blowjob. I'm at the Beasties concert, downtown, in the middle of the pit, and she's flickin' her hair at me, stickin' her ass all up in my jock. And before I know it, I'm in her parents' bedroom, on fucking Fifth Avenue."

Some boys at the table salivate, some hide physical discomfort. Alex is more than comfortable continuing, "She goes down on me, and she's going strong, right?! So, then I ask her to play with my balls."

Eddie Groth, a rambunctious nebbish with attention deficit disorder adds some much needed punctuation, "Chah, Chah, Chah!"

Alex resumes the recitation of his epic tale.

"She looks at me all weird and's like, 'is that what guys like? I mean, like, it's kinda gross down there.' And I'm like, 'are you fuckin' kiddin' me? That's the gold at the end of the rainbow – and you're the lucky leprechaun.' So she gives them a tug, and I just blast all over the place. Like a super soaker. My load hits the ceiling fan and splatters around the room – like shrapnel."

Everyone is astonished by this story and too amateur to call its details into question, so they do their best to conceal their ignorance. The last thing they want is to appear as novices, so they smile nervously and nod their heads a little too hard. But Eddie can't help himself, he's on Ritalin, although that lengthy regimen doesn't appear to have had any impact on his personality.

"I came in a fucking key-hole once," Eddie states.

Thomas contemplates this brazen feat as everyone gawks at the little weirdo. Was this a key-hole in his own house? Was it on his property at least? Or did he violate an innocent and unassuming door in public? Were there witnesses? Did he have help? Accomplices? Was he injured in the process and what exactly was the motive? How would this act provide pleasure to a man? Thomas gets the last word.

"Cool, Eddie. Thanks so much for sharing."

The bell rings.

Thomas and Jeremy walk down the second floor hallway, past a row of dented lockers, on their way to their respective first periods. The maroon checkered floors – the color of the Fordham Ram – reek of Pine-Sol, or whatever substance the custodial service uses to burn away the pungent trail of teenage boy day in and day out.

"I'm going to start a band," Thomas says.

Jeremy's interest is piqued, something that's not exactly achieved easily.

"Seriously?"

"Never been more serious in my life, man." Thomas grins. "Just started playing with a dude from grammar school."

"Grammar school?"

"We went to grammar school together. He's in high school now – public high school – where they actually let girls attend class."

"Who needs girls when we got Jesus?"

Thomas snickers, stops at a classroom door as Jeremy keeps walking. Thomas twists back to his friend, "You going to the field tonight?"

"Yeah, man. Want me to pick you up some green?"

Thomas pulls out a crisp ten-dollar bill and slaps it into his boy's hand. It's always a little strange for Thomas when he enlists Jeremy to get him drugs and not because of the illegality of the transaction. It's during the act of exchanging money that Thomas wonders about his friend, for very explicit physical reasons. He wonders if Jeremy feels a need to display his particular stigmata, if the inability of Thomas and some of his other friends to avert their eyes is the very reason that the scars on Jeremy's wrists are so obviously visible.

Jeremy lives around the block from Thomas and they've lived right around the block from one another for the entirety of their brief lives. They just didn't figure it out until high school. Something about living in Colonial Heights, in Yonkers, the air up there connected them on a quasi-metaphysical plane. Yonkers is the second hilliest city in the country, second only to San Francisco. There's literally nothing level, everything's crooked; residents joke that the city's topography is also reflective of its political landscape. Thomas met Jeremy for the first time during their freshman year on the southbound train platform in Tuckahoe awaiting the 7:31 local train to New York with stops at Botanical Gardens and Fordham Road in the Bronx. Botanical Gardens is the preferred stop for Fordham Prep students because you're risking your life, or at least your lunch money, getting off at Fordham Road.

The two kicked off their metaphysical relationship with an experiment in lysergic acid diethylamide, LSD, an experiment that Jeremy had turned into an extracurricular hobby. Thomas had yet to indulge in it, mindful of the horror stories passed on to them by their guidance counselors, but these horror stories had not prevented him from becoming fixated on the drug and he was anxious to drop some, provided there was adequate entertainment and an adequate guide. Jeremy was the guide, and the entertainment was David Lynch's *Twin Peaks: Fire Walk With Me,* the movie prequel to the mind-bending, and some-times head-scratching, hit primetime television series. Inside a dark theater, their senses were assaulted with a well-dressed dwarf dancing backward, floods of stroboscopic light, David Bowie playing the role of an invisible FBI agent, cherry pie, and a soon-to-be-dead prom queen raped and murdered by her father, who incidentally morphs into a deranged lumberjack each time he fucks her. Perfect material for two teenagers with heads full of acid.

The first four hours of drug-immersion were transcend-ental in every facet of the word. The mysteries of life were argued, and then promptly resolved. There was no record of their revelations, and they could not recall them afterward, but that in no way diminished the experience and what was acc-omplished during it.

The inevitable fall came about halfway into the trip, when Thomas's guide urged him to supplement his high with a bong hit. It is generally understood by experts in the art of the trip that there is a perfect time to get high and that time is when you are well into the comedown. The world is getting soft and a joint or a bong hit is like that last little hill on a roller coaster, it takes you back up one more glorious time so you can enjoy the softness of the comedown all over again. But the thing about acid is that it's totally mental, for instance, if you have it in your head that you shouldn't do any other drugs while on LSD, that it will ruin your trip if you do, then it will actually ruin your trip. You must make rules and you must stick to them or else civilization as you have always understood it will collapse. This is the very origin of the rule of the comedown joint and these rules are not to be ignored. Against his better judgment, and at the insistence of his trained guide, Thomas broke one of his fundamental rules at the peak of his trip. As he inhaled the smoke from a two-foot glass bong, loaded with a belly full of ice water, he felt the rise of insanity from his torso to the top of his head, like the mercury in a thermometer dipped in molten lava. He instantly regurgitated everything in his stomach. Unmercifully, it didn't end there. His mind was convinced he had poisoned himself, even though this was clearly preposterous. It kept triggering his gag reflex, expelling the toxins from his body, but there were no more toxins left to expunge. After he puked all the bile his stomach lining was able to produce, he kept going, gagging on nothing, and subsequently cutting off the airway to his lungs. He doubled over on the ground, struggling for breath, unable to get even a single panicked word out.

Jeremy approached Thomas, as he knelt on the porch outside his friend's house. Jeremy's mother worked graveyard hours as a nurse, ironically, and she was working at the time of this incident. The typical things Thomas heard might happen on a bad trip started to happen, though it didn't seem quite so typical to him. Should have listened to those goddamned guidance counselors.

Jeremy looked right at his friend, his metaphysical neighbor –

"Hey neighbor!"

He asked him if he was all right, if there was anything he could do, anything he could get him, a cold beer perhaps? A Zima? Some chewing gum? Of course no product on the face of the Earth could have any appeal for Thomas at this moment, each name, each product concept, seemed absurdly useless to Thomas, comical to the point of desperation, and this comical collection of product names set off a cascade of psychological echoes in Thomas, reaching back into his childhood and extracting punchlines from the Bazooka Joe comic strips that came with that product, setting these punchlines up as a bit of poetry and then bending them into darkly existential verses expressing the folly of all human exploits, like something Samuel Beckett might write, Qua, Qua, Qua. Time itself seemed to have ground to a halt for Thomas and created a vantage point from which he could see the scope and foolishness of human history, reaching back to some primordial state before the caveman and then leaping forward into the distant future, to a place where the very world under his feet had become a product, the dirt and grass replaced by a vinyl substrate that breathed with the life force and intelligence of some superhuman computer. Thomas didn't want to know about the vinyl computer world, he didn't want to see the glory of human achievement snuffed out by the relentless crunch of a future technology beyond our control and understanding, but there was no way for him to get away from it; his body seemed ironed into place, here on this porch, a short step from his slowly hardening puke, so in his head he devised a way to flee from the bell jar of frozen time, a way to propel his crumbling mind into another place and he did this by imagining a huge boot, a boot of his own devising, a boot that looked like something a coalminer wears. No, what a cowboy wears. Yes, no, that's not it, like something a Beatle wears, or wore when they were still together, the kind with the elastic, the laceless kind, and this boot was him, but not him, exactly, a boot that represented him without destroying him and he pictured this boot coming down on the accelerator of a car, but not a regular accelerator, an accelerator that more closely resembled a lava lamp than something you'd find in a car and all of this was being designed by Thomas in the instant of his greatest need. The boot came down on the lava lamp accelerator with crushing force and the mind of Thomas Harrison left our world, left our solar system, our galaxy, maybe even our universe, crossing through this threshold by means of a tiny wrinkle in the cosmic fabric. The mind traveled to black holes and blue stars going supernova and it drifted in this celestial plane for every bit of time that ever was and ever will be. The mind became all of space and all of time, it was both immense and smaller than a quark, it existed as all experiences possible and it knew the perfect silence of no existence whatsoever.

As time and space swelled the recesses of his mind, Thomas couldn't tell if he had passed through a wrinkle in the universe or a wrinkle in time, and he began to imagine that he had passed through a wrinkle in his own face, his face at one million years of age, suspended in the heavens like a sign of the zodiac, and the speed with which he folded into himself threatened to pull his entire essence inside-out, like the way his mother folded his socks when she did his laundry, and he couldn't stop it, at all, from happening, all he could think about was the inevitable moment when these two versions of himself would integrate into each other, the younger version and the older version, and what parts of himself would then dominate the other, whether or not his younger face would become his older foot, or whether his older face would become his younger foot, and in considering what he might do to prepare for these possibilities, he became incredibly annoyed that he had worn boots, because he should have worn sandals, so that whatever part of him ended up as his foot would be able to breathe, and this made him wonder about lost socks and whether the part of him that had drifted into the wrinkle of space, or the wrinkle of face, would ever find its way back to the sock drawer or if it would be eternally adrift in sock purgatory.

Thomas thought of how his life might be forever disproportionate due to the missing other sock of himself.

Eventually, the head of the person that was once Thomas Harrison opened its eyes and saw his friend standing over him, with something a lot like worry etched on his face. Jeremy said something about the effectiveness of yogurt on the effects of the bad trip, but from Thomas's perspective, Jeremy's mouth wasn't even moving. It was as though Thomas could hear his thoughts through telepathy or some kind of supernatural phenomenon, as if the acid allowed Thomas to tune his brainwaves into the brainwaves of the people around him, astonishingly circumventing the shackles of verbal communication. Thomas begged Jeremy to take him to the hospital, to drop him at the emergency room and be done with it. He had no concerns about getting into trouble with his parents or the cops, no concerns that his young, fragile life would be derailed in ways that would be completely unforeseen from where he stood now, he was certain that immediate medical attention would be well worth the few months of being grounded or the obligatory stint in rehab. Jeremy began to cry, tears began pouring out of him, perhaps that Lynchian dwarf had crept back into his psyche, dancing backwards along the heightened plane of his consciousness, and he grabbed Thomas and hugged him. He hugged him as tight as he could, and said he was sorry.

Was this the reason why the hippies were so touchy-feely? The reason the peace and love generation was so loving? Because they were so fucked-up on acid that each of them needed to hold onto another human being for fear of falling off the cliff of individual consciousness?

Whatever it was, it was no bullshit. Thomas's mind had convinced himself that he must vomit, and with nothing left to vomit, he had merely been choking. If one stops breathing, one will die.

Not a good realization to come to with six hours left on your trip.

Now, after disappearing into the vortex of his mind and reappearing an instant later, while at the same time having experienced the entire history of the universe, Thomas realized that Jeremy's embrace was the only thing that helped, the only thing that made sense in a nonsensical state of mind.

"I'm sorry, Tom. I'm sorry…"

Jeremy takes the ten bucks from Thomas and crumples it into the pocket of his beltless pants, which are in danger of slipping past his ass, and he continues down the hall of Fordham Prep to his class. Of course Thomas wants some weed.

Jeremy turns, strutting backwards just like that damned dwarf, and shoots Thomas his trademark point, underscoring it with an, "Aiiight."

***

Bridget is parked in art class, surrounded by her classmates at their individual easels. Ms. Sheehan, her skinny, exceedingly longhaired, Earth-mother of a teacher, makes her rounds from student to student. She stops behind Bridget, eyeballing her canvas. While others concentrate on drawing bowls of luscious fruit, glistening and ripe, Bridget touches up an image of fruit, apples and such, impaled on several razor-sharp meat hooks. Ms. Sheehan surveys the depiction with interest, "Do you think you'll ever actually follow the assignment, Bridget?"

Bridget adds some luster to those metallic hooks, "Not likely."

"I do kind of like it."

"It needs more blood," Bridget observes.

"Of course."

Sheehan shakes her head, but has to smile, as she continues along to another student. Bridget places her pencils down, closing her eyes, and exhales. Bridget exhales for the therapeutic value of the act.

Bridget has been prescribed anti-depressant medications, many different medications, a bounty of medications, medications as plentiful as Baskin & Robbins ice cream flavors, medications in all shapes and colors, in colors much more numerous than the colors of the rainbow, medications in quantities nearly equal to the many languages of the human race, a tower of Babel of medications and she has been on this laundry list of medications since she was eight years old. What childhood malady could have justified this salad bar of meds being visited on Bridget? Sure, a casual observer with an eye for analysis might have detected her lack of motivation on the soccer field at an early age, like the way she'd shy away from the ball whenever it was kicked anywhere near her, or noticed her brittle temper, like the time she smashed all the windows on the garage door with a hockey stick. An ever-increasing percentage of the medical community views these childhood failures as justification for testing new wonder drugs on innocent children. Bridget suffers much, there's no doubt about it and most of all from a debilitating anxiety. The bone-chilling anxiety that accompanies her while being forced to give classroom presentations. The gastrointestinal stomach ailments that she swears are there, but no doctor can officially confirm. The anxiety of her compulsive drawing and erasing, drawing and erasing. Bridget suffers.

Just breath. In. And then out.

The phenomenon of syncing one's breathing with another's is seldom discussed, but is a considerable fear held among the anxiety-ridden. It's something Bridget obsesses over: the idea of someone other than herself controlling her breathing. It is simultaneously smothering and freeing. During an anxiety attack, breathing becomes front and center, you can actually convince yourself to stop breathing if you're anxious enough. Or so you think. But it's what you think that matters. It matters enough to actually cause you physical pain and discomfort. And that's a problem. Inevitably, nobody thinks you're crazier than you think you are.

In an attempt to combat her anxiety while giving a presentation on earthquake preparedness – an endeavor not worth the chalk when you live in the northeastern quadrant of the country, but an assignment is an assignment, and who knows what part of the country one will abscond to when free to abscond – Bridget focused on her classmates around her. She attempted to picture them in their underwear, a ridiculous cliché, but one that had worked for her in the past. It didn't work this time. She couldn't picture anything. No boxers, no panties, no edible thongs, no pierced labia or Prince Alberts; just her breathing –

And the sound of other people breathing.

Bridget became deaf to her own rhythm as her classmates began breathing in the same tempo. At least that's what she thought was happening. In actuality, it was Amanda Welsh, and only Amanda Welsh, overweight by acceptable Westchester standards, with dimples the size of pomegranate seeds and the crease of her belly pinching the plaid of her uniform with every exhale. Her breathing eclipsed that of her peers, thunderous sound waves created at a distinctly lower frequency and emitted from the inner depths of her flesh.

She was like a bag of bagpipes squeezing itself.

Bridget could hear nothing but her breathing; in fact, she honed in on it, on the wheeze of air passing through a crowded windpipe.

Inhale. Exhale. Inhale. Exhale.

Like the equalizing knob on her stereo, Bridget's brain shut off the treble and turned up the bass, louder, louder, louder; all the way to the max. Every word out of her mouth was garbled, as if she was speaking underwater. The only frequencies allowed into her ear canals were those from the bagpipes. As a result, she adjusted her breathing to mimic those of the bagpipes, because if she didn't begin and end her breath at the precise moment the bagpipes did, she would cease breathing. And, of course, die. The bagpipes were her assisted breathing machine: at this very moment, standing before her class, every movement, every word, every breath, being judged by her peers, her teacher, the loiterers in the hallway passing by, and her breathing was regulated by a bag of human bagpipes.

She was a stock car stuck in its groove, unable to change lanes. Then she stopped. Breathing.

Either the overweight girl she was listening to stopped breathing, or Bridget mercifully broke free of her often unforgiving burden. Either way, the end result was the same: Bridget's knees buckled, her legs collapsing underneath her, and the side of her head smashed into the corner of her teacher's steel desk. She was knocked instantly into blissful unconsciousness.

She likes this moment the best.

***

Thomas sits attentively at his desk in English Class, somewhere in the middle of the room. His posture is honestly something to behold. As with a lot of things with Thomas, it isn't entirely clear if the posture is an indication of his serious nature, or purely a necessary ruse. His teacher, Mr. Markham, sits on the lip of his desk as a Hispanic slacker with a goatee, Elias Santoro, stands at the front of the room holding a crinkled piece of loose leaf.

As he addresses the class, Markham lets out a sigh that is two parts ennui and one part pain. "Since Mr. Santoro so shamefully disrespected his fellow classmates by wearing headphones during our poetry presentations last week, I felt it was fitting for him to explain himself. Apparently, the music he was listening to was more important than the poetry we were reciting, so he's now prepared to analyze the song and critique its poetic value."

Markham leaves it at that; he doesn't turn toward Elias, the culprit, the bad seed, the rabble-rouser, the loose cannon, the loner, the misunderstood, he doesn't acknowledge him in any perfunctory way, just lets the painful silence extend in the class until –

Elias shuffles, looks down at the paper, which he crinkles even more. This kid is such the rabble-rouser that he actually likes the awkward silence.

"*Drain You*', by Nirvana."

The teenager looks up at the class, assessing his prey. A few kids scratch their heads, a few pick their noses, all with their middle fingers, and one grabs a hold of his crotch. Elias looks back down at the page, clearing his throat – for a small kid, he's got a rasp, a smoker's rasp, like he's been smoking since he was about two. Hey, kid, happy birthday, here's a hot wheels and a pack of Lucky Strikes.

Markham waves a limp hand, barely lifting his extremities, as he commands the attention of the class. "So, Mr. Santoro, what's it about?" he asks.

Elias doesn't miss a beat.

"Sex."

Markham flexes the muscles in his upper lip as though he just bit into a sour gummy worm. "Excuse me?" he asks.

"In fact, the whole album's about sex," Elias contends. "*Smells Like Teen Spirit*, what do you think they're smelling? *In Bloom*, fertilization. *Come As You Are* is self-explanatory. *Breed*, come on, you don't need a Ph.D. to figure that one out. *Lithium* is about being horny; in fact, it's horniness that ultimately leads us humans to happiness. *Polly* is about rape. *Territorial Pissings* is a comment on the biological propensity to 'mark' your mate. *Lounge Act* is about jealousy and smelling your girlfriend's vagina on your best friend's breath—"

Markham explodes, "That's enough!"

"But I'm not finished."

"Yes, you are."

"I didn't even get into *'Drain You'*."

Everyone laughs; this is pretty much the only reason these kids get up in the morning, this is the stuff that makes the torture of high school academics a little bit less intolerable. They love the blind rebellion of adolescence. Markham points at the classroom door.

"JUG."

Thomas watches Elias slink out of the room. As the school bell rings, the rest of the class shuffles out and Markham waves Thomas over. There's much more enthusiasm in Markham when he waves at Thomas; this is the case with the students he hasn't totally lost hope in, the ones who still have a chance to do something productive with their lives.

"I mailed your Georgetown recommendation this morning."

Thomas, nonchalant, "Thanks, Mr. Markham."

"You're an excellent writer, Thomas, your analytical stuff is fantastic. But, to be honest, your poetry could use a little more *oomph*...more emotion, I mean."

"I'll work on that."

He knows it's just what Markham wants to hear.

***

The ritual of dining in the Harrison house is not to be missed. The Harrisons' believe in the family dinner, in the simple idea that eating together can bring a family together and they've been following this belief with reverential fervor for over fifteen years. The dinner is right next to holy; it's the breaking of bread. But it is a crucifix for any teenaged kid. To the teenager, the dinner is where family converges to push the illusion of interconnectedness like crack-cocaine on the corner, in the hopes of actually being able to relate to people as detached from one another as strangers on a train. It's the place where the parental units are most likely to pull out their microscopes for a close inspection of the viral failures infecting their children.

Thomas, Bridget, William and Maureen assume their designated positions around the kitchen table. The focus is on the food. The focus, whether they like it or not, is always on the food. Tonight's meal is sautéed pork tenderloin encrusted with rosemary-infused breadcrumbs with a side of roasted butternut squash. The culinary presentation is beautiful, each plate is artful in its own right, and it's evident that Maureen spent considerable time preparing it. Which is why she must restrain herself from chopping Thomas's fingers off as he reaches across the table for the bottle of ketchup. Instead, she looks up and changes the subject, and in doing so, breaks the silence, "So, Bill, tell us about work."

William chews, and then speaks, while continuing to chew, as if to add punctuation to specific points in his story. "Had an interesting arraignment today. The defendant, Deena Rangarajan, a research scientist over at Packard Pharmaceutical, is being accused of attempted murder. Apparently, this woman, Rangarajan, and her husband, Vikram, were playing what the prosecutor referred to as a—"

He extends his hands and makes a dramatic gesture with his fingers, mockingly indicating quotation marks.

"—'kinky game,' in which one player, handcuffed and blindfolded, had to guess what items were touching them. I believe Vikram poked her with a pencil eraser. Then, when it was his turn to be cuffed and blindfolded, Rangarajan stabbed him twice in the chest with a paring knife."

Bridget shakes her head in disgust, "Jesus."

Thomas pretends to be interested. He's accustomed to the advantages of assuming a posture of interest, and he wears it well, like the tweed jacket with suede elbow patches that used to be his grandfather's. Bridget's overreaction provides an opportunity for William to shove another quick bite of dinner into his mouth.

"I know. It gets better," William insists, enthusiastically.

Maureen smiles; she tends to smile the instant a conversation takes a turn for the worse. If she can counteract verbal darkness with visual lightness, she does so. Perhaps both extremes will cancel each other out. Like charged particles, positive and negative, eliminating the other's inherent dominance. A dichotomy of living: the sun and the moon, 6am and 6pm, the Madonna and the Whore, dinner conversation that ruins your appetite – and the smile to encourage one last bite of your potatoes, or in this case, butternut squash.

"She pretends to call 911, puts him in the car, telling him, insisting, it was an accident, and drives him to Hawthorne Medical Center. But, instead of going to the emergency room, she parks around the block and stabs Vikram, again, puncturing his heart."

Bridget plunks down her fork, "What the fuck?!"

"Bridget," Maureen pleads.

William is unfazed by his daughter's crude interruption, and continues on with his story. "Then, she takes him to the hospital, thinking she's finally killed him, or at the very least put him in a coma. The police question her, and she states that when her husband came home, he'd already been stabbed. The cops then proceed to inform her that Vikram is alive – that he's woken up and told them all about the game and the multiple stabbings."

Everyone keeps on eating.

"Pretty crazy," Thomas says, feigning interest like a pro.

"What's really crazy is, the guy ends up living, and now he's defending her in court! Have you ever heard of such a thing? He's claiming she suffers from depression and bipolar disorder. That it's not her fault."

Bridget slides her chair back, her plate still full, "May I be excused?"

Maureen nods, and Bridget hops up from the table.

"I set bail at half a million, which she posted, to my amazement. She can't go within a hundred yards of her family and she'll have psychiatric supervision."

Maureen watches Bridget stalk out of the room, and then turns to her son. "Any plans tonight, Thomas?" she asks.

"Hanging around Bronxville."

William, through a mouthful of food, "I think the word is 'loitering.'"

"Can I have twenty bucks?"

"It costs money to 'hang?'"

Thomas turns to his mother, filing his appeal. She often enjoys playing the role of judge in her own house.

"I have some curtains you could 'hang' for free," Maureen says.

"Loitering is illegal," William notes, enjoying the ersatz prosecution. Thomas stands up, taking his plate, and also the plate his sister left behind, and marches to the sink.

"It's not worth the aggravation."

William chortles and pulls out his wallet. He plucks a fresh twenty-dollar bill and bestows the greenback upon his son.

"Here. Don't waste it."

Thomas grabs the bill and bolts.

Later that evening, an itinerant group of teens gather in *the field*. It's the field because they've named it such. There are similar fields in which teenagers hang in every county across the country. They could name it something else, something unique, something less obvious, something like Hark's Point after Timmy Hark the beloved former leader of their pack, the man who started their great tradition, who now calls South Bend, Indiana his home and inexplicably became a college football fan. They could honor Timmy, they still like Timmy, despite the college football thing, but then it wouldn't be *the field*. The remarkable thing about kids in the nineties is that every kid felt alone, alienated – from their schools, from their family, from themselves – but they were all alienated together. They found solidarity, community, through alienation.

Alien Nation.

In lieu of bald bulbous heads and red birthmarks, these aliens wore converses and cardigan sweaters, these aliens felt the perennial teen certainty that their generation was different, different from those that inhabited the eighties, the seventies, the sixties, and so on, in their teenage years. Teens in the nineties ignored the fact that they shared a lot in common with these other generations. They swore that their generation was changing the world and the evidence was all around them: in the invasion of their music, their ethos, into the broader culture, not only the American culture, but the global culture; the evidence was in the implicit discordance of punk rockers wearing preppy garb and it was in the fact that no one even blinked at that idea. Post-modernism was a part of their wardrobe, as it was a part of their mind set.

The aliens of Westchester County, all under the age of twenty-one, gravitate around their planet: a metallic beer keg, strategically positioned within the maze of trees. Their choice of sustenance for the evening is Coors Light; the silver bullet of beers, assuring no werewolves will fuck with them tonight. Thick brush forms a natural barrier from the road, while the opposite side of the field converges on the bank of the Bronx River. It's the kind of place that kids always choose, a place that seems hidden to those who are hiding but obviously exposed to anyone who might be looking for them. The party is barely controlled chaos – a litter of red plastic cups, a surplus of smokes, and way too much noise for what's supposed to be a hush-hush party. Thomas, Jeremy and Alex hover in a circle smoking a blunt.

"Dutchie?" Jeremy asks, as he inhales a massive cloud.

Alex nods in the affirmative, so it's not technically a blunt, it's a Dutch, a distinction marked by the type of cigar wrapper in which the marijuana is rolled. To a stoner, this is the best kind of semantics, the kind that revels in the accoutrements of the act of getting high.

"Vanilla Dutchmaster…toasted."

Thomas glances around at various couples strolling the field, holding hands, cuddling, kissing, and engaging in an array of PDA [Public Displays of Affection]. He zeroes in on a scuzzy guy lurking through the area in Birkenstocks with distractingly hairy toes. He's got a towel slung over his shoulder, and is ogling random girls who pass him by.

"Who's the shady looking dude?" Thomas asks.

Alex squints at him, recognizing the kid, "That's Beau. He's cool, man, I play hockey with him. Carries a towel around 'case he gets lucky and lays a Betty down in the bushes."

"Confident, huh?"

"He's hung like a Scud Missile."

Jeremy looks at Alex, dying to delve deeper into his observation, but he figures it's best for all of them if he holds back. Alex tries to save face, a remedial act he might as well have stopped attempting years ago. The line Alex crosses, and the frequency with which he crosses it, is an enterprise to behold, as his line is painted miles away from the streets traveled by common man.

"So I've heard," Alex maintains.

Jeremy can barely contain his laughter. Thomas continues scanning the area, peep watching, and spots Elias straddling a tree-stump, downfield, strumming an acoustic guitar. He inches his way out of the circle, "I gotta piss."

"Breaking the seal, already?" Alex asks. "You're gonna be pissin' all night…"

Thomas tips his cup back, chugging the rest of his beer. Just as he's about to finish, he holds a mouthful. Alex scrambles, but he's too late: Thomas sprays the beer on his buddies, but mainly all over Alex's brand new Simple sneakers.

"Douchebag! Hope your piss burns," Alex shouts.

Thomas stuffs the cup into his back pocket, crinkling the plastic, and treks over to Elias. The grass becomes more overgrown, more and more out of control, as he negotiates his way toward the Fordham Prep pariah, at least in the eyes of the faculty; specifically, the chair of the Language Arts department, Mr. Markham. Thomas shakes a foot as he steps into a particularly unkempt patch of grass, hyper-aware of potential predators, like ticks or other fanged vermin, hiding in blades stunted by their proximity to the exhaust fumes of the Bronx River Parkway. Thomas has always felt that the suburbs around cities like New York are a massive Darwinian experiment aimed at discovering exactly how much rubbish, chemicals and pollution the native wildlife can withstand before mutating into a new species. He dances and sidesteps around substantial bushes and clumps of grass, a dance that is a clumsy charade, in an attempt to avoid eye contact with the looming figure with the blunt instrument in his hands that he's rapidly approaching.

"Fuckin' ticks—"

Elias wears a stained white tee with "Fuck T-Shirts" hand-written across it in magic marker under a black pleather trench coat; his aesthetic is less slacker than it is grim reaper. He watches the tips of his fingers, like he's mesmerized by them, tracing their movements as they navigate the guitar strings. He is also singing, rather quietly, but sounding pretty damn good:

"Gather 'round, in the gym, people clapping, not for him./

He's not popular, he's to blame, he seems normal, he's insane./

Blow your whistle, referee. Damn you're late, he broke his knee./

I'm not gone, I'm just so far away, and then he said you got a beautiful team./

Kill the team, kill the team, yeah, kill them all for me...."

Elias pauses his instrumentations, and looks up at the nearing teen. Thomas assesses him, more like judging, "So, you're like that dark loner who comes to parties and doesn't talk to anyone?"

"Dude, you don't know how many girls I get doing this," Elias replies.

Thomas can't help laughing, even if it's only briefly. He knows this song is one of Elias's originals. Originals. There's a nice ring to that. Thomas realizes that, until this very moment, he has never actually heard any friend, acquaintance, or even the novice musicians in Sam Ash testing electric guitars and distortion boxes, play anything other than cover songs. He squats down next to Elias Santoro, eager to pick what's left of his brain, "Ever think about joining a band?"

Elias gives this some genuine thought, taking his time – like he's contemplating chaos theory.

"From time to time," Elias says.

Elias strums a chord; Thomas persists with his inquiries, "I'm looking for a singer." If Elias's expression changes, it's undetectable to Thomas.

"You're in my English Class, right?" Elias asks.

"Yeah."

"Here's some 'English' for you..."

Elias immediately rips into a verse of the Sex Pistols' song, *"Bodies,"* picking it up from a line that has more "fucks" in it than any other lyric. Thomas smirks, recognizing this classic of bygone British punk. He attempts to sing along, too, with his best anarchist intonations.

Thomas puts the brakes on his boyish excitement, though; not wanting to let on in any way that he thinks this meeting has developed into a momentous occasion. In his expertly repressed youthful exuberance there is such optimism, such blind faith in the potential of tiny things, that Thomas actually believes history might judge this as a momentous occasion. Like one of those stories about when John met Paul or Peter and Roger found Keith, a yarn that takes on majestic dimensions as the bit players mature into icons of the world stage. Some people would call it a delusion, but Thomas, in this moment, thinks of it as a vision – a prognostication of the heir to their musical throne.

At the very least, Thomas knows this motherfucker can sing the word "fuck" as good, if not better, than the very fucking best of them.

He has just found his front-man.

***

Jeremy takes another hit off the smoldering Dutchie – these things seem to burn without ever ending – as he watches Thomas and Elias fraternize amidst the trees in the recessed corner of the field. He figures his friend is probably up to something.

Alex downs the rest of his beer, tapping Jeremy on the side of the shoulder, regaining his attention, "Who am I?"

Jeremy faces Alex as he flips his plastic cup into the air and holds out the top of his hand. The end of the cup smacks the edge of his fingertips, then tumbles haphazardly to the grass below.

"I don't know," Jeremy replies.

"Greg Louganis."

NO ALTERNATIVE

Alex bursts out laughing at his own joke, and what a brilliant joke it is.

CHAPTER THREE

The political climate of the 1990's stands in stark contrast to the decade it succeeded. In the 80's, nuclear war was at the forefront of everyone's consciousness. This is reflected in the leaders elected at the time: it was an entirely republican decade; in the most general sense, republicans run on fear, democrats run on hope. The Commies were the villains. They were public enemy number one, the basis for our fears, and the threat that eclipsed our collective hope as a people. The only sure thing safeguarding freedom's frontier at that time from being attacked by the Ruskies was MAD, an acronym for Mutually Assured Destruction: a policy described by Ronald Reagan himself as a *suicide pact*.

The simple calculus of this policy was if the Russians launched a nuke at us, we'd launch a nuke right back, blowing both of our countries straight into two of the seven circles of hell. And the same went for us launching a nuke at them. This was actual foreign policy, not political satire or a clever cartoon in the New Yorker or a black comedy out of Hollywood featuring a multi-talented British comedian. This was existence.

The policy completely ignored the legitimate possibility of inadvertent attacks, rogue launches, simple human error and the potential confusion of missile launch tests – because if nuclear warheads were to be the center of our foreign policy, then the missiles that carried them had to be built and tested. Thankfully, the Ruskies shared our core human values; they're heathens, but they value their no good communist lives enough to protect themselves from oblivion.

For Reagan, suicide wasn't quite scary enough; it read more like a passive/aggressive threat. It didn't have nearly enough teeth for the United States of America and its Department of Defense. Reagan used to play cowboys in Hollywood Westerns and he had an image to uphold. The U. S. of fuckin' A. had an image to uphold, standards of machismo to meet. He needed to up the stakes, raise the drama, and load the Smith & Wesson – the whole episode was shaping up to be a good old-fashioned ten paces, turn-and-draw shootout. Have you ever seen a cowboy commit suicide? Cowboys don't commit suicide. They stick boots up asses, and in this case, the redder the ass, the better. Reagan could have been listening to the Butthole Surfers airin' their lungs about Chairman Mao, doo-doo and the atomic bomb in their song *"Moving To Florida."* Reagan could have been inspired by it at the time.

Scratch that, there's no way Reagan listened to this song, nor anything else off their album *Rembrandt Pussyhorse.*

It's safe to say he probably never listened to anything close to the Buttholes, and most of the country was right there with him. Especially since their punk rock aesthetic might easily be confused with communism to the untrained ear. They were part of a burgeoning underground movement in indie music, along with bands like Sonic Youth, Dinosaur Jr., and Big Black, all who went largely unnoticed. Which meant poverty, more or less, as the big corporate labels simply weren't interested in what they were selling. The Buttholes lived in one cavernous room, its walls painted silver, and they slept on plywood platforms suspended by chains from the ceiling. They refused to be paid individually. If one member wanted to buy a pink bandana, all five of them bought pink bandanas; if one member needed a new pair of shoes, they would all buy new pairs of shoes. You get the idea. They were always together, for meals, everything. Like the longhairs of the 60's, they were outcasts, but they were outcasts together. However, their rebelliousness didn't result in an equivalent countercultural movement. Not even close. Not in the face of *Mutually Assured Destruction*. The threat of nuclear obliteration has a way of fostering a widespread sense of apathy.

Reagan would be damned if he'd let this indifference infect the hardworking, God-fearing, wholesome citizens of his part of the country. He needed a way to combat this enemy, this threat of apathy, manifesting itself culturally as the stagnation of the Cold War, in his eyes. He needed to bring this war into the future. He needed to give us – his faithful, idealistic, and patriotic citizens – a specific enemy, and a specific manner by which we were going to kick the Commies' asses, an innovative and technological approach that only the U. S. of fuckin' A. could deliver. The answer, the skeleton key, the administration's foreign policy solution:

Laser beams.

It was laser beams that would destroy the Russians; it was laser beams that would destroy communism. And, accordingly, it was laser beams that would destroy our sense of apathy. We would vanquish our twin enemies of apathy and communism by scattering satellites strategically throughout low Earth orbit, powered by combustible nuclear energy that would engage a series of laser-emitters designed to shoot down any number of incoming enemy warheads. The technology would allow for the simultaneous neutralization of nukes that entered our spatial boundaries, functioning like a protective armor wrapped around the entirety of our country. More like Saran-Wrap, considering the armor was invisible. It was like the deflector shield employed by the Death Star in *Star Wars*, and it was derided as such. But since Westerns were now passé, much to the disappointment of the commander-in-chief, why not turn to science fiction as a storytelling genre through which the theater of politics could spin its morality tales and perform its international vaudeville?

Since George Lucas owned the *Star Wars* franchise, the administration decided to label their foray into sci-fi as the Strategic Defense Initiative, or SDI. This completely obviated the benefits of MAD, which assured that each superpower competed on an equal playing field. With the advent of SDI, the United States could, theoretically, launch a devastating nuclear attack on the Ruskies, and when they retaliated, blast their nukes out of the sky with our laser beams, giving us the clear advantage. This program and the accompanying public announcement, this raising of the stakes, had the chilling effect of tempting the Russians into launching a nuclear attack preemptively before we were able to complete the technology, which would force us into the MAD scenario of our nightmares. Supporters of SDI embraced the idea that countries without the technology would be forced to the bargaining table, rather than be the ones to launch the first suicidal strike, which would then lead to genuine talks of disarmament, ones that didn't involve the assured destruction of anybody, communist, or capitalist.

Reagan waved the idea of sharing the laser beam technology in front of Mikhail Gorbachev's face, but the Soviet leader balked, refusing to believe Reagan would ever deliver credible information. Gorby instead demanded that Reagan give up the pursuit of SDI in favor of returning to the shared apathy of MAD. What Gorbachev failed to appreciate was that his demand was like stopping a cowboy at the ninth pace and insisting he stand there until sundown without ever turning around, without ever drawing his weapon.

As long as both gunslingers are armed and ready to turn around, without actually turning around, all will be right in the world and the tumbleweeds will just keep on rolling through bloodless plains.

Fuck off, Gorby – If I want laser beams, I'm gettin' me some goddamn laser beams.

As a result of Reagan's cowboy posturing, Gorbachev began pumping money into the international arms race, attempting to develop Russian laser beams. Their beams would surely be red; their red lasers, against our blue. George Lucas had no ownership of the colors of his characters' lightsabers, so if Reagan wanted to be Luke Skywalker to Gorbachev's Darth Vader, then this was exactly how he would live out his fantasy. What happened next, whether intentional or not, was both triumphant and fortuitous. The only way for a capitalist to fight a Commie and win was not with nukes, but with money. It turned out that what America could afford, at least in the short-term, the Soviets most certainly could not. No matter how outlandish or scientifically fictitious the goal was, only the American economy could maintain the ruse. The reforms implemented by the Soviets to level the playing field and acquire the much sought-after laser beams, ended up bankrupting the entire country and leading to an abrupt end of communism. Or this is just what the Reagan-backed revisionist historians would have us believe. That the Soviet Union was a corrupt, bloated, and grossly mismanaged totalitarian state ready to be toppled by a force no greater than a mouse fart is an alternative version of that same history. Either way, they lost, we won.

Capitalists, 1; Communists, 0.

So the nation transitioned into the 90's with no clear-cut enemy to revile, nothing left to fight for – outside of the enemies inside us. We got what we wanted. Careful what you wish for. There was that brief altercation with Saddam in the desert, when he fleeced Kuwait of its land and its black gold, but that was like swatting a fly with a spiked mace. That was over in a couple of days, or so it seemed. There was no longer a reason to vote for a republican president.

Enter, Bill Clinton. Baby-Boomer-In-Chief.

The sacrifices the boomers' parents had made, through World War II and the knuckle-busting hard work that followed, finally paid off and now their children could sit back and enjoy the spoils. The economy was flourishing, there was no threat of nuclear annihilation, and welfare had been turned into workfare. Had the Age of Aquarius finally arrived? Had all the celestial treasures and hidden riddles that have remained unsolved for generations finally been uncovered? What was left for the children of this generation to achieve? When you're born into a world that vanquishes the strongest existing communist state and follows that with an explosive boom in wondrous technology and a red-hot economy, what do you set your sights on?

For the generation coming of age in the 90's, there were no simple answers to these questions. There was no process of elimination, no educated guesses. There was no clear-cut path beckoning them. No modus operandi. So they perfected the art of being slackers, an aphorism that future revisionists will surely rephrase as *the art of their culture*, and earned a label that was just about as vague as their sense of what to do with their lives:

Generation X.

***

Bridget lies in bed, lights out, wide-awake, staring at a constellation of self-adhesive glow-in-the-dark stars stuck to her ceiling. There may no longer be a threat of star wars incinerating her neighborhood and her hamster, but there is a distinct possibility that one of these suspended plastic stars might unpeel from the paint and crash down onto her in her sleep, landing in her mouth, slipping through a gap in her teeth and sliding past her tongue, like that fucked-up statistic of the voluminous amount of spiders we unknowingly inhale every year while sleeping. Bridget sleeps with her mouth open, a habit evidenced by the pools of dried drool she discovers embedded in her jersey-knit pillowcase each morning. Her sheets depict a graphic design of the sky, with blue atmosphere and cotton-white clouds. It's kind of like climbing into a Magritte painting every night, then stepping out of it again in the morning. Her drool pool blends in seamlessly with the clouds, so sometimes she can't tell how much of her pillow is stained. Not that she'd wash it any faster if she could tell, not when there are more pressing issues, like foreign objects raining down on her as she slumbers. One of these fucking stars could lodge in her throat and cause some kind of unusual sudden death syndrome. Then, what does it matter if it glows in the dark? It won't help the coroner determine the cause of death any faster, or if she didn't succumb to the death star, it wouldn't help the x-ray specialist locate it any better either, even if he used a black light to assist the ENT as he performs an emergency tracheotomy to remove this accessory of childhood interior design. Bridget feels like her best bet, the most rational approach to the problem, is to simply stay awake all of the time, to just never go to sleep, because who needs the hassle of dealing with such an unpleasant eventuality. Plus, they're so pretty to look at, she's always loved them, from the time she helped her father stick them to the ceiling, hanging in his arms halfway up a tottering step stool.

Bridget brings a small battery-operated Dictaphone tape recorder to her mouth, recording herself, as she gazes up at her cluster of stars:

"It's 4:45 a.m. Such beautiful trees in the suburbs. Sky is clear. Stars shining. But my thoughts are with a man named Giacomo who, in 1836, was the first in his family to die of fatal familial insomnia."

She speaks precisely, measuring her words, like her brother might measure the timing of his drumbeats. She imagines the ordeal that this man went through. Because insomnia is like a vortex of recursion, once you find you can't sleep, you start to think about not sleeping and thinking about not sleeping starts to prevent you from sleeping, so it's only natural that eventually Bridget would contemplate the ordeal of Giacomo. Imagine you can't sleep. Not just for one night or a couple of nights of poor sleep, but you can't sleep at all for days and days. You try napping, but that doesn't work. Your blood pressure rises, pupils disappear, if you're a man, you become impotent. After many days of desperately trying to sleep, the tiredness goes away – you're awake, you're awake all of the time, you're the most productive human being you could have ever imagined yourself to be. It's as if sleep was nothing more than a widespread conspiracy; there's simply no need for it. This period of lucidity is rapturous at times, but in the back of your mind you still know that not sleeping can't be healthy. There is a reason people sleep. There is precedent. That much your mind cannot ignore, no matter how much it tries to. After a month of no sleep at all, your speech suddenly goes, motor skills quickly follow, you lack even the most infantile ability to crawl or suck a nipple. Your townspeople abandon you, thinking you're cursed. They're absolutely convinced of it. As you slip into a coma, you think you've escaped it, that you can finally put your mind, body and soul to a compassionate rest. But, tragically, your mind is perfectly clear, hyperaware of the horror of the situation – you've become a witness to your affliction, but are unable to testify in your own defense.

"Poor Giacomo. I wonder if he had music in his life – if he was able to listen in his last hours. Did it soothe him? Did it help at all?"

Bridget's words drift invisibly into the pinhole microphone of the recorder. As she clicks it off, she closes her eyes. Visualizing...visualizing...

She begins to whisper to herself, "One Giacomo, two Giacomo, three Giacomo, four Giacomo, five— "

Bridget is younger than Thomas – younger only by a couple of years, but to them it might as well be a millennium. She just missed the minimum requirement for Generation X, and she felt too old to be categorized as Generation Y, if there was to be a Generation Y. She supposed there would be, eventually, but she found herself stuck in this nebulous gap in history that seemed even more apathetic than her brother's generation. If Gen-Xer's were nihilistic, what did Gen-Y and their non-existent subcategory have to live for? It was a crisis of existential proportions.

Several years prior, William was involved in some controversial decisions regarding the construction of low income housing in residential, middle class, Yonkers neighborhoods. Ultimately, he issued a decision in favor of the construction, which sparked a fervor among those working men and women in these demarcated zones who had recently taken out second mortgages on their homes. It also didn't help matters that the opponents of the project were entirely white and the prospective tenants – their underprivileged new neighbors – were largely black or minority. When Thomas and Bridget were much younger, a contingent of the privileged public, at least people who were more privileged than the truly underprivileged who were riling them up, organized a protest outside the Harrison home. William knew about it; you can't just show up at an elected official's house wielding signs and shouting epithets without some kind of forewarning, so the cops were there, and orange cones with reflective tape were placed down. It was a little bit more like a block party than a witch-hunt. William sat in the kitchen, reading his newspaper, unconcerned by the protest, the police having assured him that it would only last an hour. They would make sure it did. But a mob surrounding your house is a deeply visceral experience for a couple of kids. It's exciting, real exciting, but also off-putting in the most extreme sense.

The siblings gathered in Bridget's room, as it provided the optimal perch from which to view the shenanigans unfolding on the street below. The two of them huddled by the window, cautiously twisting the rod on Bridget's horizontal blinds, opening the slightest crack in the barrier, careful not to draw attention to themselves. They peered out the glass at the life-blood of the Yonkers' economy, which was walking vigilantly in a repetitive loop on the blacktop upon which Thomas and Bridget once did figure eights in their matching Roller-Racers.

"Hey! You! I see you!"

Thomas ducked, mortified, as he realized he'd blown their cover, having been seen by one of the marchers, a particularly chubby specimen drinking out of a thermos that almost certainly did not contain coffee. The shouts continued, mounting in volume and in a decidedly aggressive tone, the mob apparently assuming that it was William peaking out of the window, not his curious offspring. Bridget hit the floor beside her brother and inspected his demeanor. His face had turned bright red and she could tell he was embarrassed. He couldn't hide from the shouts, which kept on coming, and he wanted so desperately to hide. So Bridget, growing increasingly more annoyed, went ahead and exercised her right to not give a fuck – a welcome side-effect of whatever mental illness her therapist had decided to diagnose her with the previous week. This week might have been borderline personality, a symptom of which was a type of sociopathic behavior involving indifference toward other human beings. An indifference tailor-made for a moment such as this. Bridget sprung up, retracted the blinds, stood up for her big brother and extended her middle finger toward the bigmouth below. This shut him up, pronto – most likely because the bird was being flipped at him by a little girl, and not the big, bad, bleeding-heart judge.

Bridget just smiled at the man, whose face had turned a bright shade of red as well. Even the cops laughed at him.

If Bridget had to choose a letter, she'd be Generation Z instead of Y. It was something about being last, being cataloged at the conclusion of the modern generational alphabet that was satisfying to her. At amusement parks she'd always preferred sitting in the last car on a roller coaster, something about seeing all the assholes screaming uncontrollably and flailing about in front of her gave her an added thrill not typically associated with the ride.

The position gave her perspective, and she liked the fact that no one could look over her shoulder. No one was physically in a position to judge. No one could observe her when she inevitably lost control.

***

In the garage, Thomas crouches behind his wall of drums. There's a sanctity about the space, its placement in the corner, the storage boxes stacked around it, like it was arranged that way on purpose. Outside this area of percussion, Connor cranks his amplifier as Elias tapes a microphone to a makeshift stand.

Elias straps on an electric guitar, tinkers around with it, adjusting knobs and flicking switches, "I have a song that's only about four chords."

Thomas, grinning like a kid in a porno shop, "That's just what we're looking for."

"It's a love song," Elias says. "I call it 'Chummin'."

"A love song about chum?"

"Chum is what love carves you into – after it's over."

"That's out there," Connor says as he vigorously nods his head, totally with it. "I like it."

Elias proceeds to strum a succession of four power chords. Thomas and Connor listen as intently as teenagers can. Elias steps to the mic, "Then I change it up, when I go into the words—"

As the band experiments with the song, waves of sound resonate through the walls and are carried deep into the house via a network of electrical wiring, copper tubing and foundation beams, building into a physical force that is new to the house and which sets it to trembling in the way that tectonic plates tremble in the first blush of catastrophe. The structure is being shaken to its core. William and Maureen escape the clamor, realizing that negotiating with the teens to lower the volume is an exercise in futility and they welcome the excuse to get out of the house. Bridget hops onto the couch and watches her parents drive away through the living room window, the dimensions of which resemble the two-way mirror of an interrogation room.

The guys halt the music, resulting in a cacophony of discordance. Connor spouts words of encouragement, "Good, man. I dig it."

Connor tinkers with the chords on his guitar, trying a minor or two, like a chef taste-testing ingredients for a gourmet meatloaf recipe. *Gourmet Meatloaf,* could be a decent name for a band but for its similarity to the iconic one-named performer. Thomas replays the progression of the notes in his head, assembling and dissembling it, analyzing it like a jigsaw puzzle that has been cut improperly.

"When you come back in with the full chords, into the verse, hit the distortion pedal and belt those lyrics out," Thomas suggests.

Elias bounces it around his brain.

"You think?"

"Let's hear those pipes, big-shot," Thomas cajoles.

Elias nods, Connor looks up.

"I think I might have a good intro."

When the second-rate rock starts up again, pulsing in the air, Bridget ducks into the kitchen. She opens a cabinet over the sink and pulls down a bottle of Stolichnaya Vodka, the preferred brand of her grandfather. Stoli Martini, straight up, very, very dry, no fruit, rocks on the side. For some strange reason she could always remember the specifics of his signature drink, from back when he was alive to order it. He treated his body like a theme park, the theme was alcohol and there were never any lines for the rides; he died when he was seventy-five of emphysema and complications to adult-onset diabetes. *"You never really tried to help me…"* Elias's screaming voice is unavoidable, *"…understand those things you do,"* as it vibrates the countertops. Bridget extracts a prescription bottle of lithium from her pocket, opens it up, pops a pill into her mouth, and washes it down with the vodka. *"And when I close my eyes, I'm still thinking about you…"* Elias continues, *"…and when I look inside, I see there's nothing I can do…"* Bridget places the vodka bottle under the sink faucet, filling it with just enough water to compensate for the booze she drank. *"...it doesn't ever end, so God please help me make amends, the story never ends..."* She opens a sliding door, and steps outside onto the back porch. She lights up a cigarette. The sounds of nature are blunted by the rock and roll as she gazes into the waving trees. She pulls her tape recorder out, pushes play, presses the miniature speaker right up against her ear, and listens.

"It's 4:45 am. Such beautiful trees in the suburbs..."

After only a moment of listening, a moment in which bitter self-judgment works its way quickly through her, like hemlock in her veins. In this instance, she can't help but regret her failed attempts at self-expression, and wonders if she had, or will have, anything worth expressing properly.

She casually tosses the recorder into the bushes, the tape inside still running, playing to an audience of pine needles.

***

A classroom, filled with boys at desks feverishly penciling in multiple choice scantron examinations. Thomas, breezes through his – he's either careless, smart, or both. One of the notable things about Thomas is that he's completely unaware of which of these characteristics best describes him. He finishes first, hands in his test.

The side of the Fordham Prep building, where the old building meets the new auditorium, is the hot spot where the daring hide and rip butts between periods. Thomas and Jeremy slink into the area and light up their smokes, while Alex, abstaining from the habit, initiates their slacker sport of choice: hackey-sack. The defining feature of a Slacker Sport is that it must be a physical activity that a person, or group of people, with very little motivation can perform while smoking or otherwise loitering in ways unbecoming of the model student. In mid-kick, Alex attempts to insert some practical motivation into his pals,

"You guys need a bassist. Then I can start getting you gigs."

"What the hell do you mean, you'll start getting us gigs?" Thomas replies.

"I'm your manager."

The bluster of this approach is something that Alex believes is a form of self-confidence, he believes that by saying something like this forcibly he has a better chance of actually seeing it come to pass. This is the same approach employed by the young entrepreneur who either grows up to become a Hollywood agent or descends into a self-perpetuated spiral, ending his sordid life as an unrepentant pimp. Either road is still an option for young Alex who, like so many unformed young men, displays flashes of great promise. Nevertheless, Thomas and Jeremy snicker at his delusions.

"Manager? You can't even manage your calculus homework."

Alex punts the sack at Thomas's groin, which he nimbly blocks with the side of his knee. Thomas picks up the sack, nods to Jeremy and lobs it to him, who kicks it back into the air.

"Dude, you should play bass," Thomas says.

Jeremy looks a bit flummoxed.

"Me? I don't have a bass. And I don't know how to play one."

Thomas scoffs at his lack of self-confidence, "Sid Vicious didn't know how to play bass and he was the bassist for the fucking Sex Pistols."

Their conversation is interrupted by the sound of a rope scraping against the edge of the building's roof. The boys look up, squinting at the bottom of a metal bucket being lowered between them. On its side is a label: CIGARETTES. The label looks like it was written in red crayon, possibly by the hand of a sentimental kindergartener trying to persuade his cancer-riddled father to quit lipping the devil's stick. The crudeness of the lettering is meant to mock the soon-to-be detained high schoolers, to mock their maturity, which is ironic, considering they're not actually old enough to buy a pack of cigarettes at the local gas station. But it's always more enticing to traffic in the paraphernalia and the substances that the authorities have decreed are off-limits, such trafficking being a right of passage for all teenagers. Dean O'Malley, the academic disciplinarian of Fordham Prep, a man who enjoys his job the way a sports fan would enjoy working the stadium of his favorite team, hunches over the edge of the roof, clutching the rope that holds the metal bucket. Thomas and Jeremy begrudgingly stamp out their cigarettes, extinguishing them under the heels of their shoes, and place them into the bucket. Alex can't hold back his self-righteous glee, "I think you guys might want to think about quitting."

Thomas grits his nicotine-tinted teeth at his friend as he and Jeremy head into the school, tails between their legs.

Fast-forward to a mute classroom, in which Thomas, Jeremy, and assorted hooligans, as deemed "hooligan" by salaried hooligan-deemer O'Malley, sit at their desks in silence. O'Malley is parked at the front of the room, his Rockport-wrapped feet propped up on the desk, reading *The New York Post*, on which a dapper OJ Simpson at his defendant's table graces the cover. O'Malley used to be a Golden Gloves boxer, back in a day that seems enticingly close to him but as distant as prehistory to the kids he oversees. His physical exploits seem more distant than his memories as they are buried under the pain of recurring shin splints, an ailment he mainly treats with Jameson Irish Whiskey. He's been known to drizzle the whiskey on his cereal in the morning. On the blackboard be-hind him, written in block letters, is: "Justice Under God." It's JUG, for short. Jeremy coughs, clearing the phlegm from the back of his throat. Dean O'Malley doesn't even look up.

"No coughing," O'Malley says.

Jeremy, barely a protest, but it's a protest nonetheless, "But—"

"No 'buts.'"

O'Malley puts his feet down, leaning forward in his chair. "You've smoked enough of them already outside."

The acronym, JUG, may not have been very well thought-out by the administrative staff of the school, considering the target audience: libidinous teenage boys. Most of them were al-ready familiar with the magazine of a similar title, the obvious difference being the plurality of the word. It's hardly surprising that a Catholic institution would unintentionally stoke the fires burning in the loins of their underage male devotees. The am-ount of repression inside the walls of an all boys high school, and an all boys *Jesuit* high school at that, is nothing short of startling. It takes loads of self-discipline not to laugh sitting amidst this group of insubordinate perverts while staring str-aight at those letters.

JUG.

Maybe that's the point.

Jeremy puts his head down in defeat, laboring to hold in his coughs, as Thomas chokes on his laughter.

***

Bridget sits across from Dr. Malcolm Brenner, a stout man whose spare-tire is tucked tightly into his pants with the aid of a micro-checkered shirt from L.L. Bean. He's balding, has tor-toiseshell glasses, and is detached to an extent not usually found in someone with a degree in understanding the human mind. Like too many successful suburban psychiatrists, he has just about reached the unforgiveable point in his professional career where he takes his patients for granted, knowing that their options are few and his fees secure.

"Tell me about your experience the other day at school."

Brenner isn't exactly Mr. Rogers, nor is he inclined to invite conversation. This is unusual for someone paid by the conversation. Bridget can't help thinking that he is constantly trying to trick her, that every session is some bullshit act aimed at passive-aggressively sifting valuable information from the coalmine inside her head, an excavation of her most private and personal thoughts, fashioned to appear like mere observation. The environment feels like a product-testing lab designed to determine whether or not she is ready to go to market, ready to be put on shelves. But, as always, if she didn't feel like talking, she didn't have to –

Bullshit.

Bridget sinks down into her chair. She grabs hold of its leather armrests, shifting the weight from her lower back and dispersing it through her shoulders. She begins talking. Just like she does every week.

"I was hanging out before first period, smoking a cigarette with my friends. And then something snapped. My feet felt like they fell out from under me, like I was on a roller coaster or the free-fall at Great Adventure, but I was standing on the ground. My heart started racing. I thought I was having a heart attack. Everyone was looking at me and I just ran inside, into a bathroom in the cafeteria, and started crying. I hid in the stall for the first three classes."

"What inspired you to emerge?" Brenner asks.

"I don't know."

Dr. Brenner goes ahead and pulls out his prescription pad, one of those pads with a hand-stitched suede case that he got as a present from some client or vendor long forgotten. Without hesitation, he begins writing.

"I want you to try this. It should help with the social unease."

He chicken-scratches a prescription, tears it out of the pad, and hands it to his nervous patient:

Excelsior 200mg.

Bridget glances from the script to the pen in her doctor's hand, which features the multicolored "Excelsior" logo on it and flaunts the slogan: "Excelling in Existence." Bridget peers at him, more than skeptical. He continues, "You can take it with the Prozac and Lithium. Shouldn't be a problem."

Bridget's face is a jumble: half-smile, crinkled nose, and a pair of raised eyebrows. Nothing, at all comfortable.

***

What the fuck is your name, motherfucker?!

The plastic prongs of tape cassette wheels spin inside a yellow Sony Sports Walkman, dually equipped with rubber weatherproofing in case its owner happens upon a waterfall on his or her morning jog. The artist is 2 Live Crew and the album is the seminal *As Nasty As They Wanna Be,* one of the first albums to feature the black and white "Parental Advisory: EXPLICIT LYRICS" warning label. The song is *"Dick Almighty."* Its guttural words are rapped over the cotton candy electronica of Kraftwerk's *"The Man-Machine,"* one of the first examples of electronica and the very beginning of the techno movement. It must have been by design that one of the first uses of sampling in Gangsta' Rap would borrow from Kraft-

71

werk. Was Kraftwerk aware of the 2 Live Crew's use of their innocent pop melody as a platter on which an X-rated tale of black cock-worship was to be served?

Dick Almighty, [SCRATCH] all, [SCRATCH] almighty; [SCRATCH] Dick Almighty, [SCRATCH] all, [SCRATCH] almighty; [SCRATCH] Dick Almighty…

This was before musical artists were required to ask permission from, and pay royalties to, another artist for the use of his or her music. If a song was recorded and played, it was assumed to be part of the public domain and gangsta' rappers could steal the fuck out of it. And then Vanilla Ice came along and screwed everything up, predictably; yet another example of the white man fucking it up for the black man. History repeating itself in a small corner of the cultural landscape.

The opening is hypnotic, almost haunting, elevating lyrics that owe more to the porn industry, than to poetry, up to a level of profound misogyny, a level on par with the strokes of a proper psychopath, a psychopath who should be kept as far away from women as the law is able to decree. The song authenticates the generous girth of the black penis and the vaginal tearing that unquestionably results from intercourse with such penises; moreover, the lyrics go on to imply that such an injury is something that's not to be feared, but rather blissfully begged for.

But when it's a young woman listening to this music, a young white woman from the suburbs – who, it's worth noting, is decidedly not part of this record's target demographic – two words from a very different musical genre can generously be applied: Punk Rock.

Bridget walks the narrow train platform in White Plains, her oversized headphones, her cans, cupped around her demure ears. She holds one side of the headphones; she's not so much concerned with the music leaking out into the unsuspecting ears of others around her, as she is with trying to push the bass deeper into her own eardrum. Everything outside of her headphones is like slow-motion, reduced to an irrelevant backstage, as "*Dick Almighty*" reverberates through the intricate canals inside her head.

Bridget plops down on a concrete bench and lights a cigarette, her eyes barely registering the arrival of a commuter train. She stares blindly at the handful of people who exit and enter the train. She just sits there. As the train pulls away, her eye is drawn to a nearby trash bin. Something is sticking out of it. She stamps out her smoke, and then ambles along the platform toward the container. She plucks a small electronic keyboard out of the top of the trash can: it's scratched and cheap, a Casio, but in functional shape. She looks around, seeing if she might catch a glimpse of the person who left this gem behind –

No go.

For a moment, she wonders about the person who might have thrown this little keyboard away, someone who had some dreams about it, some hopes and aspirations, she wonders if the keyboard is defective in some way, if it contributed to the loss of those dreams or if the person was solely responsible. Is it possible to be complicit with an inanimate object, can a tiny piece of electronic equipment really have a lasting impact on any life? Bridget tucks the instrument under her arm and walks down the platform, bobbing to her hip-hop beats.

Dick Almighty, [SCRATCH] all, [SCRATCH] almighty; [SCRATCH] Dick Almighty, [SCRATCH] all, [SCRATCH] almighty; [SCRATCH] Dick Almighty…

***

Thomas, Connor and Elias are back behind their instruments. This time, Jeremy's along for the ride. He cradles an abused Fender jazz bass, the red paint chipping off its maple body, and plugs it into a small amplifier, an amplifier so small in fact, it's unclear whether it's running off electricity or if it's powered by Duracell batteries. Jeremy stands on his tiptoes, it's as if he's balanced on some kind of precarious edge.

Thomas introduces him to their overarching band philosophy, "We only play stuff that's like three or four chords." He goes to great lengths to make the point exceedingly clear, "Five max."

If the point wasn't clear enough, Elias interjects, "And no cover songs. That way no one knows if we're fucking something up."

Connor waves a reassuring hand at the nubee, "I can teach you as we go along."

"Aiiight. Let's do this," Jeremy nods.

Elias, the singer, the front-man, the only member of the band with enough testosterone to grow a complete beard, must always have the last word, like any good front-man must, whether he's aware of this habit, and subsequent right, or not. And he must enact this privilege beginning right now –

"Let's kill this shit."

Amps crackle, as fingers hit the frets.

Bridget walks in through the front door as quietly as possible, even though barely-muted garage rock suffuses the air of the home. Maureen, perched at the top of the stairs, bent to some task like cleaning or hanging pictures, turns toward Bridget as she enters. Maureen would always recognize the arrival of her daughter in an environment, regardless of the circumstances; in the midst of a nuclear holocaust she would still feel her presence. She couldn't escape her.

"Why didn't you call? I was getting worried," Maureen asks.

"I took the train."

"I would have picked you up."

Bridget walks upstairs, brushing right past her mother.

"I wanted to take the train."

Maureen eyes the foreign object beneath her daughter's arm, the thing with the black and white keys, the thing that may or may not have been manufactured to emit some kind of musical melody.

"What's that?"

"I found it."

Maureen tosses her hands up at the vibrating house, "Just what we need...more music."

Bridget strolls into her room, shutting the door gently behind her.

After inspecting the keyboard, running her fingers along its plastic contours and testing the delicate action of its black and white keys, Bridget depresses the power button. Nothing happens. Flipping the instrument over, she locates the battery compartment, opens it up and pulls four "C" batteries out of it. She searches the drawers of her messy desk and locates brand new batteries. She carefully inserts these into the battery compartment and switches the device on, triggering a series of glowing lights peppered along the panel. She tests the keys and is rewarded with piping notes of clarity; it works perfectly, as far as she can tell. She activates some pre-programmed hip-hop beats, available at the push of several purple quarter-shaped buttons along the bottom, tinkering with them, adjusting the rhythm. She plugs her headphones into it and then straps them on her head. Her unfinished still-life canvas is situated behind her in her room, but Bridget has the feeling of a new canvas sitting in front of her as she lays her fingers on the keys.

***

There is a sterility to a courtroom that rivals the indifference of examination tables in abortion clinics, or the bureaucratic indifference of the DMV. The ceremonial room, adorned with handsomely carved cherry wood tables and chairs, is less than half full. The wood is real, everything in the courtroom lends a sense of solidness to the proceedings, but there's also a very real implication that nothing here is real, an overwhelming feeling that it's all a façade, that the very expensive wood is simply filling the empty space of this room with the veneer of dignity.

The bailiff stands, pushing out his formerly muscular chest.

"All rise."

The crowd rises as Judge William Harrison shuffles several stacks of papers and turns away from the bench; his flowing black robe makes him look like he's dressed up as Darth Vader without the mask.

"We'll resume in the morning," William says.

William steps into his chambers and goes through the ritual of removing his robe and hanging it in a small closet. The garb and the routine of donning and removing it every day at work has always reminded him of the priesthood and the vestments associated with that profession. He thinks about how the two rituals probably stem from the same origin of placing authority figures in formal wear so that the unruly masses might pay them heed. William absently grabs his litigation briefcase from beside his desk, the same briefcase he has lugged around since his days as a fledgling class action attorney in

Manhattan, and walks out into the long marble-lined hallway of the municipal building in White Plains. As the electronic security doors part for him, he gestures to Charlie, the security guard, "See you tomorrow, Charlie."

Charlie steps in front of him, as if to shield him. "Your Honor, you might not want to go out this way," he cautions.

William stops walking, emerging from the reverie he normally enjoys during his departure. He looks over Charlie's massive shoulder at a mob of picketers organizing along the curb. They brandish signs, *"Blood On Your Hands!" "Put Them Away, Not Let Them Out." "Baby Killer!!!"* William is stunned. It takes him a moment to register the fact that the barrage of defamatory remarks that the crowd is unleashing in escalating volume and intensity is unmistakably directed at him.

Minutes later, William sits behind his desk, visibly shaken and still clutching onto his litigation briefcase. His clerk, Randall Gomez, paces in a circle in front of him, worried about William, and worried about the protesters, and trying not to divulge that he's worried about the trajectory of his career opportunities as well. William is not one to retreat but he knows how important it is to avoid public confrontations at all costs – he's not just a man anymore, he's a representative of the people, he's their model of objectivity. Citizens' livelihoods, businesses, families and permanent records hang in the balance of his thoughts, opinions, and ultimately, his decisions. His sole decisions. He's no longer a man; he's an institution, and therefore he must think as such.

"News broke about an hour ago," Randall says. "It's all over the television."

"Thirty years of hard work, Randall," William reflects.

"It'll blow over."

"I made the right call – any judge would have done the same thing."

"We all know that."

William sighs heavily as he turns, swiveling his chair one hundred and eighty degrees, and stares out the window, peering down at a bustling bus stop below, at the city streets that have felt like his responsibility for so many years. For the moment, he recognizes that this rapid turn of events has displaced his sense of community; a loss that he dearly hopes is not permanent.

***

Maureen stands over the stove, pan-frying potatoes. She slides a slew of sliced onions from a cutting board into the simmering pan as she watches the local news on a small countertop TV no bigger than a toaster. On the television, police swarm around an opulent suburban home, lights swirling as a team of paramedics wheel out several stretchers. A reporter at the scene of the crime dutifully performs the portentous voice-over, in her signature monotone –

"Only weeks ago, Mrs. Rangarajan was in court, accused of stabbing her husband, and claiming it was an accident. One thing is certain, the events that took place this morning were no accident."

Maureen watches in a trance, but doesn't stop flipping the potatoes.

"Released on bail, Mrs. Rangarajan, who was subject to a strict restraining order, returned home and stabbed her husband and daughters to death while they were sleeping. Mrs. Rangarajan took her own life shortly thereafter. Family members issued a statement hinting at a lawsuit. They believe that Supreme Court Justice William Harrison is to blame for, quote, 'his erroneous and premature decision to set this troubled woman free.' The county is launching an investigation."

The oven beeps loudly, its shrill note cutting through the reporter's narration like the Santoku Bocho knife favored by Maureen. The SB is the perfect culinary instrument for carving bulbous onions into millimeter-thin slices. Home Shopping Network offers an entire set, straight from Japan, in a commemorative ivory-hinged box at twenty-five percent off in-store prices. Maureen didn't miss out on this incredible offer. She bends down, using her legs to avoid straining her back, swings open the oven door and extracts a bubbling ceramic dish of chicken marsala. Maureen swears by ceramic cookware, ever since her Pyrex baking dish spontaneously exploded one evening. Pyrex claims their cookware can withstand both the environs of the oven and the freezer, but what Maureen found was after transferring a freshly baked casserole from one environ to another, it was too much for the rapidly expanding and shrinking molecules inside the glass to handle. While sipping red wine some forty-five minutes later, Maureen and William had to duck for cover as the dish exploded, splintering into dangerous shards, like some kind of improvised demolitions device. It had been sitting in the sink, its bottom pressed against the cold, damp porcelain. Luckily for Maureen, William's Green Beret training kicked into gear, and he threw her to floor and blanketed her with his body. That's how she remembers it, anyways. Pyrex glass is awfully thick and William got a couple of pieces stuck in his back. The wounds blended in with the rest of his scars, including the pockmarked remnants of the horrendous acne he had as a teenager. Maureen carefully places the piping hot ceramic dish on the counter. She blows on it gently, before tossing her oven mitts back in the drawer and turning off the television.

Thomas, William and Maureen assume their usual positions around the circumference of the circular kitchen table, a small carved pumpkin as its centerpiece, candle flickering inside. Bridget is conspicuously absent. The three family members sit in silence, until William breaks it; it's always William who breaks the silence.

"Is Bridget having dinner?"

Maureen is measured in her response. Self-discipline in such moments is what she has prepared for throughout their lives together.

"She said she's not hungry," Maureen replies.

"I don't care whether she's hungry or not, she should sit at the table."

"Leave it be, Bill."

"I will not leave it be, goddamn-it!"

Maureen and Thomas default back into the previously established silence. William stands, getting a hold of himself. He gently pushes in his chair, folds his napkin over the seat-back, and politely addresses them, "I'll be right back."

They watch him leave, on tenterhooks.

"Your father had a bad day."

"No shit," Thomas remarks.

Bridget sits on the floor of her pigsty of a bedroom, headphones strapped on, playing her keyboard, spastically writing lyrics into a marble notebook beside her. The door to her bedroom sticks at the top corner, from years of fluctuating northeastern temperatures and improper insulation, the wood has warped, convexing the corners. To open it, a simple turn of the doorknob won't cut it; you really have to rap at the top of the door with a closed fist. This gives even the most benign entrance a decent dose of dramatic flare. That is, if the door is closed tightly, and when Bridget is writing music, it's closed as tight as architecturally possible.

William stands outside this barrier of her bedroom door, attempting to speak through it, "Please come down to dinner."

No answer. William turns the knob, leans into it, but gets nowhere. He shakes his head and slams the top corner of the door with an open palm. The door bends inward, its molecules oscillating, like those within Maureen's Pyrex as it shifted temperatures, and it flutters open. William doesn't need an invitation to enter any room, no matter who's occupying it, not in his own house. He walks in, stoically. Bridget's momentarily startled, and then proceeds to ignore the invader.

"Please come down to dinner."

Bridget looks up, scrunching her face at her father, "What?"

She removes a single headphone, irritated, leaving the other cupped in place as music continues to blast from them.

"Please come down to dinner," William pleads for the second time.

"Fuck you."

William flips, his face turning crimson red. The trigger has been pulled – the Queen of Diamonds spinning rapidly around in his head. He rips her pair of headphones off, hurling them against the wall, pieces of their plastic shattering into even smaller pieces of plastic.

"No. Fuck you! Fucking bitch!"

Bridget snickers to herself as she turns back to her keyboard.

"I loved those headphones; they were, like, part of my head," Bridget says.

"Not anymore."

William leaves, about as quickly as he entered, slamming the door behind him; court adjourned.

Back in the kitchen, the headquarters of the humble household, Maureen and Thomas are jolted by the sound of the door slamming upstairs. Footsteps echo. William strides back in, reclaiming his seat at the head of the room's table. He resumes eating as if nothing has happened. He turns to his one and only son, "So, how was your day, Thomas?"

Thomas regards him uncertainly, before venturing a response, "Had to be better than yours."

William chews.

CHAPTER FOUR

Rockin' Rex is a hole-in-the-wall record store plastered with new and used vinyl, tape cassettes, and compact discs. If you looked really hard, you might find an eight-track or two floating in one of the dustbins on the floor. Vintage posters with yellowed edges and curling corners line the walls, and the place just smells cool, as if such a thing could be manufactured in order to attract the desired clientele. In the evenings, bands play on a small stage, a plywood platform propped up by milk crates in the cluttered corner. Through the narrow hallway in the back, you can make out a small sink, refrigerator and some rotting Hostess "Fruit Pies" on a stack of dirty plates. It's clear that whoever owns this Mecca of punks around Westchester actually lives here, too. It reeks of a modern day commune, of a place where music rules and its followers come to worship.

Proponents and practitioners of grunge, as movement and lifestyle, frequently malign the hippy generation, but they share much more in common than most of them would care to admit: their mutual lack of concern for cleanliness; their disdain for established methods of interacting and conducting business;

a general contempt for the American worship of money. The grunge generation is almost exactly the same, except that they are a whole hell of a lot angrier – a sentiment clearly reflected in the tone of their music. This has less to do with lifestyle than it does with the consequences of lifestyle. The hippies bought into the peace, love, and music marketing scam in the late sixties that resulted not in utopian bliss, but in holes in their brains. The net result of the LSD, opiates and assortments of amphetamines that they washed their souls with in what gonzo journalist Hunter S. Thompson observed as their romantic, but nonsensical, search for the real American Dream.

Their search for enlightenment resulted in Swiss Cheese being made of their Medulla Oblongatas.

So fuck them.

We must play louder, voicing our complaints as a generation into our elders' rusted ear canals, screaming them as loud as possible, because any softer and they simply cannot hear it, the vibrations will be lost in the holes inside their heads.

We reject you.

We reject you and the fucking flowers in your hair.

Grunge-folk and punks of various ilk watch *The Left* perform on the rickety stage in the corner of Rockin' Rex. The Left boasts a female singer; the rest of the group is male, and they do one hell of a Letters To Cleo impersonation. Thomas and Connor weave their way to the front of the teeming crowd of teens.

Connor cases the place, "This joint gets more and more crowded every time I come in here."

He hops onto a shelf, comprised of sardine-packed vinyl. Thomas stands, surveying the band on stage, absorbing their presence, their je ne sais quoi. The singer, a metal bone inserted through her nose, confronts the microphone.

"Thanks for coming out. There are probably much cooler things you could be doing right now, but you boring mother-fuckers came here to listen to us."

Smatterings of cheers and claps ricochet off the walls.

"Let's do another one."

They break into their song, *"Take It Back"* –

"Let's skip the good part,

returning to start,

I'll press the reset so we can play, again..."

As the spectators pogo, springing themselves up and down to the pulse of the song, a young girl is hoisted atop the animated crowd. This is Jackie O'Brien, petite Betty, trying hard to hide her preppiness. She's restless and risky and offsets camouflage paratrooper pants with a tight white tank top, showcasing her ample bosom. She also crowd-surfs like a pro. Thomas' eyes lock onto her as she floats over the writhing youth, his eyes, with a mind all of their own, cannot be moved away from her as he stares and stares and continues to stare. Connor looks down at Thomas, noticing his stare. It's the kind of stare that's hard not to notice.

"...Get in, get out, I can turn this around./

And keep my feet on the ground."

Connor hops to the floor, dropping to one knee. He looks at Thomas and points his finger toward the ceiling.

"Take it back./

Take it back this time./

Give me some breathing room."

Connor nods encouragingly at him.

Thomas looks at the crowd; in this moment of hesitation lies all of his angst, all of his teen uncertainty, all of his fear of ridicule, the fear that every sane teen has when confronted with the distinct possibility that he will be noticed by his peers, noticed in a way that is not wanted. This fear can destroy the best moments of our lives. If we let it. All Thomas has to do is steal one more glimpse of Jackie and the hesitation is reduced to ashes. It's reduced to ashes via flame-thrower. He steps up onto Connor's leg, contracts his quads, and catapults himself on top of the crowd.

Thomas crowd-surfs to the front, squirming toward Jackie. They inch closer and closer to each other, as best they can while under the manipulation of other peoples' hands. His focus is momentarily derailed as he recalls a hole in his jeans, a hole he tore in them the other day while tightening his bass drum pedal. It's dangerously close to his ass, but it hadn't yet occurred to him that he should sew it up – or plead with his Mom to sew it – as there didn't seem to be any good reason to do so, it seemed like a hole in his pants near his ass was an adequate badge of his grunge ethos and he thought that leaving it there was probably cool in some way. Strategic rips in wardrobe are fashion statements, a sign of the times, and snafus in general are to be embraced rather than fretted over. At a practical level, there were simply no occasions that he could foresee where other individuals would be eye-level with his undercarriage. Until now. Maybe this tiny rip was the basis for his hesitation to expose himself in this way to this crowd, the reason that he didn't think of in time to avoid his current predicament. Thomas simmers at himself, angry that he didn't listen to his own reasonable sense of caution. In his anger and increasing fear, he imagines that there is a distinct possibility that a finger might slip through the tear in question, circumvent his flimsy boxers, and insert itself into his unassuming asshole. While the likelihood of this is probably on par with being randomly struck by an asteroid, it still seems like a very real possibility to Thomas as he frets and glides along the top of the crowd. Just as they're about to meet – not someone's random finger and his orifice, but the girl he's rapidly floating toward, this Jackie O'Brien girl – a portion of the rambunctious mob throws Jackie on top of Thomas. His attention is immediately rediverted back to his target objective; colliding into a supple bosom can have that effect. Their combined weight sends the teens crashing to the concrete floor. Jackie's firm body ends up draped over Thomas as the crowd forms a circle around them. Thomas shakes it off. Jackie doesn't have to; Thomas broke her fall quite valiantly, even if his valiance was unintentional. They look at each other, through the stars and the clouds, making sure they're both physically all right, before breaking into a simultaneous fit of laughter.

Just outside the gates of Rex, Thomas, Jackie, Connor and the singer and guitarist for The Left, Gretchen and Zack, smoke cigarettes along the dilapidated sidewalk. Thomas tries his best to connect with the rock stars of the evening, "You guys drew a great crowd."

Zack moonwalks past Thomas.

"We didn't get any crowd." Zack goes on to insist, "Opening for the InSINerators got the crowd."

Gretchen blows a smoke ring into the air between them, something she is expert at and a skill that her tiny fan base wants to believe is easily transferable to other aspects of her personal life.

"Zack's brother is the bassist for them; they took pity on us," she says.

Thomas, shaking his head, "Nepotism is so anti-establishment."

"Ain't it, though?" Zack replies.

Zack heads back inside with Gretchen. Connor grabs the door, holding it open with his foot as he turns to Thomas, "You gonna watch the other bands?"

Thomas looks at Jackie, thinking fast.

"You wanna take a drive, maybe get some beer or something?" he asks her.

She doesn't even hesitate for a second.

"Yeah. Sure."

She chucks her cigarette, winking at Connor, "Don't worry about your friend, I'll look after him."

Connor smirks as he shuffles inside.

This is the moment for Thomas to tiptoe through the impenetrable miasma of awkward silence and begin wooing this lovely young lady. But he's not quite done with his cigarette and in his mind, as long as he keeps smoking his cigarette, inhaling its poisonous exhaust, he doesn't have to make the next move, he doesn't have to face the possibility that the silence is better than whatever meaningless chatter he might invent. The cigarette is his hourglass, buying him a little more time.

His entire generation is buying time. His generation of suburban teenagers, living the easy life, surviving on the dole of their parents' bank accounts. The struggle of their forefathers is a distant memory, a story Grandpa would recite at visiting hours in the hospital. A story he'd recite repeatedly without realizing he'd repeated it, the repetition somehow diluting the validity of the information for Thomas, as though only hearing a story once makes it more valuable, an auditory jewel to be treasured for a lifetime. The diabetes had usurped his grandfather by that point, the veins in his left leg having almost completely deteriorated; various professionals in the medical field weighed in and performed the first of what was an innovative surgery to replace several of his veins with artificial plastic veins. It worked for a while, but eventually his body rejected the treatment. The visits to the hospital are among the most painful memories for Thomas, something stifling about the small room, the antiseptic smell mixed with an unmistakable scent of decay, the metronomic beep of the respirator. On the surface, there wasn't a whole lot to worry about during these visits, no pressing reason to feel fear, horror, or anxiety. They didn't even have to make sure Grandpa got his medication, the nurses did all of that; he was covered by Medicare. He was a mostly docile man at this point. Not so when he was raising Thomas's mother and he raged against her own period of rebellion. In the sixties, those fucking hippies were rebelling, maybe Thomas and his friends sneer at that rebellion, maybe they think it was less heroic than it seemed to their parents, maybe they think the rebellion had a wimpy quality to it, saturated with love as it was, but they were unquestionably rebelling against something. There was something to rebel against. What do these kids in this record store have to rebel against? Curfews? Their ancestors came here for the American Dream, they fought to obtain it, shed their own blood for it, and now their children are living it. So what's left for the children of those children? What's left when you think you have everything you've ever wanted?

Thomas's cigarette has burned down to his fingertips; his smoldering cherry's on the verge of falling out. Only a moment left with his desperate thoughts.

What's left for the teenage slacker to want? The answer is simple. Sex. Even the most aimless of slackers shares in the desire. Sex. It's the one undeniable adolescent constant. Sex.

Biologically speaking, the human species really hasn't evolved all that much over the years. Some studies report that teenage boys think about sex approximately once every seven minutes. Some also say once every seven seconds. Sex. Maybe it's once every seven words. Johnny Rotten may have been outspokenly anti-sex, despite the name of his band, but the majority of punk rockers, bona fide and posers alike, did not share his sentiment. For Thomas, it was less Generation X, than it was Generation Sex. And this whole music thing, he's now beginning to think, is his entry into the subject that he cannot stop thinking about. Sex. A subject with enough power over him that it is even capable of freeing him from his normally mute behavior.

Thomas watches the burning ember fall from his cigarette, as though in slow-motion, its ash disintegrating against the pavement. He blows the residual smoke from his lungs and looks up at his charge.

"Where should we go?"

Jackie hits him with the hint of a puckish smile.

***

Thomas's car, his parents' gold Toyota Corolla bequeathed to him when he turned 16 and it hit 100,000 miles, sits alone in the empty parking lot of a closed CVS Pharmacy, its engine running and headlights suspiciously off. In the backseat, Jackie and Thomas tumble to and fro, kissing each other with what can only be described as the unrestrained vigor of youth.

Jackie suggests to him, "I have a belt, you know."

He looks at her belt, attempting to pluck the perfect response from the tree of his testosterone-flooded mind.

"You want me to tie you up with it?"

"No. I want you to take it off, along with what it's holding up."

Thomas undoes her metal-studded belt and slides her pants off. He looks at her, in her black lace underwear and tight white tank: she's quite possibly a vision of perfection. They both pause, clumsy, unsure, their blood being redirected to the appropriate parts of their bodies. The segment of our culture that raves about values and tries to tell us all what to do with our lives and our bodies may think that the blood was rushing to inappropriate parts of the bodies of these young lovers. But biology knows better, and in its rush to create new life, it will send the blood to the place where the blood belongs. Thomas reaches in, bringing his hand toward the crevice beneath her panties. As he slides his hand up along her flawless thigh, she grabs his knuckles, roadblocking his fingers. He looks her in the eyes, as if to distract her from the route his hand continues to travel, but it's no use – she's thrown street-spikes down in front of him, shredding his freshly inflated tires and stopping him in his tracks.

In high school, there's a thin line between virgin and slut, and it's a line every girl is forced to strut agonizingly across as though it's a high wire act, with her reputation hanging perilously in the balance. In high school, much like prison, your reputation means your life. If you've had no experience, the smell of lameness will envelop you. It gets into your clothes, the fabric of your car seats, your textbooks, your backpack, your locker, your hair, and others disperse away from you in the cafeteria, and before you know it, no guy with a quarter of an erection will want to get in those pants. On the flip side of the coin, if you sleep around, chalk up those valued lessons and get the palms of your hands on that golden knowledge, you risk being labeled a slut. Once you've entered the gates of whoredom, there's no coming back. There's no reinventing yourself. You're used up, damaged goods; those gates are locked, chained together behind you and it might as well be a cemetery, because your social life is as dead as the carcasses underneath each and every one of those tombstones.

Thomas shifts around, restless. He decides to take a different approach: he leans back, unzipping *his* fly.

From the point-of-view of the teenage girl, boys have it so much easier as teenagers. High school is like an enormous vacuum where time, and the reality implied by our pointless efforts to measure time, is suspended. In one of the great ironies of human existence, high school is a time when almost no one worries about the future, where everything is taken moment by moment. This despite the fact that one's future is never impacted more by what he or she accomplishes there. In elementary school, you're completely clueless and generally not worrying about anything, except whether you can spend more time eating candy and watching cartoons. Likewise, in college, you're worrying about getting wasted and watching cartoons. At the very last minute, in college, you start worrying about getting a job and realize that if you had only done better in high school, you could have gotten into a better college and getting a job would be so much easier. Sure, you need to decide on a major, which will invariably dictate the course of the rest of your life, but it's the flash of the university name on your resume that will open the most doors, even though so many students from the best colleges waste the positive effect of the school name on their resumes by being prima donnas. The inability to prepare for the future in any way is why the college application process is always such a downer, and always the number one thing parents will push their kids hardest to complete. It's like the teenager's mind is physically predisposed to ejector-seating reality and kamikaziing into sex, drugs and rock'n'roll. There's nothing their parents can really do, except hope, and if they're religious, pray, that their kids stay alive long enough to make it to college and, at some point within those four years, commence the use of their brains. If only girls weren't so fucking worried about walking the tightrope of their reputation, a tightrope that's like a thong they're unable to remove from their universal ass, they might be able to enjoy the pit of anarchy and despair that the boys swim through. They could swim through it together. And what a beautiful, and ripe, world that would be.

Jackie peers up at Thomas, noticing his uneasiness. It doesn't appear as though the blood is flowing as quickly as he'd like it to.

"Are you all right?" Jackie whispers.

He tries to cover his outrageous nervousness with some earnest, but so obviously unmastered, masculine mimicry, "I'm better than all right."

She smiles at him and then drops her head into his lap with all the grace of an anvil. Thomas springs back slightly, his reflexes naturally reacting to something heading that fast toward his testicles. Just as he begins to relax, his muscles loosening, a rapping sound fills the air. Thomas is so enthralled in what's happening that it takes him a moment to realize that there is an unidentified set of knuckles tapping on the window beside his head. After a second or two, Thomas turns into a circle of light, aimed right at him – there's an intensity about it that pierces into his pupils, almost blinding him instantaneously. He brings his hand to his brow, blocking the light. As his vision adjusts, he stares up at a police officer shining a flashlight into the car. The two kids quickly cover themselves up, flinging their articles of clothing back on with bumbling haste.

Thomas grabs a hold of the front headrest, hops back into the driver's seat, and rolls down his window – he pretends like he has just been pulled over for a minor traffic violation.

"Hello, Officer."

Jackie makes her way into the front passenger seat. She kind of takes her sweet ass time. Thomas tries to will her to go faster via his admittedly limited powers of telepathy, but it's as if the sheer thinking of such a thing encourages the opposite. Thomas briefly contemplates how this act, in varying levels of degree, might very well be a recurring experience that plagues a man, with respect to his relationships with women, throughout his life.

"License and registration."

Thomas gropes around the glove compartment, hands the uniformed officer his license and registration. The officer stalks off to his vehicle, leaving the teenagers frozen in thought about what might happen to them, about whether their simple acts of affection might constitute some kind of felonious act.

"Are we in trouble?"

Thomas can hear the trepidation in Jackie's voice.

"Could be. I'm not sure."

Thomas looks at Jackie and a sudden need to protect her overwhelms him, so he adds, "It'll be okay. Don't worry."

Before they know it, the officer is standing at Thomas's window again.

"Step out of the car, please."

Thomas steps out, planting his feet firmly on the cement.

"Hands against the car."

Thomas complies as the officer shines the light inside at Jackie.

"Any weapons in the car, miss?"

"No. Of course not," Jackie insists. "We're just having some fun."

The officer drops his eyebrows and looks down at the license again. His eyes scan the syllables of the "Harrison" moniker.

"Thomas Harrison. Any relation to Judge William Harrison?" the officer asks.

"Do you know him?"

"Sure. Voted for him. Twice."

Thomas considers this, pretending to take his own sweet ass time, and then responds accordingly, "Never heard of him."

The officer smiles, and then turns Thomas back around to face him.

"Sure you haven't."

He holsters his flashlight and goes ahead and exercises a little of his power to be a prick. There are fringe benefits in any line of work. And he's got just under an hour and a half left in his shift before he meets the guys over at Durty Nelly's on McLean Avenue for a round of Irish car bombs.

"He's in some hot water. Should'a never released that crazy cunt."

Jackie leans over, as if this is her cue to inject the female standpoint into the conversation, a conversation that's very much on its way to devolving from conversation to pissing contest.

"I don't think it's her vagina that's crazy."

Thomas winces the way only a girl can make you wince. The police officer just smirks, the closed-lip kind, probably because he's gritting his teeth behind them. In all likelihood, he hasn't had a girl around in his life that could make him wince that way in a long time.

"You're right...excuse me, miss."

The officer hands the license back to Thomas, tips his hat like some detective in a 1940's noir, and ambles back to his cruiser.

"Have a good night. I won't tell your Dad about this."

Thomas climbs back into his car, he can't even look at Jackie. Under his rapid breaths, he mutters, "Fucking asshole."

Jackie could respond with a clever insult, further tarnishing the cop's reputation in the eyes of the teens, as if that might be necessary, while also supporting Thomas, in an effort to boost his ego in that kids against authority kind of way. But she doesn't. She doesn't even say a word. She just places her hand on Thomas's shoulder.

Truth is, nothing could've made him feel better than that.

***

Thomas's car snails along a recently paved suburban street, passing the latest models of Sports Utility Vehicles – Izuzu Troopers, Jeep Grand Cherokees, Ford Explorers, and one Land Rover with all the bells and whistles – all parked neatly along the unblemished curb. He's observing the traffic laws and speed limit to a nerve-wracking tee. Jackie's eyes are glued on the passing houses, all of which are bigger than the houses on his block, and she surveys each of them.

"Okay. Pull over right here," Jackie says. "Try to be quiet, if you can."

Thomas pulls over to the curb, putting the car in park.

"Is this where you live?"

"No. It's a friend's house – she left the back door un-locked."

Thomas shoots her a strange look; he hasn't even started to understand her.

"Her parents are clueless," she responds.

"Can I call you?"

Jackie lets the question register, lingering, then grabs a pen from her purse and scribbles her number onto the dashboard. She kisses him and hops out of the vehicle. The kiss distracts Thomas, his focus drawn to the notch in the center of Jackie's top lip – the notch between the top lip and the nose, the notch whose biological name is the philtrum and upon which the sides of Jackie's sensual lips hang like velvet curtains. But this fleeting fixation is only enough to distract him for a moment before his eyes snap to the vandalism this zaftig girl has just committed on the inside of his automobile.

"Hey!"

But, shit, he has to smile, at the boldness of this simple action, at her poise and her charm, at the way she has made her mark on both him and his car. He sits there and watches her trot around the side of her friend's house.

As Thomas returns home, driving up his quiet street, he makes out an unusual shape on his front lawn in the dim night light. As he parks, scuffing his tires against the curb, his eyes becoming adjusted to the dark suburban landscape, the shape begins to take on a recognizable form and he gradually realizes that the shape is a body, a human body, sprawled out in the grass. Panic hits him instantly. He leaps out. Rushing up to the body, he slows down, digging his heels into the grass, uncertain as to what to do next. He leans down, placing a hand on its shoulder, and as he's about to turn the body over, Connor springs to life, eyes rolled back and hands protruding out like a zombie. Thomas jumps back, grabbing his chest.

"You scared the crap out of me!"

Connor laughs, but he's also super fucking pissed.

"You deserve a lot worse. You just left my ass, you motherfucker. I live in fucking Katonah, for Christ's sake – how the hell am I gonna get home?"

Connor stands up, lopsided, and stumbles over to the side of Thomas's house. He squeezes between the bushes, unzips his jeans and proceeds to urinate all over the aluminum siding.

"What're you doing? You drunk fuck!" Thomas shouts.

"I should piss in your ass," Connor replies.

"Lamestain. Where have you been?"

Connor shakes his head, flinging his hair about, "I went out with those cock-heads from that band."

Thomas grabs Connor, extracting him from the bushes. Without making any physical contact and with only the most brief visual inspection, he makes sure his friend's member is tucked neatly back in his pants, then he drags him inside the house.

"Sleep on the couch."

***

Thomas lies in his bed, mostly motionless, but for the twitching of toes, enjoying the plunder of his dreams. Dreams he will not remember by the time his eyes have opened and adjusted to the morning light. His mother stands over him, gently tapping the edge of his pillow with the back of her hand.

"Thomas. Wake up. You have to drive your sister."

Thomas is half-asleep, gripping onto his down comforter like he's choking it to death.

"Huh?" he mumbles.

"We have your cousin's Christening to go to," Maureen says, "Your father and I are leaving, and we're leaving now. You have to drive your sister to school. I already told you this. You have Aunt Caroline's number, right, if you need us? If not, I taped it on the fridge."

Thomas reluctantly rouses from slumber, bleary eyes meeting the eyes of his mother. He blinks away the glue sealing his lids together and peers down at the horizon of his sheets, staring at the tent he's pitched with his morning erection. He hurriedly turns onto his side, bringing the comforter along with him and clamping it between his knees, as he attempts to conceal his shame from the person who spawned him – the person responsible for making him into the degenerate that he is today.

"School? Umm. It's Sunday."

"She's running one of the booths at the 'Fall Festival.'"

Thomas tries to suppress the resentment of the older child, the child who is always asked to do more, who is asked to baby-sit and clean the house, to take on the role of quasi-parent so that the real parents can begin the process of gradually removing the tether that has tied them to home and offspring for nearly two decades. Thomas knows, intellectually, that his parents deserve such respite; he just resents them for making him grow up ahead of schedule and at inopportune times like Sunday morning.

Thomas drives his car, still in the midst of waking up – this is an intricate process on Sundays – while Bridget sits dutifully in the passenger seat, a large portfolio case between her feet. Connor's passed out across the backseat with his limbs sprawled about, snoring his black lungs out.

"So what's this booth you're running?" Thomas asks.

"A kissing booth," Bridget responds.

"Really?"

"No. It's just something dumb for my art class."

"Sounds fun."

"Not even close." Bridget laughs as they pull up to the entrance of *The School Of The Holy Child*. "You can take my place if you want," she says.

A gaggle of girls meanders along the sidewalk in matching plaid Catholic schoolgirl uniforms, their pleated skirts rolled up extra high in an effort to make the restrictive uniforms into mini-skirts. As Thomas rakes his eyes across this gathering of budding young ladies, his eyes freeze and widen, a moment of panic stealing into his heart; Jackie is walking among them. Trying to remain calm and appear distracted, even disinterested, Thomas points the girls out to his sister, "You know them?"

"Yeah, they're in my class," Bridget responds.

"They're sophomores?"

"Yeah. Bunch'a posers."

Bridget watches as her brother continues to stare at Jackie. As much as Thomas tries to hide it, tries to come off cool and detached, the stare is conspicuous. Bridget glances at the dashboard and sees the phone number written on it, along with the name "Jackie" in script beside it. Displaying poise well beyond her years, she changes the subject, vying for Thomas's preoccupied attention, "You wanna come inside and buy some drawings? We're raising money for retards."

"I can't," he responds, "we got band practice."

"You guys are wasting your time."

Thomas hears her, but still looks out the window, fixated on Jackie.

"What the hell do you know?" he barks.

"I know the shit they call alternative isn't an option anymore – it's a requirement, and when it becomes a requirement, it's not an alternative to anything."

Bridget grabs her portfolio case, stumbling out of the vehicle. She twists back, leaning into the car, "If you want to be a musician to express yourself, Thomas, then you have to actually express yourself."

She shuts the door, loudly, defiantly, an act that's entirely in keeping with her character. As she walks away, she can't help but toss a parting zinger his way, "You're just another follower."

Thomas is used to ignoring his sister and his sister's unstable and volatile behavior. As he watches her enter the school building, he reaches into the backseat and shakes Connor awake.

"Yeah, yeah, what?" Connor mumbles.

Thomas is all jittery nerves, and not because of Bridget's defiant attitude. He points out Jackie as Connor sits up. "She's in my sister's class." In the haze of his hangover and his som-nambulant state, it takes a fair amount of time for Connor to pick Jackie out of the crowd, to focus on the fact of who she is, and to tie Thomas's statement to that fact.

In the interim, Thomas elaborates on his statement, "Two words: statutory fucking rape." Connor's eyes widen.

"You fucked her?!"

"Well, no... uh... not yet," Thomas responds.

"When do you turn eighteen?"

"Couple months."

Connor gives his buddy a hearty slap on the back.

"Plenty of time. Besides, the old man's a judge, you got nothing to worry about; as long as you rape her in his juris-diction—"

Thomas winds up and punches Connor in the arm, hard, then shifts his car into drive. As the remaining Catholic sch-oolgirls file into the school, Bridget walks back out, bringing her portfolio case with her, and heads into the street.

Bridget breezes into *Slave to the Grind*, a hipster café with an under-underground vibe. It's a Bavarian-themed hangout that caters to the most expensive liberal arts undergraduate school in the country, Sarah Lawrence College, located right around the corner. Lisa Bonet went there. It has a neat sculpture in its main quad, which doubles as a series of steps, but they're steps that lead to nowhere in particular. Steps to endless debt. Then again, if you're currently enrolled in SLC, it's because your parents can flip the bill for it. This is Bronxville, this ain't a state school, nor the locale for it. This is the campus where the Yonkers kids drive through Saturday night drinking forties and shouting "fag" from the windows. Which is why Slave to the Grind can charge out the ass for a single shot espresso. A red, white and blue bandana-wearing lesbian server – the bandana being an unsanctioned part of her uniform, since the rest of her outfit is a German barmaid getup – turns as Bridget approaches the counter.

"What can I get ya?"

"Black tea."

This employee has made the outfit hers. Her stockings have been ripped, either by her own hands or those of an energetic girlfriend. Her peasant top features the traditional puffed sleeves and cheap embroidery, but her black velvet bodice is laced up tight with blood-red leather straps. Her shelf-like hips flaunt a tattered forest-green velour skirt with a lace trimmed apron that's covered in coffee stains and a button pinned to it that reads: "*I inhaled.*"

"You want it black, right?" the server asks.

"Uh-huh," Bridget replies, nodding her head vigorously. "Black."

As the barista turns away, Bridget glances at an accumulation of flyers on a bulletin board hanging over the milk and sugar station. There is one particular flyer that stands out, like it's floating above all the rest:

"OPEN MIC NIGHT – EVERY SATURDAY"

It's part of a new marketing campaign to get customers into the shop. It's designed not only to capitalize on the recent alternative music craze – there are more indie bands crawling out of the woodwork than termites – but also to differentiate itself from the newly opened Starbucks that set up shop in prime real estate at a major intersection just down the street. The managers of Slave To The Grind had no idea what a Starbucks was except for the fact that the company was opening a new store somewhere in any one of the fifty states at a rate of about two a day. And that there was always a line to get inside to buy something they called coffee, but which apparently included the active ingredients from crack cocaine as well. Some college hooligans took it upon themselves to desecrate the sign, altering the "B" to an "F" with a thick coat of iridescent green spray-paint, so it now reads Star**F**ucks Coffee. The kids that attended SLC were precisely the right demographic for Star**F**ucks to target. They were the kind of kids who could afford to pay their inflated prices. However, these kids weren't going to give in that easily, not just yet. They had principles. They refused to capitulate to the manipulations of this environmentally corrupt, labor-abusing, anticompetitive, monopolizing, unfair-trading, and politically amiss corporate behemoth from Seattle. This was ironic, since their lives were predominantly funded by their fathers' considerable nameless corporate earnings. The way they saw it, if Lisa Bonet could cast aside her wholesome image, and the wholesome paycheck that came with it, on *The Cosby Show* to get naked on the silver screen with Mickey Rourke – a career choice that exhibited a proclivity for insubordination she surely picked up at school – the students at Sarah Lawrence could take a pointer from Lisa and rise up against the establishment, too.

One corporate behemoth from Seattle at a time, for Christ's sake, Bridget keenly thinks to herself as she grabs the "Open Mic Night" flyer and rips it down. She crumples the homespun advertisement up into a perfectly round ball and stuffs it into her pocket.

***

The band is jamming on their heavy grunge-pop tune, *"Chummin."* Their guitars are so over-driven the sounds being produced from the amplifiers bring to mind sheet metal being pressed through a meat grinder, which by some kind of cruel design, ultrasonically reduces it into a phalanx of metallic shards flitting into the recesses of your ears. Alex, Johnny-comelately, is sprawled out on a threadbare couch in the corner of the garage, something the Salvation Army might sell if the Harrisons felt charitable enough to donate it to them. He is asleep, astonishingly so, amidst the relentless noise. Elias sings a foot away from the garage door, like the wood is a paying audience watching him perform.

"I'm through,

you always take for granted those things I do./

It's always the same stupid bullshit lies..."

The song grinds to an abrupt halt, chords and rhythm going astray, and Elias looks back at Jeremy.

"J, man, what the fuck?"

"Hey, I'm trying..." Jeremy replies.

Thomas shakes his head from side to side as Elias directs a scowl toward his fellow bandmates, his brethren in song.

Elias is a bit of a pedal-head, a predilection one might assume purists of punk rock would disdain. Some do, as effects pedals have mostly seemed the province of hair-bands and metal, toys Eddie Van Halen would trifle with. But as punk progressed into hardcore, and from there into post-punk, the use of analog effects became a way to destroy the sound, not slicken it like the Van Halens of the world. J. Mascis of Dinosaur Jr. used a ton of pedals. His sound was so big, and incorporated about as many turning points as a Raymond Chandler novel, that it resulted in his first breakthrough record, *You're Living All Over Me*, being completely distorted – and not just the guitar, but the entire recording. The record company hesitated to release it until Mascis convinced them that if it was okay to distort guitars, it was okay to distort the entire recording. Play the album in your car, it'll blow the speakers out – just as it was intended to do. Elias recently got his hands on the "Grunge" distortion pedal by DOD, the settings of which consist of four knobs: loud/butt/face/grunge. The manual that comes with it outlines a variety of settings that can supposedly give you the *Green Day* sound for a specific song, or the *Smashing Pumpkins* buzz. The sound of a generation in a box, just plug in your guitar and dial it in. It's tempting to think that it's that easy, and Elias was tempted by that thought, except for the fact that Elias doesn't really think like that, Elias never puts much forethought into anything at all, really. His musical credo and something that has guided him in most aspects of his life to this point is, just pick it up and play it. There could be a meta-ironic use for the pedal, grunge playing grunge; perhaps he could just let the pedal play itself. These thoughts, as valid as they might be, never occurred to Elias. Neither did the lame-ness of buying such a pedal. He simply didn't care. And that attitude was about as close to encapsulating the shared sens-ibility of those kids filed under the label of Generation X. Whether they knew they didn't care, or not.

Elias not only has the Grunge pedal, he also has a RAT – a more authentic and less commercial conduit to grunge – that he often uses at the same time. He also has a wah-wah, chorus, flanger, delay, phaser and, of course, volume pedals. He likes to stomp things while he plays, and the more reasons to stomp the better, a trait that's likely hereditary. His father, Carlos, was an aspiring tap dancer who grew up performing on street corn-ers in Brooklyn. He studied under the tutelage of Ernest Bro-wn of the Tapping Copasetics. Carlos knew Ernest as Brownie, and he even tapped with him at the Newport Jazz Festival in the 60's; this was before *tap* lost its luster in the public sphere, which at the time was being bombarded with new-fangled stimulation like the British rock invasion, LSD and newsreel footage of the Vietnam War. Tap dancing had officially been left by the wayside, much in the way the 90's checked hair-metal at the curb; though Elias would argue that his father's brand of artistry was far superior to the crimes against humanity committed by rock'n'roll in the 1980's.

Brownie had to take a job as a security guard, as his passion wasn't likely to pay the bills anymore, and Carlos started selling shoes. But he didn't just sell shoes, he opened his own shoe store, and within ten years he owned one in each of the five boroughs of New York City. *Santoro's Discount Shack of Shoes*. He never attended college because he never completed high school, and even though his immigrant parents loved him dearly, they never had any expectation that he would achieve such a level of success.

Although his bank account began to reflect his achievement in the footwear business, Carlos never became complacent. In an act resonant with the times, he decided to relocate his family to the affluent Westchester suburbs. He still hadn't let go of his dream of tap dancing; he simply redirected it. He invested a healthy portion of his savings into a tap shoe that would revolutionize the craft and delight the dancers who wore it. It was going to be a shoe with a space-age graphite tap plate and synthetic leather upper that would flex along with the muscles in your foot without permanently stretching the material out. Body temperature and physics played a part, too, the specifics of which were a trade secret that Carlos had been formulating for years. He hired an expensive Park Avenue attorney and was about to file the patent. As Elias was getting ready for his eighth grade graduation – he attended the prestigious Horace Mann in Riverdale – he entered the family bathroom and found his father lying dead in the bottom of the bathtub. Carlos was nude; however, the disconnected shower curtain covered most of his body. At least some element of his dignity remained intact when his son discovered him in this state. Streams of water continued to pelt his body from the dangling showerhead, the type you can hold and utilize in its massage setting on your back. There was no blood to speak of, at least none that could be recalled by Elias; all he could focus on were the two of his father's eyes retracted back into the alcoves of his ocular sockets. Carlos had slipped on a patch of soap lather on the side of their porcelain bath. He had grabbed the curtain in an attempt to regain his balance, but ultimately brought it down with him as gravity slammed his head into the wall and broke his neck on the lip of the tub. A man so light on his feet slipped in the shower.

Elias had always meant to follow-up with his father's pursuit, with his patent application. Perhaps to honor his memory. Perhaps to make money. Perhaps to leave something behind. He just never got around to it.

Elias shouts at his bandmates, "Let's do it again."

Thomas stands up, seconding Elias's notion, "Let's do it again, guys. From the beginning."

Elias jumps onto his *grunge* pedal with both of his feet, practically busting the little piece of equipment apart.

William and Maureen turn leisurely into their driveway. As they climb out and approach the house, the level of abrasive garage rock increases in volume. William stops abruptly, staring at the front of his house. Maureen stops beside him on the short slate path. They both stare at their property in unmistakable horror. Maybe it's the music; despite their vocal support of Thomas's musical ambitions, it's possible that it has finally become too much for them. It isn't such a stretch to believe that two hardworking parents such as the Harrisons would have a breaking point when it comes to the aural assault being perpetrated in their home. Tranquility in the latter years of one's life should really be more of a right than a fringe benefit.

The band continues to struggle through the chorus –

"I've been begging for admission, but you won't let me in..."

The Harrisons open the door at the top of the stairs, interrupting the rehearsal in the garage. Their disposition is more than a bit prickly. The inexperienced band grinds to a halt again, except Elias; he has his back to everyone else.

"Fuck!"

He turns around, a head full of steam, meeting eyes with the Harrisons.

"Oh. Hey. Sorry."

William, sighing, looks down at his son.

"Thomas, a minute please.

Thomas's parents are usually pretty together people, they-'re not likely to show much in the way of vulnerability, at least in an external sense. A politician and his wife are blessed with this innate ability; they have to be, and so it's an unusual occasion for Thomas to sense that they are slightly off in some way, that they could be described as being in something of a state. It's hard to even recognize at first glance and Thomas immediately doubts his perception. If William's heart has ever bled, Thomas has never seen it. He climbs out from behind the drums.

William, Maureen and Thomas stand atop their manicured front lawn. Now they all look like something is amiss, they look offended, even angry; they look like they might all break off into a loud and misdirected argument, the kind of argument that you later regret for a whole host of reasons. On top of all of this, the three of them look especially scared.

Scrawled across the front door in graffiti is the word:

"MURDERER."

The word is in bright red bubble letters, red letters that bleed in the way that the title of a cheap horror film might bleed, a title that is supposed to be written in the blood of the many victims in the film. The "D" in the word MURDERER is carefully sprayed around the door's antique copper knocker, but not so carefully that its aged green patina reminiscent of the finish on the Statue of Liberty is also stained with this paint. *The Knocker of Liberty*. That's what the family has always called it and its patina is what William likes about the knocker and it's why it adorns his door. It's an adornment that he expected would be enjoyed well into his retirement. And now it has been defaced.

"Well, I didn't do it, if that's what you're thinking," Thomas says.

"I know you didn't do it. Did you notice anything, hear anything?"

Even as he says it, William knows the answer. Thomas waves a feeble hand at the garage, frustrated with the performance of the band.

"We've been...practicing."

"Maybe if you spent less time 'practicing,' and more time focusing on reality—"

"Bill, please." Maureen interrupts.

Thomas shrugs his shoulders, recognizing the inadequacy of the gesture and his very thoughts on the subject of this desecration. William walks inside; his agitation is getting the best of him. He closes the door behind him and locks it.

"Oh, come on," Thomas sighs.

William habitually locks the doors and windows in his house, whether he realizes he's locking his family out or not. That's less important than ensuring the security of his house – that structure with the outlandish mortgage. The net effect of this act, the fact of locking his family out of their own home, is less important to him than the possibility of a security breach on his property. He's unlocked and relocked the doors in his sleep, double-checked the alarms, reset the motion detectors in the basement, and he's totally unaware that he's doing it most of the time. It's become part of his muscle memory. There's nothing like a lapse in security to set the neurons firing.

Thomas plops down in the grass, picking at some dead leaves on the ground, as his mother walks up to the door and rings the doorbell.

***

William and Maureen sit across from their litter, Thomas and Bridget, the nuclear family gathered as one, save for the oblong living room coffee table separating the generations from each other. The tension that radiates between them is a palpable heat wave, one that Thomas and Bridget could use to warm their hands if they weren't frozen in fear across from their father. When you grow up with a man who was a Green Beret in Vietnam and whose day job now consists of putting hardened criminals behind bars for extended periods of time, it's easy to develop a healthy fear of your father. William leans forward, into the glow of the sodium vapor streetlamps seeping in through the considerable bay window beside them, "When public officials, like those involved in the judicial system, are threatened, it's a security risk, it's something that our federal, state, and local governments take very seriously. I don't want to alarm you about this situation, so I'll cut right to the chase here – I've got a handgun."

Bridget rolls her eyes in disgust. Thomas feels that his role here is to be the stoic and understanding son, so he keeps it together like a pro.

"As much as I hate the idea of bringing a gun into this house," William says, "the chief of police recommended I carry one. They've issued me a government carry-license and a standard .45 caliber pistol."

As a judge, William has the gift of gab and he can tell a tale, embellished with great humor and a smattering of healthy anecdotes, with the very best of them. In this situation, however, he feels a need to rush to the end of his presentation.

"Your Mom and I felt you needed to know."

Into the silence that follows, Thomas nods, "I understand. I'm cool with it."

Bridget scoffs at her brother's apple-polishing approval, "This is so not cool; shootings are ten times more likely in—"

"Don't lecture me about crime statistics," William retorts.

"Fine. Just please don't shoot me by accident. That's all I ask."

William is stunned by her frank remark. As a man knowledgeable about firearms, trained to use them by the finest fighting force in this history of the world, and as a responsible pillar of his local society, William cannot even imagine how his daughter could think for a moment that he would allow the accidental discharge of his weapon and that she might think such a discharge could somehow be directed at her. The family members drift away as William sits and broods on these thoughts.

As night descends on their neighborhood, Thomas wobbles upstairs, buttoning up his plaid flannel pajamas, and knocks on the outside of the bathroom door. He can hear the faucet running as he spies a rectangle of fluorescent light seeping out from underneath the door.

"Bri, you almost done?"

"Yeah, hang on," Bridget responds.

The door pops ajar, opening a smidge. Thomas slowly pushes it all the way open, stepping inside. Bridget stands in the corner, flossing her teeth, fidgety. The nightshirt that she wears stops well short of her panties. Thomas looks down at the magazine rack on the floor as he bumps the door closed with his hip. He never understood why his parents read Conde Nast's *Travel Magazine*; they never travelled anywhere. Anywhere that required the assistance of a magazine. Unless their imaginations were powerful enough to transport them unaided to the exotic destinations illustrated in the publication while taking a shit.

Thomas looks up at himself in the mirror, scratching at the thin stubble that camouflages his chin.

"It doesn't make you look like him," Bridget says.

"Who says I'm trying to?"

Bridget delivers a dismissive snort in his direction. Thomas looks at his sister through the mirror – his eyes drawn to her underwear, her off-white panties with a subtle peach lace fringe, a reflex that afflicts all teenage boys whether they're related to what they're looking at or not. He's momentarily taken aback by her state of undress and the utter disregard she has for his awareness of this state. Thomas has always known his sister to be flighty, distracted and, at the most basic level, a little disturbed. But in this instant of ritualized intimacy, he sees her for the first time as a confident young woman, a woman possessed of feminine bravado. In the moment of his perception of this, however, her vulnerability returns in force, as it most always does, sketching the outline of fear onto her face as she lifts her eyes to meet his in the mirror. He is compelled to ask, "You okay?"

Bridget tosses her floss, smiles, trying to sell it.

"Million bucks."

Thomas laughs, grabs his toothbrush and toothpaste.

"Let's talk," he says.

Bridget is ready for this and she jumps right in.

"This whole thing. The crazy woman killing her family, the fact that it's all over the news, and the way Dad told us the story, that first time, while we were having dinner…I mean, I know he likes to entertain us with these stories of his and maybe I'm looking at it in hindsight, but it seems like he knew there was something wrong with this case all along."

"I think you're reading too much into that part of it."

"Maybe. But the graffiti and Dad getting a gun – this is bad shit."

"His job has some risks," Thomas tries to reassure her.

"How can you just brush this off?"

"It's not that I don't understand how serious this is; the fact that this is not just some crazy news story, that it's actually happening to us. But Dad needs to know we can deal with it – that's what he's looking for from us."

"I don't know if I can deal with it."

Thomas turns away from her and starts brushing his teeth. Up and down strokes, massaging the gums gently. He uses his own special brand of toothpaste, a formula without SLS – sodium lauryl sulfate – which is, technically, a detergent that's used to remove stains from the teeth. For Thomas, and many others who suffer in agonizing silence, SLS is an irritant that is the root cause of canker sores, which for him are rampant. If using a rare and extremely pricey brand of toothpaste that can only be found in specialty drug stores decreases the severity or frequency of the hellish mouth ulcers, he is willing to give it every possible chance. When he does have an outbreak of canker sores, he tends to stick his tongue into them and explore them, rooting around in the little craters as if prodding them might bring them to an early demise – it seems to calm him, sooth his nerves. Even though it's exceedingly painful.

"Doesn't it bother you?" Bridget asks.

Thomas stops brushing, leans over, and spits a frothy puddle out into the basin of the sink. He pauses just long enough to compose himself, which he needs to do, because he knows exactly what she needs to hear.

"Yeah. Sure. It bothers me."

He understands how different she is. Like anyone who is even a little self-aware, he wonders if the difference he feels is in her or in him. The way Bridget flaunts her emotions has always been a sore spot for Thomas, her dramas having eaten up huge swaths of the lives of the Harrison family. Does that drama mean there's something wrong with her, or does Thomas's reluctance to share his feelings with Bridget, with his parents, with just about anyone, mean that there's something wrong with him? He wants to connect with his sister, but knows he can't. So he simply pretends to.

"It'll be okay."

He goes back to brushing. He smiles at his sister in the mirror; it's like smiling at a stranger on the street. As Bridget finishes up her nighttime routine and walks out of the bathroom, his eyes drop once again to her panties, the elastic bands pressing into her thighs and causing a little bulge of flesh, a bulge that will grow as her cellulite does over the next twenty years or so, as she bears children or simply eats too much, he can see the Victorian pattern of lace imprinting itself into the surface of her flesh, imprinting a tiny mandala that causes him to flash back to his bad acid trip, which thankfully yanks him out of this troublesome and inappropriate reverie. He looks back into the mirror, thoroughly disgusted with himself. His tongue prowls the inside of his mouth, searching his gums, the backs of his lips, the roof of his mouth, anywhere with a mucus membrane, for the first signs of an abscess.

Thomas jogs out to his car, parked under the cover of Grandview Avenue's foliage, a corduroy jacket thrown on over his PJ's. He opens the driver's side door and leans inside, the dome light illuminating him. He whips out a packet of lime green Post-Its from his pocket and transcribes Jackie's phone number, the scrawl of which is still ever-present on his dash.

Moments later, Thomas finds himself sitting cross-legged on the floor of his bedroom cradling his phone and looking at the scrap of paper, nervous as all hell. He has one of those see-through plastic telephones; the kind with the neon colored electronics, circuit board, diodes, wires and capacitors, all view-able through a clear plastic shell. The item is a relic from the summer between eighth grade and freshman year at Fordham Prep, a moment in time before he had pubes, but he's still very fond of it, maybe because of its connection to his more inno-cent past. He tries to pump himself up, gazing into his phone's glowing electronics, nearly chewing off his bottom lip, "Fuck it."

He dials rapidly, in Guinness-Book fashion. It rings.

"Hello?"

The woman's voice on the other end of the line is defi-nitely not Jackie's; it's stiff, much more formal, but still some-how inviting.

"Hi, may I please speak with Jackie?" Thomas asks.

"May I ask who's calling?"

A boy calling for Jackie: her voice just became a little *less* inviting.

"Tom Harrison."

What seems like an eternity of awkward silence passes. For a moment, Thomas thinks she simply hung up the phone on him, as if a boy calling to speak with her daughter is such an affront to her dignity that her only option is to end the call without another word spoken. Just as Thomas is about to test this theory, she speaks.

"Hold on—"

The second eternal silence is marked less by uncertainty than by anticipation. Thomas can feel the sweat breaking out on his palms and he wipes them absently on his pants, as if preparing to shake someone's hand. He feels hyper-aware of the dingy little bedroom he's sitting in, piles of CD's and magazines, dirty socks, unread books. He wonders if Jackie would think his room is lame, if she saw it and saw the way he lives his life, would she think less of him? The thought disturbs him only until he realizes how little the state of her room would affect the feelings he has for her.

"Hello?" Jackie says.

"Oh, hi, Jackie. It's Tom. Harrison."

"I know who you are."

Thomas smiles, their intimate contact from the other night rushing back to him, arousing him all over again so that he lightly brushes his lips against the grid of miniscule holes in the plastic receiver, as if doing so will get him closer to nibbling the ear on the other end. "Right." He can tell she's smiling, too, wherever she happens to be in her house, her words just have that kind of feeling to them as they settle softly into the space of his ear.

"I wish you'd've told me you were calling," Jackie says.

"Sorry," Thomas says, in a teasing way, "but how could I've told you I was calling – without calling?"

"It's okay."

"I was wondering, you know, if you wanted to go on a date. Like a real one."

"Sure!" Jackie blurts.

Another small moment of silence follows, not quite as eternal as the previous two and this one is the best one of all, because it isn't awkward, nor is it ripe with anticipation, and it isn't causing him to wipe his sweaty hands on his pants and rue the inadequacy of his tiny bedroom. This silence is comfortable. Until Jackie sets Thomas to worrying all over again by dropping a tiny bomb on him.

"But I should probably tell you something—"

***

Thomas sits beside Jackie, squirming like a worm with a fishhook in its body, crammed in the middle row of an overcrowded multiplex movie theater. Thomas wants to be holding Jackie's hand, rubbing her legs, slipping his hand up her shirt and making out with her, touching her in any way she will let him. But he can't do any of this, because sitting in the row to their immediate left are Jackie's parents, Fred and Diane O'Brien.

Fred passes a tub of artificially buttered popcorn to the kids –

"Popcorn?"

Jackie takes the popcorn, internalizing her embarrassment, doing her best to hope that Thomas won't flee her and her helicopter parents, that he'll be willing to put up with this madness long enough for her parents to become comfortable with him. Jackie knows her parents and she knows that once they become comfortable with something, they let their guard down. Then Jackie can take advantage of them and she and Thomas can have a lot of fun together. She extends the popcorn to a nearly paralyzed Thomas.

After the movie, back at the O'Brien household, Thomas and Jackie sit across from Fred at the kitchen table as Diane slides steaming cups of Earl Grey tea in front of everyone. The table is wood with a glass top. Between the glass and the wood are hundreds of Christmas cards, many of which feature pictures of their friends' families, left over from the previous holiday seasons. Fred takes an elongated sip of his tea, and then addresses the young man courting his daughter, "So, Thomas, what are your plans, as far as a career goes? Jackie tells me you're a musician."

His delivery of the word *musician* might as well have been fired through the barrel of a Colt .45. Thomas adjusts his plaid button-down shirt as though he's adjusting a bulletproof vest.

"Well, I play drums in a band. Nothing too serious; just a hobby, really," Thomas insists. "Right now, my focus is getting into a good liberal arts college, then maybe applying to law school somewhere down the road. Extracurricular activities look good on the application. So I'm told."

Fred shifts his weight from one jowl to the other. Under intense interrogation he might be willing to admit that this answer was almost impressive.

"I see," he says.

Jackie's mother sits down; for some reason Thomas can't take his eyes off her wrinkled cleavage. Like every boy his age, Thomas is constantly dealing with his voracious sexual desire, and the frequency with which this desire seems unusual and even perverted has been bothering him a lot lately. If he was better at relating his feelings to other people, he might realize that such oddball feelings are as typical in teenage boys as the Converse sneakers and plaid shirts are to popular fashion. But he's never had the chance to realize this.

"Jackie still has some time to think about college. She's fourteen, after all – won't be fifteen until January. So, we're not putting the pressure on her just yet. But you sound like you've thought things through, Thomas."

Thomas writhes in his chair. It feels like a bullet has just slipped past his vest, and this one's a hollow-point.

"Thank you," he says.

He is trapped in one of those situations where any information divulged is both too much and not nearly enough. By talking about college, which seemed like a mature thing to do, he had simply accentuated the age difference between Jackie and himself, which is only exacerbated by the fact that Jackie was such an exemplary student in grade school that she was allowed to skip eighth grade and advance directly to freshman year in high school. Jackie wanted to do this, despite her insatiable need to conceal her academic prowess from her peers, concerned she might turn them off with what could be perceived as nerdiness, mental intimidation, or an air of superiority. She is younger. And at this particular transitional age, she is *a lot* younger. She is younger than Thomas and younger than all the other girls in her grade. So her parents, Fred and Diane, have every reason to be protective.

Fred smiles, attempting to liven up the quiet room, "Who wants to play 'Six Degrees of Kevin Bacon?' Anybody?"

As Jackie escorts Thomas out of her house, he cordially waves back to her parents. Jackie slips out onto the stoop, closing the door softly behind them.

"Thanks for being a sport," she says.

"That was really fucking weird, Jackie. I feel like a pedophile," Thomas laments.

"You're not."

"Maybe we shouldn't do this."

"Who cares about my parents? They fucking suck. There are ways around them—"

She grabs him by the collar of his shirt and pulls him close. Thomas goes in to kiss her, but she stops him within a millimeter of impact. She gazes up at him, white cradling the bottoms of her eyes.

"Not here."

Thomas is frustrated, but also entranced. Jackie's vulnerable, for the first time, for the first time from Thomas's point-of-view, at any rate. One of the things that attracted him to Jackie was her brazen aggression. This vulnerability is a departure from his initial impression of her, so it takes a moment for him to process it.

"Please don't tell anyone about this," she implores. "About my parents coming with us to the movies and everything."

He realizes that it can't be easy for her, exposing him to her relationship with her overprotective parents whose methods of child-rearing are harmless enough from an objective perspective, but these methods are also the teenager's kiss of death. It's the kind of thing that spreads like a contagion once it gets out, an infection that can contaminate the entire microcosm of her high school in the blink of an eye, an infection that can spread further, potentially reaching as far as all of the other high schools in the social network of greater Westchester. It's the kind of information that would subject her and her dating life to relentless ridicule. Unfortunately, you can't really do anything about your parents, and every kid that has a parent has to live by the rules that parent sets; every kid has to *seem* like they're living by those rules.

Deciding that he likes this vulnerable aspect of her personality, Thomas takes her hand and kisses it like some chivalrous knight.

"Your secrets are safe with me," he whispers.

Jackie slips back inside as Thomas retreats to his car parked just down the road, preoccupied by one of those moments of reflection, a chance to inspect himself to determine exactly what kind of man he is, and what kind he wants to be. It's not difficult for him to recognize that there are aspects of his relationship with Jackie that are completely ludicrous and embarrassing. Shame crawls around his neck and shoulders, creeping its way down the rest of his body, weighing him down to the ground. But he shrugs it off as quickly as possible, his body taking over and forcing the image of her lips into his mind, the smell of her hair, the press of her body against him. While he wonders if there is something legitimately wrong with him for being attracted to a girl so much younger than he is, he's also happy to surrender to the feeling.

Thomas's romantic life has not been the stuff of novels; a lonely man can forgive himself for his sins.

CHAPTER FIVE

A hipster crowd is scattered around Slave To The Grind, a small contingent gathering around a tiny stage. A college intellectual with a Burberry cashmere scarf and Buddy Holly glasses sits catty-corner to the stage, immersed in <u>Franz Kafka: The Complete Works</u>. Everyone in the place sips oversized porcelain mugs of coffee. The MC hops up on stage and grabs the dented microphone.

"Hey, welcome to open mic night here at Slave To The Grind."

There's spotted applause. The Master of Ceremonies looks like he's about to pass out from dehydration, the result of a previous night's bender.

"We've got some interesting folks lined up," the MC slurs, "but first I'd like to introduce someone new to our stage."

He reads off an index card, and it becomes obvious in a second that he hasn't proofread it yet: "Born and raised in Harlem, moving rock and pimpin' ho's, he's come to spit his big-dicked styles. Ladies and gentleman, Bri Da B."

No more applause, just a whole slew of really strange glances as Bridget approaches the stage, weaving through the modest audience, looking as white and preppy as ever. She sits on an oversized barstool, looking like some wayward child who snuck into a nightclub.

She slaps her Casio keyboard across her lap, and leans into the microphone –

"Yo niggas. I'm Bri Da B."

The audience is flummoxed. Bridget, *Bri Da B*, blasts the pre-programmed beats from her keyboard through the room's hodgepodge PA system. And then she starts rapping, busting out her tune, "*Gravy On Top*" –

"B R I D A B, uh-huh, I'm not a playa, but the ladies like me—

I make one dolla, two dolla, three, four./

Don't try to stop this, I'll make five dolla more."

The college intellectual looks up from his compendium of Kafka.

"Harlem life wasn't givin' me nothin', uh-huh,

now every night I eat turkey with stuffin'./

I got the gravy on top mixed with the greens,

I got the peas and carrots and lima beans, yeah./

I keep the ladies laced with zirconia,

their response is 'baby, let me bone ya.'/

I keep the streets alive and lit,

'cause my '89 Honda ain't never gonna quit, no."

Onlookers shift uncomfortably in their chairs as they sip their coffees. From the looks on their faces, tonight's brew seems a bit more bitter than usual. Bridget keeps on rockin' her flow –

"Being a big-dicked man was never easy,

now I got the one, two, three baby fosheezie./

The ladies are attracted to my dirty foreskin,

I'll hit you from the back, just let me in, yeah./

I'm not a playa, I just crush a lot, no.

I like my fish and I ain't gonna stop, uh-huh./

My dick is fat, ready and ripe,

so get in line, bitches, but don't fight, uh-huh—

Bri Da B."

The song ends, rather abruptly. The crowd is stunned. The college intellectual claps enthusiastically. Bridget catches sight of her one fan –
"Thanks. Bitch."

Bridget leans against a wall outside Slave to the Grind, gripping a cigarette tightly with the tips of her fingers that are poking out of fingerless gloves. Her keyboard is stashed under her arm. A small group of college girls trot past, shooting an assortment of sharp looks, a whole kitchen set of knives, at her.

"You're fucked in the head," one of them mumbles under her breath.

"Nope, never been fucked there," Bridget replies.

She turns her back on the bitches, whose steps are in unified stride with one another. Bridget stares at a ripped poster plastered to the brick wall, the one adjacent to the alley where the one bum in Bronxville spends occasional nights. It's an anti-smoking poster comprising of two teenage girls, one who's smoking, one who's not. The girl who's not smoking is a tall blonde, with a pearly smile and pristine posture, and dressed in a white cable knit sweater; the girl who's smoking is a short brunette, who is slouching, scowling, tattooed up the arm, wearing torn jeans and a ragged black t-shirt. The caption on the poster reads: *Who Would You Rather Be?*

The coding of colors in advertisements, television, movies, magazines, newspapers, zoetrope, and every other form of entertainment, has facilitated the media's manipulation of viewers for centuries. In most cases, the use of black and white is pretty black and white, which is why we say that something is black and white, because we can all see the stark contrast between the two. White is associated with good; black is associated with bad. The Hollywood Western immortalized the great white American hero, sporting his ten-gallon hat, his stirrups and calfskin boots, chasing after those wretched Indians, who are, in reality, a light reddish tan in color – but in the ancient days of black and white film, they never looked blacker. One wonders how John Wayne always stayed so white, given all those hours galloping around in the blazing desert sun. Cowboys on the frontier didn't have access to the kind of SPF-50 blocking cream Wayne's make-up artists applied to him. His skin was as white as an Irish immigrant baby's bottom dipped in the head of a Guinness Stout. Because in the face of the darkest of evils, only the bright, pale, ashen, vanilla, creamsicle-colored, fair as the milk from a freshly squeezed teat, requisite face of God can possibly prevail. This is the image that film producers, along with their bankers and sponsors, wanted to convey to the viewing public and circumstances really haven't changed. Turn on the evening news and you will find your finely polished white news anchor reporting a story about some black guy breaking the law. But to those watching at home, you can put your minds at ease. The chocolate-colored culprit has been apprehended and is currently locked behind a cold set of iron bars and, based on the profiles of the American prison population, you can rest assured that he will remain there for a period of time that is greatly disproportionate to the nature of his crime. There is no need to panic; there is no longer an imminent threat to the general public – to those residing in the hills, there's no longer a need *to hide all your white women.*

Please stay tuned as we continue our coverage of scaring the ever-living shit out of you – after a word from our sponsors.

It's not that Bridget necessarily thought of herself as black, she just felt black, in the most abstract sense of the word. People often neglect the plight of the woman in American history. African-American men won their right to vote in 1870, as ratified by the Fifteenth Amendment; whereas, women – white or otherwise – did not win their suffrage battle and gain that same right until four amendments later on August 26th, 1920. The passage of the Civil Rights Act of 1964, while known for its landmark legislation outlawing discrimination against blacks, also marked the prohibition of discrimination based on sex.

The bill had not originally included women, until Howard W. Smith, a Democratic Congressman from Virginia, added the amendment at the last minute on the floor of the House of Representatives. Smith and his supporters argued that the law would protect black women, and prevent white women from enjoying the same protection – a distinction that was patently unfair. Historians speculate as to whether his concern for the opposite sex and their struggle was sincere, or merely political rigmarole; a strategy to embarrass those northern democrats who opposed the civil rights of women to placate their labor union base. His motives, and whatever sincerity or lack of sincerity was behind them, were inconsequential; when Smith introduced the amendment on the floor, it was met with re-sounding laughter from his congressional colleagues. And this was a mere thirty years ago, a chronological blink of an eye – it was the age Maureen was when she gave birth to Bridget.

So, in many ways, John Lennon spoke the truth in his controversial song, "*Woman Is the Nigger of the World.*" Even after the 1964 bill, it was clear the struggle was far from over.

After an abridged class on albinism in biology, Bridget began some research into melanin, which is not to be confused with melatonin, the chemical in the brain that stimulates sleep, a stimulation that Bridget is sorely lacking. Melanin is the primary determinant of skin pigment in human beings. Bridget became fascinated with the effect of this natural polymer, coming across some information, reliable or not, on Melanin Theory, the premise of which asserts that black people are superior to white people, in the strictest of biological terms. Albinism, for example, and the affliction of pale skin in general, is a result of a lack of melanin, a classified deficiency; whereas, an abundance of melanin, found in darker skinned individuals, especially in those of African heritage, is seen as not only physically advantageous, but also indicative of some potential superhuman ability. Melanin is a semiconductor, and some theorize that it can absorb electromagnetic radiation; following that, voluminous amounts of it may convert light into sound, bypassing interaction with the brain entirely, opening up higher, more evolved, forms of communication; and, additionally, that it is the biochemical basis for what's commonly referred to as "soul." On top of the rhythmic improvements resulting from such a primal relationship with sight and sound, as evidenced by the clear dominance of the black man over the white man on the dance floor, it opens up a door to a vastly greater dominance as a race within the human species.

Bridget figured it's not that far a leap from electromagnetic radiation to nuclear radiation. And, what if, the African-American community, the minority, was simply laying low, concealing its power, and waiting for the white man to destroy himself. The war in the Persian Gulf, the threat of nuclear proliferation in the hands of Saddam and his thugs, among countless others in that godforsaken desert region, introduced the possibility of global catastrophe in our future, both near and far. Perhaps the Towel-Heads are the new Ruskies? They're sure on they're way to getting there. And when that time comes, and the nukes hit, the black man will be the last one left standing on the planet. The melanin in his skin will absorb the radiation and transfer it into energy, an energy that will lead to the rise of a new superspecies of human begins, redefining and raising the bar within the Homo genus of bipedal primates. And this species, this superspecies, will be the black man. The black man – and woman – will rule the world.

And soul brothers and soul sisters of the universe, you may consider Bri Da B your sibling.

Bridget always pined for a black superhero, someone other than a concoction of some seventies exploitation film like *Shaft* or *Blacula* or something. Someone comparable to Superman.

And the thought of this happening, not in the guise of entertainment, but in reality, was a thrill to extinguish all other thrills. Even if the theory was utterly preposterous, just the thought, the notion of such a thing, such a coup d'etat, the intimation, was powerful. It lent us hope – hope to those outsiders, hope to disenfranchised groups and subgroups around the world, hope to Bridget that someday, even if the black man didn't rise to superspeciesdom, that in the meantime, perhaps she could become a black superhero.

Bridget garnered a profound respect for the power of community among black people. The shared struggle within the history of the African-American community created a bond among blacks that seemed to transcend actual community. Bridget noticed that black people who had never met could immediately strike up a conversation and be laughing like old friends within a matter of minutes. By contrast, it seemed like most white people barely recognized the fact that the human being is a social animal. Her family seemed especially suspect in this regard, where conversations were always forced and flat, bouncing off irrelevant parts of the human condition rather than speaking with any level of revelation and intensity. Bridget has always wanted to go to a black church in Harlem and revel in the powerful bond of soul that is celebrated there on any given Sunday.

So, her answer to the question, *Who Would You Rather Be?*, is obvious.

Stewart Francis Boyle, Kafka-reading college intellectual, squares up beside Bridget and peruses the poster himself. He extends his enthusiastic endorsement of the chick wearing black smoking the cigarette.

"I mean, come on, who would anyone rather be?" he says.

Stewart twists around, nodding at Bridget, "Whoever came up with this add campaign should be fired. It makes me wanna have a cigarette."

Bridget extends her pack of cigarettes to Stewart as she keeps her eyes on the poster, focusing on the line of text at the bottom, the advertisement's attempt to hammer the point home:

"DON'T SMOKE!"

As Stewart lights up, Bridget reaches out and tears the bottom left corner of the poster, removing the "DON'T" from the ad. She crumples it up and tosses it into the alley, leaving only the emphatic "SMOKE!" under the provocative picture on the brick wall. Stewart smiles.

"That was so punk rock I can't even handle it," Stewart remarks.

Bridget cocks her head at him, "Vandalism?"

"No, no."

"Vandalism is so…pathetic," she grumbles.

Stewart backs it up a bit, attempting to flip to the same page this girl's on. He will soon find out that this is a difficult task; the book she's reading is dense, completely lacking a table of contents.

"I meant the show. Your performance."

"Bollocks. It was shite."

He guffaws, "Everybody in there takes themselves way too seriously. They only care about what someone else thinks is cool – if it's not grunge, or whatever it is they call it, they could-n't give two shits."

Bridget starts to walk away, having had just about enough of this guy; however, for some inexplicable reason, and against her better judgment, she decides to go ahead and give him a chance. She abruptly looks back over her shoulder, "I'm gonna watch the trains. Wanna come?"

Stewart is slightly perplexed by the suggestion, but what the fuck.

"Um. Yeah. Sure."

Bridget and Stewart sit on Bronxville's commuter train platform, on a concrete block of a bench, southbound side. The air around them vibrates in a subtle way. If you were there, you might think there was something powerful developing between these two and it was expressing itself in a palpable way in their immediate orbit. But then the rumble would hit you and the shimmering train would whiz past with a concussive slap of wind and sound, before fading down the tracks. Bridget and Stewart stare at the red taillights as their iridescence disappears into the night.

Stewart is a mass of contradictions, all of which are bundled into a young man just starting to understand himself. An affinity for someone like Bridget, who possesses even more contradictions, like her off-the-wall music and her undefined intentions as an artist, seems to make sense to him.

"People don't realize Cobain was a prankster," Stewart says. "The guy wore a 'Corporate Magazines Suck' T-shirt on the cover of a corporate magazine. Record companies are looking for the next Nirvana and fans all think they're from Seattle, wearing thermal underwear and shit. The reason people wear thermal underwear in Seattle is 'cuz it's fucking cold and wet all the time."

Bridget laughs, extracting a bottle of whiskey from her bag.

"Success sucks," she says.

Stewart snickers, "Kurt used his music to react against the assembly line of crap that the eighties dished out, only to become exactly what he was reacting against."

"Must've hated himself for it."

She takes a sip of booze, offers it to him. He waves a hand.

"No. Thanks."

She looks at him, furrowing her brows. She takes another swig. Stewart is used to having to defend his sobriety, he's a college student after all.

"I quit. Been sober eight months."

She tips her bottle at him, "Now that's punk rock."

Stewart sighs a smile as Bridget lights up another cigarette.

"Where do you go to school?"

"Sarah Lawrence. I'm majoring in Surrealism," Stewart responds.

"Whatever happened to Surrealism—"

"It was an anti-art movement developed in reaction to the rationalism that led to World War I. It was, no pun intended, an *alternative* to the formalistic painting of the time."

"So you think Kurt Cobain was a modern surrealist—"

In an article Stewart wrote for his college music zine, *The Note*, he didn't quite suggest that Cobain was a surrealist, but he did imply that his mere existence, and its place in history, may in fact be surreal. His music brought rock and roll back from the dead. Literally. Rock and roll up until that point was dominated by schlocky, vampiric hair-bands, who for all intents and purposes, resembled the featured extras in a homoerotic remake of *Night Of The Living Dead*. Zombies in tight sparkle pants. And mullets galore.

Cobain made rock real again. He made it tangible. Ironically, he made it just tangible enough to be manufactured in factories worldwide. Stewart theorized that Cobain threw his life away to escape the version of himself that was being packaged and sold for $19.99 in Wal-Mart. Fast-food psychoanalysis, possibly, but a valid point. He did become a pop icon, the voice of a generation, and in the eyes of corporate America, an indispensible cash cow. He wore a 'Corporate Magazines Suck' T-shirt on the cover of a corporate magazine, but it was still *him* wearing that shirt – on that corporate magazine. Until he could eliminate himself from the commercialism that was attached to his hip, it would never be anything more than commercialism. Ergo, the shotgun blast to the head –

By killing himself, he killed corporate America, if only his version of it.

The ultimate irony and the most surreal element of his story, is that by killing himself, he made his public persona that much stronger and that much more grossly profitable, introducing brand new people and their money from the farthest reaches of the world to his music. Kurt Cobain ceased to be Kurt Cobain, fulfilling the prophecy of his music: he became his songs. Existence is subjective, such is the basis of the term, and his songs still exist –

And, of course, these songs are all for sale.

"Maybe—"

Stewart looks at Bridget, contemplating her question; posing one right back at her, "Perhaps Bri Da B is a surrealist?"

Bridget burps, blowing it right at his face.

He smiles, "I knew it."

***

The band smokes under the shallow lip of the roof just outside the Harrisons' garage, their collective cloud of cigarette smoke curling around the ivy that's developed along the brick on that side of the house. It's raining, but there's just enough room to stay mostly dry, but for the few rogue drops leaking down from the gutters. Elias ashes his C-I, prying into Thomas's personal exploits, which have until now remained intentionally undisclosed –

"You get in her pants last night?"

"We went to the movies," Thomas responds curtly, hoping to end the investigation at that.

Connor ashes his C-I, he's not letting his friend get off that easy, "Did you get in her pants?" he asks.

"Are you guys serious about this band, or what?" Thomas spurts.

Everyone nods, there are even glints of enthusiasm in their eyes. Thomas, in this instance, is just thankful that he diverted them from the topic of Jackie.

"We need to rehearse twice as much and when we're not rehearsing, we need to practice on our own, every day. It feels like we're just going through the motions and that will not fly if we want to get somewhere. We need to work on our hooks. Elias, you're the front-man, you're the one who sets the tone for the band; you need to work on those vocals, that rasp."

"I'm trying to get rid of that rasp."

"No, man, use it. That can be our signature. Labels are looking for post-grunge bands – pop music with dirty vocals."

Jeremy, the dissenting voice, "Yeah, but there's ten thousand bands that sound just like that."

"Not yet. We gotta move on this." Thomas insists.

Connor pulls out a crinkled newspaper article, freshly cut from Westchester's Journal News Weekender. Connor's father is an accountant. The man lives a perfectly normal life, receives a perfectly normal paycheck, and has a perfectly normal wife; all perfectly good reasons why he encourages his kid to indulge in as much sex, drugs and rock and roll as possible. He doesn't specifically mention drugs, ever, but the phrase and the lifestyle are simply not the same without it, so Connor feels obliged to take artistic license on that part. It's not that his father doesn't adore his life – he loved the first girl he slept with so much so that he married her. Which is why he'd like his son to experience the pleasures of life that he chose not to experience personally; he didn't view them so much as missed opportunities as he did a series of choices that he'd be a fool to regret. The way he sees it, you can't have regrets if you're happy where you are in life, and he is perfectly happy. If there was some way that he could still have what he has in life now, while stepping back in time to live life a little more fully, he would do it in a heartbeat, but he's pretty sure that if he had made those choices when he had the chance, back in the day, he wouldn't be the man he is now, he wouldn't have the life he has now and when he thinks like that, it makes him sad. So when Connor's Dad spotted this article in the paper, it jumped out at him, and he just had to cut it out for his son. That's just the kind of Dad that he is. The four teenagers gather around the piece in the paper, the headline of which reads:

"BATTLE OF THE UNSIGNED BANDS."

Connor dishes the details, "We submit a demo tape and if they like us, we get to play in a battle at CBGB's – the winner gets a record deal. Alternative rock. Must be original. Those are the two rules. We have that. That's us."

Jeremy looks down, shuffling his enormous feet, which look even more enormous in his Chuck Taylor clown shoes. What Jeremy hadn't realized yet is that you're supposed to buy Converse Chuck Taylors a full size *smaller* than your regular shoe size, because they're built like clown shoes to begin with and if you buy them in your actual size, your toe won't even reach into the reinforced white rubber toecap. As a result, Jeremy's feet looked that much more floppy; though he didn't mind it all that much because the extra room gave him some space to stretch and curl his toes, which he enjoys and which he tends to do when he's restless. It's like a hidden cavern at the tip of his foot in which he can stretch out and release his stress without anyone ever seeing. Throughout our days as upright primates, all the stress and the literal and metaphorical weight of our individual worlds, funnels down to our feet, forcing us to walk on fleshy lumps of stress and tension. Finding ways to relieve that stress can be life-saving. The ultimate method to release this pressure, and by extension to release endorphins in our brains, is to partake in the glorious act of the foot massage, the dark chocolate of physical therapy, the act which most closely resembles the sexual act to the pleasure centers of our brains, placing it among the finer things in life, alongside pinot noir and cunnilingus (not that any of these dudes are familiar with such delicacies at this point in their stunted lives). But it is through this line of thinking that Jeremy can rationalize the benefit of having extra room in his shoes even though the truth is that the Chuck Taylor is an uncomfortable shoe. It's produced with very little cushioning, a super-thin sole, and a total disregard for anything resembling durability. Wearing them larger than what is recommended is undeniably responsible for the blisters forming on the backs of Jeremy's heels. Whereas, the Jack Purcell, the kicks Thomas rocks, is a much more comfortable choice – its sizing is accurate and its durability a given.

Elias puffs his cigarette, absorbing the full extent of its toxicity into every available square inch of his underdeveloped lungs. Perhaps it's the insidious drug, nicotine, or maybe the idea has actually lit a spark in the lethargic Elias, but suddenly he excitedly considers the prospect, "You think we can pull that off?"

Thomas stiffens, somewhat on edge –

"Not a chance."

Connor continues to sell it.

"We only have to record one song – it's all they want."

"We're nowhere near ready, man," Thomas exclaims. "We haven't even played a friggin' gig yet."

Thomas shakes his head, walking aimlessly to the end of the driveway. Elias sags. Jeremy continues to look down at his shoes, thinking about how much his feet hurt. This kind of lack of self-confidence is something that doesn't fly with Connor. He is forced, as if by some inner-demon, to continue his efforts to pump everyone up, "Let's play a gig then."

"Easier said than done, boy genius," Thomas says. "What venue is going to hire a band that no one has ever heard of and who has never played a gig?"

Connor doesn't miss a beat, "You know St. Joe's has that youth ministry thing on the weekends – in the church basement."

"The acoustic lounge?"

"Yeah." Connor continues, "The church has this get-together on the weekends where musicians play acoustic stuff for the neighborhood kids. Supposed to be an alternative to going out and getting all fucked up, I guess."

"But it's acoustic," Thomas says.

"We tell 'em we're gonna play acoustic, then we plug in."

"I don't know if that's a good idea."

Elias responds to anti-authority hijnks as though it's a muscle reflex, "I like it."

"What do you think, Jer?" asks Connor.

Jeremy looks up from his Chucks, standing up straight, maybe the straightest he's ever stood in his short slacker life, either because he's proud to be taking a stance on this important subject relating to the band or because he's trying to get as far away as possible from his aching feet. "I'm down," he says. "But before we play, don't you think we should come up with some kind of name for the band?"

***

140

Jeremy thumbtacks a flyer up on the bulletin board in the Fordham Prep commons, stapling it right over a flyer for Habitat For Humanity. It consists of a Xeroxed picture of an alien, which looks more like a gremlin than an extraterrestrial little green man – though gremlins are, technically, little green men, if you buy into the portrait Hollywood painted in the eighties. This one has a halo drawn above its head, adding a touch of religious mysticism to the cartoon. The heading over the creature proclaims in bold type:

"LATTERDAY SAINTS - live at the St. Joe's Acoustic Lounge - This Saturday Night!"

Jeremy takes a few steps back, joining Thomas, his partner in the rhythm section of this band, *Latterday Saints*, its name having just been christened, as they both survey the official advertisement.

"Sweet," Jeremy says.

Thomas, tapping his feet, ever the critic, "It'll do."

Connor strolls into Slave To The Grind, approaching its bulletin board. He whips his hair back and pulls out a flyer – the same Latterday Saints leaflet. In their self-deluded adolescent minds, the imagery in the flyer, with its space invader logo, will soon become iconic in the indie music scene. The amazing thing about such delusions is that they sometimes come true. Ask any successful band if they thought, when they first started out, that they would make it in the business and, if they're being honest, they will own up to the fact that the entire success thing seemed like a fluke and still seems like a fluke to this very day. The best musicians, the ones whose music retains integrity deep into their careers, are the ones who still can't believe they made it. As soon as they start believing the messianic bullshit that fans and critics start writing about them, their music starts to suck. The history of rock and roll is littered with bands whose music has sucked far longer than it was good. The clearest example of this is The Rolling Stones. Without question, one of the finest rock and roll bands in the history of music for about the first 15 years of their combined career, up until the release of *Some Girls* in 1978, almost exactly fifteen years after their debut. It is not the best Stones album, but it's a fine recording, even if slightly marred by Mick Jagger's overuse of his weak falsetto range. Fifteen years of producing some of the best rock albums ever, followed by decades of never releasing a single song worth listening to, let alone anything resembling a quality album. "*Start Me Up*," the single they released a few years later, was an interesting song to open a concert with, but its last line about making a dead man come is more of an analogy for the Stones' lifeless musical output in their latter years than an example of good songwriting. Countless hours of barroom banter have been spent exploring the bands that belong on this list. The Who, Pink Floyd, Yes, Jethro Tull, The Eagles (wait, they always sucked), REM, and, of course, Michael Jackson. Truth is, anyone starting out in the music business would be thankful to have the opportunity to be one of the bands that has sucked longer than it was good. That would mean you had a career. Connor would be fine with that. He pins the flyer into the corkboard. Lost among the countless coffee shop flyers is one of Bri Da B's, promoting an upcoming performance, which Connor utterly fails to notice.

Meanwhile, Bridget sits in her fifth period class, cemented to her seat, while ignoring the teacher at the front of the room who prattles on about ancient Mesopotamia. The instructor, Mr. Nagle, means well, but it's Mesopotamia for God's sake. Maybe there's something about the word Mesopotamia that leads Bridget to scribble the word *Pimptooth* into her notebook, in bubble letters, writing over it again and again, expanding its girth, giving it an R. Crumb trippiness.

Jackie sits at the desk directly behind Bridget. She giggles with her friend, peeking over Bridget's shoulder at her doodling. As the teacher turns his back, Jackie leans forward and whispers into Bridget's ear, "I hooked up with your brother."

Bridget freezes. Jackie finishes her thought —

"I've had better."

Bridget smiles vaguely. Then she grabs Jackie's hair, and pulls her over her desk, dropping her hard to the thinly carpeted floor. The surrounding students stand, in shock and excitement, as the teacher rushes toward them. Bridget yanks Jackie's head from the ground and starts to pummel her in the face with a closed fist. Mr. Nagle swiftly throws Bridget off her, breaking up the spontaneous chaos.

Bridget, sweat dripping down the side of her face, looks around, at the chaos she created, with what can only be described as aloof objectivity.

In her mind, she smiles; but her face remains uncreased.

***

Thomas unlocks the front door of his house, its finish having been freshly repainted, and walks inside, schoolbag slung over his sore shoulder. He hears yelling upstairs, the unmistakable shrieks of his sister; shrieking that may very well rival the decibels his band of brothers generates in the garage. He closes the door, locking it for good measure, a trait he has unconsciously picked up from his father. He drops his bag and heads straight up the stairs.

Bridget has rolled herself up on the floor of her bedroom and is crying uncontrollably. Maureen stands over her, monitoring her, watching her, unsure of what to do with this child who has brought such torment into their lives. Maureen knows that she has to stand her ground, so she is both forthright and understanding.

"No!" Bridget shouts.

She rocks back and forth, nothing short of hysterical.

"We have no choice. We told you if you lose control again we're going to send you back. Your father and I can't take it anymore," Maureen implores.

"I'm not going back!"

"You need proper care. We can't give you the kind of supervision you need."

Bridget wails. Amidst the wailing, Thomas opens her door and walks into the scene. It's a scene that's dramatic to an absolutely extreme point, to a point that if it was a movie and you were watching it on screen, you wouldn't believe it. It wouldn't seem genuine. Because most people have never encountered a human being acting like this; it's reptilian, it just seems so completely contrived, like a display of emotion only for the sake of the sensational nature of emotion – it's a spitball of undiluted adrenaline shot right at the teacher from the back of the classroom. But it happens. It is real. It happens all the time, behind white picket fences, and behind no fences at all, too. But the front door is always closed and it's always locked. It's the human impulse to throw the firecracker after it's lit and run away from it, to run when someone yells *bomb*. We're simply preprogrammed to not be around when this happens, when explosions occur, and to run away on the occasions when they do occur. So a recognition of these episodes is something the brain guards itself against, because to permit access to such episodes, to process the information and recognize it as part of the human experience, is to accept this anomaly into your life. It's to accept the fact that if one person can explode, you can explode, too.

We're all capable of sinking to the bottom, but we continue swimming, ignoring those who've sunk beneath us. Bridget, on the other hand, though seemingly at rock bottom, has become quite adept at being completely impossible to ignore. And this is an astounding showcase of her talent.

"What's going on?" Thomas asks his mother.

"Let me handle this. Go downstairs."

Bridget, spitting out vitriol, "I'm not fucking going back!"

Saliva splatters from Bridget's lips like drops of acid on the carpet, seeping through the preexisting filth in the baby blue filament and burning holes into the eroding wooden floor beneath, drool that is distilled from the wrath and bile bubbling up inside of her and erupting out of a part of her mind that can never be seen, can never be known, can never be loved by the family who are on the receiving end of her rage.

Maureen reiterates, "This is not your choice to make."

Bridget stands up, confronting her mother, the veins pumping viciously from the side of her neck, her fury no longer contained by the flimsy blanket that she has dropped to the floor.

"Fuck you!"

Maureen maintains her calm. She has had far too many opportunities to practice this sort of patience. But Bridget's aggressiveness is more than enough to ignite the kindling within Thomas.

"You better fucking relax," Thomas says.

"You fucking bitch! I hate you, you fucking bitch."

Bridget's eyes look like they're going to explode. She lunges at her mother, at Maureen, pushing her shoulders backwards –

"Get out! Get out of my room!"

Maureen's head hits the door. Thomas loses it –

"Don't you fucking push her!"

Thomas throws Bridget violently against the floor. He dives on top of her, pinning her down with his weight and jamming his forearm into her throat. He presses firmly down upon her larynx, against the soft tissue of her neck that, just moments before, held throbbing veins that spoke of her discontent. When Bridget was younger, she suffered from chronic sore throats – her tonsils would become inflamed with regularity at the very hint of a cold. She was the fragile child, the sick one, and Thomas knows that he begrudged her for the constant attention she won from their mother, attention that she still craves, and which she demands with each new and volcanic outburst. Thomas wonders if it would take less effort to suffocate her because of her enlarged tonsils, if he were to press them together in just the right way, would the history of her illness and her hysterics conspire to make her even more fragile in this moment of their sibling confrontation? She's been screaming her lungs out for what's probably been hours, and inflammation in that area is not a possibility, it's a certainty.

"You touch Mom like that again...and I'll kill you."

Bridget's tonsils, or her pending death, are the last things on her mind. The theme of her ailments, recurrent in the narrative of their family, is never far from the topic at hand. Like when Bridget was beginning her tenure as *the judge's kid* on the soccer field, a title bestowed first upon Thomas by his teammates' parents, under their breaths, while he was captain of his Westchester Youth Soccer League team *The Missiles*. The team their Dad coached. Thomas had moved on, moved on to eventually getting cut from his high school team, but Bridget had just begun. Because she'd been so sickly, because she was not a strong child, she'd been placed at fullback, placed by her father, into the position requiring the least amount of strength, the least amount of strategy. It was basic, instinctual, it was muscle memory, kicking the ball when it's kicked at you, and kicking it away from you, doesn't matter where, as long as it's far, and as long as you're facing the opposing end of the field. So, fundamentally, if you know how to stand and maintain your balance, you can be a fullback. Some directional sense helps; north, west, east, south, or more fundamentally, backward, forward, left, right, that's pretty much it. But anxiety disorder has a way of warping this logic, turning left into right, shaving your senses down and hanging them upside down by their tails.

The Missiles had won two consecutive league championships, so naturally, when it came time to coach his daughter in the game, her team was to be called *The Missilettes*. They hoped to enjoy the same level of success, but this was simply not meant to be, in part due to William's restrained attitude on the sidelines. He found he couldn't bring himself to shout at the girls in quite the same way he could shout at the boys – and there certainly weren't any threats of new assholes being ripped, that would be uncouth, politically incorrect, and bordering on sexual harassment. The coach had elections to consider, constituents to instill with confidence in his ability to help lead the community, he could not allow himself to unleash the inner monster coach who would inspire these young ladies and he was at a complete loss as to what other methods might be employed to achieve the same results. Bridget had been to her brother's soccer games, she had seen the raging monster coach and she was afraid of it; though, from the beginning of her participation in the sport, it was fairly evident that her father had taken a backseat this time around with respect to unleashing the id of his coaching mind.

She would often set up cones in the backyard, run dribbling exercises, and practice kicking the ball toward this one special spot on their tree. It's a gigantic maple tree, a base spanning a width of seven feet, from which three gigantic limbs issue forth, each limb the size of its own individual tree. Who knows how long it's been growing, but it's likely to have out-lived her ancestors tenfold. The limbs tower over their house, and part of their neighbor's house, the largest limb hanging precariously over Bridget's bedroom; it became one of her many sources of anxiety, this around the same time that she developed a fear of thunderstorms which, in itself, is not un-usual for children but caused concern in her parents when she held onto the fear into her teens. Years ago, before her parents bought their home – they got it for something in the range of $230,000 in the early eighties – the previous owners had half-inch thick wire bolted into the tree and wrapped around its limbs, stabilizing the far flung mass of the organic structure. Bridget would line up the ball, sometimes placing it atop an inverted cone like an oversized golf tee, and kick the ball up into the tree, toward a section of wire. With a stroke of luck, she would nail the wire, sending the ball bouncing from one wire to its counterparts, from one limb to the next, rebelling against gravity's pull, bouncing wildly like the ball inside a pinball machine. Occasionally she would have such a stroke of luck, but it was an occasion of great infrequency, and when she did, she would smile. Their grandfather had a pinball machine in his basement, and she played it all the time. Something Las Vegas themed, it had a lot of playing cards you could smack the ball into, then the spades or diamonds would light up, and the red dress on the buxom cocktail waitress that adorned the front of the machine would glitter. It reminded her of this. But there was also a chance she might snap the wire, at least that's what she thought, sending the limb crashing down onto the house, squashing her room, which would give her an excuse to repaint it – after it was rebuilt, as it surely would be, given such an incident of force majeure. She'd always wanted to paint the walls black. The modification in décor might help her sleep.

Bridget was practicing outside one afternoon when Thomas trotted into the backyard, cleats tied onto his feet, shin guards strapped to his legs. She'd always wanted her big bro to give her some pointers. So they ran a few drills, got warmed up and Thomas grabbed the ball from her. He said he'd like both of them to position themselves at opposite ends of the yard, and he was going to punt the ball, attempting a drop in the middle of the yard, then when the ball hit the ground, they would make a run for it, vying for possession of the ball. Bridget was game. When that ball hit the ground, she booked, running like she never had, hoping to impress her brother with her agility, her mastery of putting one foot in front of the other, even without the spikes of cleats, even with her rubber-soled Reebok Pumps, the girly version. But Thomas was clearly not going to let his sister win, as some, if not most, big brothers in a similar situation might. As they converged, Bridget running at full speed, Thomas slide-tackled the ball, sweeping her feet out from under her, and slamming the bottom of his cleat into her unprotected shin. She flopped to the ground, like a skirt steak tossed to the counter by a butcher. She cried, one of those cries you can't really ignore, that most of the neighborhood probably couldn't ignore, the cries that cause people to jerk their heads up in response. It's a sound the likes of which humans can understand, which sparks the empathetic response in people. Bridget didn't think Thomas empathized with her at all. He encouraged her to get up, to stop crying; he encouraged her in a way that sounded like an order, an order with no hint of love behind it. He told her she'd never survive on the soccer field pulling shit like this, until their mother came running out, kneeling to Bridget's rescue – it was then Thomas was able to empathize. Or at least act like it. So their mother could see that he cared about his sister, and not just about demonstrating his superiority as an athlete, as a competitor, as a sibling. No, he didn't *just* care about that. She hoped he didn't. He cared about his sister's hairline fracture, an injury for which he was responsible, and presumably he cared about the fact that she would, from now on, wince every time a player on the other team dribbled toward her. Presumably.

As Thomas pins Bridget against her bedroom floor, the siblings stare into each other's eyes, attempting to bridge the gap between them that has been growing wider for years and years, attempting to transfer some air of human understanding. But all that's transferred between them is hate.

Thomas removes his arm, startled by his own strength, startled by the depth of his anger and his willingness to take that anger out on Bridget in a way that could have severely injured her, or possibly cost her her life. Bridget catches her breath and begins weeping hysterically once again. It's as though she doesn't need to breathe when she weeps, the tears and the breath rushing out of her without stopping. It's a flood, the inexorable rush of a Tsunami bucketing forth from Bridget's tortured face. Thomas stands over her; he is teetering, balancing on the precipice of something steep, something that's been brought out of him, something his sister brought out of him. Maureen sees it, whipping her hand out toward her son.

"Go downstairs. Now!"

Thomas departs, storming his way downstairs. His departure is Bridget-esq, actually, and if she was in a better frame of mind, she might admire his manner of exit. Maureen squats down next to Bridget, wrapping her arms around her. She holds her daughter as tight as she can. Maureen starts to cry along with Bridget, as though the pitch of her cries is in complete harmony with Bridget's. Perhaps, if she can't reach her daughter through reason or through simple maternal love, there might be a way to reach her through sound, through the music of their shared despair.

"I hate you. I hate you so much."

They rock back and forth with each other.

"Please don't make me go," Bridget begs. "Please don't make me go."

In the farthest corner of the kitchen, William sits alone at the table, sifting through piles of paperwork, cases currently being cited as precedent by the attorneys in an ongoing trial. He ignores the chaos above. This is a feat he is accustomed to achieving at this point in his career as a father. Thomas enters the room.

"I don't understand what's wrong," Thomas says.

He stands there, trembling. His father glances up at him, regarding his question for a second, but not for much longer than that.

"She's handicapped, Thomas," his father maintains. "Your mother and I have been dealing with this, this problem, for years. She's been on anti-depressants since she was eight years old, if you can believe it. There has always been so much anger, so much rage. She could never control her feelings. Just relentless mood swings, never any logic to it. We did everything we could to shield you from it."

Thomas sits down at the table.

William looks at his son, "She has our legs. But she could never figure out how to use them." He leans back in his chair, its wood creaking. "You had a lot of the same...well, similar...issues when you were younger, but you were able to find a way to deal with them. You were disciplined. Your sister. Well, she's just different."

Thomas's eyes are locked on nowhere. It's a cold, and particularly blank, kind of stare. He could be mad, or afraid. But William doesn't see it; no one ever sees it.

The patriarch turns back to his pile of paperwork.

***

Sequestered on the floor of his bedroom, not dissimilar to the position his sister was in on her floor upstairs, Thomas speaks softly into his phone, exactly loud enough to get out a sentence, one that's out of earshot from the rest of his family. He has Jackie on the line. He digs his fingers into the carpet, massaging it, scraping his obsessively clipped nails along its coarse surface.

"What did you say to her?" Thomas asks.

"Nothing. I was just joking around. Typical girl shit."

"My sister is manic-depressive. She can't handle jokes."

"I realize that…" Jackie clears her throat, "she punched me in the fucking face."

Thomas is empathetic, or at least pretends to be, "I'm sorry she did that. I really am. There's been a lot of stress on our family recently."

He realizes he can't make excuses for his sister, he can't explain the unexplainable, rationalize what's irrational; it's easier to just brush the whole thing off.

"It's okay," he insists.

But the thing about brushing things off is that what's brushed off most always comes back, and when it does, it's accumulated more of itself and becomes an even greater nuisance than before.

***

Bridget sits in therapy, this time accompanied by legal guardians, namely her parents. Dr. Brenner listens intently from behind his mahogany block of a desk to Maureen and William elaborating on the various family dramas and bothersome issues concerning Bridget, most of which are recurring and will not be going away any time soon.

"William has been experiencing work-related—"

William interjects, cutting his wife off, "A particular decision I made has been criticized publicly."

Dr. Brenner leans back, almost imperceptibly, in his leather-bound Herman Miller "Eames" chair with hydraulic tilt adjuster, which is seemingly an unmistakable throwback to the lifestyles and indulgences of psychoanalysts in the seventies. Is there a better profession to be so self-referential?

"Yes, I've read about it," the good doctor replies.

It's only been a handful of years since professional offices brought the hammer down on smoking indoors, and only a handful more until that same hammer is brought down on bars and nightclubs. Otherwise, this character, the good doctor, would have a hickory pipe planted between his lips smoking a pinch of tobacco, the imitation Irish bacon-flavored kind.

William grunts at the revelation, "The papers have had a field day. While we get death threats."

Dr. Brenner shows no sign of compassion; his objective is objectivity, "And, Bridget, how has this affected you?"

"It has nothing to do with what I'm going through," Bridget says, rolling her eyes at the doctor and the room at large. "I don't like it. Who would like it? But, at the very least, it's been kind of exciting."

William is sickened by this sentiment.

Bridget continues, "The problem is I'm so fucking bored with my life I can't even sleep. When I lie down, I can't think about anything else except why I'm not sleeping. I can't remember the last time I had a dream."

"Anything else?"

"The only thing I can really say for sure is that, most of the time, I can't feel anything. It's like the whole world is encased in a bowl of pudding and I'm just stuck in the middle of it all."

Maureen fights back tears as she listens to her daughter's every syllable.

"I want to be able to dream again."

Bridget looks to her parents, borderline desperate –

Maureen is from a different generation, a generation where rebellion was an antidote to woe. The Baby Boomers often refer to the late sixties as the pinnacle of their lives, the high-water mark of their counterculture, if they could only just re-member it. Maureen remembers. She remembers experiment-ing with group sex and how that experience resulted in an un-expected passion for painting. These were the days before rampant sexually transmitted diseases and the spectre of AIDS, the days when love was actually free. Perhaps the sins of the parents must be atoned for through the suffering of their chil-dren? Maureen believes in God, the one the Pope believes in, and she believed in God when she was being sixty-nined by a Hispanic roofer and an Afro-American legal assistant. It's pro-bably more appropriate to refer to the position as a six-hundred-and-ninety-six, since Maureen was in the middle, sand-wiched between these two men, whose heads met at her bot-tom, each pleasuring her nearest orifice. The roofer was, of course, on top.

In the midst of Maureen's arduous task of simultaneously stimulating their two members, members belonging to men whose last names were unknown to her, she was able to find time to notice some art. The art hanging above the bed of this wannabe commune in upstate New York near the state capital was what appeared to be a Jackson Pollock. A lot of paint dribblings and lines of splotch. This was no Jackson Pollack, but Maureen would defy you to tell the difference.

As the boomers boomed, climaxes occurring in almost perfect sync, Maureen couldn't look away from the painting. She thought it spoke to the very moment she was experiencing. If she could imagine the simultaneous climax of three individuals, gyrating as one unified organic being, and the resultant fluids implied in such a deed, this painting could not have expressed the visuals any better. In fact, Maureen thought, after their post-coital consumption of marijuana and mushrooms, if they were to remove the bottom sheet of the bed and hang it out to dry, a similar painting, albeit slightly more organic in technique, might materialize in the fabric. Even if they had to employ the aid of a black light to bring out the intricacies of the design.

As they passed a roach clip, Maureen stood up, residual cum draining down her inner thighs, and stepped good and close to the painting. The Hispanic, after a nice, long toke, encouraged her to, "Take it down."

Maureen reached up, stretching herself, and dismounted the painting from the wall. She glanced behind the canvas and noticed two sets of wall hanging wires: one at the top and one at the bottom.

"Bought that at a garage sale. Owners couldn't figure out which way to hang it, so they installed two sets of wires. Every week or so, they'd just flip it."

Maureen went ahead and flipped it. She flipped it again. No discernable difference. This was the beginning of a lifelong love and pursuit of painting in the style of Realism. Abstract Expressionism was an unfulfilling, masturbatory, waste of time – that was the lesson, the deep understanding, that she took away from this collective encounter.

In college, Maureen set about taking a number of painting classes and worked hard enough to commit a portion of her costly liberal arts education in Manhattan to a minor in Classical Art. Her thing was portraiture. Specifically, Rococo, which then merged into Neo-Classical Portraiture, in the Age of Enlightenment, the Age of Reason. She was near expert at analyzing the works of the Eighteenth Century masters like Boucher, Reynolds and Gainsborough, and her exploration of the "Portrait of Napoleon" by the neo-classical Jean-Auguste-Dominique Ingres earned her an A- in her advanced Classical Art tutorial.

Her eye for portraiture ended at analysis – she was unable to make use of her vast knowledge and actually draw portraits of the human face. Something about the eyes. Either getting the eyes correctly, or looking in them if she did. It was just something about the eyes. But she could draw portraits of canines with enhanced skill. Dalmatians, Irish Setters, Bulldogs, you name it. Every dog in her family growing up had been immortalized, in portraiture, on canvas, then framed, and promptly hung, around the corridors of her childhood home. Oil, charcoal, watercolor, all were utilized to depict the minutiae of every hair sprouting from the bodies of these creatures, these extensions of the human clan, the humble animal who bears the indignity and the responsibility of being referred to as man's best friend.

She was just unable to reproduce the minutiae of man.

But she was good, damn good, especially by the measure of those who have no gift for this kind of thing. Maureen was not going to find her work hanging in any legitimate museum, not in her lifetime and not ever, but anyone could see that she had a gift and she would often indulge this hobby as her children were growing up. In the yard, amidst the green backgrounds of their garden, she would break out her easel, her palette of paints, a canvas, and produce something that her children would marvel at. She never painted her kids, she focused solely on the dogs that swarmed around them in their various phases of growth. And through the growth of the dogs, as depicted in the pictures, she could determine the specific phase of growth of her children. She once displayed a retrospective of her work at the Sunshine Retirement Villa across town, and got paid for it. Regardless of the venue, compensation for art is a rare and welcomed accomplishment. And perhaps her point-of-view, in this case the portraiture of thoughtfully posed Pomeranians, helped add a little levity to the last days of this establishment's ancient and incontinent residents.

If you can affect one person with your art, if you can reach across the divide of awareness and touch one person, you've succeeded as an artist.

Unfortunately, one of the people Maureen touched, was her daughter. Bridget, whether through casual exposure during her upbringing or simply through inherited genetic talent, took quite naturally to painting. However, she was never able to keep up with her mother's talent and this was a point of frustration for Bridget, perhaps another of the myriad pressures in life that contributed to her anxiety. It never registered with Bridget that she was simply young, that talent grows slowly, like her body, that it must be nurtured, practiced, and imbued with experience. With experience comes point-of-view, context, originality, all of which informs the talent. The only thing that ever registered with her was: she was not as good as her Mom.

So she put down her pencils. Not Bridget, but her mother, Maureen. She gave up her pursuit so as not to compete with her daughter. Parents often sacrifice for their children; sometimes it's their ambition, sometimes it's their health, sometimes it's their lives. Or however one quantifies it. It's almost always their own sense of youth. Maureen gave up her artistic passion, the one thing in her life that gave her joy. And Bridget never noticed the sacrifice.

Dr. Brenner jumps back into the therapeutic ring, his eyes passing over Bridget, while craning his swollen head toward her parents, "I'm confident this can be solved with medication. I hesitate to send Bridget back to the hospital – she's been making progress."

Maureen finds a measure of relief in this.

"I think I'll take her off the Prozac and switch her to Zoloft; it's new, let's see how she reacts to that. We'll keep her on Lithium and start her on Neurontin, it's an antiseizure medication, but a few of my colleagues prescribe it to stabilize mood and have chronicled wonderful results in their patients – it should help smooth out the Zoloft. We'll continue with the Excelsicor for anxiety. As for the insomnia, I'll prescribe a sleeping aid, half dosage, to start. We'll monitor closely and see where we stand in a month."

Bridget chimes in, "Sounds like more pudding to me."

This desultory statement galvanizes William –

"Are these prescriptions really the answer? She's been taking this stuff for so long, and yet we keep having these issues."

Dr. Brenner writes the prescriptions, already on autopilot.

"Mm, hmm. Medication remains the most effective treatment."

Bridget stares out the window –

An SUV drives into the parking lot, plowing through what appears to be a thick layer of chocolate pudding.

CHAPTER SIX

St. Joseph's Church in Bronxville, New York, is a gothic mini-cathedral sitting directly across the street from the local grocery store, an A&P whose name has recently been changed to *The Food Emporium*, in an effort to appeal to the ever-increasing upper-class clientele of Bronxville and to add a percentage or two to the margins of its retail prices. The clientele can afford it. With respect to both the rate of recurrence and clarity of timbre, the church bells cannot compete with the frequency or effervescence of the store's cash registers. Teenage skater punks and slackers in grunge-wear, who all reside outside of Bronxville's city limits and don't give a rat's ass about the gourmet salsa or fake butter the Emporium is peddling, walk right past the automatic doors of the supermarket and descend into the neighboring church, Bronxville's house of the Lord, in a parade of restless youth that might seem incongruous in a slightly less liberated community.

A makeshift sign along a stone path by the church reads: *St. Joseph's Youth Ministry presents: The Acoustic Lounge.*

The disenfranchised file into the church basement, an old pale yellow seventies era gymnasium lined with tables of coffee and a variety of calorie-filled five-and-dime store munchies. Fritos recently expanded their artificial flavor market: cool ranch and bbq; both styles are quickly surpassing their competitor, Dipsy Doodles, as the suburban stoner's preferred choice of midnight snacks. The tables are filled with these flavors. The room, though lofty, is extremely narrow, the walls only a foot or two from the basketball court sidelines. Consequently, there are large pads, vinyl coverings stuffed with foam chunks, deliberately hung over the walls to absorb the blows from the off balance elementary school student who might stumble off the court and take a header into the wall while going after a ball. The aesthetics vaguely recall the interior design of an insane asylum. Ministry staff and Father McSweeney, a priest in his early 30's, another unusual sight in a conservative suburban church, fix their stares at the cast of misfits infiltrating their place of worship.

Onstage, behind a well-worn curtain, the band sets up, securing their plugs into the appropriate power surges. Connor tunes his low E-string for the fifteenth time, while Thomas tightens the head of his snare drum. They're careful not to make too much noise, as that will ruin the anticipation of the crowd. If those in the crowd were to detect any hint of the music before the music is presented to them, there's no telling what could happen – this is show business after all, and the foreplay of the crowded lines, the smoking of pot, and the compression of bodies against the barricade at the front of the stage, is all part of the experience. The music is the climax, and as such, should be postponed as long as physically possible. They also don't want to give away the fact they're using electricity.

Elias peeks through the dusty curtains at the increasingly rowdy crowd, "Bunch of fucking losers."

It's not that the band is popular, it's just that their flyers had gotten around and the rumor that they weren't going to play acoustic had gotten around too, and this information reached just the right audience that appreciates it when their peers undermine the system and strangle the status quo, no matter what it is they're doing.

Their nerves spike, Thomas's leg pumps. He asks, "When do we go on?"

"Alex is finding out now."

Connor smiles, pacing, pumping himself up. He straps his fender to his chest, brings the scratched pickguard to his mouth, breaths condensation onto it, and shines it up with the sleeve of his wool sweater – the kind with the single stripe across it, a style that will soon be popularized by Billy Joe Armstrong in the music video for Green Day's *"When I Come Around."* Connor is ahead of the curve, not surprising when it comes to fashion, and this will be a personal vanguard he will undoubtedly pat himself on the back for when MTV releases the video in January 1995. It will be a validation. Green Day released their breakthrough album, *Dookie*, in February 1994, two months before Kurt Cobain committed suicide, and they were still releasing singles into the subsequent year. Music was the hottest commodity going, hotter than cocaine was in the eighties, and it was much easier for kids to persuade their parents to buy them a record by a band called *Green Day* than by groups calling themselves *The Sex Pistols* or *The Buzzcocks*, notwithstanding the fact that *Green Day* was a reference to marijuana, a fact that was lost on most parents and a lot of the kids who bought the record.

"This is it, guys." Connor pipes.

The crowd metastasizes. The staff grows more and more worried. Jackie and two girlfriends, an ice-blend of punk and preppy, push their way through the crowd to the front. Jackie's face is bruised, but well hidden with strategic make-up. She cuts in front of a particularly handsome guy, kind of a jock-type, in form-fitting cargo pants. She notices him noticing her out of her peripheral vision and, with the subtlety of a horny teen, flips her stringy hair into his face. She purses her lips, pivots, grazing her rear ever-so-gently against the outline of his crotch.

Her friends observe this, and one of them, Megan, sighs, "You're such a bitch."

Jackie smiles as she rubs her ass into his groin some more.

"What are you talking about?"

This guy's boring night just got exponentially better.

Alex chats with Father McSweeney by the picnic tables that are supporting vast vats of cheap coffee. The asylum feel of the gymnasium, the cheap coffee and cheap snacks, the lights that are way too bright, all of this coalesce to make the gig seem more like a class at school than a rock and roll debut of great promise. Maybe Alex, assuming the role of conniving concert promoter, is one of the more authentic aspects of the evening. It sounds like he's trying to sell the humble servant a used car with tampered mileage.

"The band's prepared to play about six to eight songs. Depending on the feeling afterward, they could do an encore. How does that sound to you?"

"We'll see." McSweeney's eyes are glued to the bubbling chaos that's on the brink of spilling out around him.

"Please just get them on in five minutes." McSweeney says, as he walks away.

***

Alex leaps onto the stage at the front of the gymnasium, taking the steps two at a time. He grabs the mic and taps a finger on it a few times.

"Ladies and gents, girls and boys, hold onto your butts..."

The PA system is already feeding back, just a small taste of the onslaught of noise that is about to come.

Clearing his throat, Alex proclaims loudly, "The Latterday Saints!"

The moldy velvet curtains open to a mixture of scattered applause and sarcastic quips. Elias steps to the microphone.

"Thanks for coming."

The band, for the first time, is alone on a stage. They squint at the sparse lighting fixtures, orienting themselves; all eyes are on them.

"We were Jesus Christ and The Latterday Saints...but he got lost on the way to the show." Elias continues, "We're here tonight to absolve you of your sins, but only if you forgive us for not playing acoustic."

Elias performs the sign of the cross, and he's pretty sure he can see the excess blood flushing through the veins and capillaries of Father McSweeney's face.

Then all hell breaks loose.

Thomas counts the sticks and they rip into "*Chummin.*" The crowd cheers. The staff looks confused, the music much — *much* — louder than expected. McSweeney leans in to a junior staff member, "I thought this was acoustic?"

"Supposed to be."

Father McSweeney shakes his head as he stalks off down a corridor. The band head-bangs as they begin to play. The crowd jumps up and down, sweaty bodies ramming into each other, testosterone and estrogen discharging like a Mentos dropped into a bottle of sparkling soda, as they mosh to the music. Elias sings his lyrics, like charcoal scraping against a bricked wall, his words whipping into the compressed blur of the crowd –

"I'm through,

you always take for granted those things I do./

It's always the same stupid bullshit lies, you never really tried to help

me understand those things you do."

The band, sounding like a real band, feeds off the audience – these gypsies, these scavengers of the suburbs. The staff tries to politely insert themselves into the middle of the youngsters to quell their riotous behavior, to hopefully prevent the dreaded mosh pit from reaching critical mass, but it's overwhelming. Their efforts are useless. *Slam dancing.* The term alone implies impenetrability; it's adamantine. It's the suburban version of the dance, but there are still some fists involved.

"And when I close my eyes..."

Jeremy sings a very adequate back-up, but he's easily over-shadowed by Elias's uber-aggressive lead vocals –

"...I'm still thinking about you."

"It doesn't ever end, so God please help me make amends, the story

never ends...with you."

Jackie, dancing in the labyrinthine crowd, makes eye con-tact with Thomas and Thomas likes it, he thinks that this is a tiny slice of the rock and roll fantasy, to have a young, spirited, and incredibly sexy girl staring at you from the crowd. But he's so worried about losing his timing that he breaks his gaze with her, and he looks around the place: an entire sea of kids, their bodies cresting like a wave, as they dance simultaneously to his rhythm. Unlike his counterparts, there is no microphone, no PA system to amplify him, no electricity carrying his sound waves into the ears of his followers. He immediately connects to his audience the second his stick hits the plastic skin. There's no rerouting, no middleman – he's one with everyone. He's riding the wave with them, but it's as he realizes he's riding it, that he's connecting with this massive crowd, as he looks down into the crest of this protoplasmic surf, he's over-come with nerves. His muscles all stiffen at once and he feels like he can't get a good deep breath. Playing the drums is a physical workout, especially when you're playing this style of music, and not being able to breathe when you're playing is like trying to run the hundred meters while holding your breath. You may start out okay, but you can't sustain it. Thomas closes his eyes, focusing on the rhythm, letting his body do what comes naturally and gradually he fights his way through the minor panic attack.

"My time is fragile by what I've known,

what I've known./

I can see through your shit,

bored and old, bored and old."

A spectator hops on stage, circling Elias like a strung-out shark. Elias is working it, working the crowd, and as he sings, he grabs the kid by the back of his shirt. The kid smirks, going with it, playing along with Elias. As Elias pulls the shirt back, the kid bends at the knees and then launches himself into the crowd. He's caught, just barely, the crowd sagging as they pass him around, too fast, without enough control. People are screaming, dancing, moshing, as the fever and tempo of the song builds.

"It doesn't ever end, so God please help me make amends, the story

never ends."

In an effort to control the surfing kid, the crowd careens into the refreshment table and knocks it over onto its side. Piping hot coffee waterfalls onto the floor, chips and cheap snacks float into the steaming black liquid, soaking it up and creating a soupy and sticky mess on the ground. It's become unqualified mayhem.

"I've been begging for admission, but you won't let me in."

Jeremy and Connor glance at the sides of the stage and see the staff beginning to flank them. They're not happy and they-'re well beyond incorporating social niceties into their intervention tactics. It's guerrilla warfare time; kill or be killed. They've already turned the other cheek.

"You're a short-term obsession, borderline a sin."

Elias, looks at the staff, then turns sharply back to Thomas who keeps thundering away at the beat.

"I'll be yours for the weekend, that's where it ends. And I'm still

waiting for my time..."

At this precise moment, Father McSweeney cuts the power. He literally disengages one of those old-school circuit breakers, the kind Doctor Frankenstein used to bring his monster to life. He closes the box, locking it for good measure. The sound goes out and the place goes completely dark. The exception being, Thomas, because he is still drumming. It's like he's unaware that anything has happened; he will not be handcuffed by electricity, or manipulated like a puppet by those who control the switches and plugs. He only realizes something's amiss when the crowd begins to boo loudly. He looks up at his bandmates, who are staring at him, and staring at his instrument, with what he can only perceive as jealousy, since of all their instruments he's playing the only one that is technically acoustic and, therefore, audible. That piece of information does not stop the Holy Father from ripping the sticks out of Thomas's hands, putting them in his back pocket and pointing his finger toward the door. Coffee cups, and what's left of the munchies, have achieved flight as they're thrown around the room. The bowls they were in are floated up to the ceiling like UFO's, eerily resembling the kind deployed in the low-budget sci-fi movies of the fifties.

The staff fires up flashlights, shielding themselves from the flack, illuminating the exits and corralling the cattle out of their facility.

Outside the entrance to the church, Alex stands impatiently alongside Father McSweeney, who can't stop pacing around in a circle while the staff kicks everyone out of the sacred building.

"Father, I thought we said six to eight songs?"

"Get the hell out of here, before I call the cops."

Alex joins the mass exodus of teenagers, disappearing inside them, and turning to address them all, "Everyone, party at the field!"

***

Their party spot is packed to the brim with the underage crowd from the show, plus the field's usual stragglers and neighborhood scallywags – it's a juvenile delinquent's dream. All under the cover of autumn trees. Connor, Elias and Alex make a beeline for the keg at the center of it all.

Connor's jazzed like Coltrane, "That was fucking awesome!"

Elias has to snicker at him, "It was real awesome getting cut off in the middle of our first song."

"Who cares? Did you see everyone moshing?"

Alex particularly enjoyed the moshing, "Did I see? I felt up at least ten different asses in that mess."

"You committed sexual assault in the basement of a church," Elias says.

"They were into it," Alex insists.

They approach the keg and notice an enormous line, but, to their surprise, the kids at the head of it wave them in.

"It's all you, dude," mumbles one of the kids.

Elias tilts his head at the young follower.

"You sure?"

The impressionable follower digs his knees into the grass and begins bowing, doing his best *Wayne's World* impression, "I'm not worthy." Though it's a parody, the intent is most earnest.

He hands Elias the tap, and he starts filling their cups. Elias nods his head, his chin raised ever so slightly, as if he's considering the notion that he could probably get used to this kind of treatment. Jackie and her two girlfriends are not far behind the boys as they scamper to the head of the line.

"Hi boys," Jackie pronounces. "You wanna pour me some of that stuff?"

"Got ID?" Alex asks.

She sticks her tongue out at Alex, and he pours away.

"Where's Tom?"

Elias points over to the river. Alex hands her the beer, overtly eyeing her bodacious figure. She notices and gives him a smile, tossing her hair as she walks away from them. She gets this a lot, and her reaction has become stock, as she's practiced it to perfection in front of her mirror.

Thomas and Jeremy huddle together, squatting down on the bank of the Bronx River, smoking a freshly rolled blunt. The crisp air rolls off the surface of the modest tributary, wafting the marijuana smoke into their faces.

"That was fucking embarrassing."

Jeremy hesitates, stumped by Thomas's sudden pessimism.

"It was fine, dude."

Thomas takes a substantial hit off the blunt.

"We sucked. We should have practiced more. A lot more."

"And we should have used battery-powered amps," Jeremy responds, as he cracks the fuck up. He is bleary-eyed, and somewhat frazzled, but Thomas remains stone-faced, his eyes glued to the ripples rolling along the oily surface of the Bronx River, the river he thinks of as his local river and the only one in the area that can compete with New York City's East River for the prize of foulest river on the East Coast. If you could tally up the sum total of chemical sludge, radioactive isotopes, household appliances, beer cans, bicycles, cars, condoms, syringes and body parts, you'd have your winner and the sclerotic river could stand at some imaginary podium and give an acceptance speech for its award, a speech littered with inappropriate nature references and punctuated by wheezing coughs. If the Bronx River won, it would claim that the syringes and body parts that it carries flowed from the Bronx into Westchester, a gross generalization that most Westchester locals would be quick to accept, despite the fact that the Bronx is south of Westchester County and the river doesn't flow that way. The condoms are another story entirely. The River has to own up to that tally and perhaps it's proud of its role as a repository of condoms, just as the young men who deposit them there are proud of their shallow sexual triumphs.

Jackie sneaks up behind the two boys, draping her arms around Thomas. Jeremy stands; he knows what time it is.

"I'll leave you two kids alone. Keep the herb."

Jackie plops down on the grass next to Thomas, rubbing the side of her body against his. He passes her the weed as he contemplates the curvature of the breast resting against the lower quadrant of his shoulder blade.

She smiles at him, "You were great tonight."

Thomas is immediately dismissive.

"Usually, drumming is the one thing I can do without thinking. I can just shut my brain off and do it. But tonight, it felt all wrong."

"You're stoned," Jackie laughs.

Thomas looks down, pensively, "See these two fingers..."

He holds his left hand out toward Jackie, extending his index and middle fingers.

"I can't fully extend them. Fine for holding a drumstick, but can't play a power chord." He chuckles, "I always wanted to play the guitar."

Jackie takes his hand into hers, and rubs his fingers, massaging his knuckles.

"What happened to them?"

"My Dad used to coach my soccer team, you know, when I was younger. He put me in the goal, cause he said he could 'rely on me.' Couldn't rely on anybody else on the team, but he could rely on me. Dove for a ball once, jammed these two fingers into the ground, cracked 'em up pretty bad."

He looks up, smiles at her.

"He wouldn't take me out of the game...and I wanted to tough it out for him."

His eyes tear slightly, much against his will.

"We won."

Jackie senses his consternation, and so she changes the subject, changes the subject to the one thing that can always raise the sun in an adolescent boy's moonless, bible-black night: she guides his fingers down to her pierced bellybutton, "Check it out. Got it in the city. It's a barbell."

Thomas raises his eyebrows, "Do your parents know?"

"You *are* stoned."

Thomas kisses her, as the invitation is crystal clear, but he is cautious. Unusually so. The two teens press their lips together, as if testing their biometric pressure. Then Jackie suggests, in a tone that's anything but cautious, "I know something you can do with those fingers."

She looks at him reassuringly, then whispers into his ear –

"Rape me."

She pushes his hand down into her crotch.

"I give you permission."

Thomas, pulling his hand back, like his elbow is spring-loaded. "Jackie, you can stop coming on so strong. I know you're not really like this."

Jackie lets this sink in. People don't usually talk to her like this, at least those she's trying to impress. She drops her head; she can't even look at him. Her guard is completely down, or so it seems.

"What if I told you I want you to be my first?" She whispers.

Thomas leans in and cradles her porcelain face, looking directly into her eyes, and through to whatever may be behind them, "What if I told you the same thing?"

Jackie glows like the glow-worm she got for Christmas as a toddler. With the palm of Thomas's hand bonded to her belly, like it somehow caught itself on the barbell, she thinks if he squeezes, her stomach might glow and her bellybutton ring might shimmer, just like her glow-worm did when she hugged it, in its felt green pajamas and floppy nightcap, its cheeks bubbled out in inexplicable joy and reverence, as if it was celebrating that particular moment in the life of a child, a time that embraces naïveté, and wonder, and peanut butter and fluff sandwiches. She pulls Thomas down on top of her, into the cover of the surrounding brush. It hasn't been that many years since she held her glow-worm, since she cuddled with it under the soft and peaceful embrace of her oversized down comforter, since the idea of what she has been longing to do with Thomas would have seemed like some kind of nightmare or joke. It hasn't been that long, but it feels like several lives and half a world away from her now.

In a twisted kind of paradox, you feel older as a teenager than you will ever feel in your entire life, not that you think you won't age or think you won't gain some level of wisdom as you pile on the years, but it's at this age that you think you have all the answers – and you get to write the questions, too.

Making love is the exception, insofar as burning questions and their corresponding answers go. All teenagers know one thing about sex: that they don't know anything about sex. If it can ever be said that there are two kinds of people in the world, then it can be said that there are those who have had sex and those who have not and they are distant relatives at best. Conceptually, it should be like the way the Beach Boys described it in their popular love songs – if you substitute the word "surfing" with "fucking," they paint a pleasant picture of the experience. But they never wrote lyrics about all the sweat involved. Thomas soon learned that, really, he couldn't possibly concentrate on that stuff – the concept of lovemaking as crooned by lyricists, as poeticized by the romantics. He was more concerned with two things: 1) maintaining his erection; and, 2) ensuring he lasts longer than ten seconds. His asinine remedy for the latter was to think of dead squirrels. Namely, the dead squirrels he and a neighbor friend of his, Ulysses Sweller, who he'd call Ulee for short, used to make dead by shooting them with BB guns when they were young and unrepentant sadists. One time, Ulee shot a squirrel – the thing must've been perched up a hundred feet high in an oak tree, seemingly oblivious, eating its nuts – and the bugger dropped like a bowling ball, hit the ground, and bounced three or four times like it was made of condensed rubber. To their wide-eyed amazement, it ran away as though it had barely been injured. It would've been easier to open fire on the creature, at that very moment, having fallen right to them from the sky. But they couldn't possibly attempt another shot; the fall most likely resulted in some internal bleeding, and they were far too transfixed by the comedic and tragic act of its apparent soon-to-be death.

Thomas imagines his penis is the BB gun powered by a single silver CO_2 capsule, its casing punctured when loaded and cocked, releasing its carbon dioxide, pressurizing the innards of the weapon, the pellet suspended in perpetuity waiting for the trigger to be pulled by its faithful owner. Just as he'd once resisted shooting that squirrel, he is going to wait to pull his trigger in this instance, because he is in control, in control of his trigger, though the pressurized capsule and its unstable elements seem very much in control of him.

In his particular case, there is no safety for the weapon.

As Thomas imagines the displaced innards of the rodent, picturing what it would look like if his pellet struck it point blank, and recycling this image in his mind in an effort to distract his raging hormones, Jackie's friends, Megan and Abigail, congregate by the keg. They fawn over Elias, Connor and Alex, the heroes of the hour, the closest thing these meanderers will get to brushing flannel with full-blown rock stars in a dewy field in Bronxville. This is not necessarily the case for Alex, but that doesn't stop him from relishing in their moment.

"When they open the box and that gimp pops out!" Alex exclaims.

He's recounting the famous scene in *Pulp Fiction*, the epitome of the early nineties indie film movement, a film that tuned into the apathy of the alienated teens that saw it and turned the hippy ideal of violence is bad, into the grunge-era attitude that violence is cool, at least violence via the make-believe weapon of art. For Elias, the film also tuned into a personal fetish of his, "I'd like to own a gimp."

Abigail, with a very specific antenna that is tuned to an altogether different frequency, says, "I didn't really get that movie. Too much violence. And the dialogue: n-word this, n-word that."

Alex points out, "Someone should tell Quentin Tarantino he's not black." Despite the fact that Alex doesn't think this at all, the thought never crossed his mind until Abigail made it plain that she had taken offense to Tarantino's free usage of the most loaded of racist terms. Alex sees this as an opportunity because Alex is the kid you knew in high school, the predator who will do anything to unburden himself from the chain of his virginity and Abigail is cute. He's got decent looks, and he actually does get a variety of ass, he just hasn't gone all the way yet. That would require a higher-level of dedication, since the longer girls hang around him, the quicker they catch on to his schemes. But he's got that kind of confidence, that swagger, that piques girls' interests at first, but soon after suffers considerably from the law of diminishing returns. Alex could do a lot worse than Abigail, in fact the lot worse that he could do is what he has been doing lately, spending the majority of his nights alone, clutching himself in his bed and fantasizing that any girl that he knows might some day bless him with her erotic pleasures.

"Are you kidding me?" Megan adds. "I loved it. The last thing I saw John Travolta in was '*Look Who's Talking 3*,' which don't get me wrong, is one of my favorite movies of all-time, completely snubbed by the Academy by the way, but this tops it. When he stabbed Uma Thurman with that needle. Oh my God. I thought I was gonna pass the fuck out—"

Connor, lying in wait for an opportunity to show off his encyclopedic knowledge of the history of film, and lo and behold, here it is on a silver platter, "That scene's a rip-off of Martin Scorsese's 1976 documentary, '*American Boy*.' Ver-fuck-ing-batim. Steven Prince, Neil Diamond's road manager, the movie's about him, and he tells this real intricate and unique story about giving a girl, a girl who OD'd, an adrenaline shot the size of a cannon to the heart. Same fucking dialogue, down to the consonant. Same goddamn scene."

"So what?" Alex retorts. "Am I ever going to see this stupid film? No. I don't watch any movies made before 1986. '*Top Gun*' is my absolute limit." He finishes chugging his beer, "And who the hell is this guy Scor-se-se?" Maybe if Alex hadn't already chugged three beers, or if he really had any true sensitivity to the needs and desires of the fair sex, he would have noticed the way Abigail looked away at this comment. But he didn't notice and doesn't realize how much more effort he will now need to expend if he has any chance with her at all.

Connor shakes his head, genuinely saddened by the total lack of intellectual curiosity reflected in Alex's comment, as Megan continues, "Nothing's 'original' anymore. I mean, think about it. Everything gets recycled. But, I guess, really, it's what you recycle it into that matters."

Connor is actually somewhat impressed with this thought process and is prepared to concede that Tarantino took a snippet of dialogue from an obscure film and turned it into a gripping action sequence, but his opportunity to expand on this thought is lost in a fog of red and blue lights that slice through the field from along the road. A dozen teenage heads snap around to the lights, like deer tuned to the sounds of the forest, and they see uniformed police officers trudging into the sides of the field wielding industrial flashlights. They sidestep through the terrain, scaling into the field and zoning in on the offending miscreants. Most of the officers are wearing black, pimped out in some kind of faux-SWAT getup, as if this is the most action these Bronxville cops have seen all year and the targets of their hunt are the local equivalent of the Gambino crime family. They live for this kind of shit, for the opportunity to wear these outfits outside in the real world instead of exclusively at the departmental Halloween party.

Alex takes the hint and chucks his cup.

"Let's bounce!"

Teenagers bolt in every conceivable direction. Connor grabs Megan's delicate hand and he leads her off into a dark corner of the field, running at a remarkably fast pace. Elias, opting for the slightly bolder approach, picks up Abigail, hoisting her into his burly arms.

"Do not fear, fair maiden, I will lift you to safety."

Abigail slaps him squarely across the face, and it smarts. She actually made his ear ring. He drops her. She runs.

"You'll get us both caught, you fucking idiot," Abigail chides.

Elias, clearly taken aback, "So much for chivalry…"

Thomas and Jackie are in the throes of making love. Within the coarse thicket, crinkling the fallen leaves on the ground, they are totally absorbed in the moment as Thomas thrusts his young self into Jackie and she wraps her legs tightly around him. Thomas recognizes a keening emotion in himself, something he is unfamiliar with and it dawns on him that this is what it feels like to be happy. Any notions of a BB-riddled squirrel have been dismissed by the overwhelming presence and physical beauty of Jackie, by the incredible joy of her moist vagina engulfing him in warmth and welcome. There is only so much ammunition in his teenage clip to combat such a visceral force and he feels it fading, he senses that he can't hold it any longer, he's torn by the desire to make the moment last forever and the desire to feel the glorious release. Thomas is on the verge of orgasm when he sees the police lights, their spinning luminescence slashing through the shrubbery, hitting his eyes.

This, as a method of distraction, works much better than a dead squirrel.

He promptly jumps off Jackie, zipping his pants, a tall task given his engorgement. But anything is possible under the right circumstances. There is only half a moment for half a smile; then his senses kick in.

"Come on. Get dressed." Thomas implores.

He spots hordes of kids scattering throughout the field, many being grabbed by cops, mowed down by the scythe of the law, stuck like flies on field-sized fly paper – this is just too easy for the man. Jackie rapidly tidies herself up, brushing the leaves off her jeans as she keeps one eye on the police, who are inching their way steadily toward them.

"My parents are gonna kill me." Jackie says, in a panic.

"Not if they don't catch us."

Thomas gestures toward the only barrier in this little field, a barrier that has always remained uncrossed during these parties: The Bronx River. Thomas is suddenly a changed man, the memory of sex still hard upon him, he feels somehow daring and reckless, a complete contrast to the quiet and withdrawn Thomas of yesterday. He can't help flashing a devious grin. Jackie doesn't like what he's implying.

"No fucking way." Jackie says.

Jackie knows as well as anyone the toxic nature of this estuary and the idea of wading into it is utterly repellant to her. Perhaps it's because of the recent intimate contact with Thomas, as if she thinks the evil stench and pollution of the water will find an easier way into her, a way to infect and corrupt her further than she has already been corrupted. She was happy to be violated by Thomas. The violation of the river is unwelcome, like a real rape or a cancer. Her face goes pale as Thomas grabs her hand and leads her to the river.

Thomas and Jackie submerge their bodies in the waist-deep water, immediately shivering as they wade across the unpleasantly cold canal, stepping between loose stones and other unidentifiable objects along the riverbed. Jackie strains to see through it, trying really hard to make out what's beneath the surface, "Are there any leeches in here?"

"I'm more concerned about the rats," Thomas quips.

Jackie whimpers.

Three-quarters of the way to the Yonkers side of the river, flashlights shine on them from the Bronxville side. The voice of authority bellows from behind the bouncing beams of light –

"Stop right there and come on back."

Thomas looks back at the cop, but keeps on moving.

"What are you gonna do? Shoot us?"

Thomas can't help but provoke him, still feeling reckless. Still feeling. The cop stands there, his feet planted in meta-phorical cement.

The kids struggle to the opposite bank, shimmying up through the mud and the stunted brambles. Sopping wet, they both climb out and shake off all the excess water they possibly can. The couple laughs as they scuttle away down a stone path, hand-in-teenaged-hand.

Meanwhile, Jeremy searches for his bandmates, like a soldier in the shit, but they are nowhere in sight. He's as lost as he thinks they might be, until he thinks he hears something. He turns around, at the sound of stamping feet, right into the face of a police officer –

"Party's over," the public servant bluntly informs him.

Jeremy, his sweaty palms pressed against a squad car, stands there as the officer meticulously searches through his backpack. The cop halts, smirking like they always do when they find something that they were really hoping to find. The cop yanks a zip-lock bag of pot out and slaps it on the hood of the squad car.

"What's this?"

"Uh. Oregano?" Jeremy replies.

"It's a misdemeanor, that's what it is."

He cuffs Jeremy's skeletal hands behind his back and opens the door of the black and white, roughly pushing Jeremy into the backseat, the tip of his nose brushing against the steel partition as the officer shuts the door summarily behind him.

Connor, Megan, Elias and Alex walk along the main street of Bronxville, trying to camouflage themselves as aimless pedestrians, which is mostly pointless since there really aren't any aimless pedestrians in this sleepy little township, given the strictly enforced non-loitering laws. The elderly certainly aren't walking to any movies this late, not without matinee pricing or a double shot of espresso. Anyone out walking this late is either a degenerate drinking in the field, or someone out to score a dime-bag from one of the degenerates drinking in the field. From a suitable hiding place, Connor peers back at the canopy of trees, under which rests the field, their arena of nihilism, their bastion of newfound manhood and womanhood, the place where they work so hard to soil the purity of their reputations.

"Where the hell are Tom and Jeremy?" Connor says frustratingly.

Megan slaps Connor in the arm.

"And Jackie?"

"And Jackie. Shit."

Connor kicks an empty beer can into the middle of the street.

***

Bridget rolls out of bed and steps into her slippers, both of which are shaped like the snouts of Boston Terriers. She strolls to her window and opens it all the way. She pokes her head outside, leaning a cheek on the sill, and lights a cigarette. She stares into the glare of the rising sun.

Though there's no school on weekend mornings, a reality that's to be exalted, Bridget does bemoan the absence of Howard Stern. The Howard Stern that used to exist on actual radio, before selling his soul to satellite. 92.3 K-ROCK. It was a classic rock station her mother listened to, on a rare occasion or two, when Bill was at the office; however, she didn't listen to Stern – but her daughter sure as hell did. To supplement his absence on the weekend, Bridget would often tape his bits and anthologize them on best-of mix tapes. Howard was a bit of a boys club, but his trailblazing Channel 9 TV show, featuring such timeless skits as Homeless Howiewood Squares, Stuttering

John and Kenneth Keith Kallenbach blowing cigarette smoke through his eyes, opened his sensibilities up to a much wider audience of lunatics, weirdos and teenage girls like Bridget, even though the majority of his female audience was comprised of lipstick lesbians. Or so his male listeners very much liked to believe.

What attracted Bridget to Stern was pretty simple: he was saying everything her parents wouldn't say to her, nor would want to be said to her by others. Which is why Stern had so many problems with the Federal Communications Commission in the beginning of his career.

But, really, it was also Jeffrey Dahmer. Every era has its iconic killer, and the nineties had Jeffrey. By the summer of '91, he was killing a person a week – and eating them.

"Don't you dare have lunch with Jeffrey Dahmer!"

The above plea is the title of a parody Stern wrote to the melody of *"Mrs. Brown You Have A Lovely Daughter."* Peter Noone, the lead singer of Herman's Hermits, and the person who performed the original version many years ago, sang the song live on the air. The benign plucking of a ukulele provided the rhythm to Noone's melody and the backdrop to words that cautioned individuals against dining with Jeffrey due to the high probability that they would become the next course.

Bridget caused quite a stir one Christmas Eve during dinner – an extravagant meal of New Zealand rack of lamb, cooked to a medium pink, accompanied by mint jelly – when she asked if she could put on some Herman's Hermits records. Bridget knew her Mom was a fan when she was younger. Maureen, remembering she'd had a few LP's in the living room cabinet, responded eagerly to the request, "Sure!" There's a natural desire in parents to expose their children to the cultural influences in their lives, especially when it comes to music since every parent finds the music of their children largely unmelodic, violent or dumb. Bridget hopped to attention, kneeling down at the stereo and pretending to put on a record, but substituting it with the audiotape of the parody. As the ukulele kicked in, and Bridget hopped back into her seat, Maureen sighed in appreciation: "ahh, Mrs. Brown you have a lovely…."

Then William stopped mid-bite, teeth halfway into the meat, holding his chop by the bone like his Nordic ancestors in the dead of winter at some medieval Icelandic barbeque. Probably around the time he heard the line about body parts, specifically the sections most suitable for being grilled and eaten as steaks.

"Go to your room!" shouted from a mouth with the chop still in it.

Thomas smiled bigger than he had all year. It was one of those moments, those "in" moments, those had-to-be-there times, when he and his sister just looked at each other and *got* each other. They both cracked up, helter-skelter-like.

The 'rents eventually calmed down, and of course, Bridget was allowed to eat Christmas dinner alongside her family, though something was certainly left to be desired about those chops after listening to the song. It didn't help that the recent revelation in the news involving the case against Dahmer was that he had drilled holes into some of his victims' skulls, while they were still alive, and injected hydrochloric acid into their frontal lobes in an effort to transform them into *zombies*. Afterward, Thomas asked Bridget for a copy of the parody. She gave him hers, having accomplished the kind of random act of impunity that she felt fit the tape perfectly.

Flicking the butt of her cigarette out the window, over her neighbor's fence and into the birdbath in their yard, Bridget opens the Journal News to its front page, zeroing in on the freshly pressed headline: "Investigation Launched Into Fatal Supreme Court Bail Hearing." She wields a scissors, spinning it around her finger like a cowboy would his six-shooter, before snipping the article about her father out from the newspaper. She carefully sets the piece aside.

Bridget begins a small ritual that she has only recently developed, but which is starting to feel like a really important part of her. Kicking off her Boston Terrier slippers, she clears some room on the floor. She gathers her tools into the cleared space – her little lost and found keyboard, her favorite headphones, a small microphone and a battered Tascam four-track mini-studio that she salvaged from the garage, from a pile of recording equipment that the Latterday Saints had been hording like nuts in a squirrel nest. She squats down onto the floor, straps the headphones over her ears – its broken right speaker is being held in place with a delicate strip of duct tape – and leans into the microphone that's connected to the four-track. The electro-beats pump into her ears as she begins to rap her latest material, which she calls, "*Republican*" –

> "*My Daddy's a Republican, his daughter's a pimp, I got dreads in*
>
> *my hair and I walk with a limp.*/
>
> *Supreme Court ain't nothin' when you live in the hood, the ladies*
>
> *want your dick and they want your goods...*"

Bridget presses stop on the four-track machine. She leans over, cracking the back of her neck, and whispers the lyrics as she scribbles them into her notebook, committing them to hip-hop history –

"...the ladies want your dick and they want your goods."

She springs up, and steps over to her hamster cage. She removes the soiled newspaper lining the floor of her pet's confined domicile, and replaces it with the rather lengthy article about her Dad.

"Pee on that, Bumpy."

***

Sunday may be reserved as God's day by some, Thomas's parents included, but in the Harrison household it is also reserved for band practice. There is reverence in that that rivals the reverence of piety. There is reverence in appointments. There is reverence in study. There is reverence in aptitude. There is reverence in any time that is spent with friends or loved ones in pursuit of shared dreams. There is reverence in transferring sound, and the emotion nested within that sound, to another person so that person may reverently attempt to decipher meaning from the sound. Thomas, Connor and Elias are once again in the garage, inside their laboratory of sound, setting up their instruments for the morning's rehearsal. They are hung-over, sore, and for the most part soaring from last night's gig, which, by most accounts, was successful despite the brevity, a brevity that might be verifiable as the shortest gig in the history of rock and roll music. Jeremy would likely agree with this assertion, if he was there, but the bassist of the band is conspicuously absent.

Connor breaks the cloudy ice, "I looked into booking some days at 'Big Sound,' a studio upstate."

Thomas recognizes the name as the name of quality, the name of rock and roll. In other words, the name of a league they ain't playing in.

"In Saratoga?"

"Yeah."

Thomas, nodding away, "Hendrix recorded there. Talking Heads. Iggy Pop and the Stooges. I know a little something about it."

His words are delivered in a cadence that implies they'll never sound like those bands. Connor doesn't pay it any mind and continues to disseminate his plan to his brethren, "I figure we can take a weekend and go up. No distractions, just music. There's an apartment above the studio where the bands get to stay."

"Sounds cool," Thomas says limply.

There's a faint knock at the garage door. Thomas cranks it open; Jeremy is standing there at the precipice of their cave. He has looked better. Elias, tilting his head at his bandmate, inquires, "Where have you been, man?"

Jeremy ambles in, a solemnity to his gait, as he places his artificial leather bass case gently on the floor. "Got caught with pot," Jeremy responds. "A lot of it. Probably gonna get it reduced to possession, but still, my Mom's super fuckin' pissed."

Jeremy had spent the night in jail, and when people – especially kids below the age of consent – spend the night in jail, the experience tends to leave an indelible mark, an impression that will not be altered by time or sympathy. No one really knows how to react; none of these fortunate youths have ever rented a room in the big house or even a house the size of the tiny one-room cell in the Bronxville police station. The closest Thomas comes to this reality is that his father checks unfortunate youths into all kinds of these houses for a living.

"Maybe I can talk to my Dad, see if he can do something," Thomas offers.

"Don't worry about it...I'm not."

Jeremy takes out his bass, plugs it in. He doesn't take to favors. The less he takes, the less he owes – because in his mind, he doesn't have that much to give. Indentured servitude is not an agreeable option for him. In reality, no real friend would demand from him what he could not give, but it would be his self-imposed demand to make it up to his friend that would lead to unending bother. True to his nature, he would rather not be bothered.

He pulls a crumpled piece of paper from his pocket.

"Something good came out of it, though. I wrote a song."

He roughly tunes his strings.

"About Leslie—"

The group shifts uncomfortably. It's surprisingly strange how, when your physical freedom is taken away, your mind reacts as though on reflex, and it compensates for it. In order to escape the shithole he was sitting in, Jeremy simply disappeared inside his head, and let his mind take him away. It transported him back to the time he visited Mexico last year, over Easter break, spring break for the Catholics, when Leslie broke up with him. Leslie was his first girlfriend, the first girl he made love with, when they had volunteered their virginities to each other on a hammock in the backyard of her best-friend's vacation home in Martha's Vineyard. Her friend's parents were in Europe that summer, so she provided the locale for this pinnacle event. They lied with each other, wrapped in each other's arms, while wrapped within the crisscrossing rope of the hammock. They just reclined, their flesh leaking through the network of fabric, imprinting its rigid New England colonial design into their backs, and just stared at the stars. The break-up moment in Mexico served as the bookend to the beginning of their relationship, so far away in that glorious hammock, and it seemed appropriate to Jeremy that these respective moments occurred on opposite ends of the continent, the sun rising on one, setting on the other. Even in the most callous break-ups, a review of the relationship, the good and the bad, the cherished and the reviled, the joyous and the painful, is an obligation of the parties involved. Whatever editing is to be done to the relationship in the minds of the lovers must be undertaken now, the footage must be loaded, viewed, rewound and subsequently fast-forwarded through, ultimately landing on the end credits as the couple parts. In some cases, the running time of this review is much shorter than others. This break-up was the bittersweet kind, as if there is any other kind, but a kind nonetheless, and this kind fell into a specific subset of the bittersweet break-up, one that is typical among teenagers who have professed their love for one another, exchanged sterling silver rings, broken heart pendants, leather jackets, punk rock mix tapes. It's falling head-over-Converses in love at an age when we're still growing, physically, mentally, and emotionally, but more than just growing, expanding at breakneck speed, finding ourselves at a pace that is downright alarming and which will never be duplicated for the rest of our lives. It's guaranteed that no love will last, but this teenaged love feels like heroin in the brutal rush of its power, its ability to commandeer the body and the mind and its ability to make you feel like a steaming pile of shit when it comes to its crashing end. It's not that teenaged love is more powerful than any of the other types of love we experience throughout our lives, it's just that we will never feel that way again, never feel that rush of addiction, the certainty that we have found our proper place in the universe and we feel that way precisely because we haven't completed our physical and mental maturation. That's what makes it unique. That's what makes it addicting. That's what makes it so enervating when it starts and so heartbreaking when it ends. And it always ends. And when it does, what was once there, what was once perfect, becomes irretrievable –

It's lost forever.

Jeremy and Leslie were on the beach, kissing tenderly and gently, the way a couple that is not brand new starts to do at some point before they stop kissing altogether, kissing for what was soon to be the last time. It was the fact that they knew it was going to be the last time that made the kissing even more tender, as though there were memories tied up in it, as though there were regrets, not of times gone by but of times that would never be. He could feel her face, their cheeks grazing against each other's, their tears mixing together, and he remembered how he licked them off his lips, tasting them. He tasted the salt; it was like he dipped his tongue into the expanse of the Pacific Ocean. As Jeremy sat in his dank little holding cell in Bronxville, it was like the break-up was happening to him all over again, like he was replaying the events in his mind with Technicolor clarity, not the cheap rewinding and replaying of a VHS tape, but the hyper-clarity of a laserdisc, right down to the depiction of the blood dripping into the sand after she left. It was as High Definition as hi-def could get back then. Before there was Blu-ray and plasma televisions, there was the clarity of regret.

"But this time, when I remembered it, it was different. I could write about it. Instead of doing something stupid like cutting my wrists."

The band looks at their bandmate, Jeremy, considering him and considering his experience, his subsequent journey back from the dead, as he buries his head into his bass and starts plucking its strings. Then he sings the lyrics of the song, the song he wrote while he was imprisoned –

"Through rusted bars, uncertain pain,

the brightest smile you tossed my way./

It stung my eyes until I cried,

melted the bars, the devil died./

The time has come to take my hand,

and through my heart you send a sign, a warning not to rearrange the

life I've sworn has been too strange..."

Jeremy continues to sing as the band watches; everyone is just short of mesmerized.

"It's been too strange./

It's been too strange."

It's difficult not to be moved by this performance, especially when they know the backstory to every word and they are discovering that his haunting vocals are in perfect synchronization with the story they know so well —

"The time has come to say goodbye,

the light of your smile never bends./

Too good for me I'll keep in mind,

reality can't help but fall./

Quick to stand, you're in my reach,

I'll walk with you until you say,

'I've played it safe until the end, and know that I've found you

finding me..."

Jeremy is not emoting the way a teenage boy might think is appropriate in such circumstances; Jeremy does not think he is the second coming of Dylan, Bob or Thomas, he knows that his lyrics don't scan like the kind authored by a professional; Jeremy is simply telling the truth, and when a person with an instrument finds a way to tell the truth with sincerity and honesty it can be very unnerving, it can be moving, and it beats the hell out of all the posing that is so common in the business.

"Since we can't escape the verse,

It's making things a whole lot worse. /

She said that I can't take much more,

Plus, I've seen your kind before. /

There's no waking from this dream,

It is actuality. /

You think you've made it to the end,

Or till it comes around again. /

I'm wasting my days with nothing to say to you. Yeah, would've and should've and if I had left you./

I'm wasting my days with nothing to say to you./

Yeah, would've and should've been."

As he finishes, Jeremy looks up at Connor and Elias, sniffing back a gob of offending snot that he is not even aware is bubbling out of his nose.

Thomas, taking shelter behind his mountainous drums, taps the tips of his fingers on the top of his knee, as if in a trance, resetting his body's rhythm to its default tempo. He might be measuring out the rhythms to this new song in his head or he may be distracted by some other thought. He might be trying to recall the post-coital exhilaration and wonder he experienced along with Jackie last night, as a means of tapping back into the bliss and leading him away from his darker thoughts. Either way, he is unwilling, or unable, to look Jeremy in the eyes.

***

Inside Stewart's closet-sized dorm room, Bridget drums on an <u>Introduction to Psychology</u> textbook with a pair of mechanical pencils. The walls are lined with cult classic movie posters like *A Clockwork Orange* and Brian De Palma's *Blowout*; the latter is Stewart's way of paying tribute to De Palma, who was a graduate of Sarah Lawrence College. Alongside the movie posters are various reprints of surrealist paintings from Magritte and Dali, along with the photograph of that woman crying glycerin tears by Man Ray. In addition to these pieces of decorative flare, there is a bright red rubber lobster glued to the handset of his phone and positioned in such a way that when he speaks on the phone he is forced to speak into the lobster's ass, a placement that was very much intentional. Bridget is sitting at Stewart's desk as he stands, piping-hot coffee in hand, pacing restlessly around his room. The side of his ceramic coffee cup bears a silk-screened image of "Guy Smiley," the preeminent, and exceedingly cheerful, game show host marionette with the big black grin from *Sesame Street*.

"In October, 1986, CBS anchorman Dan Rather was assaulted on Park Avenue by two men wearing suits and sunglasses," Stewart observes. "He was thrown to the ground and one of the men started kicking him and asking, 'Kenneth, what's the frequency?' Rather was confused, he didn't answer, and they ran off."

"Maybe if he'd answered, they would have gotten caught?" Bridget responds.

Stewart is thrown off by this comment.

"But no one caught them, see? I did some research and found a guy in an upstate prison taking credit for it. He was recently arrested for killing an NBC stagehand outside *The Today Show*. He claims he's from the future."

"We really don't understand the nature of time."

"No, you're right, we don't. But the guy says that everyone in the future has a double in the past, and he'd mistaken Rather for his future double, Vice-President Kenneth Burroughs. He's convinced the news media is beaming hostile transmissions into his head, to prevent him from returning to his own time, and he wanted Rather to divulge the frequency of the signals, so he could stop them."

"He's right, of course – the news media is very hostile."

Stewart smiles at her, a general glow about him. Bridget is eager for him to get to the point, "Where are you going with this?"

"It's what Michael Stipe said about the incident. He said: 'It remains the premier unsolved American surrealist act of the Twentieth Century.' Then R.E.M. wrote their song about it."

"That's a stupid song."

Stewart sits down on the edge of his bed, crossing one leg over the other and seizing a moment to sip his coffee.

"I quote the lyrics in my thesis."

Bridget begins crying uncontrollably. Stewart hops to attention, immediately trying to lighten her up, "Come on, it's not all that bad." He's never really seen this side of Bridget before, the side her family is so devastatingly familiar with. But the role of court jester is a character he's not unfamiliar with playing.

Stewart realizes his mistake, "Are you okay?"

"I don't know what's happening. I just feel...nothing."

Stewart puts an arm around her, as she continues to vent, "Nobody understands."

"The best artists are the most misunderstood," Stewart says.

Bridget starts laughing, through the tears.

"I'm not a fucking artist."

Stewart already knows Bridget well enough to know he shouldn't argue with this statement, regardless of the evidence that points to the contrary, evidence that he has witnessed firsthand on the stage at Slave To The Grind. He tries to console her, rubbing her back and just trying to be there for her. Bridget looks up at him, the crook of his nose casting a shadow over her face.

"What's the one thing, in your life, you're most afraid of?"

Stewart responds, "To die alone, never having found true love. What are you afraid of?"

Bridget, without even a second's thought –

"Bears."

Stewart cracks up; they laugh, together.

***

As organized as Thomas likes to think he is, he always leaves packing to the last possible minute. It's almost like he never actually believes he's going anywhere until he's there. Thomas squeezes his see-through phone between his ear and shoulder, talking a mile-a-minute to Jackie, hopping over its telephonic coil, as he throws balls of clothes and various drumming accessories into a duffle bag in disorderly haste.

"I'm not gonna say it."

"Just say it," Jackie pleads.

Thomas pauses, exasperated with her —

"Fine. I promise not to look at any other girls. Are you happy now?"

"Yes."

"It's in the middle of fucking nowhere."

Outside the Harrison house, a car beeps impatiently. Through the window, Thomas catches a glimpse of Connor's SUV idling at the curb, waiting for him to get his shit together. Connor and the SUV are accustomed to this waiting.

"I gotta run."

"Bye!" Jackie snaps.

"Bye, Jackie O." But Thomas just stands there with the phone, waiting for her to hang up. "Will you hang up already?!" he urges.

"You know I hate to hang up first. I like hearing the click — it gives me closure to the conversation."

Thomas can't decide whether to laugh or be annoyed.

"Bye!"

Thomas finally hangs up the phone, grabs the duffle and sprints out of his bedroom. He flies through the hallway and slides to a stop on the beaten paisley rug that lies by the front door. As he grabs the doorknob, Maureen swiftly sweeps into the foyer, envelope in hand.

"You're not leaving..." she says.

Thomas's muscles tense as he pivots toward his mother. She hands the envelope to him. He drops his bag to the ground.

"...until you open this."

Thomas takes the missive and glances at the return address, **Georgetown University** in bold blue and gray letters. William follows Maureen into the foyer, standing behind her and putting his hands on her shoulders. They're both clearly anxious. Thomas looks at them. His mind is already on the road, already focused on the recording, already not interested in the contents of this letter. But maybe that's a defensive posture, an attempt to prepare himself for the possibility of disappointment. Whatever his own misgivings, it's clear that he's not going to be allowed out of the house without opening the letter. William could level sheer brute force against him, if necessary, to coerce him into opening the letter, but Thomas understands the pivotal nature of this moment, knows that he must perform the role of the obedient son. He opens the letter slowly, prudently pulling out its contents, being careful not to crease anything, and he quickly scans the correspondence –

"'Dear Mr. Harrison...'"

As he reads, the words pass before him like they're being typed on an antique typewriter, each letter being violently stamped upon his forehead: *Georgetown University's Admissions Committee regrets to inform that you...*

In the brief instant of this quick reading, Thomas attempts to grasp the magnitude of that short sentence. That short half of a sentence. He wishes that there were more lines to read between, but the words are perfectly clear and there is no need to read any further. He allows his brain to summersault around the verbal landmines and regain its balance as he plans his counter-assault. Then he reads the letter aloud to his parents, who are both standing there in front of him, waiting on tenterhooks –

"Georgetown University's Admissions Committee is pleased to inform you of your *acceptance* into the class of 1999."

He looks up, dutifully putting on his show. Maureen rushes up to Thomas, hugging him warmly, "Yay!! Wonderful job!"

William lays a heavy hand upon Thomas's back, pinching the back of his downy neck. Thomas's choreography in this instance, however improvised, is deft. The anticipation and expectations of the audience involved are so high, it clouds their judgment, and any hint of fraudulence in his act, in his performance, goes undetected by their normally adroit radar.

Bridget materializes at the top of the stairs, looking down into the foyer, as Maureen and William shower Thomas with beads of praise. She stares into this rare moment of familial intimacy, not connected to it in any way.

"We're so proud of you, Thomas."

Bridget watches and listens, it's all she can do, she doesn't feel enough of anything to have any desire to be a part of the moment, to share in the joy of her parents or the conspiracy of her brother's bold lie. She watches William, who adds some weight to the hand he has draped on Thomas's shoulder, as if pressing this hand harder against his son will help him to connect with the boy in a manner that has eluded him over the years. William feels the need for a solemn statement, something that will define the moment, define the success that he has enjoyed in his life and the success that he now envisions for his son, "You have my legs, my father's legs, and they've carried us a long way."

Connor, waiting outside, beeps again. Thomas folds the letter, stuffing it deep inside his pocket.

"I wanna show this to the guys."

He picks up his bag, plasters on a smile and exclaims, "See you soon."

He glances upstairs, meeting eyes with Bridget. The siblings just look at each other, with nothing to say, silence like a vast marble obstacle, like it almost always is between them. Thomas turns his back and walks out the front door. Bridget drops her head, deflated in every sense of the term, and fades into the confines of her room. William disappears back to wherever he came from. Maureen twists her body around, looking upstairs – no one is there.

Connor drives as Thomas props his feet on the dash, adjusting the band-aid on his battered shoe. The back of the SUV is stuffed to the ceiling with musical equipment; every turn, every stop, every cigarette ash out the window, is marked by some kind of rattle from the trunk behind them.

"I got into Georgetown."

Connor cocks his head back, then slowly nods, compressing the stubbly folds of his chin into his chest as he replies, "Nice. 'Grats, man!"

"Thanks. My parents seemed really happy – happier than me."

"You should be happy."

Connor waits about a second or two, then tests what could be potentially stormy waters, "What's gonna happen to the band when you go away?"

The question just hangs between them.

"If I go away," Thomas says, as he puts his feet on the floor. "One thing at a time. First, let's just win this contest."

Connor carefully navigates the treacherous highway entrance as he finally asks his drummer the question that's been on
the edge of his mind, a question that has also been at the forefront of Thomas's mind, before it got sideswiped by Georgetown and its pro forma rejection letter –

"What do you think of Jeremy's song?"

Thomas doesn't even have to think about it: "It's our
number one."

"Yep," Connor agrees.

Thomas, however, is resolute in his response.

"But he can't sing it."

Connor glances at Thomas, hesitantly nodding his head,
"You know Jeremy wants to sing the song."

"I know."

A busted-up van pulls up next to them on the right. It's
the kind of van with a raised roof and equally raised flooring,
meant for handicapped riders, which seems counterintuitive
because the raised aspect of the vehicle looks like it should
make it more difficult for the disabled to board. Elias has no
physical disabilities, though his bandmates often question his
mental faculties. He spent all summer painting houses in order
to save up the money to buy this van and he is driving it, as the
state of New York has sanctioned him to do. He's also smoking an absurdly huge blunt, an act not sanctioned by the state,
as Jeremy grins in the passenger seat beside him. Elias and
Thomas simultaneously roll down their windows. Elias tries to
pass the blunt to Thomas, while driving sixty-plus miles an
hour, through the blasting wind. They shout over the sound of
the rubber on the road.

"Have a hit of this shit. It's outta this world!"

"No thanks, man," Thomas replies, waving a hand at Elias.
"I'm straight."

"Yeah, I know you're straight. I just want to know if you want a toke of this mar-i-jaun-a?"

"I'm cool."

"You are definitely not cool."

Elias shouts past Thomas, over to Connor, "How 'bout you?"

Connor, an outspoken proponent of the direct approach, replies, "Stick it up your ass, Cheech."

Elias begins to roll up his window.

"Ungrateful puntas."

He floors the van, pulling out in front of Connor.

"Fucking wack-nut," Connor sighs. He shakes his head vigorously, his eyes glued to the back of Elias' bumper as he speeds away. "That asshole didn't put his blinker on. I hate that shit. In fact, I don't think there's anything I hate more than that. Why do people think that's okay? It is definitely not okay. I think you should be allowed to hit people who don't put their blinkers on."

"That makes a lot of sense."

"Just put your fucking blinker on, okay?"

Despite his consistently souring mood, Thomas has to laugh at his friend's obsessive peeve.

***

The entourage of vehicles pulls up to a solitary building, which looks more like a farmhouse than a recording studio. The structure is surrounded by unending woods. The band gets out, breathing in the late autumn air. As they step to the laborious task of unloading their gear, Lance Ward, a robust fellow with a long red goatee, tattoos on his temples and huge tribal earrings, waddles up to them.

"Welcome to Big Sound, fellas," the fat man expounds, "where we make your sound…really goddamn big."

The boys are silent; they're serious about their music, serious about grunge, and also serious about not seeming like a bunch of punks who don't know shit. They wonder if there is any room for humor, for whimsical behavior and witty jokes, in this business of making such serious music. This is a potential career path for Christ's sake.

Lance finally laughs, dispelling the tension he takes so much pleasure in creating as part of his job description.

"I'm Lance. Let's have some fun."

Yes, there is room. There has to be. They all slap hands and grab their share of equipment, lugging it inside.

CHAPTER SEVEN

Jackie dresses in front of her full-length mirror. She tightens her black lace bra, pushing her breasts up, increasing her cleavage. She presses on the sides of her breasts, trying to maximize the effect. She picks up a pair of tweezers and carefully tweezes a number of offending hairs from her eyebrows. With each yank, she winces slightly and her eyes involuntarily tear. It's been a while since the discovery of pubic hair in her nether region, but she's taken good care of them ever since, recently having fashioned them into a grouping that is referred to in the porn industry as a *landing strip*. For many voracious young women, it's not so much a runway as it is a cheese grater, rubbing the grunge off the less-than-hygienic private areas of teenage boys who insist on grinding back and forth against it while pursuing entry into them. Jackie is half Italian, on account of her completely Italian mother, so an excess of hair in unwanted locales is a constant concern. She once found a stray hair, about an inch in length, sprouting out of her areola. She plucked it away with such haste she nearly ripped off her nipple.

She heads downstairs, a vintage Vietnam-Era military jacket draped around her shoulders to conceal her skimpy clothes, and turns into the living room. Her parents lounge on opposite couches, each curled up with a hardcover book. Since they are avid readers and collectors, both of these books are first editions by some darling of the literary world who is famous only among writers and the tiny population of people like Jackie's parents.

"I'm going to the movies. Abigail's sister is driving us."

Fred turns, addressing her firmly, "Be careful. And bring back a ticket stub."

She shakes her head, before her mother adds punctuation to the predetermined house rules, "Be back before midnight."

"Don't want to turn into a pumpkin," Jackie whispers.

"What did you say?"

Jackie's ass is already out the door.

"Nothing. See you later."

The door closes jarringly behind her as she jets across the front lawn and touches down on the sidewalk, moving at speed down the street.

Right from the start, Jackie experienced the worst periods in the history of periods. She has only had to endure them for two years and seven months, but they have not improved at all in that time. It isn't the pain of the experience that bothers her so much, although the pain is substantial, but rather her complete lack of control over the damned experience, her inability to erect even the most modest defense against the unwanted intrusion of blood. It was guaranteed to arrive monthly, like a credit card bill you open and let sit on your desk, putting off writing the check for three to five days. But it was nature that had its grip on Jackie, not vice versa – a notion Jackie spent many nights roiling over and revolting against in the hormonal stew of her brain.

NO ALTERNATIVE

The first time her parents took her to the emergency room was the month of her second period. The time she first cut herself.

She refused to let her body make her bleed. With a deep desire to counteract nature and subvert its laws, she was determined to be the one to make her body bleed – she was determined to be in control. If she was going bleed, it was going to be a decision, it was going to be controlled, and she was going to bleed everywhere, not just from the abyss between her legs. If pain was to be a constant, might as well get used to it and build up a tolerance. Life is all about tolerance.

Her first cut was approximately three inches in length, a trench she dug into her inner thigh with an Exacto blade. Jackie couldn't say why she chose this exact location. She might have thought that it was in a place where it could be concealed, or that the pain might be easier to control there (it was not) or perhaps she designed the cut as a gutter to collect the remnants of her shedding uterine tissue. It's just as likely that there was no reason at all to choose her inner thigh.

Her parents were eager, downright anxious, to believe that what had happened was that she had cut herself trimming the pubic hair around her vagina with her father's disposable Gillette razor. This was the excuse she gave and it was accepted just about as quickly as it was conjured up. To draw this repartee out further meant to indulge in the dismantling of the illusions that have taken several lifetimes to assemble. The only one who seemed skeptical throughout the entire event was the doctor, the one who sewed up the crooked slash, though his looks of skepticism were expertly ignored by Jackie's father, who simply refused to look this professional man in the eyes. The doctor had to know, he sews up these kinds of wounds with increasing frequency and wonders about the odd collision of social pressure, cultural angst and self-hatred that lead the young female population of this affluent suburb to take up arms against themselves. And it's almost exclusively the practice of young women. Young men might cut themselves, but it's usually on the wrist in an attempted suicide, not this intentional scarring, this self-mutilation. The subsequent times her parents took her to the ER, the dread resided not in the fact that Jackie was injured, or that she might be doing this to herself, but rather in the chance that they might run into the same doctor. They staggered their hospital visits between the three hospitals in the county. They triangulated their routes. A shape, incidentally, Jackie once carved into the top of her foot.

Jackie's parents are self-proclaimed bookworms, a proclamation they would shout from the rooftops if they were more extroverted. If they could wear a book like the kids wear cardigans, they would. Because of their devotion to the world of books, they've limited the family's consumption of television to ten hours a week: five during the week, allowing for one hour of primetime viewing per weeknight; then a generous five hours of viewing on the weekends, allowing for the occasional three-hour-plus movie or miniseries on cable. Movies involving dramatic recreations of the Bible, up to and including depictions of Christ on the cross, are subject to exemption.

Jackie is a reader herself, a closeted science fiction fan, a personality trait that she has perfected at keeping secret. She's a quick reader, she taught herself to speed read in order to minimize the chance of being caught reading by those who might judge her. Her tastes range from the classics of Heinlein and Sturgeon, to the drug-addled and post-modern Philip K. Dick. Her latest hidden treat is the supremely trashy <u>The Drive-In 2: Not Just One Of Them Sequels</u> by Joe Lansdale. She's just reached the chapter where Jack and his friends encounter a town where public suicide is encouraged by Pop-along Cassidy, a cowboy with a television head, whose church of film and pain is presided over by the alien drive-in gods.

Needless to say, if her predilections had gotten out, she may have remained a virgin until well into her forties.

Jackie thinks about writing, about consigning one of her own stories to paper, enchanted by the idea of unconcealing herself in a way that only words can help facilitate. But the notion of archiving her private self, her geekdom, is simply another way to be exposed as a fool and a fake or to be ridiculed for the strangeness of her thoughts, so she recoils from the idea at the same time she's seduced by it. She convinces herself that the risk of exposure is the best reason to stay concealed. This is before cell phones and the internet, where one fateful photograph transmitted via text message could mean social, personal or professional suicide. Most people never have to worry about such things, but at this time Jackie's thoughts consist of recurring imagery of her dissecting her own body and it's reasonable for her to conclude that the reading public is not ready for her to expose herself in this way. She imagines operating on herself with tailor-like precision, taking a scalpel and starting at her wrists, slicing up along the arms, into the armpits and down through her torso, and so on. Once she is properly incised, she imagines peeling her old body off to reveal a much prettier, more powerful version of herself, someone who is able to strut her stuff from the inside-out, a version of herself unafraid to speak her mind – an unmitigated megaphone for the repressed teenager trapped inside of her and inside of us. In years past, the Catholic Church considered self-flagellation as something that might put one on the shortlist to sainthood; they considered it an act of selfless faith, a tribute to the suffering God's only son endured for all mankind.

Is there really that much of a difference between whipping oneself or slicing an arm with a razor? Is this an argument her parents might accept? Jackie has considered this line of reasoning, but is pretty sure that her self-mutilation fantasies would not be received with the same level of beatification.

Best to not even mention it.

Jackie's Aunt, a tenured professor of anthropology at the University of Michigan, is fond of saying, "When you buy something new, like a piece of clothing, after you take the tags off, do something to damage it. Right away, when it's right out of the box. Scuff up the toe, tear a hole in the knee, put a crease in the brim." Her point being, "nothing lasts," and the sooner we shatter the delusion that purports otherwise, the better it is for all of us. She's not a Buddhist – she's an Atheist, actually, a spiritual decision derided by Jackie's mother and Jackie's mother's mother – but she subscribes to a similar philosophy rooted in the idea that when you hold a glass, be assured that it will eventually break. It was made to break, not to last. Clothes are an extension of yourself, a reflection of your personality, and just like your body, your threads have a life expectancy. Subconsciously, according to her Aunt, human beings in post-1950's consumer America use clothing as a shield, a way to extend youth, to cover the flaws of the aging process; that is, to ignore reality. Your clothes will age, decay, fall apart, just as your body eventually will. Ashes to ashes, dust to dust. But by taking the first step and proactively beginning the decay ourselves, by taking ownership of that decay, we can enjoy our clothes more. Rather than worrying about that stain or that rip, we can live free of concern and focus more on living; we can enjoy our own bodies that much more. That initial damage frees us from the burden of eternal life and all the effort that goes into fooling ourselves into believing in it in the first place.

And to think her extended family didn't consider her spiritual. Jackie always likes what she has to say and makes a point of making her affection known, which never ceases to incense her parents. That predictable result does cast suspicion on the motive of her fondness for her Aunt, because attaining that result may very well be the reason she feels such fondness to begin with.

***

Jackie, Abigail and Megan stand on an obscene line outside the doors of "The Pinewood," a college high-dive of a bar and haven to underage drinkers, and not just a little underage, but a bar that caters to genuine teenagers. The Pinewood is in Riverdale, the Bronxville of The Bronx, its location parallel to the elevated train at 242nd Street and Broadway. This place is like Tijuana for Westchester kids. Just south of the border of their idyllic neighborhoods beckons a place where terrible fake ID's and a cover charge buys you access to adulthood, adulthood as perceived by the teenager: kamikaze shots, pot in the bathroom, and wasted girls, each grinding to hip-hop at decibel levels guaranteed to obliterate any attempt to learn the names of your dance partners before you make-out with them. It eliminates the awkward name-learning moment entirely and encourages everyone inside the packed room to move directly to tonsil-hockey. Provided no one pisses himself or herself, or pukes on their romantic interest, graduating to blowjobs and lousy finger-fucking in the back alley is the natural progression of business in the evening's events.

Connecting-the-dots of hedonism doesn't get any easier than at this shithole on Broadway in the Bronx. Jackie and the girls pass around a metallic tube of red lipstick, each tarting herself up.

"If we didn't have to stop to buy tickets to a movie we'll never fucking see, we might'a got here before it got so packed," Abigail barks.

Jackie insists, "I'll get us in."

The bouncer, a black guy with enormous trapezius muscles bulging out between his neck and shoulders, and the bar owner, a middle-aged Irishman who might as well be pregnant the way he's let himself go, his perfectly spherical belly stretching through his pink Izod shirt, flank the entrance of the joint. Jackie bypasses the bulk of the crowd and saunters directly up to the powers that be –

"Hi guys."

"We're at the max right now," the owner mumbles.

He's not even looking at her. Jackie leans forward, pushing her chest out and bumping it into the owner. He looks down into nubile cleavage.

"I was wondering if you can squeeze me and my two girlfriends in there?"

The owner leers, trying not to think about his wife or the cops. He glances at the bouncer, who gives an imperceptible nod.

The inside of The Pinewood is packed with kids, kids that are drinking, kids that are smoking, kids that are gloriously on the edge of losing their minds. Jackie, her friends in tow, has infiltrated this stronghold and despite the underage crowd, even she can tell that no one in the place is more underage than her. She struts triumphantly to the bar with put-on confidence and stands behind Alex, who's obviously been sitting on a stool in this establishment for quite a while.

"Hey there," Alex says, turning and handing a shot to Jackie.

Jackie, squinting at him with pleasant recognition, grabs the shot, downs it, and tries to carry on the conversation through watering eyes, "Aren't you supposed to be upstate with the band? I thought you were their manager."

"Please."

Alex hunkers down over another shot, clearly not happy with the subject of discussion. Jackie steps toward him, wedging herself between him and his neighboring lush, and talks loudly into his ear, "With all the groupies that hang around those recording studios, I naturally assumed you'd want to be there."

A seasoned lawyer might object in this instance, claiming that she's leading the witness, but there are no lawyers in this dump and no one to alert Alex to the host of problems he could be setting himself up for, only a bartender earning minimum wage sliding another beer in front of him. Alex responds to his friend's girl in the way he sees fit, knowing just what to say to set her off –

"They'll be too busy with the band."

Alex chuckles, washing the laughs down with the alcohol. Neither he nor Jackie can tell who is playing who at this point, partly because of the drinking, but mostly because they are rank amateurs at this game. Jackie looks away, back at her friends stuffed in a corner across the saloon, the wheels of insecurity only having just begun to turn inside her head.

***

The members of *The Latterday Saints* play in separate glass-enclosed cubes that can hardly be called rooms as they lay down the tracks to Jeremy's song: Connor strums the guitar, crunching the chords; Elias plucks specific notes on his guitar, positioning his head close to his amplifier, listening to the effect; Thomas pounds the drums with mechanically precise timing; Jeremy picks his bass, mouthing the lyrics to his song. They look like ants in an acrylic ant farm, busying themselves with their respective jobs, focusing on their individual contribution to the larger whole. Little musical communists, competing together in their own kind of arms race, attempting to produce the next alternative hit, attempting to beat the other kids doing the exact same thing in the recording studio one town over, attempting to out-grunge grunge, attempting to etch their names into the everlasting pages of *Rolling Stone*, or *Spin*, or *Kerrang!*, with a printing press of nuclear-powered inter-galactic lasers, like the ones that Reagan and Gorbachev used to dream about.

Attempting to become *the next big thing*.

Hours later, after the repetition of takes has ravaged their nerves and deadened their ears to the melody, rhythm and sound that they love about the song, the music continues to play, its distinctive genetic nature committed to a length of magnetic tape that plays back from the reel-to-reel, blasting through the high-end speakers sitting in front of the band as they stand around the mixing board, listening to their mutual creation. It feels as though they've played these notes a million times tonight and now it's time to listen to them a million times. The sound flows through the unoccupied space of the glass-enclosed recording cubes, weaves its way through their ear canals, through the hallways, through the rooms, as though the rooms are a microcosm of their shared brain as a band, the sound is assessed, broken down by instrument, by beat, by notes, by volume, by effect pedal, by cymbal crash. Each element is put into its own category, inside its own cube and that cube is reorganized into another cube, and then compressed into another, then bounced into another, building and rebuilding, one track on top of the next, until they arrive upon something resembling the final product that they were seeking. The song becomes an auditory representation of their collective mind and the construction of this collective mind is like brain surgery, with their brain being dissected and splayed out before them to analyze. What was once a primal, sacrificial, ritualistic orgy of rock and roll, rock and roll with a maximum limit of three chords in a garage, has now become a process. It has become a scantron test.

Lance presses stop, the reels clinching to a halt. "Sounds good, guys," he commends. "Real tight. I'll compress the drums and really beef up that low-end. We can also crunch the rhythm guitar a lot more when we mix."

He rewinds the tape, getting right back to business. "Give me a little bit of time to set up vocals."

Jeremy turns to Elias as the pair wobbles out the door, punch-drunk on the evening's activities, "Let's do some vocal exercises."

Elias replies, a blank expression on his face, "Smoke cigarettes?"

Jeremy chuckles like a schoolgirl with a mouthful of Pop Rocks while Thomas shoots Connor an apprehensive look; Thomas doesn't want to do what he's about to do, but it has to be done. It's the adult thing to do. In his mind, they're not kids anymore, even though it does seem like the music business requires its stars to channel the sensibilities of children in order to appeal to a mass audience of children. Connor nods, as he and Thomas reluctantly follow their friends outside.

The band members smoke cigarettes as they kick around a hackey-sack on a landing outside the studio. The air is particularly cold. There's a mist in it, a fog at their feet that mingles with the smoke spiraling off of their cigarettes and rushing in exhalations from their mouths, thinly lit by the security lights overhead. The loose sack connects with an ankle and darts through the air, cutting through the vapor of smoke and fog, and funneling the haze into ethereal helixes that spin in slow-motion around their heads.

Connor breaks the ice, "We really should start thinking about how to sell ourselves. If we're serious about doing this thing right, we need to have a signature sound, a voice that ties all the songs together."

They stop hacking.

"We need to start thinking about packaging ourselves."

Elias picks up the sack, squeezing it almost therapeutically in his hand. Thomas inhales a significant puff of his cigarette, while implementing his knack for driving points home, "That means a single lead singer."

Something begins to percolate in Jeremy's brain. "What are you guys trying to say?" he asks.

Connor tries to temper Thomas's brusqueness, he tries to exhibit a degree of reason with his fellow bandmates, as he elaborates, "We think Elias should sing everything. You know, so there's a glue connecting the music." He can't help but clear his throat nervously. "And that includes your song."

"Why?"

"The business side of the band is just as important as the music, because it's what allows the music to be heard." Connor is trying hard to talk some sense, or a form of it anyway. "Bands have plans, they just don't all of a sudden appear on the radio one day, no, they need game-plans, tactics, campaigns, just like politicians, love 'em or hate 'em. It's going to take a lot of work to get to where we want to go."

"You're so wrong. I mean, the music is all that matters. We're not fucking politicians." Jeremy retorts.

"This is standard stuff, man."

Jeremy silences himself, seething. When Jeremy is really mad, his anger manifests itself as sweat and it's this anger sweat that is seeping from his pores now, creating a sheen of visible anger on his forehead. In an effort to get back to the hackey-sack game, Elias tosses in his two cents, "If someone writes a song, and they want to sing it, they can sing it." He tosses the hack into the air, only to watch it fall victim to gravity and plummet to the concrete.

Thomas is not a big fan of the passive/aggressive approach to anything; he disdains it. He was raised to disdain it, in spite of the fact that the parents who taught him to disdain it are also guilty of employing it against him from time to time. But it's a lesson that has stuck and he has spent a good deal of energy in his short life fighting against it. He fights on now, "This competition, this is our chance to get signed. Record companies are not signing bands with multiple singers. They're looking to market one voice. And Elias has the voice."

"What about The Beatles? Someone signed them, right?" Jeremy says, choosing to enter the ring with Thomas.

"That's fucking ancient history," Thomas replies.

Connor, backing Thomas up to the extent he can, "Elias sings most of the songs anyway, so it would make sense if he sings all of them, right?"

There must be order in this world, or chaos will destroy us all.

"This isn't personal, dude, it's just the business," Connor assures him.

"This is not a business to me. This is my fucking life!"

Frustration is getting the best of Thomas, taking him down a pitiless path to believing he has no choice but to take direct aim at Jeremy, a path that will not give him room to reverse course if he changes his mind –

"Elias is a better singer, okay – and it's about time you wake the fuck up and realize that."

"Is that right? Who the fuck are you to judge?"

"You sing like a fucking pussy."

Jeremy steps right up to Thomas, like he's ready to mix it up. Toe-to-toe, in the literal sense of the idiom. Elias sees their heads getting hotter and steps between Thomas and Jeremy, though this is mostly a symbolic gesture because Elias is a good deal shorter than his bandmates, so their line of sight remains unobstructed and they continue to glare at each other in an unnecessarily aggressive fashion.

"You sing like someone who tried to off himself but didn't have the balls to do it right. That's what you sound like," Thomas spits.

Jeremy lunges past Elias at Thomas, smacking him sharply in the side of the head with a half-closed fist. Thomas springs back, instinctively choosing flight over fight. But then that little something inside snaps and he reverses his choice, pushing Elias aside with manic strength and knocking Jeremy hard to the ground. Thomas looms over Jeremy, breathing hard, heart pumping like the pistons on an accelerating train. Connor wraps his arms around Thomas in a bear hug, and somehow pulls him away. Jeremy scrambles up, disheartened by the words spoken, disheveled by the scuffle and disgusted with his friend. He lopes off toward the woods.

Thomas shouts after him, "You're a voice that no one wants to hear."

He glares around at his remaining band members, like they're all part of the problem, like he's officially recognized a virus and has set about immunizing them all from it. But now Elias is steaming, too. "Dude, what the fuck is your problem?! That was so completely uncalled for."

"He hit me first!"

"He had every right to hit you for saying that bullshit."

"Do we wanna be just another garage band wasting our fucking time?"

"No, we don't! But who fucking died and anointed you the god of the band? Is this really how we want to resolve our problems, like bullies and assholes?"

Connor is still clutching Thomas's shirt. Thomas pushes his friend away and storms back inside the safe haven of the studio, slamming the glass doors closed behind him. Maybe he'll find reason in there, maybe peace. The studio as the United Nations of band bullshit, where musicians who are at each other's throats can unite under the banner of song. Or maybe not.

Connor lets out a deep breath, shaking his head. "Man, I didn't see that coming," he observes.

Elias flicks his cigarette, looks into the woods.

***

Jackie, Abigail and Megan bounce up and down in the middle of an honest-to-goodness meat market. Even though this particular market is not refrigerated, it is populated by dim-witted drunks who appraise the meat hungrily and lick their lips as if anticipating a scrumptious meal or clearing away globs of barbecue sauce. The hormones, pheromones, and testosterone have raised the temperature in the room to approximately the same degree as the body temperatures of its occupants, and the girls are encircled by a mass of grinding bodies as alcohol-fueled singing fills the stifling air around them, because everyone's a singer when they're drunk. Joining the rest of the patrons in the Pinewood, the three of them sing along with the quintessential jukebox bar song blasting from the ceiling's speakers: Bon Jovi's "*Livin' On A Prayer.*"

In bars, the eighties are still alive.

Jackie looks around her at cavorting couples swapping each other's saliva, the chances of these people knowing one another's names: low. She takes a swig of her beer, spinning around to face her ladies, screaming like a constipated infant –

"Wooooooooooooo!"

Abigail "Wooooooooos" back at her, prompting Megan to roll her exhausted hazel eyes into the back of her head. Jackie is enough of a handful sober, but when she's this inebriated, all bets are off the table. Alex weaves hastily through the perspiring crowd and hands a fresh set of Jägermeister shots out to the girls, who are beyond feeling the booze.

Megan habitually glances at her watch, and when she does so now she is compelled to lean into Jackie's ear, "It's eleven fifteen. We need to leave soon if you want to get home before twelve."

"You're such a buzz kill."

Jackie holds up her drink, looking wantonly at Alex.

"Here's to cheap thrills!"

Alex downs his shot, ignoring Jackie as he slams the glass upside down onto the top of the bar. He swaggers away, almost irritated, though it's difficult to tell whether he's simply so smashed he's lost control of his facial muscles and their ability to convey mood. Jackie watches him as he heads into the back of the place.

In the bathroom, which barely deserves such a regal title, Alex empties his bladder into a urinal that is caked with scum, piss and chunks of what appears to be fecal matter, however impossible that may be. The owner of the Pinewood is known to brag that his joint is the only bar in town that can charge five dollars at the door and *not* put toilet paper in the girl's bathroom. The demand to get in is that high, and that unselective.

Jackie shoves open the door to the men's room and confronts Alex from behind, her equilibrium in desperate need of ballast.

"I don't think I like your attitude."

Alex turns slightly, as he shakes out the excess urine from his urethra, "What is it you don't like about my attitude?"

Jackie rushes toward him, pinning him against the urinal.

"You haven't tried to fuck me yet."

She grabs him by the neck and rams her tongue down his throat. Maybe if Alex hadn't had a half dozen beers and as many shots he might have had a moment's hesitation, he might have thought for a moment that this girl is dating one of his best friends and displayed the character and integrity that exists in us all, or most of us all, but he's immature and whatever ability he once possessed to think lucidly has been blurred by the mind-warping effects of the demon known as alcohol. Alex reciprocates, immediately, pulling Jackie's shirt up and grabbing hold of her breasts. The two of them stumble toward the stall so awkwardly their interaction seems to morph into a kind of Dionysian square dance reserved for dance floors upon which only those afflicted with muscular dystrophy are allowed to stomp. Alex grabs his beer bottle off the edge of the sink and they lock the stall door behind them.

Cheap thrills. Cheap thrills as defined by whom? There's a difference between the cheap thrills imagined by a teenage girl, especially one as young as Jackie, and those conjured up in the throbbing brain of an 18 year-old boy; there's a disconnect between language and experience, between desire and expectations. The sexual peak of a man takes place around the time he is 18, whereas the peak for a woman will not occur until she is closer to 30. 18 year-old boys everywhere use this factoid as the only evidence needed to justify the creation of an idyllic sexual institution in which 18 year-old boys are paired off with 30 year-old women at random, or grouped together by similar interests in hobbies or tastes in movies, for the express purpose of engaging in mutually consensual sexual intercourse. (There are also plenty of 30 year-old women who endorse this fantasy and decades later they will get their own television show in order to capitalize on the mutual fantasy and its advantageous demographics in the eyes of an insatiable media empire.) But when it comes to sexuality, the cheap thrills of a teenage girl chiefly revolve around expectations, the expectations she might have about how to relate to boys and the expectations she might imagine the 18 year-old boy as having: like fucking in the bathroom of the Pinewood, an act that is imperceptibly more classy than anal in a church confessional. It is of no personal merit to any girl to strive for and achieve such a benchmark, but they do such things in a vain attempt to quantify expectations, to see what they are willing to do, how far they are willing to go, how much it bothers them to go so far, as a means to secure the approval or idolization of some random boy by aiding that boy in achieving his own personal fantasy. Sexual pleasure doesn't even factor into it. If it did, she would wait for the opportunity to fuck this 18 year-old boy in the bathroom of the Pinewood until she was 30 years old. In the case that is unfolding here, next to zero sexual pleasure is being derived from the exploit.

And exploit it is.

As Jackie leans her buttocks onto the metal toilet paper holder, the one with no toilet paper, she props her foot against the toilet tank, hikes her rumpled skirt up and unzips Alex's Abercrombie & Fitch stonewashed jeans. She grabs the beer out of Alex's hands and drinks it, caressing the bottle's opening with her tongue as though it's his erect member, and sucking in its barley goodness like she's sucking nectar through the straw of his vas deferens. She doesn't know why she does this except that she vaguely understands that guys like this kind of thing. It's a visual aid, and this is certainly an increasingly visual culture. Her representational efforts are rewarded as she watches the exhilarating way Alex's eyes widen, his head tilting back as he inhales a fevered breath into his lungs, and as if there was any doubt that he would stop there, together they share in the subsequent reward of Alex ripping her panties off, its little lace remnants falling softly to the floor. He is unsure if the panties were designed to snap off, as though they were a disposable prop a stripper might wear and tear on stage, or if he actually tore through the fabric – either way, the effect is the same, propelling him further into the void of unthinking wish fulfillment. She doesn't protest. And it happens so effortlessly. Ripping underwear should really be more difficult, a proper article of clothing should allow for a greater challenge. Maybe the emergence of the Wal-Mart culture is to blame for this flimsy undergarment. Regardless, he doesn't give it a millisecond's more thought – he sinks his mouth into hers, licking beer from the chapped creases in her lips. She wraps her hands around his throat and pushes him back, digging her thumbnails into his Adam's Apple and looking him in the eyes, trying to match the animal lust germinating in his pupils, trying to fulfill those damned expectations. Then, in a strikingly bold maneuver for a girl of such delicate age and pedigree, she takes the remainder of his beer and pours it onto her exposed vagina. She douses herself, marinating her labia with every fermented nuance of the microbrew. Alex's salivary glands rev into overdrive, enough that he spits a loogie into a puddle of piss that has formed on the floor before diving to his knees and plunging his face into her pungent crotch.

Dehydration is a result of many things; in this instance, it has less to do with alcohol consumption than with the genitalia being unable to lubricate itself due to lack of sexual longing, ample evidence that Jackie is in over her head, that she doesn't want to be here. And perhaps there's a little guilt peppered in there, too. In the absence of a K-Y Jelly type of friction alleviator, saliva is the preferred substance to combat the dry vagina, but it's a substance wasted by the inexperienced male partner presently between her legs; however, the frothy head of a Samuel Adams Boston Lager can add a certain amount of lather to an age-old problem and enhance the cheap thrills of any 18 year-old boy; in this case, of one Alex Pappas.

CHAPTER EIGHT

Bridget and Stewart chill outside of Slave To The Grind. Inside, the unassuming coffee shop is packed to the brim, it's standing room only, there's even a line outside to get in, which is unheard of for a café like this. And there are never any lines in Bronxville; lines are for the proletariat, not the privileged. Bridget, sporting braids in her hair, each strand adorned with multicolored Jamaican beads, and wearing a T-shirt with OJ Simpson's mug shot screen-printed on it with *Free OJ* written in block letters above it, glances through the window at the spectators.

"There's a lotta people."

Stewart is digging the buzz, "Word of mouth, it's how it happens."

He is evidently more excited than Bridget. She pulls a compact bottle of whiskey from the side pocket of her bag, a faux-flask shaped container filled with Irish swill; Stewart's eyes are glued to it. He feels he should probably say something, so he does, "Maybe you shouldn't drink before the show."

"Maybe you should shut the fuck up," Bridget barks while tipping the bottle back and taking a swig.

She gargles the whiskey, glaring at Stewart, and washing away any bothersome food particles left over from the micro-wavable mac'n'cheese she had for dinner. Stewart, more than a little concerned and adequately offended by her shitty attitude, slouches inside the coffee shop.

Tucked away in the corner, Stewart has arranged an ela-borate picnic table with a neon green sign displayed on one of Bridget's easels that reads:

BRI DA B. PRICE: 5 Bones.

Next to the sign is a stack of cassettes. He hoped the gre-en motif would subconsciously imply cash money, would en-courage people to spend, and the fact that patrons stand in a zigzag line to purchase the coveted debut album is all the evi-dence he needs to prove his theory is working. Bridget walks inside, ignoring Stewart completely. She struts to the back, careful not to make eye contact with anybody, careful to remain tucked snugly inside her shell of indifference, as if the freak show isn't ready to be looked at, to be heard, or to be judged just yet. Bridget likes to think of herself as a freak compared to these people who are here to see her. She likes being weird, she likes feeling different, this is what sustains her and makes the stupidity, or genius, of what she is doing palatable. Bridget is pretty sure that she would never come see herself perform; if it wasn't her music being performed she would not have any interest in it at all. But before she gets on with her freak show, she needs a few minutes to herself, so she slips quietly, and hopefully unseen, into the unisex bathroom.

Bridget locks the door and hunches over the sink. She looks up into the mirror built into the wall, a clean and simple piece of reflective glass, unscathed by the young patrons of the establishment except for a cutout picture of Woody Allen that's pasted to the center of it, Woody's head, floating in the ether, the spaces between his glasses where his lenses should be and where his eyes should be are cut out, allowing Bridget to line her eyes up to his. Looking at herself as Woody might look at her is an unnerving and slightly disorienting experience, like she's seeing herself through the eyes of someone else, the eyes of one of the patrons waiting for her outside, except this patron is a world famous filmmaker, not that his fame adds to the experience which she would find unnerving even if it was just some random guy, but Bridget wonders for a moment if Woody is looking at her the way he might look at Soon-Yi, the adopted daughter of his ex-girlfriend Mia Farrow, who was about the same age as Bridget when he allegedly began his affair with her. Somehow, this thought makes her feel better; it blunts the unnerving effect of the picture with her eyes looking out of it.

Stewart got that Woody Allen poster from Kim's Video downtown, cut out his head, and glued it to the mirror when he worked as a barista at Slave for a half a semester during his freshman year. And it just stuck. Or no one was able to get it off. Stewart's father, an English-born Protestant who wants desperately to be a self-hating Jewish intellectual like Allen himself, was attending a screening of *Sleeper* in Greenwich Village during the fateful night of his son's birth. Some people embrace a stereotype, even if it doesn't apply to them. It's easy to spend a lifetime finding yourself and maybe never even getting there, so why not pick a personality you like and just go with it? In some intellectual circles of Manhattan, the irony of such a choice was not only respected, but lauded. The religious aspect, the difference between Stewart Sr.'s religious background and Woody Allen's religious background, was merely circumstantial; what he believed was irrelevant, as it seemed to be irrelevant to Woody as well. It was what others believed that mattered. Not in the way of impressing others, but more along

the lines of fucking with others. His shicksa wife, as he'd affec-
tionately refer to her in bed, Stewart's mother, began to encounter labor pains inside the movie theater with her husband, as
substantiated by increasing moans of anguish that no male will
ever know or understand in his lifetime. Despite the onset of
labor, Stewart Sr. refused to leave the movie and bring his wife
to the hospital until the conclusion of the film, in which Woody
proposes a future where red meat and cigarettes are among the
healthiest things for you and an *orgasmatron* is the only appliance
you'll ever need to get your ya-ya's out. It was just too damn
funny. He watched fifteen more minutes of the film before
taking her to the emergency room (her cries eventually became
too severe to ignore), which he wouldn't have been able to do
if he'd acquiesced to her earlier.

But there was also something to not acknowledging reality,
to evading the responsibilities implicit in such acknowledgment.
Sort of like Stewart's obsession with Surrealism. Maybe it's that
apple and tree thing.

Bridget stares at herself in the mirror, through the besp-
ectacled eyes of the still slightly young Woody Allen. She picks
her nose, wiping the booger onto Woody's schnoz.

***

The MC stumbles up onto the stage, flaunting hair, make-
up and wardrobe that suggest he is disheveled in accordance
with some perplexing prerequisite of dishevelment, since he
more or less looks like this all the time. Tonight's ensemble
features a white t-shirt with yellowish armpit stains that have
hardened over time. The garment really completes his outfit.
There are some instances where this kind of patina is considered antique – this is not one of those instances. He leans over,
cracking his back, and speaks into the house's dented micro-

phone, "Back by popular demand, everybody…he's here to spit his sweet love and drop some pants."

The MC pauses dramatically, allowing enough time to pass that the audience might be led to believe he has had an aneurysm.

"Ladies and gentlemen," he eventually continues –

"Bri Da B!"

There is actual applause this time. But Bridget is nowhere in sight. A group of African-American men assemble at the back of the house, a clientele that did not frequent this establishment, generally speaking. They huddle just inside the double-doors of the entrance, their presence distinctive not only because of their skin color, but because they're the only people in the place who aren't talking. The MC looks from one side of the room to the other, scanning the multitude of faces around the stage.

"Ladies and gentlemen… Bri Da B?"

Bridget finally appears, twisting her way through the crowd.

"Here he is, everybody!"

Resounding applause bounces off the stucco walls as she takes her stool, sets up her keyboard and adjusts the mic.

"This is off my new album, 'Around The Motherfuckin' World,' which is for sale right here, right now, for five bones. Why smoke the rock when you can smoke yourself some Bri Da B?"

She starts her preprogrammed beat, beginning to bob her head to it and going right into her rap, "This here's *Pimptooth*" –

"They call me pimptooth,

they call me sucka the toe,

they call me time after time as I'm rocking my flow./

They call me eyebrow,

and a rugged one at that,

they say chump finger give us rum and make it fat."

Spectators also begin to nod to the music, while sipping their steaming lattes, and making sure not to spill one frothy drop. The participation of the crowd is sincere, they're actually enjoying the show, even though it's really not so much a show as it is a happening; primarily in the sense that it's as good as guaranteed that nowhere else on Earth is this same thing occurring – this girl doing this, this white girl, dressed up like a black man, acting like a black man, a black man who's got a big black cock, born in the hood, rapping like she is actually a black rapper, a street hustler, a gangsta' – nowhere else is this happening except right now and right here, inside this small suburban coffee shop called Slave To The Grind.

"They call me lipnose,

they call me fuckey the dick,

they call me nose hair,

they call me slick finger Rick./

They call me lymphnode,

they call me crusty eyeball,

they call me pubic bone,

they call me leggy the tall. /

They call me bunion-toe,

they call me strand of hair,

they call me lickey-tongue,

they call me brussle-supple-fare. /

They call me nipple-tit,

they call me ass of the shit,

they call me bend a knee,

but most of all, they call me Bri Da B. /

Uh-huh, uh-huh, yeah."

The crowd applauds, emitting hoots reminiscent of those produced by the audience of Arsenio Hall's recently defunct show.

"Thanks, niggas."

The black men stand motionless in the back.

***

Bridget and Stewart run the merch table, partnering again after her most well-received show to date, selling demos. It's a cliché, but music can do that, it can bring people together. It can also help sell stuff; entering into evidence every commercial jingle ever written and the fact that they're almost out of tapes. One of the black men approaches with his two buddies not far behind, all of whom exhibited a great deal of patience by waiting in line and not cutting to the front from the get-go. This man's name is Lincoln, and Lincoln's an extra-strength package of rage, wrapped loosely around a permeable heart of gold.

"Where do you get off using the word 'nigger' in your raps?"

The duo looks up at their critic, both trying hard to figure out how to play the next move. There's an elephant in the room. It's standing right in front of them, and this makes Stewart very nervous. In this nervous state, his mind races to the realization that the *elephant in the room* metaphor, which he believes is English in origin and which his father uses to no end, might be racist in this context, or at least in poor taste. Stewart is grateful that he didn't blurt it out loud to Lincoln, but just the thought of it and the fact that it was the first thing that sprung into his mind, with its loaded jungle connotations and accompanying images of Kunta Kinte, calls into question his ethnic bias, which until this moment he thought he never had. Kunta Kinte was kidnapped, raped and reduced to a slave because he journeyed into the African jungle to find the appropriate wood to build a drum. He was persecuted by the white man because of his search for music. And now Stewart is pimping out music that is enslaving the music of the black man – or so he thinks, or so he thinks someone else might think – music that eluded the grasp of Kunta Kinte, music that the modern black man has taken ownership of and for which he is finally enjoying success and public acceptance, and music that this little white girl is trying to steal back from them. Just like those white men stole the black man's freedom centuries ago.

Stewart figures he'll stand up. It's unclear whether he's

standing up to protect Bridget or to run away. Lincoln waves a limp hand at him.

"Sit down," Lincoln says. "She's a big girl, she can answer for herself."

Stewart sits right back down, like what the hell else is he going to do? As it happens, Bridget doesn't know the character of Kunta Kinte and she is more than eager to respond, "Well, I don't actually say 'nigger,' I say 'nigga.'"

Lincoln is more than visibly irritated.

"My name is Lincoln – after Abraham Lincoln. Right? See it? My mother named me that because her great-grandparents were slaves, and he freed them. He freed them so they wouldn't have to be called 'nigger' anymore."

Bridget listens thoughtfully, sincerely interested in the position that Lincoln is taking, to the point where it almost feels like some kind of experiment to her, like a part of an introduction to Sociology that she had recently in school. A dispassionate part of her recognizes how condescending this is, how completely lacking in empathy for Lincoln's position, for his actual plight as a young black man in a very white world, a plight that includes the very real facts of his friends and relatives being shot and stabbed on urban streets and being incarcerated in the ever-expanding prison system of these United States, a prison system that has taken on the most sinister attributes of a cancer and whose malignant growth, rather than being monitored and abated by a caring physician, is aided and abetted by the insidious introduction of capitalism into the management and operation of this system throughout the country. The more people put in prison, the better it is for business. Nevertheless, even though Bridget knows she's judging Lincoln in ways that are not entirely fair, she also thinks that he is probably doing the same thing to her. What might be hard to recognize for someone like Lincoln, or for anyone coming across the strange phenomenon that is Bri Da B, is how organically her alter ego emerged from the person she has always known herself to be, how similar the two parts of her personality really are. Bridget, as perceived within the demographic she technically falls into, should be watching *Beverly Hills 90210*, not listening to rap music and not modeling her personality on the overt aggression of the black male who dominates the rap scene. But color is subjective. The shade of blue perceived by one person is not the exact shade of blue as perceived by another, there are a potentially infinite number of gradations of every color that we all perceive differently, color blindness being the most dramatic example of this. Color also means different things to different people, its textures and emotions expressing themselves differently in all of us, and the facts of this expression often prevent us from getting to know another person and realizing how alike some people are. Pigment is a dictator, a ruler of roosts, a measuring cup inside of which standards are set and expectations are routinely and inaccurately forecast. Shorthands have saved time and saved lives. We understand *yellow* to mean caution, for instance, in our experience with road signage and traffic lights at intersections, but in the case of racial colors, shorthands have divided generations of human beings and will continue to divide us from Generation X to double-X to triple-X and beyond.

Bridget looks Lincoln directly in the eyes and speaks to him just as directly –

"Let me ask you a question, if you're named after a white man, why can't I take the persona of a black man in my music?"

"Two totally different things, and I bet you know it. You don't have any idea what it means to be a black man in America," Lincoln replies.

"I'm sure you're right about that," Bridget sighs, "but all the same, that's some self-righteous bullshit."

"What?"

"I love rap. I love African-American music. To me it feels like real music – *real* music – not like all the other crap that's on the radio, the kind of music that reaches inside me and shakes me, that speaks to me, that wakes me up from the stupor of living in suburbia. Creating roadblocks between me and the music can't be a good thing. If it makes me want to express myself the same way you express yourself, isn't that nothing but a good thing for both white people and black people?"

"You don't understand what the word means to us."

"Well, that's fine, so maybe if the rappers I listen to stop saying 'nigga' in their songs, I'll stop using it in mine."

"It's not your word, so it's not your place to decide that."

"But it's not your place to tell me how to think either, is it?"

Lincoln just stands there, arms crossed, looking good and pissed. But that doesn't stop Bridget from treading on, nothing much does –

"So, just chill the fuck out, honkey, and grab yourself a vanilla latte."

Lincoln's face sinks into itself, as if he has been completely bowled over.

"Did you just call me a honkey?"

"I'm a white chick, I can use that word, right?"

He is silent, for just long enough to be considered awkward in any social circle, whether of varying ethnicity or not. Then a thin smile creases his lips, "You're one crazy ass nigga."

"Aw, thanks." Bridget returns the smile, as if she was expecting the response; she always reacts like this, and obviously Lincoln could never know that. It's almost impossible to argue anything with Bridget unless there's common ground that's been established prior to the argument. Otherwise, don't even bother. She says what she says and simply hopes she'll end up on the right side. It takes far too much thought to think things through.

She grabs one of her tapes and holds it out to Lincoln –

"On the house."

Lincoln hesitates, then gives her an inch. Just from a standpoint of pure entertainment value and unabashed boldness, he's got to give her some props. He's got to respect that. And he does.

"Some of that shit is on the edge," he says.

"Take it, enjoy it. Not every white person is an evil asshole."

He takes the demo, which is about as DIY a product as it gets, and hefts the plastic case his hands.

"My cousin, Sean, outta Mount Vernon…you can throw a stone from the roof here and hit it, but none'a'you Bronxville folks like to admit it's that close."

"*Money earnin'* Mount Vernon," Bridget responds.

"Money earnin'," Lincoln nods his head, "That's right. Sean, he just started a label, and it's blowing up right now."

He holds the tape up.

"Maybe I'll pass this along to him."

Bridget beams.

***

Bridget and Stewart once again find themselves loitering atop the cement platform of the Bronxville station watching the trains pass them by. Stewart looks up at Bridget, "I'm proud of you."

"Get off your high horse," she replies.

She pulls out her bottle of whiskey, takes a nice, elongated sip. He watches her as she grasps the tops of her feet and pulls her legs up onto the bench, folding them neatly beneath her rump.

"I'm not on any horse," Stewart responds.

Bridget starts to giggle, looking back at Stewart as he sits down beside her.

"I always liked seahorses," Bridget says. "I like the fact that the male seahorse carries the eggs and gives birth to the baby seahorses. It takes the pressure off the female."

Stewart smiles, crossing his legs. Bridget scans his lower limbs, wrapped in his tight black jeans.

"That's a nice image," Stewart observes.

Stewart contemplates the seahorse. He thinks about its name, seahorse, and whether the name is somehow derived from this attribute. While he considers its confused state of sexuality, struggling to pinpoint the origin of its name, the basis for which is probably as simple as the thing looks vaguely like a horse, Bridget leans in and kisses him.

The incident lasts for an incredibly brief instant, it's over before it even began; but moments like this that are measured temporally are computed differently by opposing parties, moments like this beg a comparison to the ticking clocks of dreams and the unreliability of such clocks. If one encounters a clock in a dream and focuses on the digits, the numbers will prove to be unreadable. What's a flash of lighting for Stewart feels like a lifetime for Bridget. What's the same: the result. He instantaneously pulls away, taken so completely by surprise.

"Sorry—" Bridget shakes her head. "That was stupid."

She takes another nip from her booze, drinking not only for herself but also for the countless other young women who have felt a favored young man pull away from them. If she had a forty of Olde English, she'd spill some of it to the ground in honor of her forgotten sisters. Here's to fellow victims of the great unrequited illness.

"It's okay." Stewart hesitates, then he takes her hand. "I'd like you to come to an AA meeting with me. I go every week. You don't have to participate or do anything, just sit and listen."

Bridget jerks her hand away, her demeanor transforming effortlessly into the visage of contempt.

"If you get to know me better, Stewart," Bridget cautions, "you'll figure out that I really don't like people telling me what to do."

"I'm not telling, I'm just asking."

She looks down the tracks. Far away, a vector of light glows, increasing in dimension. A train is coming.

"Fuck off," Bridget snaps.

She hops down onto the dimly lit tracks. Stewart springs to the edge of the platform, leaning over the side, "What the fuck are you doing?!"

Bridget shimmies across, skipping through the spaces in the tracks like a kindergartner playing hopscotch, as if she has done this many times before. Time seems to slow down again, but this time for Stewart, as it telescopes into this crazy moment, a moment that hangs in the air like smog, a moment in which it seems like it's taking Bridget forever to get across the tracks, but it's one hundred percent certain that time hasn't effected the oncoming train one bit, that fucker's still moving at speed, barreling toward an exposed Bridget in a way that makes Stewart feel like he's going to regurgitate. Maybe it's just his perception that's making the train move faster, as a kind of safeguard, a self-preservation mechanism, a result of his biology that he tries desperately to rationalize, because he doesn't want to admit that he's a coward, a complete fucking coward, a recognition that runs in direct contrast to the hero he sees himself as in his own head, the hero we all think we are in our own heads; he possesses a cowardice that he believes he inherited from his father because he has to blame someone, someone other than himself, and he wants to kill this coward, not his father, but the gutless biology that prevents his body from moving until after the train passes. It is a fail-safe switch that's been flipped by the part of himself that he hates, the part of him that prevents him from risking his own life and jumping down there onto the tracks after Bridget.

In reality, Bridget is already at the other side of the tracks and up onto the platform in under a heartbeat. She yells at the top of her lungs from the opposite side, "I'm going home, Stewart!"

She waves at her friend as the train whizzes between them, wiping their silhouettes from each other's sights. Stewart paces restlessly along the cement, rattled to the bone. As the train finally passes through the station, it reveals an empty platform across from him. He turns away, a frazzled wreck, and peers down at the keyboard she abandoned on the bench.

CHAPTER NINE

Elias sits alone in a vortex of sound. He has headphones on and adjusts a microphone as Jeremy's song reverberates through the wall-mounted speakers in the cavernous mixing room. The foundation of the music industry was built upon the concept of artists singing other artists' songs. It's as old as the Gregorian chants. As much as the modern music industry is a show, it's also a business. A song may be indisputably good, but the way that it's delivered – the way it's sold – is an entirely different ball of wax. The song must be sold in order to keep the whole world of records spinning on its axis. It's that incestuous relationship between art and commerce that breathes life into the melodious organism of song.

Lance sits behind the mixing board, like a trucker behind the wheel of his rig, while Thomas and Connor lean over his shoulders. They're the backseat drivers on this road trip and they peer through the windshield at Elias, who reads off of a crumpled piece of loose leaf paper, the very same piece of paper that bears Jeremy's original lyrics. Elias mechanically sings Jeremy's words as Thomas and Connor try to will the song to another level, the level that's recognized as having the grunge stamp of approval in the industry, which is their ticket to success and fame. They stare at their front-man through the thick pane of soundproofed glass as if to plead with him to unleash the naked aggression that he brings to his own songs, the same aggression that inspired them to recruit him as their lead singer. But Elias is not paying any attention to them, which is not to say Elias isn't doing his job, and doing his job well. He didn't refuse to sing the song, which he might have done given his relationship with Jeremy and his empathy for him in these circumstances. He is singing the song. He started out tentatively, as if he was picking his way down the path of the words, finding the nuance, finding the places he could make his own. By the third take, his performance really takes flight. Maybe Elias is honoring his commitment to the band, as its lead singer, or he's honoring the lyrics his friend wrote, lyrics that were unquestionably written from the heart. In some way, to refuse to sing the song or to not sing it well, would be to dishonor the heart from which the song emerged. At least this is how Elias rationalizes what he's doing. In his effort to be professional, he has put the needs of the band ahead of his conscience and as he warms up to the song, as he makes it his own, he finds great pleasure in the result, as if there is a cannibalistic part of him, an element hidden well below the surface, that he didn't consciously know existed before but which he is embracing as it emerges, a Darwinian part of himself that relishes the opportunity to devour the work of his friend and present anew as if it were his and his alone.

Thomas sighs, more heavily than usual. He is getting what he wants, what he came here to get, but he can't help visualizing the events that are unfolding here as a form of vehicular homicide. Not manslaughter, with its connotations of the accidental, but a premeditated kind of murder because Thomas knows that there's no way he can pretend any of this is an accident. When he closes his eyes, the waves of Jeremy's sound bounce around the inside of his skull like bumper cars, minus the childhood nostalgia.

There is nothing innocent about this.

Outside the recording studio, where a frost has formed atop the terra firma, Jeremy has extricated himself once again from the proceedings, from the work, from the vehicular homicide, and from the scratching distress of feeling betrayed by his best friends. He leans against a tree, the moonlight illuminating his silhouette. He cradles a smoldering cigarette in the cupped palm of his hand, menthol, a tobacco flavor spurned by most suburban slackers, a taste savored predominantly by those in the urban community, or those with a fetish for inhaling fiberglass shards into their lungs, as the myth suggests. But Jeremy happens to like it, enticed by the swoosh of menthol into his lungs, the way it feels both warm and cool at the same time.

He slides down the tree, his back bumping along the bark as he breaks into convulsive weeping.

***

Later, Jeremy squats in the middle of the living room of Big Sound Studio's residential quarters playing video games. While invigorating for some and mind-numbing for others, gaming is a kind of meditative experience for Jeremy, bytes of yoga, electronic rosary beads. The upstairs of the studio has a Williamsburg, Brooklyn feel to it, when it was still seedy, before it got gentrified and trendy. It's a huge loft with plywood flats separating the small bedrooms, like cubicles in an office but absent any commercial value or architectural integrity. There are large canvases of makeshift modern art attached to the walls from floor to ceiling, art of wildly variable styles and skill levels, art that seems a little lost in this out-of-the-way recording studio in upstate New York, as if it had been hoping to find its way into a hip little museum but accidentally slipped into the music industry instead. The pictures are not hung with great care and Jeremy can't be sure if they're being displayed for their artistic value or to function as thermal insulation. Thomas walks into the living area, leaning on the couch at the back of the room.

"The song came out great," Thomas says, trying to be encouraging, trying to bridge the divide that he created. Jeremy is trying not to hear him, and he's doing a damn good job of it, with the help of Sega CD.

Jeremy is immersed in *Night Trap*, the first of a revolutionary series of full motion video (FMV) games from a company called Digital Pictures. These games integrated live action video footage that was filmed like a regular movie, with additional footage that was shot in order to provide various outcomes to the ends of scenes, to produce a gaming experience akin to the *Choose Your Own Adventure* book series they all read as kids. In the case of FMV games, instead of a reader skipping around to different chapters, a game player is able to skip around to different video clips and alter the narrative of the story by the way he plays the game. In *Night Trap*, Jeremy plays the role of a member of SCAT, Sega Control Attack Team, who is in charge of protecting a group of girls whose slumber party is crashed by a vampiric enemy called "Augers." Jeremy toggles between hidden cameras located in eight different rooms of the house, switching from camera to camera, monitoring the girls and their activities as they proceed through the game in various stages of danger and undress, while being hunted by Augers, brutes dressed in black that use cylindrical scythes with a series of tubes to drain the blood from the unassuming girls' necks. Every time one of these lumbering Augers gets close to a potential victim, Jeremy activates a booby trap in the room that prompts a portion of the floor to drop out, or triggers a bookcase to spin, or flattens the stairs into a slide, ensnaring the blood-thirsty bastards and endearing Jeremy to the ladies whose lives he saves. But sometimes he misses, and an innocent girl gets the hemoglobin sucked out of her.

The game player's contact is Kelly, an undercover SCAT agent who is played by Dana Plato. Plato, the former teenaged star of *A Different Strokes* and prepubescent crush of Jeremy's, will overdose on painkillers just before the turn of the millennium, an overdose that will initially seem like an accident, but will later be ruled a suicide in accordance with Oklahoma state law. She will die on Mother's Day, May 8th, 1999 and leave behind a son, who will die by his own hand almost a decade later to the day. Afterward, her son's friends and surviving family members will mention that he was always saying he wanted to be back with his Mom, and how Mother's Day was always a difficult day for him to endure.

The game was controversial for its time. In December, 1993, the Senate Judiciary and Government Affairs Committee hearing on video game violence declared *Night Trap* "ultra-violent" and "sick," which made it even more appealing to teenagers. Along with a handful of other games like *Mortal Kombat*, which Big Sound also has in its library, it helped effectuate the first official rating system for games. The controversy that erupted as a result of these hearings, the fervor that ensued in the gaming community, and the accompanying spike in sales, were the reasons Jeremy got the game in the first place. In his more honest moments, Jeremy would also admit that he got it so he could masturbate to Dana Plato now that his body had finally caught up with his crush.

Jeremy is much closer to his Mom than he is to his Dad. One Father's Day, he made his Dad a *Star Wars* greeting card, which read: "Luke had Darth Vader, and I have you! Happy Father's Day!" Jeremy thought the card was very funny, but his father didn't appreciate the comparison. The fact that he'd refer to his Mom as Princess Leia didn't win him any points with his Dad either. He got his sense of humor from his Mom. She thought the Father's Day card was funny, too. His parents have been divorced for most of his life and he lives with his mother. While the rest of the band was recording his song, Jeremy sequestered himself in a closet in the living area and called his Mom. He told her what the band had done to him and he cried as he told her. She remains the only person in his life who knows how to calm him down. His bandmates might have said that he should be honored that they're recording his song and not any of the others, but if they had said that he would have ignored them. When his Mom said it to him, it meant a lot and it made him feel a lot better. It calmed him down enough so that he could concentrate on playing this ridiculous video game. It's this kind of closeness that Jeremy has always had with his Mom that makes Mother's Day a special holiday to him and will help him appreciate Dana Plato's son's troubles a decade and a half from now. At the present moment though, playing *Night Trap* isn't working as a distraction as well as he'd hoped it would.

"You should be really proud of it," Thomas says. "It's a song we can all be proud of."

Jeremy pauses the game, just before an Auger is about to wrap his stick around the neck of a particularly well-proportioned woman. He realizes that any effort to further curb his response is pointless.

"I am proud of it," Jeremy retorts as he puts down his game controller. "I was proud of it when I wrote it."

Thomas, shaking his head, "Do you have a name for it? We need a—"

"Turbulence," Jeremy says, cutting him off.

Jeremy takes *Night Trap* out of the Sega CD console and grabs *Mortal Kombat* off a shelf. He probably should have been playing this game all along. If he can't rip Thomas's head off in reality, he might as well perpetrate a similar act of violence against video game characters in his stead, like a video proxy.

There's nothing else for Thomas to say. He's sorry that he created this rift between them, but he also believes that it was the right thing to do, believes that if their relationship is as strong as it has always appeared to be, then they will find a way through it somehow. People who grow up together and go through tons of crazy shit together have a way of finding a way back to the crazy normal of their lives. As Thomas turns around, trying to leave as nonchalantly as he arrived, he realizes that perhaps saying anything at all was a bad idea, that maybe he hadn't given Jeremy enough time to come to terms with what had been forced upon him.

Thomas heads down the hallway, passing a line of bedrooms. He peeks inside one and spots Elias sound asleep, passed out in all his clothes, oblivious to the tensions that are worrying Thomas and Jeremy. A muffled laugh, something like a snort, sneaks out of the side of his mouth, as if he can't resist laughing at everything that Elias is or as if the tensions that stand between Jeremy and himself require some kind of release and the sight of the animal Elias is just enough to let some of that tension out.

A toilet flushes from a nearby bathroom. Thomas continues walking down the hall, absently scratching at his groin. The bathroom door opens and Connor totters out in his tighty-whities and rubber bath slippers.

"I must've drank ten cups of coffee today, black as black, and my piss is crystal clear," Connor says. "Why is that? What the hell happened to the black?"

Small talk is awkward under any circumstances that find your friend standing in front of you wearing only underwear. The conversation can only be awkward. Thomas shrugs his shoulders at his unkempt friend.

"Good job today, dude," Connor says, as he slaps him on the back. "The drums sounded tight."

"Thanks. You, too, man."

"Night."

Thomas walks into the bathroom, steps to the toilet — Connor has thoughtfully left the seat up for him — and unzips his jeans. He scratches himself once again. Preparing for his pre-slumber urination, he peers down at his penis. Rubbing a finger over its tip, his fingernail grazes something with a texture that is alien and out of place, a tiny lump that feels like a rubber pencil eraser protruding from his flesh. Whatever this lump may be, he knows it's not supposed to be there. Thomas faces that moment of fear and denial in which he doesn't look down, the moment during which his mind simultaneously avoids the potentially awful truth and enjoys the last moment of life before the revelation of that truth. But where self-preservation is involved, you can't remain long in denial. He holds his penis straight up and squints down at it, bringing into focus an unambiguous blemish.

"What the fuck is that?" he whispers.

He squints harder, blinking the blemish into sharpened clarity. It's sort of like a pencil eraser, though smaller and less smooth, like the end of the rubber has been scraped vigorously against gravel or concrete. It's cauliflower-like in texture and has a recognizable three-dimensionality to it, an entire system of microscopic grooves running through its surface, pockets and miniature canals in the top of this tiny mountain that are rerouting bacteria in some complex orderliness known only to the bacteria — and it's a fucking cesspool of bacteria, this much is immediately clear to Thomas, a seething cauldron of alien invaders that are laying siege to undiscovered portions of his rapidly retracting phallus. The penis will retract in response to specific physical stimuli such as very cold water, a terrific fright, or a threat. But it also retracts in response to emotional trauma, when something threatens its potency, its usage, or when the owner of the penis is himself likewise emotionally distraught. Perhaps this current situation is a combination of these two responses, the fright of the physical growth and the emotional impact of it in the mind of Thomas. The offending growth is pinkish in hue and with each blink of Thomas's eyes, the swelling seems to multiply as if the discovery of this growth and the recognition of what it means are calling forth its brethren, in the same way that physicists have claimed that the universe does not exist until there is a conscious mind in place to observe it. There's not only one blemish on the tip of his penis, but also three on his shaft, and several at the base, where the hair begins to take over and where the shaft of his penis fuses with the sack of his balls. In some primal way, the idea that these invaders are advancing toward the sanctity of his seed sets off another wave of panic in Thomas. He frantically pulls back his pubic hair, inspecting the hidden portions of his skin. He grabs a plastic comb off the sink. It's Connor's comb, but that fact is irrelevant to Thomas in this moment of complete panic. He combs back the tufts of hair for a better look. He cranes his neck, straining his spine, bending down toward his retracting penis, getting closer to it than he probably ever has, except for that one vain attempt he made in middle school to get his lips on the damn thing, a thought that is truly repulsive to him now with his penis festooned in disgusting cauliflower growths. He takes note of several more of these invaders, these illegal aliens that have raided his body and are squatting inside his cellular structure. These new discoveries sit at the base of his hairs, hugging the hair follicles, clinging to them in the way drunken sailors who have washed overboard cling to a buoy at sea, adrift yet never giving up. These ball-sack blemishes are significantly slimier than the rest as well, reminiscent of albino Brussels sprouts, like something his Mom might have steamed for dinner on some feverish occasion in his nightmare youth, a nutritious side dish that complimented a Thanksgiving turkey from hell. Thomas's mouth begins to water, generating a surplus of saliva, not as a result of appetite or thirst, but rather from intense nausea. The urge to spit comes and goes as quickly as the projectile vomit that he discharges from his stomach, a soul-cleansing heave that leaves him gasping for air because of the length and violence of the peristaltic contraction.

Through teary eyes, the result of realizing that his world has just changed, Thomas is somehow proud to recognize that most of his puke actually made it into the toilet.

***

Jackie enters her room in her pajamas and makes a beeline to her bed, throwing herself onto the thick down comforter. Her bed is the captain's kind, the kind with drawers in the side of it, drawers that Jackie has reserved exclusively for her panties, a clothing accessory that has increasingly become related to her bed in ways that she doesn't really stop to think about. Her thongs, which have become a staple of her most sluttish outfits, are thoroughly hidden at the bottom of the least accessible drawer. There's something sublime about the hint of a thong rising above a metal studded belt while bending over, and this is a fashion theme that she has implemented whenever she could get away with it.

It's well past her curfew and there was a confrontation, an accusation from her father and a denial from her, the same repartee that they have engaged in nearly every weekend for the last year. It's amazing to Jackie that her mother still seems so willing to believe her, to forgive her, and she can't help thinking that her mother must have been the most boring girl in the history of the world. How else could she believe the litany of lies that Jackie unleashes in her feeble defense? But dealing with her parents fails to compare to this moment – the moment when she must deal with herself, the moment when she's finally alone, alone with herself, alone with her choices, with the consequences those choices have birthed. With a shudder, she realizes that she should wash the Pinewood off of herself, but there's too much symbolism involved in the act. She doesn't deserve to be washed, in any way. Betrayal is the kind of grime that's tough to scrub off, no matter which part of it touches you.

Jackie curls up into a fetal position, pulling her comforter over her folded limbs, and cries. She ferociously wipes at the remnants of her lipstick with her fingers, digging her nails deeply into the crevices of her lips as though the lipstick is the real grime, the real evidence of her betrayal. Jackie had read recently that women ingest close to half their bodyweight worth of lipstick over the course of their lifetimes and that many lipsticks contain lead. The genuine risk of lead poising, bearing in mind the percentage of lead and the volume of ingestion spread out over such an extended span of time, is a remote possibility, but the statistic isn't a good one. Sometimes cleanliness trumps guilt. Sometimes they hold hands.

Jackie burrows her head into her pillow and ceases her cries, her blood replacing her tears, as it streams from her battered lips down to the bottom of her chin.

***

Bridget lies still in her bed, beneath her checkered quilt, looking oddly at peace. There's a knock, her door creaks open. Maureen pops her head into her room.

"Bridget."

Bridget inhales deeply, slowly opening her eyes to the day. It's the first time she has slept well in quite a while, ending a streak of several nights with no sleep at all. It was one of those sleeps where your body thanks you in the morning. She might not have had any dreams, or at least none that she remembers, but she is refreshed.

"Bridget, we're going to church. Would you like to come?"

"No, thanks," Bridget yawns.

"We'll see you later, then," Maureen says.

Bridget sits up, arching her back, "What time will you be home?"

"A couple hours."

Bridget smiles at her mother.

"I love you, Mom."

"I love you, too. See you later."

Maureen is heels up, just about to leave the room.

"Mom?"

Maureen twists back, the tone from her daughter drawing her in. It's so rare that Bridget's voice achieves the childlike purity it's evoking here, a tone that is strikingly similar to what her voice sounded like so many years ago and a mother can hear such things, a mother can gauge the nature of need in the voice of her child.

"Yeah?" asks Maureen.

Bridget sits still in her bed, a complex web of thoughts tying up her mind, competing for purchase and expression. But her face remains utterly blank, still a little puffy from sleep.

"Nevermind…"

Maureen smiles, closing the warped door behind her.

Bridget turns to the bedroom window as spots of dappled sunlight disperse across the curvature of her face like a lustrous camouflage.

***

Thomas, Connor and Elias lean on a big, blue United States Postal Service mailbox – if fatigue was measured in gravitational weight, the huge metal container might be in danger of buckling beneath them. Thomas clutches a multi-stamped padded envelope, the kind with the air bubbles; they even wrapped the tape inside of it with newspaper, just to be safe. The package in hand is addressed to: "BATTLE OF THE UNSIGNED BANDS;" a New York mailing address written below it. They are thoroughly exhausted and they look it. Connor opens the mail slot and Thomas slips the envelope inside, the parcel dropping to the bottom with a thud. These boys might spin a joke at the quasi-religious nature of mailing this package, if their minds had been adequately rested to practice such wit. Perhaps they'll all laugh about it some years later, when telling the particulars of this story to their children and their children's children, the time that the old man was in a rock and roll band and had big dreams. For now, even laughing among themselves requires too much energy and the combination of exhaustion and solemnity about the potential future of the band keeps them silent.

They stumble back to the van, ready for a break from the non-stop efforts of the weekend and thinking only of getting away from each other. Jeremy stands next to the van, slouching against the side of it, the heel of his left sneaker tucked under his ass and propping him up as he stares blankly at his approaching bandmates. They stop a few feet in front of him.

"I quit," Jeremy says, matter-of-factly.

Jeremy climbs into the van, sliding the door closed on the vehicle and on any attempt at further conversation, pleading, reasoning, bargaining, joking, reminiscing, etcetera. Thomas can only stand there, arms dangling at his sides. The small sense of accomplishment engendered by the success of the recording had already been in rapid decline due to the far more serious calamity that had befallen him, the calamity of the horrific growths on his penis, and the awful extent of this calamity was still taking shape in his mind when Jeremy dropped his little bomb on the band.

There is a hole of teen angst and despair opening up inside Thomas and he is starting to feel a forbidding fear that he may never be able to climb out of this hole, that this entire situation may simply be beyond his control.

***

Bridget waddles into the upstairs bathroom, still adjusting her eyes to the morning light. She stretches toward the mirror, cracking cartilage in her elbow, and opens the medicine cabinet it adorns. She blinks at the contents, the stock of her mini-pharmacy, the endless towers of prescription bottles cluttering the compact shelves. Her eyes pass over them, scanning the labels, all of which she has become so familiar with that an inspection of the drug names and dosages is hardly necessary. There were times when she thought of these bottles as her friends, but more recently they have morphed into mortal enemies, as if the fact of their existence is the reason she suffers the way she does, not the other way around. Intellectually, Bridget knows that she has had problems and that the pre-scriptions are intended to address those problems, but the more she takes them the more she feels that taking them is the real problem. In most cases, a random investigation of a med-icine cabinet would reveal a number of older prescriptions with faded labels and expiration dates that are well in the past. In the case of Bridget Harrison, *all* prescriptions are up to date and meant to be ingested simultaneously, as if a bowl of fresh pharmaceuticals in the morning in place of her Cheerios is the most nutritious meal for her. The idea of pills as a breakfast cereal has a certain appeal to Bridget, but most of these pills are not to be taken with milk, as it can cause severe intestinal dis-comfort and diarrhea. But at least consuming the pills in this way would allow her to pretend that they were something other than what they so clearly are, maybe it would help her feel differently about the pills as the cause of the problem. It might be worth the runs.

Bridget holds up a large canvas purse, a Gap purse approx-imately two seasons old, and she dumps all of the prescription bottles into it. It's a testament to the depth of her problem that this action empties the cabinet almost entirely. As she stuffs the bottles into her bag, her gaze rests on a solitary stick of lip-stick standing a barren shelf. She plucks it from the cabinet, closing the mirror, and stares at her reflection.

She wishes she saw Woody Allen's reflection instead; her motivation to ingest her regimen of pills would be much clear-er.

Bridget's eyes, staring out of her own face seem to under-stand her significantly less than those same eyes staring out of the cut-out face of Woody. She needs a persona to hide beh-ind, she needs a mentor, someone like Woody, she needs something other than the life that she is living right now and the requirements that come with it. She needs motivation.

As she continues to focus on the image of herself, she takes the lipstick in her hand, pops the cap off of it, twists the bottom of the tube and gradually extends its bright red tip toward the surface of the mirror.

***

Connor slouches in his driver's seat, reclined as far as the seat will allow and further reclined in the epic slouch of his body. He has only twenty percent of one hand on the wheel, a tepid pinch of thumb and forefinger, and it's something of a miracle that he's able to navigate the terrain in his SUV with so little contact with the wheel. Thomas sits in the passenger seat staring vacantly out the window at the passing landscape on the idyllic I-87, the New York State Thruway; though, the further south you go, the less pleasant it gets. It is one of those roadways that is equally tranquil and treacherous, and it's easy for the driver to find himself taking his eyes off the road and staring into the passing trees. It's even easier for the passenger to do that, since driving isn't his immediate concern, but Thomas is having a hard time seeing the trees – it's like he's looking past them into whatever's hiding behind them.

"He'll come around," Connor says. "He'll change his mind."

Thomas shakes his head, "No. He won't."

Thomas slouches down as well, the interior of his mind spinning. It's not quite the queen of diamonds, like his Dad, but it's pretty damn close. It's not a marker, because he has yet to encounter this feeling. What exactly is spinning is something that Thomas can't pinpoint, but can acknowledge he's never experienced it before. And it's this something that Connor notices.

"You okay, man?"

"Jackie is seeing someone else," Thomas responds.

"What?" Connor digests the comment. "I don't understand. Why do you think that?"

Thomas looks down between his legs.

"This is kind of fucking embarrassing, but I have to tell someone. This is just between us, okay?"

"Yeah, of course."

Thomas breathes in deeply, shaking slightly, and pausing for a second to wonder if he really needs to share this, even if he is sharing it with his best friend. Fear of dealing with all of this alone overcomes his fear of the embarrassment, so he comes out with it, "Something's growing on my dick."

Connor shifts awkwardly in his seat. He plants both hands firmly on the wheel and sits up a bit, as if concentrating more closely on driving might spare him from the alarming account his friend is sharing with him.

"Kind of looks like...a fungus."

"Shit, man." Connor replies.

"I'm really freaked out about it."

"I bet you are," says Connor. He wants to console Thomas, he wants to say something helpful, to be the right kind of friend at this agonizing moment, but he's also got to say something quickly because the silence is worse than talking. It's in his nature to seek immediate and direct solutions to the problems that confront him: "Get it checked out at a free clinic or something."

"Mind dropping me there? I don't want my parents to know. I think there might be one on Central Avenue."

Connor checks the digital clock on the dash; there's plenty of time.

"I can hang with you for a while," Connor says in his friendliest, and most supportive, of tones. Thomas tries hard to smile, a gesture that's poor cover for someone so ill at ease.

By the time Thomas is sitting in the crammed waiting room of the Central Avenue Free Health Clinic, the very idea of a smile is as alien as the nasty little buggers growing on and around his penis, the little buggers that he can't stop thinking about and which fill him with apprehension. Thomas sits next to Connor, both of them squeezed uncomfortably into bleached yellow molded plastic chairs that inexplicably have a groove running through the middle that feels like it's flossing their asses, threatening to split them in two. The room is also considerably less sterile than one interested in proper hygiene would like it to be. Connor decides to shoot the shit, attempting to get his buddy's mind off this room and the reason he's waiting in it.

"Would you ever get a tattoo?" Connor asks.

"Maybe," Thomas replies, nervously. "You?"

"If we make it big, I'll get a tattoo. Not sure what, but I'd get something."

"Where would you get it?"

Connor slaps the inside of his left forearm, where he'd shoot heroin, if he were into that shit. "Right there. So I can show it off when I play."

"Dave Grohl has one there."

"And Dave Grohl was a guitarist before he became a drummer."

A nurse opens a door, stepping into the waiting area with a thick clipboard in her hand. "Thomas Harrison?"

Thomas blinks, flaps his hand a bit, as if he was planning to raise it but then had second thoughts. He stands up and shuffles down the hall.

Inside the unpleasantly cold examination room, Thomas lies on the steel table wedged in its corner. He's dressed in a pale blue paper gown and staring up at the cheap industrial foam tiles in the drop ceiling, honing in on the infinite dots inside one of the squares. He had been counting them, tallying each of the dots, hoping to distract himself from the physician poking around his privates underneath his gown, until the cracks and ridges spidering through the tile started to remind him of the texture of the growths on his penis. When he abandoned his counting exercise he had reached one hundred and twenty-eight dots.

"I've only been with one girl. She was a virgin."

Doctor Pradham, a young Indian physician in a burgundy bowtie, stands up straight in front of him.

"One of those two facts is wrong," the doctor responds.

Thomas stares at him, unable to respond, rendered mute for the moment despite a pressing need to communicate with his doctor. Thomas is simply trying to put all the broken pieces of his thoughts into an order, a bigger picture, a road map, an outline that he can trace logically from beginning to end and that will help explain the series of events that brought him here today. But based on what the doctor just told him, no scrupulous retracing of steps is going to bring him to a satisfactory conclusion. None of it will help him cope. None of it will help him understand. This fact, this revelation that no amount of questions will elicit the answer that he is looking for, it is this pointlessness, he understands completely.

"How would you prefer them to be removed? I can either burn them off or freeze them off," the doctor says dispassionately.

Thomas drops his forehead into his hands. His palms are sweating so profusely that his head slips right through them, but he regains his grip, holding himself up while simultaneously holding back the tears that are so eager to trickle out of the ducts in which they're generated.

***

William and Maureen sit side-by-side at mass, inside the majestic St. Joseph's Church on Kraft Avenue in Bronxville, a church that is majestic only to the extent that a suburban house of the Lord can be majestic. Maureen looks at William and he turns to her and smiles; it's a closed mouth smile that appears to border on sour, but church isn't the place for showing off shiny white teeth. He takes her hand, weaving his fingers through hers. They shift their focus toward the altar as Father McSweeney blesses the gifts of bread and wine.

> "*Lamb of God, you take away the sins of the world:*
>
> *have mercy on us.*
>
> *Lamb of God, you take away the sins of the world:*
>
> *have mercy on us.*
>
> *Lamb of God, you take away the sins of the world:*
>
> *grant us peace.*"

Father McSweeney addresses his congregation as he raises the moon-shaped Eucharist, "This is the Lamb of God who takes away the sins of the world. Happy are those who are called to his supper."

The voices of his parishioners echo back, "Lord, I am not worthy to receive you, but only say the word and I shall be healed."

Maureen and William are religious in the way people who care about their community often are, you wouldn't find them in deep discussions about the veracity of the Bible, about whether the church is as pure as it demands its flock to be, about whether the word of God is truly from God or whether it's a compilation of human efforts, but they believe in the ritual and they believe that such rituals make a community stronger and more moral. They believe in morality, without being pedantic about it. After their visit with the Almighty and a pit stop to Topps Bakery for a box of raspberry Linzer Tarts, a local delicacy, William and Maureen pull into their driveway and step out of their SUV. As William brushes a splotch of powdered sugar off of his suit jacket, he notices a small dent on the driver's side door. He rubs his hand over the damage. Maureen bends down, looking at it, too.

"When did you do that?"

"I have no idea," William says as he scrutinizes the scratch. "Must have happened in the parking garage."

They shake their heads in unison and approach the house.

The burner on the Harrisons' stove is heating a teakettle and the water is already at the boiling point. The modern culture of the 20th Century has really given teakettles a bad rap. What used to be a benign sound intended to cue a tea drinker into realizing that the water is ready, has become an almost universal signifier for the ominous, for the foreshadowing of tragedy, for letting a psychopath know when his provisions are prime for the burning of his victim's flesh – his victim's oozing flesh. The specifics of oozing flesh may not be universally associated with a whistling kettle, but the Jungian archetype of a teakettle in recent decades, implanted into our brains by horror movies and television drama, rings true in the minds of most people. Something bad is going to happen. Although they're middle-aged and not familiar with the deluge of horror films that have saturated the market over the last decade, William and Maureen did see *Fatal Attraction* in the theater, a movie that incorporated an ominous teakettle into the pivotal confrontation scene between Glenn Close and Anne Archer: while Michael Douglas is downstairs, he's oblivious to his wife's screams because they're drowned out by the sharp whistle of a teakettle. So it's possible that thoughts of oozing flesh or concealed knives cross their minds as they open the front door, entering their humble home, and hear the teakettle whistling in its penetrating and painful pitch, the water within bubbling in a raging boil.

"Bridget?"

Maureen and William walk swiftly into the kitchen, projecting their fears into the space as if it is already the scene of some crime.

"Bridget, where are you?" Maureen projects her voice into the unoccupied air around her, filling the kitchen and the better part of the house.

"Jesus Christ," William mutters.

The kitchen has been abandoned. There are no signs of any misdeeds or transgressions of the law. William shuts off the stovetop and shifts the kettle to a cold and empty adjacent burner. The whistling abruptly fades, leaving the kitchen and the house with a distinctly empty feeling, something that might be even more ominous than a whistling teakettle if they were inclined to stop and think about it. William surveys the stovetop and the narrow counter, looking for objects that could have caught fire. In the realm of domestic safety, this constitutes a security breach, but it's mostly a misdemeanor, a crime only in the respect that family members are always committing such minor infractions against each other. That William makes a living categorizing the meaning, extent and impact of criminal acts has been a pain point in his family for a long time. While he's very effective at weighing the relative merits of any disciplinary issue that arises in the family, his belief in the infallibility of his judgment, combined with an authoritative approach to the application of punishment, creates a certain distance between him and the people he loves more than any other people in the world. From his perspective, the discipline is good, it's healthy, and it will make his children that much stronger as they head out to face the challenges of the real world. To his children, it means he's distant, calculating, less prone to show affection and this has always had the effect of making them wonder if he really loves them at all. Maybe all children feel this way about their fathers, as the father will often take a harder line, will often be less forgiving. But when the father happens to be a judge and a Vietnam War veteran, the feeling can be that much greater, that much more stifling.

Maureen walks to the sliding glass door and sees Bridget on the back porch, smoking a cigarette. Bridget turns to her mother and casually waves. William glides open the door, and pokes his probing head out.

"The kettle's boiling – didn't you hear it?"

Bridget smirks and shrugs her shoulders. William shakes his head and retreats, correctly realizing that his rising anger will not serve any purpose at all. Maureen steps outside to join her daughter on this agreeable Sunday morning.

"Put that cigarette out," Maureen quietly decrees.

Bridget lifts her foot and extinguishes the cigarette on the bottom of her boot.

"Your father and I thought we'd do a little shopping. Would you like to join us?"

Bridget turns, looks at the trees.

"I could use some more paints. I think I might like to paint these trees."

Bridget nods, glancing at the undulating branches and their quivering leaves, picturing all of the things that the leaves could look like, the intimations she could conceptually add to her painting, a tangle of kites, a school of fish, a flock of birds fluttering madly in the mind of the artist. Maureen puts an arm around Bridget, partly out of protection, partly in an effort to break her reverie.

***

Thomas and Connor walk quietly down the clinic corridor toward the exit. For two young men, there's simply no way there is any comfort in this moment at all, it's nothing but anguish, nothing but awkward. Thomas spots a payphone on the wall, next to a large dispenser of free condoms. There's plenty of reasons to stop, but he also knows it would be good for he and Connor to be apart for a few minutes, that it would be a good thing for them both to be alone, so he stops and turns to his compadre.

"I'll meet you at the car."

Connor gets it and he welcomes the respite as much as Thomas does, so he scoots out the door. Thomas picks up the payphone, digs into his jacket pocket and plunks a quarter into the apparatus. There's no hesitation in his dialing, he simply dials, like punching in an activation code for a nuclear warhead with the confidence of a cowboy whose finger is on the trigger.

It's ringing. And it's Jackie who answers.

"Hello?"

Thomas spits it out, blunt as hellfire: "I was diagnosed with genital warts."

There is silence on the other end of the line and the silence in these types of moments immediately feels like it's stretching into minutes, the minutes into what seems like hours, as though the time is elastic, threatening to whip itself back into your face at the agonizing moment when it ends.

"What?" Jackie replies.

"I'd suggest you get your ass down to the clinic and get checked out." Thomas sticks the knife into her deeper. "Don't worry, they can burn 'em off, but I'll warn you, it stings like a bitch."

"Thomas..."

It sounds like Jackie is choking. Thomas is actually enjoying this moment, however sadistic the gratification might be, however deranged that feeling is, and he's not proud for feeling this way about it, but the gratification is instant and it's pure and he doesn't fucking care how she feels.

"I'm sorry," she squeaks out meekly.

"Too late for apologies."

Thomas slams the receiver down, giving Jackie all the closure to the conversation she could ever need and putting the cherry on top of his serving of small-minded satisfaction.

He stares at the public phone, at the worn black plastic of its mouthpiece, and he can't help wondering how many mouths full of myriad illnesses and bacterium, nasty shit that should be subject to the use of a hazmat suit, have spit onto the surface of that receiver, how many conversations went down just like this one, delivered by someone infected just like he is infected, broken-hearted, just like him. He wonders how many phone calls like this Jackie has already received, how many genitals she has had intimate contact with, whether male, female or rabid animal. Thomas knows that she was unfaithful – he feels it in his heart and in the pain of this hospital experience – he knows that she had intimate relations before, during and after the time she spent with him, relations she obviously took great care to hide from him, although the physical evidence of these indiscretions may have finally become too difficult to hide, as demonstrated by the warts that were just burned off of his cock.

Connor drives up the steep residential hills of quiet Colonial Heights, glancing at Thomas, who is slumped over in the passenger seat. Thomas has his mouth tightly closed and two fingers pinching his nose, as if he's a scuba diver adjusting to the pressure of the depths, but since they're ascending the hills of Yonkers, he knows that Thomas is attempting to blow air into portions of his inner ears and pop them as he adjusts to the increase in altitude. Heights can bring pressure in the same way as depths.

"Did it hurt?" Connor asks.

"What do you think?" Thomas says, mockingly, as his ears finally pop.

"I think I'd rather not."

"Then why the hell are you asking me?"

"I can't help myself. Morbid curiosity, I guess."

In normal circumstances, Thomas would have to laugh at this, it's what he has always liked about Connor, his bluntness, the way he runs headlong into anything, without second thoughts of consequences or hurt feelings; but it's also a bluntness that's watered-down with humor, and this makes his personality, which is inherently straightforward, endearing. It's just the way he is programmed. But Thomas can't even bring himself to snicker, as if laughing might pop out another wart or intensify the contagion of this particular sexually transmitted disease, in the same way that he remembers his father aggravating his hernia further with an untimely fit of belly laughter. Thomas can't remember what prompted his father's laughter, which resulted in outpatient surgery and the implantation of a mesh patch. He can't remember what was being discussed or what funny thing he or Bridget might have done, but he wishes he could remember. Thomas is cursed with only remembering the lows, remembering the pain, the suffering, the embarrassment and never remembering the highs that often precede or follow the lows. Especially when the stories involve pain, as if pain has a way of overshadowing everything around it, eclipsing the brightness with shadows of doubt, regardless of whether the good part of the story deserves more credit, if the good part is greater than the pain in weight, in length, in volume, in duration. It doesn't matter. It's always the pain that sticks.

The scruffy kids pull into the Harrisons' empty driveway and climb out of Connor's car. As soon as their soles hit the pavement, Thomas engages an electronic opener and the garage door slowly cranks itself up. Connor enters the garage, followed by Thomas lugging endless pieces of drum equipment from the trunk. The drummer always gets screwed because he's got the most stuff, and the guitarist won't be caught dead carrying percussion, not when he can have one hand on a guitar case and the other on a beer. Even though the Latterday Saints have yet to book a paying gig, Thomas has heard the stories and he's attended shows, and he imagines their future gigs ending similarly to the way gigs end for most bands, an ending that involves the singer, guitarist, bassist, and anyone else not involved in drumming, macking it to chicks and scoring numbers at the bar as the drummer, sweat streaming down every part of his body, breaks down his kit next to the stage while being cursed out by the drummer of the next band for being too slow. Then when the drummer, whose energy and passion have been completely depleted, confronts the other preoccupied members of the band, an altercation that's inevitable, they insist that he doesn't understand, that they're doing him a favor, that they're indeed helping matters: *they're working at expanding their fan base.*

The drummer is the backbone of the band; he's the skeleton of the sound, and he risks breaking every one of its bones before and after each gig.

This is why the rehearsal space is always at the drummer's house. So it's not just enough to know how to play drums to be in a rock band, it's making sure you've got a family who doesn't mind putting up with a group of degenerates shaking their house to its foundations every Sunday with the devil's music.

"Dave Grohl may have been a guitarist before he was a drummer, but the tattoo on his arm is John Bonham's symbol," Thomas observes.

Thomas feels a need to talk, but there's no way that he wants to return to the subject of his personal problems; he would rather focus on the drums and nothing but the drums, no matter how unfair the responsibility of being a drummer is, and even if it means heading back into an ancient argument. In fact, the ancient nature of this argument between them is mildly comforting to Thomas, it suggests to his battered body and mind that there's still a slight possibility of normal in his life, even if that possibility is more remote to him than it ever has been in his life.

"Led Zeppelin's John Bonham?" Connor asks.

"There is no other."

Thomas stacks his drums as he explains, "The three rings – trinity of mother, father and child. And it even looks like a drum set."

"Nice try, but that one's on his wrist."

Connor drops a hardware bag onto the floor, without concern for anything inside of it that may be soft, and therefore breakable, "The one on his forearm has nothing to do with drums."

Thomas stops to rest, hunkering down on some stacked storage containers. He stares listlessly at Jeremy's monolithic bass amp that dominates the dusty cement floor in front of him. There's an unusual symmetry to this amplifier, a presence, like it's a magnet and everything around the room is leaning toward it, including his eyes. He continues to stare at it. He feels like he's trapped in an illusion, as if there's a magician on the other side of the door distorting every single thing in his line of vision, the way some conjurer might bend a spoon or some other kind of trick utensil, and Thomas is struck by the feeling that he's in some significant danger of being smacked in the back of the head by random debris, by the flotsam of his family's life that is stacked and stored in crates around him, by the accumulation of unnecessary rubbish overflowing in every home like his in the neighborhood, in the town, the county, the state, the country, by the remnants of ancient Rome, the rubble after Nero burned it to the ground – everything that is and ever was is in serious danger of being pulled into the void of this fucking amp. The conversation, the old argument involving Dave Grohl, ground to a halt a while ago and Thomas didn't even notice, he is not even capable of noticing such a thing right now. Connor must have said some vague and unacknow-ledged goodbye, because he is speeding off down the street now, unleashing a departing beep, a sound that barely works its way into the awareness of his damaged friend. Thomas doesn't wave; Thomas doesn't even know how he got to the front stoop, he just closes the front door behind him, making sure it's shut, but doesn't lock it. He's not entirely sure that Connor has actually left, he's not sure he's completely alone yet. His memory has become spotty and irrelevant to his current state, like his mind has become a vagabond that is wandering aim-lessly inside his own body. From moment to moment, he doesn't remember the last few minutes, or was it a few hours?

Couldn't have been, his parents aren't home yet – and they don't stray far from home for very long. Maybe the monolith erased his memory. Maybe it possesses some alien life force intent on controlling the minds of American youth, an invasion exactly like the theories that accompanied the birth of rock and roll. Thomas wishes that the alien inhabited amp, the monolith, could be used to erase memories selectively, like the mixing board in the studio, increasing the gain on some parts of his life, while taking others out of the recording altogether.

Thomas doesn't feel like the engineer of his own life, he doesn't feel capable of controlling the things that have happened to him, the things that have been troubling him, the things that he cannot seem to escape. Thomas notices the stillness of the house. He notices, because that's all there is to notice.

"Hello?"

There is no response. Part of him knows perfectly well his parents aren't there, but with his currently compromised grasp on reality, he feels he must verbalize something.

Dropping his duffle bag to his floor, Thomas sprawls out on the top of his twin bed. As the bedsprings absorb his tumble, his eyes pass over an enormous Nirvana poster tacked neatly to the wall: Kurt Cobain's unshaven, strung-out face looms in the foreground, as his bandmates, Krist and Dave, hunch down insignificantly behind him as though they're an afterthought.

Kurt was 27 when he took this picture, and he looked ancient. He looked like he was dead already.

In the street, Thomas opens his car door, leaning into it. Gripping a tattered dishrag and a spray bottle of Clorox, he rubs the dashboard like hell, painstakingly erasing Jackie's phone number. Even after the number is gone, he keeps rubbing, bleaching the color from the factory-installed faux-leather.

Thomas trundles up the stairs of his house, hitting the hall-way, the main drag of the second floor, and heads into his sister's room. He stares at her unoccupied and audaciously un-made bed, the twin of the bed that he has in his room, but so different, as if the years that have passed since the two beds were bought together have altered them beyond recognition. Thomas wonders if an object can take on the personality of the person who owns it, if his DNA can be found in his bed, not just in the hair follicles that he has shed, but in the wood itself, absorbed in a way that would mark the bed forever as his own. Bridget's bed certainly expresses her personality. The remnants of the hurricane.

Thomas approaches the bed, sits on the edge of it. By her stereo, he notices a stack of Bri Da B demo tapes. He picks one up, looks long and hard at it. The oddness of the cover, and the foreign genre of music it implies, barely fazes him and his predetermined sensibilities, but he's intrigued nonetheless.

Thomas opens the tape deck to her stereo, pops the tape in, and listens —

"My Daddy's a Republican, his daughter's a pimp..."

He snorts in disbelief at what he's hearing. His sister? A rapper? A gangsta' rapper? Is that what she's doing? Trying to do? Was she ever even into music? Really? The evidence that she is continues to play and Thomas can't help wondering why he didn't notice her interest in music. He's smothered with that feeling that you just can't know people, no matter who they are.

As the hip-hop song continues to thump through the spe-akers, inserting its rhythm into his ears, he steps over to her hamster cage.

"Your name's Bumpy."

He pokes a finger through the cage, and the rodent licks his fingertip, its sandy tongue momentarily allowing Thomas to feel the ridges in his fingerprint. He glances at the newspaper article written about their father at the bottom of the cage, the print of which is covered in Bumpy's prolific fecal matter. Thomas recognizes the humor in this and if you knew him well enough you might be able to detect the hint of a smile in the way the edges of his eyes wrinkle ever-so-slightly, but he does not laugh, as he might have in better times. It feels to Thomas as though laughter has been reduced to a function of mechanics, a set of mechanics that are unfamiliar to him now, that he would have to relearn in the same way that an injured body needs to relearn how to move. The missing ingredient is emotion, and the spontaneity that comes along with emotion, and this is lost in the haze of injury that he carries.

Thomas walks into the bathroom, looks at the mirror – on the glass, written in bright red lipstick, is:

"NO ALTERNATIVE"

Thomas doesn't blink; it's like he has been hypnotized. He reads the angular phrase, these hieroglyphics of Bridget's, the crude violence of the letters and the gorgeous red of the lipstick standing in sharp contrast the way only the best marketing strategies are capable of doing. His eyes move from the first word to the second, and back again, taking in the statement repeatedly, each time with a greater depth of meaning, the phrase burrowing deeper into his mind, alighting on a primal plane where connections are made that are beyond the conscious mind.

A solitary tear emerges from his eye, spilling over his lower lid and rolling helplessly down his cheek.

He enters his parents' room – the *master* bedroom of the house – and steps to his mother's antique burnished oak dresser. He opens a small drawer in her jewelry box, sitting like a crown atop the head of her chiffonier, and extracts a miniature key. He heads over to the closet and opens it, haphazardly pushing through clothes and a voluminous amount of clutter for a room so small. He's searching and not finding what he's looking for. His movements grow a bit wild, almost panicked, as he thrashes around in the claustrophobic closet. He has passed well beyond the point at which he could reasonably expect to reorganize the little room in a way that would escape detection by his parents, the point of no return has been reached and ignored: he has totally trashed his parents' closet.

Finally, he kicks something distinctly metal. He kneels down and pulls a lockbox out from the bottom of the mess.

Thomas stumbles back, slamming his hip into a bedside table, causing one of the two matching bedside lamps to wobble and consequently crash to the floor, but he doesn't even notice what he's done. He's not ignoring it, it just doesn't register that he's broken anything, just as he hadn't given any thought to trashing the closet. As he drops the lockbox onto the foot of their bed, he's overcome with a smell like burnt engine oil, a smell so potent it's like the stuff is suddenly lining his nostrils. As he sniffs the offending aroma into his sinuses, the odor itself seems to transform into a liquid and his nose begins to stream with it. He wipes his nose with his sleeve and then swipes at his eyes, which are also unexpectedly leaking, and he doesn't understand how a smell can be doing this or what the smell is. He can feel his heartbeat everywhere, in the ridges of his fingerprints that so recently touched Bumpy, in the hair follicles that are standing up on the back of his neck, inside each of his eyeballs where the tears are coming from, the tears which bounce out of his eyes with each beat of his heart. He shakes his head, focusing through the tears, focusing on the lockbox. He looks at it, like he hates everything about it. Opening his hand, he looks at the key, the tiny cheap key that is barely needed to open this box. He unlocks it and pulls out his father's .45 millimeter handgun. The thing is spit-shine new, so new that it has probably never been taken out of the box before, and as soon as he holds the gun up he recognizes the smell that had assaulted him a moment ago. But now the smell is attractive, soothing; the essence of the smell is almost welcoming. He hefts the weapon in his hands, sitting down on his parents' bed.

The gun itself does not merit description, since Thomas doesn't really spend much time looking at it. To do so would add reverence to the *instrument*. It's a gun, the physical outline of which is recognized by Jung and the rest of the quacks as being universal, transcending cultures and languages; a gun is a gun, and everyone knows what it does. It cuts through the bullshit.

Thomas is done with reverence, done with worship, done with false idols, done with his expectations and the expectations of others, done with worrying about how he is perceived, with worrying about his looks or if he has said something stupid, done with eating and shitting, those mechanical acts that now take on a plastic hollowness in his mind, he's done with the seasons and wondering what the weather will do, he's done with talking to people about the weather, the most vacant of conversations, the conversation that denies any hint of human connection, he's done with what everybody else in the world around him thinks.

What matters now is what he thinks: he thinks he wants not to think anymore. So, in one swift, fluid, natural motion, he twists the gun around in his hand, swings it up, inserts the barrel into his mouth and –

Pulls the trigger.

Blowing his fucking brains all over his parents' comforter.

CHAPTER TEN

Suicide is the thing; the goal; the beginning and the end; the next big thing; the be all, end all; the eye in the sky – it's the Tylenol bottle with the 20 bonus pills, because swallowing an entire bottle of Tylenol can kill you.

Suicide is an option; it's an alternative; it's aqua seafoam shame; it's dead of a .45 millimeter blast to the head.

CHAPTER ELEVEN

Being dead isn't something Thomas planned for; more accurately, it isn't something *I* planned for, even though, technically, I did plan for it, had to plan for it, in fact, in order to carry out the act. But that's not how it feels. I wasn't really myself until I did it – which is why I didn't cop to constructing the narrative until now.

Why did I commit suicide? That's the question that everyone asks of a suicide, the question that seems implicit with the very word *suicide*, the question that most people who have experience with suicide simply cannot answer with any level of satisfaction. You might think that someone like myself would have something to offer on the subject; as someone who has experienced the act of suicide and who has gone to great pains to record the facts of my life preceding my suicide, I should be able to answer the question, right? The problem is that it's not a simple yes or no answer. It requires a lot more. What you've read so far and what you're reading right now is the best that I can do with the question. At the most basic level, I think the real answer to the question was ejected from my brain the second I put a hole through it.

There's nothing like death to distill the essence of a person. That's the bare bones of it. Death is a final stamp of completion on your life and it ushers in a whole series of effects. The body begins a brand new journey at the very instant of death – nature immediately begins breaking it down into its elements, like an automotive manufacturing plant working in reverse, dismantling the vehicle of yourself, a vehicle that had been painstakingly assembled over a period of years or decades, taking everything apart, bit by bit and piece by piece. Just like the demolition of an automobile, where the pieces are sold as scrap and melted, reworked into different forms, the molecules of the body continue to evolve, or devolve, degrading and combining themselves into a state that will eventually rejuvenate the world, fertilize the earth, nourish the soil, as a means of creating the basis for future organic life. The memory of your life is also fertilizing, nourishing, and creating a legacy – the legacy that will define you above the ground, back in the real world. It's the legacy that will live on. There's nothing like dying young to perpetuate the guise of genius, the myth of expertise, the enlightenment of a soul that so clearly touched everyone around him or her while it was alive.

And, man, will there be a long line at your wake. Just you wait.

DMV line long.

Closed casket, obviously, because of the bullet in your brain.

The living have a notion that death has something to do with light: *look toward the light, walk toward the light, float toward the light.* This is largely the result of theological obsessions with light that date back millennia, but contrary to popular opinion, death is anything but light. As it relates to death, light is a misleading concept that's romanticized more than the cowboy in the golden age of Hollywood Westerns. Even in life, it's light that we hide from, preferring the shelter of shade. We squint at light and use innumerable forms of shading devices to reduce its glare. It's the source of the melanomas on our flesh, the wrinkling of our manicured, made-up dermis. The sun is the single most dangerous object we encounter on a daily basis. There would be no life without the sun, but try believing it's a beneficent entity the next time you find yourself in the desert. It causes headaches, sunburn, disorientation. It causes car accidents. Look at the bright side, and you'll strain to see it.

On the other hand, is the darkness: the darkness comforts, it relaxes, it eases. The darkness allows for sleep, rest, reinvigoration, thought, inspiration, dreams, it brings things into focus, it is security, safety, a womb. In the womb, the shared place of our origins, nothing is visible, it's about as dark as the word darkness can signify. We are blind in the womb, and after we have trudged through the light of our collective lives, we return to the shadows. If death is a return to birth, then it is without a doubt a return to darkness. And, frankly, darkness is more appealing. Sunglasses companies profit substantially from this premise.

The darkness is an all-consuming shadow of rest and peace, a shadow under which the Earth rests as time falls asleep. It's a microcosm of the universe. Just close your eyes.

It didn't hurt. Not exactly. It felt more like a plug being pulled from its socket, like a cessation of power, like a transition from a place that is powered to a natural and more powerless state, a transference of energy that is tailored in an entirely different wardrobe. The clothes aren't new, the style has been around since before life itself was stitched together, but the clothes are different – they're certainly not brand name, and there are no Converses. It takes getting used to, fitting into these other threads, just like it takes time for the body to decay, to deteriorate, to settle into the ensuing stage of fertilizing and nourishing the earth from which it came. You are tasked to separate your being from your body and, as this metaphysical process begins, you must grow accustomed to the idea that your body is the part of you that must be discarded, that it is as disposable as the last soda can you drank from and that it was fundamentally built to be left behind. Unless it's a Styrofoam cup, your body won't last. Perhaps that's the key to eternal life: Styrofoam. They should make coffins out of the stuff, to protract the illusion of endless living underground. Wood and metal caskets decay, but Styrofoam will last forever. There is a captive market ready to buy the Styrofoam casket, ready to invest in the very real possibility that it will help keep the elements away. The living have a market for everything and the selling of everything is right out in the open, exposed to the light of day, except for the selling of death. Death is the only market that serves every living person on the planet, yet you will never see an advertisement about death, you will never even be aware of the colossal death market until you experience the loss of a loved one and even then, the massive industry of mortuaries will protect you from the crass marketing of caskets, urns and tombstones. I foresee my parents at McGrath & Son Funeral Home shopping for my casket. Either McGrath, or his son, will recommend a casket, and he will haltingly talk about price, but only as a last resort will he show my parents a picture or, God forbid, a brochure.

I'm certain that the first time a person sees a casket brochure is a life-altering experience. It's probably difficult to look at any form of advertising in the same way after you have seen a casket brochure.

The insight of death, at least for me, is not how other people perceived me, but how I perceived myself. You get a cloudless picture of yourself in death and, even though I still had a lot to learn about life when I ended it, I gained an understanding of the person I had become. More importantly, I gained keen insight into the lives of my immediate family members, most specifically, my sister. I feel like I only started to get to know Bridget after I died. In death, time simply disappears, gone with the last blink of your eyes as if the entire concept is as contrived as a manmade lake, or a dam built to pause the flow of the inevitable. There is no such thing as the temporal. The clock halts its hands and our consciousness becomes boundless, it becomes one with nature's elements, just as your body will, and flows like ashes in the wind.

And I got to know my sister.

All of our distractions and our limitations are self-imposed. They may be born from sociological pressures or delivered through a set of neuroses generously passed down from the genetically fucked-up bloodlines of the generations that precede us, but it is our own failures, the prison of our own making, that prevents us from overcoming our limitations. What became clear to me is that I was so lost inside my music, the music around me as well as the music inside my head, that I failed to notice the other human beings in my life: my family. I got interested in music because of suicide, and then through suicide, I finally got to be interested in my family. I actually got to know them. Illusions are only maintained for the living, for all those in denial of the darkness that awaits. I can attest to the fact that I am finally over that denial – I shed the illusions, and I have embraced the darkness.

It is from that darkness that I compose these words.

***

Bridget browses the ever-increasing *Hip-Hop* section of Sam Goody Music in the Inter-County Shopping Center, the first mall in Westchester. The shopping hub is entirely outdoors, a vast single-floor strip mall with narrow concrete pathways connecting the storefronts, like a commercial sewer system funneling consumers from one store to the next, maximizing their desire to buy more shit that they really don't need. It's also an ideal locale for committing crimes, both petty and felonious. There's an underground system of tunnels built for the transporting of goods, which connects the retailers to each other. These arteries are off-limits to the general public, at least they are supposed to be; until a group of assailants armed with submachine guns and wearing ski masks infiltrated them in the late eighties, breaking into several stores, tying up employees and cleaning out the cash registers and the stock of Waterford Crystal. More recently, there was an alleged incident of a dead whore being discovered in a garbage dumpster in the parking lot, minus the majority of her left tit, but according to an anonymous employee, this didn't necessitate any changes to mall policy.

This is around the time when Gangsta' Rap is on the road to acceptance in the Westchester suburbs, but what would surprise most of its new white fans and what Bridget didn't know at the time, is that in just a few years, the best golfer in the world will be black, and the best rapper in the world will be white. If I didn't know any better, I would have also thought that Christ would be coming back to judge the living and the dead. It would have seemed more likely. Before we know it, there will be a mulatto president, and shortly after that, the most famous person in the world will not even be a real person, but a holographic celebrity created by the Viacom corporation. But I'm getting well ahead of myself, and yourself as well.

Right at this time, the moment shortly after my suicide, things are changing and Bridget is miles ahead of the curve.

Bridget flips through the CD's under "N" in the bins of Sam Goody, snapping through the discs until landing on a copy of The Notorious B.I.G.'s debut album, *Ready To Die*, packaged inside of an elongated cardboard box to deter shoplifters. She picks it up and surveys the album cover: a diminutive black infant, with a gigantic afro, sitting against a white backdrop. She imagines herself as a child, an infant being held by her parents, and sporting an afro. She wonders if it's possible that her parents would see the humor in this, or if they would still love her if this had been her fate. How old was I when I started to resent her for being born, for stealing my parents' attention away from me? Was it immediate, or did it grow like a cancer as I got older? Did I make this grudge worse by nursing it, instead of letting it go the way a good sibling would? An altogether normal reaction, biologically appropriate, but not something that any older sibling would brag about, not something you want rattling around in you as you pull the scales from your eyes in death. Resentfully, I always saw her mental illness as a strategy to redirect parental attention back to her, to prevent the attention she stole from ever returning to me. In death, I saw how lame this idea was, how convoluted, but I had to rationalize it somehow while it was happening to me, rationalize what made my sister so different from me. Mental illness begs intellectual analysis; after all, it's a matter of the mind, even though no intellectual analysis ever resolved any mental illness.

Maureen approaches Bridget in the store aisle.

"Are you ready to go?"

Bridget nods, grabs the CD, and heads to the block of registers.

Back in my house, *the Harrison House*, the foyer is empty. The lock on the front door attempts to spin, but the key being inserted from the outside spins nothing, since it's already unlocked. The front door swings cautiously open into the room. Maureen, Bridget and William amble inside, cumbersome snowflake-themed shopping bags in hand. For the first time in a long while, the three of them actually seem familial. But this snapshot of domesticity is quickly overshadowed by what they believe is either a complete lack of responsibility by their son, or a breach of security by an intruder of some sort. William calls out into the corridors of the house –

"Thomas?"

Maureen heads down the front hall as William closes the door, locking it securely behind him.

"You left the door unlocked," William shouts.

I have come to appreciate that it's impossible for a man with the temperament and life experiences of my father to be anything other than a stickler for security; security for his country, security for other countries, provided it's our country that's securing them, and finally, security for his family. Still, it's hard not to harbor some level of resentment for a man who is worrying about the front door being locked while his only son lies in his father's bed, dead of a gunshot wound to the head. What does it gain William to be such a proponent of keeping the bad influence out, if, in doing so, he neglects to realize that what he's locked safely inside has corrupted itself? The corruption of my suicide is like a snake that eats its own tail, like the kind of virus that thrives in isolation, and this corruption will shortly bring its toxic effects into the lives of my family.

Bridget trundles upstairs, dragging the bottom of her Sam Goody bag against the tops of the steps. As she turns toward her room, the open door of our parents' bedroom looms behind her. Bridget stops, as though sensing something, a feeling beyond the reach of normal human impulse, the kind of feeling that, in retrospect, can convince us of the supernatural, of the spiritual, of the sublime. Something that a sister senses. Maybe there's some truth to the idea that the living can feel the dead on their doorsteps, that there is a residual presence of the loved ones we have lost that remains with us forever. She slowly pivots on her feet and heads toward our parents' room.

Bridget enters our parents' room. She drops her bag on the floor. She stumbles against the bed. She is stunned by the sight.

She leans over my inert body, emotion flitting across her face and through her mind in untraceable ways. My eyes are wide open, even though they are misshapen by the track of the bullet through my head, bloodied by the resulting wound. The back of my head is like an excavated cave, hollowed out by dynamite and the remnants of my skull are scattered behind me on the bed, shards of bone, strips of flesh, chunks of grey matter and pints of blood have all become an inextricable component of the soft comforter that warmed our parents at night. Bridget crawls up onto the bed beside me like an animal nuzzling its kin for warmth in the dead of winter. She reaches for a chunk of brain, like Jackie Kennedy in Dallas. Grabbing the dripping chunk, she observes it, scrutinizing what looks like a melted marshmallow dipped in bright red corn syrup, before trying to put it back into my head.

Bridget pauses for a moment to examine this historic scene in her life.

She reaches over, grabbing my lifeless hand. Maybe she's trying to find a pulse, maybe she just needs to touch me, to make sure that it's all real, that this is actually happening. She gently lies back on the bed, scrunching the folds of the covers, and curls up next to the slab of mutton that used to be me.

Just as Mom walks into the room.

Maureen screams. It's impossible to describe the sound, but it's primal in a way that we all recognize, but rarely do we identify it as human; it's more like the plaintive cry of an animal in the wild mixed with the industrial splintering of metal, a sound more like the feedback from overdriven guitar amplifiers, from the Marshall stacks Kurt Cobain used to destroy on stage at the conclusion of every Nirvana show, a sound that Maureen is clearly not designed to produce and yet a sound that comes out of her as naturally as her first born child came out of her on the day of his birth.

It sounds like *Endless, Nameless.*

The shock and the powerful decibel range of her scream triggers a silent alarm, shutting down her body as she collapses to the ground.

CHAPTER TWELVE

The Harrison family occupies the first pew of the cavernous church, their muscles as tight as marching band snare drums. Though they're trying to appear composed, William and Maureen are a singular mess, as are so many others in attendance. Since they're in the front row, their emotions are concealed by the fact that their backs are facing the rest of the parishioners, not that their overt display of emotions are any concern to them at all. In these moments of grief, most thoughts of composure are discarded right along with loyalty to God and church. Grief is the great destroyer of faith. How impossible it is to retain one's sense of a just God when He has summarily dispatched one of the single most important people in your life, how easy to curse God with a vehemence that borders on the irrational for taking someone who matters so much, and in the days, weeks and months that follow, how hard it is not to resent the living, resent those who have been spared death when your loved one was not, how painful to see the old, the weak, the fat and the unjust continue on with their lives when they so clearly don't deserve to be alive as much as the one you loved.

Bridget, unlike all the others there, is patently stone-faced. She's an impression of a Greek statuette. An unseen tenor, obese from the sound of it, brings his thunderous rendition of "*Ave Maria*" to a resounding close.

Father McSweeney, adjusting a pencil-thin microphone on the elevated marble podium, pronounces, "At this time, I would like to invite Thomas's sister, Bridget, up to the pulpit for a reading."

Bridget stands, shuffling out of the pew. In the aisle, she takes a solitary step toward the altar at the front of the church. She's never been a big fan of the church to begin with, having only attended services when Mom and Dad forced her to on Christmas Eve and sometimes Easter. She had wanted to be an altar server, back in St. Joe's Elementary School, mostly because you got out of class once every two weeks and she wanted in on that just like I had been when I was a student there. But they're called *altar boys* for a very specific reason: you have to be a boy to be eligible to be one. Bridget wasn't allowed to be one, for no good reason, in her opinion – at least no reason that was apparent until years later when the massive abuse scandal broke and she realized that the privilege of being an altar boy had some pretty serious potential drawbacks. That this controversy would mar the image of the Catholic Church for decades seemed like some measure of justice to Bridget, but that wasn't part of what ticked her off about being excluded, it was all much simpler than that: if they can't include her in their rituals, why should she include them in hers?

Bridget stops in the aisle, turns around, and walks straight out of the church. It has nothing much to do with God, it's not that she's turning away from Him, or Her, even though that might be a suitably symbolic gesture in her current state of grief, but such a gesture would have required her to have been inclined toward God in the first place. It's not that she resents her exclusion from the inner sanctum of altar boys, even though she does hang on to some bitterness. Bridget simply wants to leave, she wants to get out of the building, a building whose owners are too cheap to keep the heat on high because it's staggeringly freezing inside there this morning, a building that suddenly seems stifling, not with heat, of course, but with the fetish of suffering. Maureen weeps, pain clogging each orifice of her face, pain in every part of her, in her bones, in her pores, so much pain that it even feels like her hair hurts. William shakes his head in irritation at the departure of Bridget, but he is not surprised that he is watching his daughter depart. Nothing Bridget does surprises William. It's the certainty of her complete lack of reliability that defines William's perception of his daughter, accepting that she will never do anything he expects is how he understands her. Jeremy, sitting torpidly with his band members in a middle row, watches Bridget leave the ornamental structure, her silhouette disappearing as the double-doors close behind her.

Bridget sits outside on the cobblestone steps of St. Joe's smoking a cigarette that's beginning to canoe. Light snowflakes fall softly around her; the dandruff of the asshole who created this whole mess. She recognizes the natural part of grief that leads her to want to blame someone and it makes her feel better. Jeremy totters out of a side door and slowly approaches his friend's sister. He buttons up his pea coat and stands his collar up around his neck as he sits down beside her.

"Only difference between me and your brother is that I was lucky," Jeremy says. "Or maybe I was just too much of a pussy to cut the opposite way – down the veins, instead of across."

Bridget looks away from Jeremy, disturbed by the honesty and by the fact that he isn't holding back his emotions; he's not one of those guys, quite the opposite.

"My parents blamed themselves for what I did to myself but, really, no one has a clue what other people feel. It's not your fault, Bridget. You just have to keep on going…keep on living your life. I know that's easy for me to say, but I wouldn't say it at all if there wasn't some kind of truth in it."

Jeremy and Bridget are similar people, similar souls. They both see through to the truth of things, and to some extent, they both saw through to the truth of me. They saw me for what I really am, or was. That's not meant to be a self-criticism. They are in the minority, as they saw past the illusions, whereas most of us crave the illusions, like narcotics – we want to see them, and we go out of our way to do so, hoping that they will prop up the edifice of our lives and keep the uglier truths hidden. We want so desperately to be fooled into believing that as long as we build a perfect white picket fence along our property line, everything will be perfect behind it.

Jeremy keeps on talking: "I used to wear long-sleeved shirts all the time, on the hottest, most humid summer days, just so I could cover up the jagged scars on my wrists."

He rolls up his sleeve, showing Bridget the evidence.

"I didn't want to alarm people, I didn't want to make people feel uncomfortable, like I was pressing the issue in some way that would force someone to ask me about it, or to feel guilty because they didn't know how to ask me about it."

The story hangs there between them for a moment. Bridget reaches her fingers out, delicately tracing the scars on Jeremy's arm. He's the one trying to be strong for Bridget, so he wouldn't want to tell her that no one has ever touched those scars before, no one but Jeremy and the doctor who stitched him up.

"I'll tell you what, from this day forward, I'm never going to cover them up again, and I'm going to do it for Thomas."

Maybe it took Jeremy opening up to her, genuinely sharing some of the fucked-up experiences that he had been through, that he had in common with Bridget, and that he had in common with me. In the days since it happened, Bridget hadn't shed a single tear about my suicide. Until this moment. I don't fault her for that. She has had her own share of demons to deal with over the years. That she shared those tears with Jeremy seems fitting to me. I always thought they should have been friends. That she also took this moment to quote a Nirvana lyric, or attempt to anyway, written by a singer-songwriter who she had always held in great contempt, that was really surprising.

"All alone is all we are," Bridget says.

The fact that she misquoted him didn't matter. Her error seemed to make the lyric better than it originally was. Jeremy puts his arm around her and they both cry together.

She doesn't push him away.

***

In the Harrison backyard, William holds a running garden hose up to my sneakers, the pair of Cons with the band-aids that I labored over nearly every day to keep together. He's spraying the specks of blood off of them. Probably should've thrown them out a long time ago, but now they've become a memento, a keepsake, an emblem of the feet his son's famous legs once deployed to guide him through what was going to be a promising life.

This is about the time when family members, relatives, friends and foes, are meant to get back to the business at hand, to press on and put the past behind them. Life goes on.

Bridget sits in front of her easel in her bedroom, staring at a blank canvas, the depth of which is intimidating. Her emotions are not as blank as they used to be, but she is still at odds with herself, still struggling to find a way to express the chaotic feelings inside, to find a suitable outlet for her manic energy. The radio plays, muted in the background, an unmemorable Snapple commercial promoting some unlikely combination of fake fruit flavors. Bridget used to drink Snapple, when Howard Stern advertised the bottles between the breasts of lesbians, propelling the unknown soft drink company into becoming the first of the new wave of challengers to the thrones of Coke and Pepsi, only to watch the company get swallowed whole by Quaker Oats in 1994. Once Snapple went mainstream and began selling their product in Lange's Delicatessen in Bronxville, Bridget stopped drinking it altogether. As she's about to change the channel, the radio returns to its musical programming –

"It's time to announce the next band to place in the top five of 102.7's 'Battle Of The Unsigned Bands.'"

Bridget perks up, which for her is barely a prickle, but in this case it's enough to remove her finger from the dial.

"With their song, 'Turbulence,' it's The Latterday Saints –"

"Turbulence" begins to play, its sparse rhythms and forceful vocals shining through her tinny speakers. Bridget turns the volume up, her eyes brightening in response to the music.

Some hours later, on the sprawling porch in the backyard, Bridget stands at the porch railing with Maureen smoking a cigarette and flicking the ashes nervously into an aluminum ashtray that rests between the two women on the balustrade. William stands at the other end of the yard, meticulously trimming the tops and sides of the hedges that demarcate their property line, a chore he takes on even though winter isn't quite over yet; he has to do something.

"I wish he was here to enjoy this," says Maureen.

Maureen grabs the cigarette from her daughter. But things have changed; changed in ways that will impact everything they do together, as a family, for the rest of their lives. Maureen doesn't judge. She doesn't scold. She takes a drag of it instead.

"I remember watching The Beatles on television when I was a teenager, about your age, come to think of it, on The Ed Sullivan Show. And it was just the best thing I'd ever seen. They played '*Help!*.'"

Maureen scrutinizes her husband in the distance, balancing himself precariously on a ladder over the hedges, while she pulls another drag on the cigarette. In this period after my death, conversations among family members went a lot like this. A memory would be brought out, just a little piece of a memory though, because as soon as the first part was articulated, each family member would see the emptiness inherent in discussing the memory further, as if my absence sucked the life out of conversations or as if the pain of my memory poisoned the wells of other memories in some residual fashion. I know that the memory of the Beatles was important to my Mom and that she had never been able to get that performance out of her head. She touches on it with Bridget, but keeps it short. Maybe it's hard for her to talk about it because she realizes it so obviously sounds like she is talking about me. Nevertheless, after my death, she remembers John Lennon, singing that specific song in front of hundreds of boisterous teenagers, bobbing up and down, their only worries stretching as far as the bubble gum they stepped in before the show and she sees the performance quite differently. Maybe she sees it more clearly now, as if for the first time, because she sees John Lennon as this wounded individual, pouring his heart out on stage, his voice filled with unbearable pain, pleading for help, but there is no one in the audience able to hear him, there is no one anywhere in the world who is able to help him.

"It's a misunderstood song," Maureen says.

She hands the cigarette back to her daughter, approximately three years before Bridget can smoke one legally, and walks inside the house. Bridget looks over at our father trimming the hedge, and then she glances down at my sparkling clean Converse sneakers sitting at the edge of the porch. Bridget picks up my sneakers and holds them in her hands for a few moments. She has the idea of misunderstanding right in the front of her mind. John Lennon doesn't mean anything to Bridget, but she can certainly relate to the idea of being misunderstood. She thinks about the attachments that I had in my life, my obsession with the grunge scene, with creating the precise look that was a requirement of that scene, she thinks about how this scene must have had an influence on the way I lived my life and the way I ended my life. Without realizing it, Bridget has wandered over to the gas grill that occupies a corner of the patio. The judge was the first guy on the block to buy the newest and most deluxe Weber gas grill, the one with the stainless steel surfaces, warming rack, the two extra burners on the side in case you needed to boil water or stir fry some onions for your burger. The judge loves his Weber. Bridget opens up the top of the grill and places my sneakers right in the center of the rack. She fires up the grill and watches as the footwear begins to smolder and melt, black smoke corkscrewing into the air. She sniffs the air, but only for a split second, testing the acrid stench of the sneakers before retreating into the house.

William turns, spotting the billowing smoke. He nearly kills himself as he hastens down his ladder at the double, tossing his clippers aside, the blades stabbing perfectly into the sponge-like ground, and rushes over to the grill. He stares at the flaming shoes, the melted rubber embedding itself into the stainless steel grate, a steel grate that he struggles to keep in showroom condition, a grate that, only a few minutes ago, might have been mistaken for brand new but now appears as if it's been the victim of years of untidy culinary abuse.

He peers at the sliding glass door, expecting to see the lurking figure of his daughter, who has been known to gloat over her little pranks, but Bridget is nowhere in sight, the house is eerily silent. The only sign of life is William's semitransparent reflection in the glass of the door, glowering with palpable unrest, as it's superimposed over the innards of an empty kitchen.

***

An AA Meeting (Alcoholics Anonymous; 12 Steps; honk if you know Bill) is underway. These are meetings that transcend description; you know what they look like. Don't pretend that you don't.

Bridget sits in a circle of about fifteen people, an eclectic group, typical for such meetings. The circle is impressively geometrical, for a circle drawn by folding chairs. This isn't surprising, considering the visible indentations on the floor from other circles and other meetings. Bridget notices the indentations, notices the number of chairs, and wonders why there are only fifteen chairs, if there had always been fifteen, would there always be fifteen chairs, why is fifteen so special? Bridget notices this so that she won't notice the people staring at her. The meeting is held in the basement of St. Joe's, the same place my band played its first, only, and now legendary gig. Legendary as far as the locals and band members are concerned. The shortest legendary gig ever, made infamous by my suicide. It makes me a little sad that my death made it more famous than the music or the performance. St. Joe's basement is also the space below where my funeral was held. The gig was a much more memorable event for me. Stewart, seated next to Bridget in the circle, stands up and addresses the modest group:

"I invited my friend, Bridget, here to listen – I told her she would be among friends and that we're all here to support her."

He turns to Bridget, who pumps her foot anxiously, clutching her sizeable purse in her fingerless-gloved hands, a pair of gloves made all the more ridiculous by the neon seahorses stitched into them.

"I told her she didn't have to speak or say anything—"

"I'd like to say something," Bridget interrupts.

Stewart plays it completely straight. "It's up to you… whatever you're comfortable with."

Bridget stands slowly, as straight as her posture will allow, while she works up the nerve to address the folks around her. She clears her throat. It's not that she's nervous, but rather that she wants to communicate to the others around her that she might be nervous, hoping that this will generate more sympathy for her and encourage those gathered to listen with an open mind. She has reason to believe that they will need to keep their minds open to cope with what she's about to lay on them.

"Stewart has been encouraging me to attend a meeting. However resistant I was at first, I now see this as an incredible opportunity."

The group nods, knowingly.

"I've struggled for a very long time, a lot longer than you might think for someone my age, and after many years of thinking about this and struggling with my problem, I've made the informed decision to take myself off all prescription medications prescribed to me by my doctor, my headshrinker, as I like to call him. After all, what's the point of living if you don't feel a fucking thing, right?"

Stewart sits up in his chair, "Bridget, if you're feeling depressed, we can help."

Bridget completely ignores him. Now that she has started, she doesn't want to stop.

"These shrinks have cornered the market – they can run circles around your average crack dealer or heroin pusher, in fact, they're the real drug dealers in our contemporary culture, dishing out FDA sanctioned goodies for just about anyone who says they're having some little problem in their lives. And I've been their guinea pig for way too long."

She opens her purse, pulling prescription pill bottles from its canvas belly.

"The way I see it, if they're gonna cash in, I'm gonna cash in too."

She holds the bottles up, displaying them as if she's a seasoned sales model on QVC or the Home Shopping Network.

"For today and today only, I'm offering you the chance of a lifetime, a chance to take a variety of legal medicine that will rock your world harder than any stuff you've ever been on. This is the real deal, the pure stuff, both uppers and downers, and you are the target demographic for such stimulants, sedatives, and mood enhancers; you're the reason the pharmaceutical companies have spent millions, maybe even billions, of dollars making these fantastic pills and I'm willing to offer you these outrageous deals because you're friends of my friend, Stewart."

Stewart shrinks in his seat, as low as he can, while others gape at the spectacle Bridget is making of herself.

"My allowance was cut off a long time ago because I'm just not very reliable when it comes to money, so I'll be honest here – I'm strapped for cash. And I'll be damned if any more of Mommy and Daddy's hard earned income is going to fund Dr. Happy and his summer house in the Hamptons."

She holds up one specific bottle, sporting a forced and cartoonish smile –

"Zoloft. 80 milligrams. Great stuff. Do I have any offers?"

There is nothing but stunned silence.

The conclusion of the meeting having arrived much earlier than is usual for such get-togethers, Bridget and Stewart trudge away from the church, slogging along the snow-covered pavement.

"You really fucking embarrassed me in there," Stewart says, visibly upset.

"Yeah, sorry. I guess."

"Why bother to come at all if you're just planning to make an ass out of yourself, dragging me along in the debacle, for shits and giggles?"

"I hadn't planned to do any of that, Stewart. I've been feeling really confused lately, and I thought, maybe, these meetings might help me, but I wasn't sure how. I didn't know what I was going to do with those pills, but I knew I wanted to get rid of them and then, suddenly, selling them to your AA friends seemed like the best option that was available to me."

"Is that an apology?"

Bridget chuckles, "Wash me from my iniquity, and cleanse me from my sins."

"I wish I had the authority."

Stewart swings off his backpack, zipping it open. He pulls out Bridget's discarded keyboard that she left for dead on the bench of the train platform. He restores it to its rightful owner.

"This is yours."

"Thanks," Bridget replies. She takes the instrument and bounces, sidestepping through the perilous sleet.

***

William assumes his position at the head of the kitchen table, sipping his piping hot cup of instant coffee while reading *the Times*. Bridget enters the room and stops short right in front of our father. She's embracing her insolence, intentionally interrupting his ritual, his weekend meditation. William knows she is doing this for a reason, so he refuses to look up at her. Bridget stands there, looking at our father, waiting, knowing that he will eventually look up at her, will lift his eyes to meet her eyes. In works of literature, in theatrical scene direction and screenplays far and wide, the descriptive look, freighted with meaning or seething with emotion, is undeniably overused but its power and the truth of such looks in our daily lives is nonetheless undiminished. The power of a look should not be underestimated. In all social situations, we are hardwired to orient ourselves by finding the eyes of another person – whether that person is sitting in front of us, is up on a screen, or in the glossy pages of a magazine. We find our place in the world through the eyes of other people. For better, or for worse. We communicate through our eyes, in a much more profound sense than through any of the words we could hope to assemble from our impressive collegiate vocabularies. A word can have different meanings, but a look is never misunderstood. That which goes unsaid in conversation and in relationships, is often transferred directly through a look. A look says everything, without ever saying a thing. As with most intense family relationships, an entire lifetime has gone unarticulated between Bridget and William, novels full of words have never been expressed because a look was enough. I could say the same thing about my father and me. Most children could probably say the same thing with respect to their parents, no matter how benign, or tragic, the relationships may have been.

William raises his eyes to meet the eyes of his daughter. This particular look of Bridget's is the kind of look that could fill the volumes of a ten part Russian epic, it could blind the eyes of an invading army, it could make a long lost brother proud of his little sister – and it will make up for the sum total of accumulated silence in both of our brief lives, with years and years, volumes and volumes to spare.

But the look, even though it's powerful, is not enough for Bridget.

"How could you let this happen?"

William pushes up his reading glasses by its wire bridge, securing them to his brow, as he struggles to address his daughter's allegation. He's used to making allegations. He's accustomed to weighing their validity. He is much less familiar with being the accused. And what father, no matter how well prepared, no matter how well versed in parrying accusations, could possibly be ready to defend himself in these circumstances?

"I took precautions," he responds, lamely.

Bridget glares at him. She's not going to let it go, but neither is he –

"You could never understand."

"Why don't you try, Daddy?"

William wonders if the truth is ever a good idea.

"I didn't think this was going to happen to *him*."

As soon as she hears it, Bridget knows perfectly well that there's nothing left to say. She understands what he has said, she can even see a little bit of truth in it, but she's pretty damned sure that she will never forgive him for saying it. The funny thing is, she realizes that most of her conversations with our father have gone this way, countless times before. The words were never the same, not even close, but the words don't mean much in the grand scheme of things. They could have recited *The Declaration of Independence* to each other, but he would still be saying the same thing, and she would still be hearing the same thing, because she could see the words in his eyes –

"I didn't think this was going to happen to *him*."

Bridget strides out of the room, leaving nothing but the ghostly echo of her flip-flops against the linoleum floor. William sits in stupefied silence for a moment or two. He's a sturdy man, a man who has always been a pillar of strength for his family and his community. The last thing Bridget would expect from our father and the last thing he would want her to see, is what he does right now. Alone in his small kitchen, with a cooling and flavorless cup of instant coffee sitting in front of him, William begins to cry. He stares at a set of matching salt and pepper shakers left on the table from last night's dinner. He tries to focus on the shakers, as a means of focusing on something, before his ability to focus goes away. He cries tears of guilt and pain, tears of untold parental regret, tears that come in torrents and are accompanied by wracking sobs; the sobs and the tears that sting his face feel like they make an indelible impression on him, an impression that will remain until all impressions fade.

He does nothing to keep this impression to himself, but there is no one here to share in his grief or bring solace to his suffering. He hangs his head over his New York Times and watches his tears stain the thin folds of the paper, each droplet spreading rapidly, expanding in circumference as they are absorbed, a whole series of wet splotches scattered across the article like Rorschach drawings, an article about Middle Eastern politics that he will not remember reading, that he cannot even remember in this moment, as the paper sucks up his tears like a sponge.

He knows these spots will eventually dry and the evidence of his emotional distress will fade, on both the paper and his face. There is no one in the house close enough to bear witness to his disintegration. No one in the house, except me. In an impossible trick of death, I'm closer to my father now than ever before, bound to him by the threads of grief.

There's a part of me that can say that I never liked the man, that I never felt his affection, I never felt the love that a father should have for his son, that he withheld that love and that I begrudge him for it, that I never felt any of the powerful emotional connections that a child should feel for his parent.

Until now.

Which is to say, until it was too late.

***

Bridget finds herself in the garage, behind my set of drums. She looks around the drums, taking in the look of them from this angle, a perspective with which she is completely unfamiliar, sitting, as she is, within the centrifuge of my life. Just as engineers use centrifuges for separating cream from milk, or for isolating isotopes in the implementation of modern nuclear weapons, Bridget theorizes that I used my drums as a means of separating myself from my family, my community, even my friends, from the construct of the world as everyone else perceived it, everyone else, but me. When I was behind my drums, did my soul separate? Was this the beginning of my inevitable end? I worked hard at keeping it all inside, keeping my uncontrollable centrifugal forces of teenage angst whirling within, keeping these forces at bay, even though I enjoyed a taste of dispensing with these forces while beating the drums and riding the waves of distorted rhythm. But there's the contradiction of the drums: while the instrument allowed me to experience some semblance of release, it kept me separated from the rest of the world, from the real world, the world in which its inhabitants bond in other ways than just making music.

It kept me from truly confronting the dangerous forces that I kept bottled up inside of me. Forces that my sister regularly dealt with also, but forces that she took great pleasure in releasing. Hurricane Bridget.

Bridget stands up, stepping in front of the kit. She takes one last good look, and then she grabs the nearby bed sheet and tosses it over the drums, retiring them to the unused status the instrument held at the beginning of this ordeal.

As she stares at this lifeless mass of musical equipment, a knuckle raps on the garage door. Bridget engages the door opener and the wooden door creaks open, raveling itself neatly into a series of tracks and suspension wires bolted into the ceiling.

Jeremy is standing there, on the other side, where the driveway roughly joins the bottom lip of the garage.

"You're early," Bridget remarks.

"Are you ready?"

There is a hunch to Jeremy's spine, like what he's carrying inside his skull is too heavy for his lean body. Bridget is obviously hesitant, but she knows she has to react, as if the question is bigger than both of them, and the answer a foregone conclusion.

"I don't know if I can…"

Jeremy reaches out, takes hold of her hand. Her arm relaxes; she lets her fingers wrap around his, grazing the scar on his wrist with her thumb. He squeezes her hand tightly and the look he gives her is calm and assured, like he trusts her in a way that he's never allowed himself to trust others before.

"Yes, you can."

CHAPTER THIRTEEN

CBGB's. Country, Blue Grass and Blues. This is where the legendary music club in the Bowery got its name. Tonight, it's none of those three and it hasn't been for almost two decades, ever since Joey Ramone and his band of brothers commandeered the modest stage in the late 1970's, shunting the more mainstream and less abrasive line-ups into musical oblivion. A plethora of punk rockers, the kind who fit into the label's current subcategories, line up along the sidewalk outside the club, the ad hoc spawn of The Ramones who have enshrined this place for twenty years.

Inside, the place is packed. The band, At A Loss, performs their song, *"Cut Before The Death Scene,"* on the main stage. They jump around, singing hard, playing hard, strutting and preening, putting on a rock show as if it was their real job. Maybe it will be, someday. The crowd crammed into the small floor in front of the stage springs back and forth, pogos up and down, some mosh, some slam dance, and a few daring ones crowd-surf.

Backstage, the music continues, muted by rickety walls covered in hyperbolic bumper stickers of punk rock bands from

A to Z. Connor, Jeremy and Elias mill about, dressed to the nines in tailored men's suits, matching grey with a subtle eye-pleasing pinstripe. The suits aren't Madison Avenue, because the boys have yet to sell their souls to the man and colonize an office cubicle, but for teenagers they look damn spiffy. The outfits are utterly out of place in a room filled with bands and music industry flunkies, all of whom are dressed in the height of grunge fashion: cardigans, torn jeans, women's sunglasses, chain wallets, Converse sneakers, Doc Marten's, wool beanies, flannel shirts, babydoll dresses, long-sleeve thermals under T-shirts. Everyone else looks exactly the same. Anywhere else on the planet, the Latterday Saints look like the establishment, but right now, in this Mecca of the world of underground music, they're the ones who look different. What used to be considered underground couldn't be anymore above-the-ground at this point and a part of this teenage trio wishes it would go back underground, to die. The boys lean against a peeling wall and stare at everyone else. A brick shithouse of a drummer from a rival band, The Posers, saunters by hauling a bass drum with a metallic mirror finish. Their reflections bend and warp in the drum, making them all feel just a little bit more unreal when compared to the rest of the musicians. Elias thinks for a moment that the drummer is dishing some attitude in their direction, but maybe it's just nerves.

At the opposite end of the corridor, Trevor Underwood, a record executive dressed down for the occasion, weaves his way through the bowels of the club like a rat in a maze and approaches the fledgling band.

"You're the Latterday Saints?"

"Yes," Connor responds.

"I heard your demo. 'Turbulence' is the name of the song."

"Yeah."

"I like it," Trevor says.

The executive looks them over, tooth to toenail.

"Nice suits. My name is Trevor Underwood. I'm head of A&R at Capitol Records," he discloses, as if it's some high-level government classification and he's bound by national security to keep it quiet. "You have a good sound...could be the new face of grunge."

Trevor says this like he's waving a strip of bacon in front of the nose of a Basset Hound. The boys can smell it; they can smell the bacon.

Trevor grins, overenthusiastically; the creases in his face stretching like condensed rubber. The band nods courteously. Trevor dispenses a series of cursory slaps to their backs and shoulders, then continues his swagger down the crowded hall-way. *The Saints* watch as he approaches a rival band, shaking their hands and performing the same song and dance.

"What a load of shit," Elias barks.

At A Loss finishes up their song, rocking it out on stage –

"I can't surrender, 'cause I've been through this before. So cut before

the death scene, 'cause they're pointing every finger at me. /

I don't remember, tragedy is such a bore. So cut before the death

scene, 'cause they're pointing every finger."

They let the chords to the chorus ring out, playing with the tipping point of feedback within the amps in a passable way, with just the right mixture of experience and disinterest. They jump up in unison, including the drummer who lifts his ass a few inches off his throne, before striking the final note on their instruments as their feet slam back onto the ground.

Backstage, the applause is muted. But there is applause. Backstage. The boys have competition; that much is clear, even as the reaction settles down to a restrained murmur. It's also clear that there are other kids their age who have their sights set on the windfall of grunge. Connor opens his faux-leather guitar case and pulls out a gleaming sunburst Fender Jaguar, strapping it on his chest.

"Had it modified," Connor says. "Cost me a pretty penny, but it was worth that beautiful piece of copper."

Elias and Jeremy both nod with enthusiasm, but their reactions are as surface as the sunburst paint on Connor's guitar. Connor had finally saved up enough to purchase the instrument – I wasn't there when he bought it, but I'm glad that he did. Right now, Connor is trying to be light, trying to remind his bandmates that the point of rock and roll is to have fun with your friends. But this is a competition and they have lost a friend and the strain hangs heavily on each of their shoulders like Connor's new fancy guitar. Jeremy looks at an oversized clock on a nearby wall and stares at it listlessly, watching the seconds tick away, feeling the weight of time as well, in the way that only happens when you are under stress in your life. I'm with them at this moment, this moment matters to me, but I can't help them in any way; it's more likely that my presence in their thoughts and in their hearts is only a distraction, something that they would be better off without.

An obnoxiously loud production assistant gripping a walkie-talkie scurries up to them, breaking the lethargy and the reverie.

"You guys are on next," the kid informs them.

***

An announcer stands in the center of the stage, his hair slicked back and a microphone clenched in his hand, as he peers into the eager eyes of the gathered crowd on the floor. Before each band appears, he runs through the same stupid little speech, as if the scripted pabulum must be exactly the same on the video for whoever wins this damn competition:

"One band will walk away tonight with a record contract. Each band performs one original song. One song, one contract—"

The cheers build in the crowd; it's standing room only and they want something to move to. Or maybe they just want to drown out the stupid little introduction.

"Let's please welcome the next band. With their song, 'Turbulence...' the Latterday Saints!"

Elias, Connor and Jeremy strut onto the shadowy abyss of the stage. There's something profound about the moment when a band steps on stage and the audience can't see them and they can't see the audience, like both parties are invisible to each other or are blinded by an air of anticipation before the band is consumed by the work of presenting their music. The audience bristles with expectation because the band isn't quite human yet, isn't entirely fleshed out on stage. There are still infinite possibilities relating to what might happen in the show, how the music will lift the hearts of everyone in attendance in some mutual rhapsody, or how you, as a special part of the audience, may find a connection to the band unavailable to all other spectators. Before the band plays, it is just the song that you know, or the record you know, because that's all there is for you to know about them, that's all that exists, the record that you've worn out from repeat listening. In that moment of expectation, there might be a camera flash or a random spotlight, just enough for you to catch a brief glimpse of them as they bend over an amp or adjust a cymbal stand. They are still a mystery, they haven't had the opportunity to ruin your perception, to slur the lyrics of your favorite song because the front-man had one too many backstage, it's still new and there's only expectation and it's one of the best expectations, like getting ready to kiss someone for the very first time; it's innocent like a kiss, not knowing like sex. Those silhouettes on stage are filled with the brilliance of your imagination, the imagination that you use to animate what you'd like to see, what you think you will see, with the aid of the collective energy from those around you, screaming into your ears, whistling, clapping, the sounds of adrenaline, the pulse of hormones, and nothing but unadulterated rock-and-fucking-roll.

It's this imagination that fuels the legend that will momentarily unveil itself before your eyes.

Then Connor plugs in his guitar.

And Jeremy his bass.

And Elias, uncharacteristically, steps to the back of the stage and sits down behind the drums.

The lights sizzle on, revealing reality and stamping out your expectations. It's the light that ruins everything, that exposes the myth as man, that illuminates the imperfections and the human frailty of our stars, that wakes us up. It's the light that blinds. Moments ago, the darkness let us drift. Its shadow let us dream. But the darkness is gone, snuffed out like the short life of a firefly and it's the light that is left, shimmering on the metallic microphone stand that protrudes from the fading darkness that lingers on the stage.

This is the moment it's supposed to begin, the instant that's ingrained in the concert-goer's mind, when the lead singer, the front-man, the star reveals himself. But this time, the paradigm is turned on its head in a disconcerting manner, in a manner that implies that this disconcerting moment is only the beginning.

A light shines on the side of the stage and a production assistant pushes someone in a wheelchair toward the microphone stand. This unidentified person is wearing a long white hospital gown and has white bandages covering arms, hands and face.

The crowd cheers, not because they know who this person is and they admire him or her, but because it's a clear homage to Kurt Cobain's famous entrance to the show Nirvana played at the Reading Festival in England in 1992. These kids in the audience weren't anywhere near England at the time, but the concert has been making the rounds in the bootleg video community after Kurt's death and is heavily featured on the first official concert film, "*Live! Tonight! Sold-Out!!,*" released by Nirvana after the front-man's passing. As the wheelchair slows to a halt at the foot of the stand, this mysterious cripple reaches out, grabbing the stand for support, and stands up to the microphone, looking very much like a ghost.

The crowd goes quiet, either mesmerized or unable to know what to make of this, unable to tell if this is a heartfelt homage or something else entirely.

"You wanna know what 'grunge' means?"

If any member of the audience had attended one of the open mic nights at Slave To The Grind over the past couple of months, they would know this voice.

It's the voice of Bri Da B.

The crowd cheers for the word, as if the word itself is a rock star, a star they can't get enough of, a star who has come to dictate the trajectory of their lives.

"I said…do you wanna know what 'grunge' means?!"

It's not a coincidence that Bridget looks like Cobain during his appearance at the Reading Festival, because she chose to reference him in this way. She was never a fan of his music and she went out of her way to chide Thomas for his obsession with Cobain and his band, but that didn't mean she wasn't curious about the music and the musician that so captivated her brother. She loved Thomas and wanted to be included among his interests. Thomas had bought the bootleg of the Reading Festival on VHS from Rockin' Rex and he watched it incessantly at very loud volume. Bridget asked him to turn the volume down, but he never would. After Thomas started playing in the garage with his band at volumes that were truly offensive, the very idea of suggesting that this recorded concert was too loud seemed utterly laughable. She felt like she had to strategically reserve such requests for moments that really mattered. She had seen Thomas watch this Reading concert several times, especially the moment when Kurt is introduced. At the time of the event, there was a lot of speculation that the band was going to break up. This was around the time the band had just started getting really famous, and up until that point, Kurt Cobain's drug use had gone largely unreported. Prior to the Reading Festival, his habit became public, along with the details of several stints in rehab the month before they were to headline. This lead reporters to conclude that the band would be breaking up, that Kurt was mentally unstable, and that he was possibly suicidal. Even Nirvana's drummer and one of Kurt's best friends, Dave Grohl, said that they were finished, expressing doubts about whether or not Kurt was going to show up at the concert. Kurt did show up at the concert and was wheeled out in a wheelchair wearing a blonde wig and a hospital gown as a way of parodying the recent tabloid reports.

Kurt was toying with his audience, those attending the concert as well as fans and foes around the world. He was going to play a show if he wanted to, he was going to do heroin if he wanted to, he was going to kill himself if he wanted to — he was going to control what happened to him and his band, not the puppet-masters spanning the globe who desperately tried to pull him one way or another. This show that everyone thought would be canceled, this show that everyone thought would be Nirvana's last, is widely regarded as one of the best shows they ever played.

This was the last performance by Nirvana in the UK, and this show at CBGB's was to be the last show for Bri Da B.

"Grunge!"

Just the word, framed by itself and without any hint of context, elicits screams of excitement from the crowd, discordant cries of sycophantic banshees. As Bridget continues, her words bounce throughout the room, reverberating through the alternately frenzied and expectant crowd.

"It means dirt, filth, rubbish. Something of inferior quality; trash — an example — *He didn't know good music from grunge*. It means a person who works hard, usually for meager rewards. And finally, it's a style or fashion derived from a current movement in rock music — characterized by unkempt clothing, and in the music, by aggressive, nihilistic songs."

Bridget stares at the audience, eerie and angelic, her eyes glowing through the slits in her bandages.

But you know what's really grungy?"

Bridget's got the crowd, she's like a living piece of performance art and they can't take their eyes off of her. They don't have any idea about the cliff she's about to jump off, or about why she needs to jump off of it.

"My big brother."

The emotion hits her. The band sees it and the band understands it. The crowd sees it too, but they have no idea why Bridget is so emotional about her brother. No one in the room thinks for a moment that the emotion is an act, because they can see it so clearly, it's like a wrecking ball slamming into her, and she's the one wielding the controls. She holds the beat before she explains, she holds it because she doesn't know if she can muster the strength to talk about it, she holds it because she can see the expectation on the faces in the crowd and she doesn't want to let them down, she holds it because it is in this moment that she can honor Thomas, while everyone is thinking about him, even people who have no idea who her big brother was. She spits the following words out like they're burning her mouth:

"He blew his brains out with my father's gun because he couldn't deal with this stupid world anymore. I respect him for that. And I hate myself for that respect. He's my hero, 'cuz I know he looked at the world and thought…"

She chokes up, unable to control her unbalanced emotions any longer, and she endures this short moment of self-loathing, a spike inside her body which is wrapped up like a mummy inside these crazy bandages; she gets angry at herself for letting the emotion get to her, for her inability to finish the sentence. It's gone in a flash and the audience is still with her.

"I know that he looked at the world and thought, 'can't we do any better than this?'"

The venue is completely silent. Some idiot claps, but someone else grabs his hands, like he must have the worst taste of any person who has ever lived, or as if he's ruining the moment, such as it is. This dichotomy grips the audience; they don't know whether what they are watching is something to be applauded or something that would be diminished by an expression of appreciation. It's the way people deal with grief, too. Not knowing how to both acknowledge and soothe the grief of a friend, they usually drift into awkward silence.

"Heard about your bother. Sorry…" Feet shuffle, eyes go to the ground. Not much else is said. Bridget has seen a lot of this lately and she sees it out there in the crowd now. Not until this moment did she know how to handle such awkwardness. She realizes, while standing on the stage in silence, that no one else matters; the reaction of other people doesn't mean a thing to her or to her memory of Thomas. She feels like a great weight has been lifted off of her chest and she knows that she can do what she came here to do. She will pay tribute to her brother by expressing herself.

"Before tonight I might have told you, if you want to stop pretending, if you want to prove you're punk rock, if you really want to prove you're alive: commit suicide. That maybe that's the only punk rock thing left to do."

She smiles, but the genuine radiance of her smile is lost in the sea of bandages; she can feel herself really smiling, something that Bridget almost never does and thought she might never do again, and she knows that her expression is in absolute contrast to the faces of shock around her.

"But yesterday is yesterday…and it's as far away from me as the beginning of time. The world has moved on and it's ready for something new, something different from the music that meant so much to my brother and his band. My brother, Thomas, is dead; your saints and your angels are dead; grunge is dead."

Bridget somberly removes the bandages from her arms, hands and face, revealing her skin, all of which is painted black. She continues unraveling the bandages until what's left on her body is a black bikini and a wig; every inch of her is dark, dark as charcoal, all topped by an unruly head of blonde hair as she tosses the last of the gauze to the floor.

In another time and another place, she might be seen as a spectre, a demon, a heretic, a witch. She might have been mistaken for a mirage atop the land. But Bridget knows exactly who she is and she's ready to share.

"I'm Bri Da B."

The audience is confused, some are even offended, but regardless of how they feel, most of the people on the floor cannot take their eyes off of her. Bridget has literally become her alter ego; at least that's how it feels to her in her own head and in her boldly black body. She will not be a coward. She refuses to submit to the cowardice of suicide; she will fight it head on, she will control what so many others have failed to control and she will do all of this in her final performance as Bri Da B. Tonight, Bri Da B will be the one to commit suicide. She will perform this symbolic spectacle for the slackers standing in front of her, for the slackers listening on the radio at home, and for slackers everywhere who are hungry for suicide and its attendant fruits of fear, angst and self-loathing. She will do this in order to release herself from the powerful grasp, the intoxicating grip, of Bri Da B.

Bridget will inject every atom of her hard-hitting persona into this last performance; and in doing so, she will deplete the alter ego of any life force it had and prevent it from ever surfacing again. She got what she needed out of Bri Da B and tonight she will put him to rest.

Elias breaks into a hip-hop drumbeat that's accompanied by Connor and Jeremy playing a funky groove on their strings. Bridget busts into *"Republican,"* her song about our father, and raps with all the self-assurance, confidence and bravado she can muster, as if she were the reincarnation of Biggie or Tupac himself, Bri Da B's larger than life personality flourishing inside her slender feminine figure:

"My Daddy's a republican, his daughter's a pimp,

I got dreads in my hair and I walk with a limp./

Supreme Court ain't nothin' when you live in the hood,

the ladies want your dick and they want your goods./

At work Daddy puts thugs in jail,

little does he know that I'm paying their bail."

Jeremy steps up to the microphone, singing back-up vocals, playing Sean Puff-Daddy Combs to her Biggie Smalls –

"Little does he know that I'm paying their bail," he purrs.

Jeremy's gentle tenor adds a bittersweet contrast, a striking melodic counterpoint to Bridget's vitriol. It's like they're engaged in an intimate dialogue with each other, priest and parishioner, she's confessing and he's listening, contemplating the gravity of her words, however outrageous they may seem.

The audience watches, confused; some are actually angry and every last one of them has become self-conscious. Bri Da B continues, rhyming with gusto:

"Surprise, Daddy Dear, baby's doing the do,

better watch out, she gonna come in front of you./

Don't you try to smack that gavel in my face,

I'll hit you with my gat and put you in your place./

So how you like me now, all grown up?

I play football but my dick don't need no cup./

So lock me up, throw away the keys,

NO ALTERNATIVE

I'll be hittin' up those ladies in security."

Bridget pumps her fist in the air like some offspring of the Black Panthers passing through white suburbia by way of grunge, suicide and the 1990's, the bellwether of a future generation in which blacks and whites will do so much fucking that they will permanently blur their bloodlines, a place where everyone is undeniably white and everyone is undeniably black, a world where color has become a point of contention only to those arguing over the settings on their holographic televisions, a world where black is only synonymous with death – nothing more, nothing less.

That is the world where Bridget is from, a world that is only imagined by people like Bridget –

"I'm a thug for life, nigga 'til the end!/

Bri Da B."

She drops the microphone on the stage, causing a pop like a gunshot blast from the speakers. This brings the song to an abrupt end. The crowd is mostly silent. There are a few boos, but these are offset equally by a couple of claps as well.

"Thank you..." Bridget whispers, to no one in particular. "Thank you all from the pit of my burning, nauseous stomach."

Bridget takes a bow, hiding her face from the audience. Now that she's done and the spotlight is on her, she feels small, insignificant and not worthy of the powerful song she has just performed. Suddenly, the light disturbs her, makes her feel exposed, threatens to burn her, like the sun would a vampire. She feels like if the audience had stakes they would storm the stage and go straight for her heart. Based on their tepid response, they probably wouldn't have the energy for rushing the stage.

At this point, it would be a relief to Bridget if they did. It's the apathy that hurts.

As Bridget stands from her bow, what is unmistakable is that she is crying. Thick, viscous tears drip through the paint on her face, carving channels of white down through her black cheeks, exposing her flesh, erasing Bri Da B and unveiling her real self, exposing Bridget, revealing a young lady who hadn't really made up her mind until this very moment on stage, whether or not she truly wanted to exist.

Bridget isn't pretentious enough to pretend that her creation of Bri Da B is some complex post-modernist critique on race relations in the United States, she doesn't see herself as a crusader for the black cause or a white interloper into the intricacies of that cause, she doesn't think these issues require any input from someone as clearly white-bread middle America as her, she's certain that the real players in that drama can take perfectly good care of their own crusade, thank you very much. What Bridget sees and what compels her into the discussion of the subject is the same thing that she thinks Thomas observed. She sees a world that should be able to do much better. So as the persona of Bri Da B is washed away by the tears she is crying, it is also peeled off by the emotion she feels, the love that she feels, for her brother. She doesn't have to hide behind anything anymore, she doesn't have to pretend to be someone else, she can finally be Bridget; she's finally able to accept herself and she recognizes that she owes that to Thomas.

Life is too goddamn short.

Bridget thinks that Kurt Cobain was like John Lennon, the John Lennon from our mother's story, how he was asking for help but no one could hear him. All the signs of Kurt killing himself were there and they were clearly overt cries for help, but no one was listening, not when his kind of tragedy helps ticket and album sales, when his kind of personal controversy sells magazines. He's worth more now after his death than he ever was in life, so the record companies, the lawyers, the accountants, managers, agents, were all complicit in his death, they were all involved in a huge conspiracy: to kill him by ignoring him, whether they were conscious of their insidious motives or not, they all stood to benefit.

Life is too goddamn short, and everyone wants to make as much money as they can and sell as much of their souls as they can, while they're here on this planet for the infinitesimal amount of time that they have. Bridget must shed her skin, her persona, like a snake shed's its skin, because she doesn't need it anymore, she has outgrown it. She thought a lot about death over the years, about taking her own life, but the obstinate mechanisms in her mind never let her confront the issue head on, she would constantly take detours around it, avoiding it with all her might, using Bri Da B as a crutch to express some semblance of emotion, to sidestep the issue of death, her fear of it and longing for it, she used the persona in the way everyone uses a disguise, except she was only hiding from herself. Bridget recognizes that once she was directly confronted with the facts of suicide, she could no longer hide from her demons and maybe that's what allowed her to finally beat them.

When I took my life, Bridget realized for the first time in her 15 years that her life is worth something, that it's worth everything, and that through my death she has been reborn. My death has become a new kind of birthday for Bridget. That is my hope, anyway. Bridget looks into the crowd, the tears streaming, as she bends down and grabs a bucket of water stashed next to the monitor at the foot of the stage. She holds the container high over her head and dumps its contents onto herself, washing the remaining layer of black paint from her body, stripping away what was.

This little girl ain't a girl no more.

CHAPTER FOURTEEN

A suburban postcard. The front of the Harrison household. Bricks, white paint, black shutters, slate path, on the first day of spring. The snow is gone for good and the ground is green again. The smell of the earth is ripe in the air. Life is in bloom.

The front door opens, and Bridget walks out. She closes the door behind her, sits down on the steps. For Bridget, the last few months of grieving have been exacerbated by the physical withdrawal from her anti-depressant medications. Her first week of withdrawal required her to be hospitalized and monitored closely, as a precaution against potential cardiac arrest. In just over a month, she reduced her pharmaceutical menu to one prescription of anti-anxiety medication, which was relatively benign in comparison to the arsenal of chemicals she had been firing into her system on a daily basis for so many years. After another month and a half, she quit the last of her medications as well. For the first time in over four years, Bridget was not on any prescription drugs and the world seemed to take on a fresh vibrancy. Spring had never seemed so fecund and full of possibilities.

The physical withdrawal symptoms from addiction to psychotropic pharmaceuticals are said to match the severity of some torture techniques. In addition to the traditional symptoms such as trembling and sweating, Bridget has been experiencing zaps inside her head, as if her brain is strapped to its own private electric chair and extremely high voltage is being randomly pulsed into the center of her cranium, as if someone plugged her central nervous system directly into a Marshall amplifier, stomped on the distortion pedal, and struck a power chord. Add to this the psychological symptoms, like an increased urge to commit suicide (which is not a good symptom for someone whose brother just committed suicide), and you find yourself in a place toxic to life. On this particular day, on the cracked front stoop of her home, Bridget can finally feel this torture receding, moving off to the horizon of her life, and the suburban spring that envelops her is a very welcome respite.

Part of Bridget thought that withdrawing from drugs would be easier when accompanied by withdrawal from her brother, as though it might serve as a distraction, allowing her to focus on one withdrawal while ignoring the other. It was a balancing act, an exchange of sorts. Being prescribed the medication in the first place was supposed to distract her from the tragedy of life. That didn't work, so now she's taking the opposite approach: using the tragedy of life to help her kick the prescription drug habit. It proved to be no more successful at altering her reality than the initial use of the drugs, but at least she is open to the idea of experiencing life in all its shittiness, because avoiding the shittiness is like ignoring reality, like ignoring life completely. The quid pro quo of her withdrawal makes her think about a Dinosaur Jr. song that I used to force her to listen to:

"Feel The Pain"

She lights a cigarette and thinks about how simultaneously right and full of shit that song is; specifically, how it purports that someone can feel everyone's pain on the outside, while feeling nothing on the inside. She's not sure which way the simultaneity tips the scale, but she's sure she doesn't care either way because she can only stomach one alternative band at a time, because one is more than enough for her, and that band, for now and forever more, is the Latterday Saints. She puts her headphones on, her cans, the ones with the duct tape holding the parts together, and presses play on her Walkman. The Saints' only professionally recorded song, *"Turbulence,"* begins to play.

> *"The time has come to say goodbye,*
>
> *the light of your smile never bends./*
>
> *Too good for me I'll keep in mind,*
>
> *reality can't help but fall./*
>
> *Quick to stand, you're in my reach,*
>
> *I'll walk with you until you say,"*

She listens carefully to the lyrics, actually enjoying the song, and bobbing her head to the beat.

> *"'I've played it safe until the end, and know that I've found you*
>
> *finding me.'"*

As the chorus kicks in, she begins to sing along with it, in spite of the tears working themselves into the performance and dancing down her cheeks.

"I'm wasting my days with nothing to say to you. Yeah, would've

and should've and if I had left you./

I'm wasting my days with nothing to say to you./

Yeah, would've and should've been."

This time there's no face paint, no smoke and mirrors, aside from the smoke from her cigarette, no one else listening to my music, and no one else listening to her. This time, it's just her –
"Should've been…" Bridget sings.
And she can't help but smile.

***

You, Bridget, are what I *should've been.*

***

As for me, I think of myself differently now. The best image I can use to describe my existence is that I'm frozen inside the album cover of *Nevermind.* You remember that iconic cover. I'm the baby, the one with the exposed prepubescent penis, submerged underwater, floating toward a dollar bill on a fishing hook. I'm back to level one, I'm a snapshot, a snapshot on my parents' marble mantle, I'm a memorial in the Fordham Prep yearbook, I'm a link on the internet. I'm an impression of an impression.

I've ceased to exist. But I remain.

Whatever was alive inside of me, whatever it was that constituted my personality, my soul, my spirit, the indescribable me that lived inside the anatomical being, whatever made me unique as an individual, ended the instant the bullet entered my brain. But it's my point-of-view that continues, the impression of me, like a footprint in the mud. After seventeen years of sculpting a personality, my presence is gone but my impression is stamped into these pages and it will be left behind for posterity, for whatever that's worth, to be mulled over, to be dismissed or embraced as fitting for you, dear reader, for I no longer belong to myself, you own me, you are the one who decides my ultimate fate, you are the one who will judge me. I lost the right to my point-of-view when I blew my fucking brains out.

The moment Kurt Cobain died, the populace bum-rushed his persona, claiming it for their own devices. Clones started appearing everywhere: rip-offs on the radio, grunge shoppers on line at Wal-Mart, copycat depressives killing themselves, just like me, I guess. Many of those depressives were the same people that were waiting on line at Wal-Mart, but instead of buying cardigan sweaters, they bought shotguns and boxes of ammunition. People seized his persona and it was their right to do so, because dead men have no rights.

When Mark David Chapman killed John Lennon, he was convicted on second-degree murder charges and sentenced to twenty-five years to life in prison. Yes, Chapman murdered a man. But it was much more than that. Lennon would have created more work, generated more art, written more songs, reunited with the Beatles, commissioned Andy Warhol to film him, Yoko Ono and his mistress, May Pang, partaking in a threesome to promote world peace from East to West and back to

East again. But Chapman took all that from him. He took that from all of us. He should have been charged with felony theft as well. He stole priceless works of art that had yet to be created, but surely would have been. It's akin to cleaning out Picasso from the Museum of Modern Art. Actually, it's much worse. At least, if all of Picasso's works were stolen, we would all still know what it had been. Chapman's act left a void.

Kurt Cobain was an avid Beatles fan. While most critics compared his music to other strains of punk rock, Cobain insisted that Nirvana wasn't punk at all, but rather a pop group and if they were guilty of imitating any band, it was the Beatles. Kurt was Mark David Chapman to his own John Lennon. With the pull of a trigger, he stole from himself and withheld the future spoils of his talent from those people who would have cherished it most: his fans, his real fans, the fans who were listening to his stuff before he transitioned into *27 Club* martyrdom, the audience who got in on the ground floor, those listeners who cared about the music written by a man, not a legend, not a martyr, not a god.

This is the tragedy of all death, the void that is left in the hearts of those who grieve and the historical hole that is created in the world by the absence of that person. It's easy to see that hole in the cases of people like John Lennon, Kurt Cobain, Jimi Hendrix, Ian Curtis and Jim Morrison, but the world changes with every death, maybe it changes even more with the death of someone so young, so promising. I'm not suggesting that I would have amounted to anything so exalted as my musical heroes, but their effect on the world was already established. When young people kill themselves, they leave before establishing an impact on their surroundings. Even if I only became a teacher, maybe I would have changed the lives of thousands of people and the world would be a completely different place. My teachers thought I was going to be a writer, and they set out to condition me to achieve that goal. I'm on record as receiving an A+ in Advanced Placement English at Fordham Prep. Despite this, I couldn't even bring myself to pen my own suicide note. The manner of my death wasn't original and it was a very impulsive act and, in hindsight, a communiqué with some sentences that sang, with a little honest emotion in it, might have added some sparkle, some nuance, to the melancholy episode. Maybe it could have eased the pain of those who cared, or helped them understand, if even just a little bit. But I chose to let the act speak for itself. Like any artist worth his salt. Or any coward.

Shortly after his death, Kurt Cobain, fellow artist and coward, was mourned in a vigil in Seattle where his wife, Courtney Love, read his suicide note to a massive group of teenagers. To her credit, when Love read the part about how *it's better to burn out than fade away*, she bookended it with admonishments. She told the gatherers, "Don't you remember this, 'cause it's a fucking lie!" She then read the quote and went on to call her dead husband an asshole for advocating such a viewpoint. In the moment that I placed my father's pistol in my mouth and pulled the trigger, neurotransmitters surged through the chemical synapses in my brain, frantically trying to find a place in my nervous system, somewhere that was safe, somewhere they could hide as death took hold of me, inside of neurons that were plotting a last ditch effort to save me, even though they knew that such a rescue was impossible, that what they were really looking for was simply a suitable space to die. As my neurons discharged like a crate of jumping jack firecrackers set ablaze, they presented me with a slide show, flashing images of the past, present and future, a future in which I saw Kurt Cobain. I was standing beside Kurt smoking a cigarette, and I asked him about that line in his suicide letter, the one about burning out and fading away, and I told him how that line left an indelible impression with me, so indelible that it might have been part of the reason I didn't write a suicide note myself, figuring I couldn't match the power of his note, and he told me that he didn't even write that line, the Godfather of Grunge wrote that line. The Godfather of Grunge was Neil Young and I'd never heard a Neil Young song in my life, or if I had I wasn't paying enough attention or just didn't care. The *Godfather of Grunge*: the alliteration of the phrase sets the worlds of religion and music on a collision course and the connection of this phrase to the suicide of Cobain, and furthermore to my own suicide, makes me skeptical that religion and music can ever be authentic when that is what's demanded by the followers, because if Kurt Cobain couldn't be authentic in the very moment that demanded him to be authentic how the hell is a puny nobody like me supposed to be authentic? Maybe the only thing that is one hundred percent authentic is death. No one has beat it yet, so it's hard to argue against that.

"Don't you remember this, 'cause it's a fucking lie!" All words are lies; to think otherwise is to endorse the notion that our feelings can be shared without any loss in quality, timber, resonance, substance and emotion. We lie to each other all of the time. Attempts to communicate feelings through words is a losing battle, which is why so many people attempt to refine the act through the vehicle of the written word. This is what I'm attempting to do now. One final, crowning effort to define myself, to reconstruct the individual self of one Thomas Harrison so that I can peacefully leave it all behind.

The *self* is what Cobain threw away, a decision based on a premise of which he was not the author, and I'm only now realizing that this is what I threw away as well. When you die, the only thing that remains of the self is memory, the memories carried by those who played the lead, supporting, and featured roles in the drama of your days. The self loses the rights to its

own persona, to its own memories and it's the supporting characters in your life, the loved ones you left behind, the friends,
the acquaintances, and even people you never knew who inherit
what is left of you, who are bequeathed with the memory of
you. In the case of a suicide, it's all inherited: the pain, the tragedy, the shittiness of the life you refused to face. The greatest
burden is placed on your loved ones, like a gift of coal on
Christmas morning. The last of that coal will be burned and
gone on the day that the last person who loved you passes away, following you into death. When I delivered that coal, when
my self was scuttling into the hidden recesses of my brain, one
thought remained ascendant, one thought took center stage above all others, it was this one inescapable thought that compelled me to the writing of this story: the thought of my sister
committing suicide.

The thought of this recursive tragedy repeats on a loop in
the cosmic theater that seats my thoughts. I imagine Bridget
drinking, it's the watered-down vodka from the cabinet above
the kitchen sink, but she's drinking way too much of it and th-
en using it as a lubricant to swallow all the pills in her medicine
cabinet. Everything that was ever prescribed to her, in one fell
swoop. I imagine my parents finding her on the floor of her
bedroom, amidst the junk, the dirty plates and cereal bowls, the
hamster shit, in a state of unconsciousness, what the emergency
response team refers to as *unresponsive*. I imagine her in a coma,
her motionless body in a hospital bed, hooked up to a plethora
of tubes, wires and prewritten prayers, the only thing doctors
are able to do is force charcoal into her stomach, to absorb the
excess toxins, because she was found too late to try anything
else. Doctors, alongside members of my family, wait to see if
Bridget's heart holds out as the drugs pass through the sum
total of her system, while her friends congregate at Slave to the

Grind and cry their eyes out, spilling their tears into elegantly spiced mugs of coffee.

What you've read to this point is preamble to this cry from the grave, this vain attempt to get through to my little sister, to connect with her and spare her the pain that she has pursued for so long, the pain that I achieved in her place. If my death is good for anything, it's in sparing Bridget.

If I couldn't write a note explaining my own death, at least I can write one in the hope of preventing Bridget's.

Dear Bridget,

The moment I'm writing this, you're unconscious in the hospital, a stomach full of charcoal, and you're on a ventilator because you cannot breathe. They say you might not make it. I don't know what I'd do if you don't, because I can't bear to think about living in this world without you in it.

I look up to you in so many different ways — ways that are so obvious to me that it kills me that you're oblivious to them. I understand you're depressed, and depression is a disease, but like every disease, it can be cured.

You're my little sister, and big brothers are supposed to protect their little sisters. And I'm weeping right now because of how incredibly helpless I feel — I'm right next to you, but still a thousand miles away.

It tears me apart to think that I somehow failed you as a brother. Out of anyone else on this planet, you're the person that most resembles me; genetically, we have the same make-up. By killing yourself, you would be, literally, killing a part of me. For you to leave this Earth is an abstraction my mind simply cannot accept. You're a tough girl, use that resilience to fight this, fight this depression – fight these fucking drugs. You can do it! I know it, damn-it, I fucking know it. My sister, my only sister, life is an opportunity, and I'm begging you, from the deepest and most genuine cavities of my heart, don't waste it.

Right now, I'm hoping for one thing, that you will be able to read this letter. I can't bear the thought that you might not be able to – that you might not make it. That can't happen. I love you so much, Bridget, more than anything, much more than myself. I might not have ever said those words, but I'm writing them right now.

If you need a reason to live, and all you need is one, here it is: I want you to live.

I'll be with you forever, whether you know it or not.

Love, Thomas

***

In death, the putrefying tongue goes purple and black and extends from the mouth in a malignant rictus, a contortion of the funny face made by an innocent child, a contortion that, in juxtaposition with our loss of animation, steals forever our ability to communicate with our loved ones, to reach them from beyond the grave and complete the arc of our lives together. I was granted parole from this universal law, parole to address Bridget from beyond this world, to share my suicide's lesson and spare visiting the exponential loss of her death on our parents. Losing the ability to speak and then receiving the opportunity to do so again, makes you get to the point much quicker. We should all be so fortunate to lose our ability to speak from time to time, because once we're given the chance to speak again, we keep it simple, we keep it true, even if that truth is in the form of a letter that mixes fact with fiction, that conflates things that happened to me with things that happened to my sister. It's a letter that I wish someone had written to me, before I went ahead and did what I did.

My father always thought that if someone in our family were to check out of life early, it would be my sister. I think my mother thought so, too, though I am sure she would never admit it. I know I thought so. I never thought it was going to be me; if I did, I wouldn't have made it those seventeen years. But the circumstances of my penance, my punishment, my redemption, whatever this might be, are tied to Bridget, tied to one very simple fact:

My sister is still alive.

In the end, it's only words that are left. Spoken, written or read, words you said, words people think you said, words people will continue to say about you for some relatively small interval of time after you're gone, words that are translated through the impressions of others, through the impressions you left on others, through the filters of the characters around us, characters who have had an impact on our lives and who've had an impact on our character. Some are more inconsequential than others.

Jackie was in attendance at my funeral, sitting in the crowd, dabbing her swollen cheeks with tissues, but her presence there meant nothing to me, despite the important role she played in this story. From this vantage point, she is not part of what I remember; she is not part of what I choose to remember. It's *deus ex machina* at the hands of the protagonist, who is, as always, allowed to make his preferences known. Those who matter are my parents and Bridget. My parents will go on, although, the name *Harrison*, the loadstone of my family history, is now burdened with a terminal life expectancy. There's an end to the line. I guess there's still some time for them to give birth to another boy, to fasten this moniker to him and urge him to carry it into another generation. But my parents will not do that. They will let the line die with me. They will feel that they owe me this much. If I was the Thomas I was before, the person who felt resentment toward my father, I may have skipped over the part where Bridget was sitting on the front steps, listening to my band's song, and my father stepped outside to join her, placing a reassuring hand atop her head and telling her he loved her. I may have skipped over that part, for some petty teenage reason, but I'm incapable of such petty feelings now and I'm hard-pressed not to say I was happy when my sister wrapped her arms around my father's legs and he looked down at her, realizing that she's a lot stronger than he thought, and she gave his leg a squeeze to tell him she loved him back. She didn't have to say it; he knew it. Before, I might have skipped over that part, but now it's my favorite part, now it's the part I want to dwell on, now it's the picture I hold in my head: my sister with her arms wrapped around my father's strong legs.

My bandmates, my brothers in song, will continue to play their instruments in assorted bands of varying styles, when they're not working at their day jobs, when they're not struggling with the vagaries of everyday life. But we did record a song together. We did leave that behind, no matter how tumultuous the circumstances were surrounding its creation. And there's Stewart, who was one of the subversives who stood and clapped for Bridget at CBGB's, but his impact on her life ended in that room, a room that several years later would be exported to Las Vegas as a tourist attraction, an act that murdered the residual grime of punk that the bands who once thrashed its stage had earnestly left behind. In the most benevolent way, Bridget didn't need Stewart anymore. She didn't need CB's, or punk rock, or Biggie Smalls, for that matter. Just like she didn't need her pills anymore. She found what she needed to go on. She found what I found. We found each other.

I have become the impression that's perceived by my sister, or that's how I'd like to be remembered, if given the choice. However Bridget remembers me. The extent of my existence, the part of me that remains and makes a difference, is captured in the colors she uses to paint me on the canvas in her head. And I hope she continues to paint. Because she's the character that counts. She's the one who matters.

She's the survivor.

WILLIAM DICKERSON

ACKNOWLEDGMENTS

My Alma Maters, Billy Mulligan, John Sarantakos, Brooke Ehrlich, Paul Yates, "grunge,"

along with special thanks to the band members of Guy Smiley, my brothers in song.

I could not have written this without the support of my family, my inspirational wife, Rachel, my frequent collaborator, Dwight Moody, who had a hand in editing this novel, and the encouragement of Sam Gowan; although he is no longer with us, he is far from forgotten.

***

Original rap lyrics by Bri Da B.
Original rock lyrics by Latterday Saints.

All lyrics used with permission.

CONTACT

contactwilliamdickerson@gmail.com
http://www.facebook.com/williamdickersonfilmmaker
http://www.facebook.com/noalternative.novel

CPSIA information can be obtained at www.ICGtesting.com
Printed in the USA
LVOW062306301012

305110LV00001B/94/P